A CARRIAGE RIDE HOME

Book One of *THE CHRONICLES OF AMBER LEAF*

a novel by

SANDRA H. ESCH

A LAMP POST BOOK

A CARRIAGE RIDE HOME
BY SANDRA H. ESCH

ISBN 13: 978-1-60039-224-5
ebook ISBN: 978-1-60039-737-0

Editor: Melissa Williams Netherton

www.lamppostpubs.com

A Carriage Ride Home

BY

SANDRA H. ESCH

BOOK ONE of
THE CHRONICLES OF AMBER LEAF

Wisdom is the principal thing; therefore get wisdom.
And in all your getting, get understanding.

Proverbs 4:7 (NKJV)

CHAPTER ONE

LONDON, ENGLAND

WINTER 1896

The dreaded day arrived.

Ollie glanced at his fiancée, took one last look at the barren countryside, and lightly flicked the reins. He steered the buggy off the main road, and through a towering gate. The horse's hooves clopped a rhythmic cadence along a tree-lined path and eased to a halt.

Emily's chatter ceased, her eyes grew wide with wonder, and then darkened like the billowing clouds greedily devouring the light.

"What troubles you, Em?" he said.

Although he already knew.

"*This* is your home?"

He grinned mischievously.

"You failed to mention you were wealthy."

He rested a comforting hand on hers. "This is my father's house."

"But he's an aristocrat," she said. "If I'm doing my sums correctly, that would make you an aristocrat, too. Ollie, I feel completely out of—"

"You're fine."

"No. Your parents will throw me out when they learn I'm a pauper."

Ollie looked up at the stately mansion with its formidable columns, cupolas, and multi-paned windows and his heart grew sad. "I fear the true paupers live here. My parents have been known to suffer poverty of the soul," he said by way of explanation. "One day you'll follow."

"But surely you've told them about me … Ollie? Why aren't you answering? You mean they don't know—"

He looked hard into the eyes of his one true love. "You are our equal. Do not for one moment forget that." He reached out a hand. "Come."

"I can't go in there."

He gave the reins to a waiting stable boy. "Henry, would you please attend to Betsy?"

"Be happy to, my lord."

"My lord?" she repeated. "Ollie …"

"My parents will be quite taken with you," he said, wishing his desire into being. He glanced at the ever-darkening sky. If by chance the gathering went poorly and snow fell, he'd have suitable cause to cut short this visit. He helped a reluctant Emily down and with a gentle hold at the elbow, guided her up wide marble steps and through sweeping doors.

Though fire hissed and spat in the hearth, he was unable to shake a chill. With Emily at his side, he viewed his home differently. In contrast to her world, which so lifted him, he hadn't before noticed the oppressing décor of muted colors. The paintings of landscapes and flowers, but none of people. The hard, cold sculpture of a horse with no rider. And though the great room smelled of roast duck, inhaling a breath in the large chamber suffocated him.

His distinguished-looking father lightly graying at the temples, and mother in her flowing gown, approached them. They wore expectant smiles.

"Father, Mother, I present to you Miss Emily de Haven."

Emily curtsied awkwardly before extending a hand.

His father undoubtedly took note of her discomfort for his, "How delightful to meet you," implied a question. "Your Emily is even lovelier than we had imagined."

As she blushed, Ollie drew her close to his side.

They made pleasantries while one servant attended to their wraps and another brought forward a silver platter. "Wassail, ma'am?"

Emily reached for a cup of the hot beverage, hand trembling. Before Ollie could help her, Wassail spilled over its sides and onto the Persian rug. "I'm terribly sorry." Her horrified gaze riveted on the carpet. "How clumsy of me."

"No need for concern," Ollie said as a servant swabbed the liquid with a linen napkin. "I've spilled a few drinks myself. Look. The carpet remains unharmed."

His father undoubtedly found the nervousness of youthful love entertaining, for a half smile cut into his cheeks.

Meanwhile, his mother lowered onto a settee near the hearth and patted it. "Tell us all about yourself, Emily, and how you and our Oliver met."

"We met at the library," he said, answering for her.

His mother nodded approvingly. "I have always deemed the library at Oxford so utterly charming."

"Not Oxford," Emily said. "We met at the British Library."

"The British …"

"I was struggling with a weighty stack of books." She broke her first confident smile. "Your son noticed and insisted upon carrying them for me. I have never before met anyone quite so gallant."

"We are most proud of our Oliver. He has grown into a true gentleman. He shall make an excellent barrister, don't you think?"

Ollie's father cleared his throat in a disapproving manner.

"And one day soon he will become a fine judge," his mother continued, "but of that I am certain you were already aware. So tell us, what course of study are you taking at university?"

Emily looked at Ollie as if pleading for help. "I do not attend university."

"You ... do not?"

"No, Lady Harrington. Ollie ... uh, Oliver must have neglected to tell you. I'm a—"

"Do you find this coat familiar?" Ollie pivoted and thumbed open his jacket at the pockets.

"No, I don't believe I do."

"You presented this to me on my eighteenth birthday, remember? It pleased me so greatly, I fear I've worn it until the fabric broke through at the elbow. Yet, I still refused to part with it. Em masterfully stitched on patches. Looks as if it were a new garment."

His mother examined the coat sleeve closely. "Yes, it does at that." She looked at Emily with an admiring smile. "So, you sew then. My, it nearly looks professional. What a wonderful hobby."

"No, mother. She's a—"

"Dinner is served," a servant said.

Ollie welcomed the interruption. Perhaps it was best to divulge Emily's family situation slowly.

They gathered together in the formal dining room. In the afternoon's dim light, Emily appeared swallowed up in a large Victorian chair. Her striking eyes and flawless complexion glowed in flickering candlelight. At the mere sight of her in the elegant setting, Ollie touched heaven.

As they dined, he shared some of the warmer tales of his youth. But when his mother turned to Emily and said, "Do tell us about your childhood," he choked down a forkful of Yorkshire pudding and chased it with a generous gulp of water. His parents needed to learn about their future daughter-in-law, but Ollie feared their questions coming too quickly and reaching too deep.

"What are some of your favorite memories?" Lady Harrington spoke innocently as if she hadn't noticed Emily fidgeting. "And tell us about your father. How does he make his living?"

Ollie girded Emily with his eyes as she lowered her fork, placing it just so next to her plate, then lifted her chin. "He's incapacitated, unable to work."

Branches of a nearby tree scraped loudly against the windowpanes, attracting his father's attention. "I wonder if a snowstorm might be threatening."

Ollie's mother said, "Yes, it does appear a bit bothersome, but at the moment I'm more concerned about this young lady's father. Emily, I'm so sorry to hear he's had difficulties with his health. I hope his condition is improving with time."

She shook her head. "He had an accident some years back. Crushed his hip. He'll never walk again."

"How very dreadful," his father said. "What was his profession?"

As Emily reached for a napkin the way a young girl reaches for the comfort of a doll and smoothed imaginary creases, Ollie held his breath. He had been wrong not to prepare her for an inquisition.

"He was a—"

His mother appeared to neither see nor comprehend the impact of the question. "Yes," she said. "Go on."

"Mother," he cautioned.

Though Emily's cheeks flushed pink, she announced, "My father was a street seller."

As his father sat mute, his mother's "I see" eased out warm and proper, but further words seemed nowhere to be found.

Ollie placed a hand on Emily's. "I'm most proud of your father. He's a delightful man worthy of our respect. Look how well he raised you." He then turned to his parents. "She is wonderfully unspoiled, is she not?"

"Yes, wonderfully," his mother said, her tone unconvincing. "And what about you, Emily? If you do not attend university, are you otherwise employed?"

She nodded. "I'm a seamstress."

"A seam …"

Ollie wasn't certain whether Emily drew strength from her professional skills, but something happened. Appearing at one with herself, she no longer struggled to gain approval. With a quick glance at him, she announced, "I take great pride in my work."

The unknown revealed, Ollie's shoulders slackened for his parents had seen her beauty and warmth before learning of her lack of social standing, and she had responded graciously. "I wouldn't be surprised to one day find her sewing for the Queen," he said then redirected his attention toward the window, relieved by the howling wind and whirling snow. "I fear we will have to cut short this afternoon's visit. As soon as there's a break in the weather, I'd best see Em home."

He got up and placed a stack of bricks on the hearth. Shortly thereafter he called for the stable master. "Would you kindly wrap the hot bricks and place them in the buggy?" He then looked squarely at his father. "I wish my fiancée's feet to remain warm during our journey to London."

Lord Harrington's Adam's apple visibly plunged beneath his collar. "Fiancée?"

CHAPTER TWO

O llie looked out across the frozen countryside thinly illuminated beneath a vanishing moon. Virgin snow in its purest form not yet stained by the wiles of man. He glanced back at the house and then at Emily who sat sullenly at his side. *Look out into a bigger, more wonderful world, Em. We are leaving the small world behind.* But then he steadied himself, for as certain as the snow subsided, it would return anew.

He tipped his hat and they bounded off. Betsy pranced like a show horse cutting a trail through a pristine blanket of white, though Emily appeared not to notice.

After they passed through the wrought-iron gate, Ollie breathed freely again. Several miles down the road he said, "It makes me wretched to see you forlorn."

She drew her hand muff close as if to secure herself. "Your parents said it was nice meeting me, but mentioned not a word about seeing me again. Did you, by chance, notice that?"

"I'm certain that was a hapless blunder on their part," he said.

"I think not. I'm not an equal to your world."

He gently flicked the reins as if gently flicking away his parents' slight. "You must learn to value yourself, Em."

"I do. It's my heritage that's the problem, and that will never change."

She withdrew again.

Gentle flurries swirled as dusk gave way to the dark of night. A brisk wind kicked up, and thick flakes hurled wildly against the road. He found it impossible to see. Realizing too late that he ought to have taken the sleigh, he pulled in the reins and hopped off the buggy.

"What are you doing?" she said.

"We mustn't take the chance of going off the road. We'd be in a real pickle."

Betsy snorted as he removed the lantern from its hook and trudged forward. "It's okay," he cooed. Seizing the reins, he patted her nose, then held the lantern at arm's length and squinted into the pelting snow. "Come, girl."

To his surprise, Emily appeared at his side, her cry muted by the bawling wind. "Let me help."

"Get back in the buggy," he shouted. "You'll catch a chill."

"No, Ollie. You need me." She tugged the lantern from his resistant hand. "You lead Betsy and follow me. You can't manage this alone."

Tufts of grass aligning the sides of the road sprouted through thickening snow. She carried the lantern low, its dim glow illuminating her path much the way she illuminated Ollie's life. He ached to reach out, to hold her. She reminded him so of the servants who cared for him, attending his every move. A feeling of melancholy swept over him for while being forbidden, that bittersweet world afforded him comfort. Emily was correct in her assessment of his parents. They had made no mention of seeing her again, and yet it was with Emily where he felt most at home. Her easy laughter. Lack of social pressure. Warmth and love from unpretentious parents. How he looked forward to indulging a lifetime of her kind of wealth.

She looked back and shouted, "We're losing the road," then forged ahead lifting the lantern high, dipping it low with every determined step. "I found it," she cried and plodded on.

Tromping through the thick white blanket, Ollie grew warm as the buggy swayed awkwardly over an occasional rock. They continued on until the wind and snow finally ceased.

He reached out to her and they returned to the buggy. He cleared small drifts, struggling through higher ones. A good distance down the road, she placed a gloved hand on the sleeve of his coat. "You asked me to marry you before I met your parents or they had an opportunity to meet me," she said. "That was intentional on your part, was it not?"

He nodded.

"You have a quality about you, Oliver Harrington, but now that I've become acquainted with—"

He flicked the reins and Betsy broke into a gallop. "Don't concern yourself with my parents. They may be aristocrats, but they aren't complete snobs."

"But they won't ever accept me. In their eyes, I'm unsuitable for your world."

"Nonsense. We love each other. What could be more fitting than that?"

She nudged the buggy blanket tighter to her throat, her teeth chattering. Her quivering could not be from the biting breeze.

"We can't risk their rejecting you, too," she said. "They may be gracious, but I would be blind had I not also noticed they are devilishly conscious of social status. That's who they are and it's not about to change."

He cringed at her ominous tone and yanked back the reins. "Whoa, Betsy." The buggy rocking to a halt, he lifted Emily's chin. "What is it you wish to say?"

She backhanded moisture from her cheeks. "I can't marry you."

OLLIE HANDED THE REINS TO THE waiting stable boy and paused before the steps of his father's mansion, Emily's final words cutting deep. 'My heart breaks for you, Ollie,' she had said. 'I come from humble means, but that has a comforting side. It will take little for me to make my parents proud. But you? I don't want to imagine how hard you must work to achieve that same end.' Then came the grim words that begged for resolution. 'You need someone more like you, someone who's wealthy, too.'

He plodded in. To his dismay, his father paced before the hearth. "You're still up? It's half past midnight. Can you not sleep?"

With hands stuffed deep in the pockets of his smoking jacket, his father shook his head. "Do I appear as if I'm unable to sleep?"

Ollie hesitated near the entry—no, not hesitated … stopped, not caring to go in. "Mother is okay?"

"Last I looked in on her, she was sitting in bed, staring at the pages of an upside down book."

He stepped up to the hearth and stretched out reluctant hands to warm them, wishing the chill in the room warmed as easily.

His father placed another log on the fire and stoked its flames. "You had enough hot bricks to keep warm for the entire journey, I trust?"

"Yes, sir."

"That's as it ought to be. But now that you're home, I believe it best we have a seat, Son."

"This sounds forbidding." He took a reluctant stroll to the settee. "The last time I sensed an imminent scolding was when I rode your prized stallion before its bandaged leg had healed." He smiled awkwardly. "I can still see you standing in front of the riding stable awaiting me and that limping horse. I swore I'd never again manage to let you down, but then I met Em. This is about her, I presume? Perhaps I can spare you a fair amount of discomfort."

"That would be welcome."

"Em is lovely, is she not?" Ollie ventured.

"Indeed."

"I assume your primary concern is with her family's social status, or might it be more accurate to say lack of status?"

"Oliver, for heaven's sakes. A seamstress? What are you thinking?"

He sat forward on the settee, elbows on knees, fingers steepled at his lips. "If that's your concern, there's no further need for discussion."

"Wonderful. You've made the decision to walk away from her then?"

"There's no turning back."

His father bolted up, red flushing his cheeks. "You stand corrected. There will be turning back. I forbid you to marry that woman."

Overtaken with calm, he looked into his father's angry eyes. "She was overwhelmed by the contrast in our lifestyles, too, even more so than I had anticipated, and now it appears I have the pitiable task of convincing her to marry me. But you would do well to know I have already married her … in my heart."

"How dare you defy me?" his father spat. "Your hasty decision will impact your life in ways you can't imagine. Emily is lovely, and I fully appreciate how you fell in love with her. But if you choose to marry, you will open yourself to being the butt of jokes and ill chatter."

"That's a bit overstated, is it not? I assume mother feels the same way?"

"She's appalled. First a barrister, and now a seamstress. Oliver, how could you?"

He steadied himself. "The aristocracy isn't all roses as we would prefer to believe, is it?"

"What's that supposed to mean?" his father scoffed.

"We're wealthy in the eyes of the world, but there's an impoverished side of our existence, too—the part that's felt, not seen."

"How dare you not be grateful?"

"I am grateful for the way you've provided," Ollie said, "but I'm not grateful for our unmitigated pressure to perform. What about our unabashed feelings of entitlement? The social snobbery of some of our relatives? Uncle Chad? Uncle Tony? You also find their behavior revolting. How is snubbing Em and her family any different?"

"We aren't snubbing Emily or her family," his father said, his words spewing out in staccato. He poured a shot of brandy and upended it in one greedy gulp. "We want to protect you, your future. Finding happiness with someone who doesn't share an equal yoke will place an unbearable strain on your marriage." He poured another. "Your mother and I don't wish you to have to endure—"

Not to be bested, Ollie got up and casually rested a foot on the hearth. "I've observed many commoners, people whose lives are simple," he said as he gazed thoughtfully into the spitting embers. "True, some live their lives off of their masters' stripes, but they also make their masters look better than they are. They aren't puffed up with self-importance, and that I find most appealing. My Em may not have aristocratic blood, but she does possess an aristocratic heart, which I find of far greater value. My mind is made up, Father. We are deeply in love, and I have every intention of marrying her."

"You will *not* marry her." His father gulped another shot. "I know from experience about which I …"

He fixed his gaze on his father's moving lips while a pained look cast a pall over the man's proud features.

"Hedy …" his father said.

"Who is Hedy?"

"My first wife."

"Your …?" Ollie returned to the settee and slowly eased down, realization rendering him speechless. His father had suffered from a first marriage he knew nothing about?

"Like you, I was a young stallion once, foolishly following my heart rather than my head, and it ended in disaster. We sought an annulment just shy of our first year."

"But why?"

His father stared off, his tone softening. "I can only assume she set out to attain what she thought she wanted and when she finally acquired it, meaning me, she decided she no longer wanted me. Overnight her behavior changed so dramatically that I had her followed." He let out an uneasy snigger. "It appeared one man wasn't adequate for a woman of her appetite."

Ollie sat quietly and pondered the weight of those words. "That must have wounded you deeply, but you've met Em. Surely you don't believe she is capable —"

"There's more. The burden of taking on someone without social and financial means shall be a weight upon our household resources." His father appeared to hold something back. "And about your question … no, Emily doesn't appear capable of misconduct, but neither did Hedy."

Ollie absently combed fingers through his hair. It was his father who had unwisely chosen his first bride. It was his father who allowed himself to become ensnared in the values of the aristocracy. It was his father who without question deemed it important to pass those values onto Ollie regardless of what he wanted. "In all due respect," he said, "I know Em's family. I feel at one with them. Now all I want is to break away from this life filled with care about things that in the end have little meaning. Don't worry, Father. I promise to succeed as a barrister and plan to well provide for my bride as soon as I complete my studies."

"Is that a fact?" His father slammed the shot glass on the bar. "How is it that you plan to pay for your last year at university?"

"Pardon me?"

His father raised a warning brow. "You marry that woman, you're on your own."

Ollie's thoughts froze. After a long moment he regained his senses and said, "I shall have to join the military then. It would appear I have no other choice."

"Oliver!"

"Not Oliver. Ollie. Em calls me Ollie and I jolly rather like it. That nickname will certainly be more suiting to my new way of life."

CHAPTER THREE

Emily stood at the threshold of her modest flat—transparent, conflicted, and determined. Persuading her would be no easy task.

"Why bother to come, Ollie?" she said.

I had to come. I have no life without you. "Why did you say yes?"

"I didn't."

He reached for her hands. "Neither did you say no."

She slowly backed to the opposite side of the living room, gazed out the window, and absently smoothed the folds in a panel of nut-brown drapery. "Lord Harrington—"

"How many times must I implore you? Please discontinue calling me Lord Harrington."

"But that's who you are."

He frowned. "Em!"

She glanced back, sparkling eyes coupling a warm grin. "Very well then, I'll stop. I promise. But it won't be easy. I rather draw pleasure from it."

"You are irrepressible."

"Not too irrepressible. I found I have a character flaw."

A grin formed. "That's highly unlikely. You're shockingly flawless."

"No," she insisted. "I'm deeply flawed. Over the noon hour I saw a street seller take a swipe at a young boy in rags."

"How did the boy manage that? Did he steal something?"

She shook her head. "He bumped an apple off a cart. Looked terrified when the seller grabbed his arm. Before I could catch myself, I accidentally gave the man a rather severe tongue-lashing."

Unable to keep any distance from her, Ollie crossed the room. "Sounds as though the seller deserved it."

"In some respects, yes," she said, her expression turning to one of regret. "But I answered anger with anger. How might that make me better?"

"You were aware of your attitude. Surely that must count for something."

Emily stopped short. "I heard someone call the boy Sven. He reminded me so of a younger version of you. He looked more Scandinavian than British. He was tall for his age. The same steel gray eyes." She reached up and fingered a lock of Ollie's hair. "Pale flaxen mane curling at the nape."

As his heart fluttered at the tenderness of her touch, she abruptly withdrew her hand.

"That was wrong of me," she said.

"No, it was right."

"But I can't have you."

"Oh, but you can."

"No, it won't work."

While she took a step back, he took a larger step forward. "I want what you have, Em. How you care. Your contentment. Warmth. Love. I find your world refreshingly different from the all-too-proper one in which I was raised." He lifted her hand and lightly kissed her ring finger. "Once again I'm asking you to marry me. Your words said no before, but your heart continues to say yes."

"Oliver Harrington, you are beyond belief. It would break your parents' hearts—"

"Do you wish to say that the errant opinions of my parents mean more to you than your love for me? Are you more concerned about breaking their hearts than you are about breaking mine? I thought you said it was *me* you love."

Moisture glistened in her warm eyes. "Please don't do this."

He refused to stop. "Their unwillingness to accept you is their task to overcome, not ours."

"But I'll never feel at home in your world."

"I'm not asking that of you. I don't feel at home there either. I want us to get a fresh start and build a wonderful new life together, just you and me."

She tenderly stroked his cheek with the back of her fingers, her touch again giving him gooseflesh. "The treasures of your world are wonderful, but the price comes too high. I would turn myself inside out to gain your parents' acceptance but that would be a fool's errand … Ollie, why must you smile?"

"My parents are no longer an issue."

She frowned. "They'll always be an issue."

"I walked away from them."

Her mouth fell open. "You wh—"

"I said I walked away from them."

"Not because of me?"

"Precisely because of you."

He gathered her in his arms and muttered adoringly in her ear. "I fear you have me stuck in a very deep and precarious hole. Have you considered the price I'll pay the rest of my life if you choose not to marry me? The thought of not having you is far too intolerable to bear."

As Emily choked back a sob and fell harder into his arms, he smoothed her hair to comfort her, and for a moment, time slowed until it seemed no longer to exist.

"I can't go off into the military a bachelor, my sweet," he whispered. "When the morning's sun arises, we shall be first in line at the magistrate's. You'll never regret saying yes. I promise you."

CHAPTER FOUR

Emily awaited Ollie at the door, her expression wary.

Hesitant to learn why, he drew her near. Defying his father's wishes had been the wisest decision he'd ever made. Each day with her presented its own slice of heaven. Waking every morning to the warmth of her smile. Coming home each evening to her welcome embrace. She cooked as well as she sewed, the flat often smelling of warm bread or hot apple pie.

The times Ollie proved remiss in providing her with adequate attention, she never complained. However, she did smile while serving unseasoned soup with perfectly burned hot cross buns. And when overwhelmed by his duties in the military, once and only once he had raised his voice in anger. She sat him down, insisting that if they were to maintain a loving home, he was to speak respectfully. Always. And that he chose to do.

"Why the troubled expression?" he said finally.

She handed him an unopened envelope, the penmanship familiar. "You received this today."

He clasped her hand and drew her to an armchair. She lowered onto his lap as he halfheartedly opened it. "Regarding your invitation to dinner," he read aloud, bile rising in his throat, "your mother and I regretfully send our …" Crushed again by rejection, he slapped the note on his knee and looked at Emily helplessly.

She touched her forehead to his. "Pen him a note," she said.

"I can't manage that."

"Where there is hatred, we must sow love." Her words softly spoken hit a nerve. "Your heart is your garden, Ollie. Pluck the weeds of bitterness before they have an opportunity to grow."

"But what would I say?"

She smiled warmly and stroked his cheek. "Be kind. Thank them for getting back to you. Offer your heartfelt blessings."

As he mulled over those words, she reached for his hand and cupped it to her abdomen. "I have a surprise," she said, her eyes glistening. "Come spring, we shall swaddle a little Oliver or Olivia."

Though the wonder, the miracle of new life burgeoned in his heart, his pleasure was short lived when the next morning he received orders to go to Sudan.

Months later, he stood in his tent, too weary to face another day. With the exception of battle, time on the front stood still and during those hours, he looked forward to receiving posts, which came in batches. Emily religiously penned one a day, sometimes two, and she always numbered them. He sorted and arranged them chronologically, and as he read, his lonely heart filled. He smiled to himself. Posts were due to arrive again today.

"Captain Harrington, sir?" The soldier stood at attention. "General Marshall has requested an audience with you. You'll find him in his tent."

Weary from yesterday's brutal battle, yet relieved it was over, victory won, Ollie said, "Thank you. That will be all."

"There's more, sir. This arrived earlier this morning."

He reached for the single envelope bearing his father's penmanship and looked about the immaculate tent as if something was out of place. Word from his father? That was strange. Yet no word from his bride? Surely a bundle must have become misplaced somewhere. He dropped the letter on a makeshift end table and set out into the blistering sun.

"Captain Harrington," General Marshall said, "I'm most pleased to inform you that the Mahdist regime has suffered a grave chink in its armor thanks to your courageous efforts. Our domination of Sudan is now imminent. I am, therefore, ordering you to return to Britain to—"

For the first time since joining the military, Ollie lost concentration. Returning to Emily? To Britain? A rush of exhilaration ripped through his weary bones, bringing with it renewed life.

A smile slicing into his cheeks, he returned to his tent, lit a lantern, and smoothed open the unexpected letter from his father.

31 July 1898

Our dearest Son:

Ollie looked up. Our dearest son? What had gotten into the man? His father had expelled him from his life not having had the decency to offer a scant goodbye. Why was he worthy of a letter with so tender a sentiment?

> *I find it difficult to believe that you have been away for get-ting on two years now. Time moves swiftly and yet it drags so. I deeply regret not having accepted your invitation to dinner those many months ago. And our last words? Although harsh and spoken in anger, at the core was a heart filled with love and care for your wellbeing. To this day, your mother and I feel tremendous remorse about our estrangement—not attending your wedding, and not seeing you off as you courageously assumed your military responsibilities. We continue to follow war news with great concern. Prayers for your health and safety remain constant on our breath.*

Realizing this was a letter he needed to consume in small bites, Ollie reread the first paragraph, fighting to the death the disingenuous thoughts niggling in, vying for attention. Regret? Remorse? Great concern? Prayers for my health and safety remain constant on their breath? Had his father become terminally ill?

Ollie lifted the letter closer and read on.

> *Other than a sniffle here and a minuscule bout of sciatica there, your mother and I are faring quite well. She said to be certain to tell you that she stumbled upon Mary Ashbury at a bazaar this weekend past. Mary inquired about you. She always was stalwart, a young lady of such fine breeding. Your mother made sure to give her your best.*
>
> *On another positive note, I am pleased to share some pleasant news. Our family assets, which had become wanting these several years past, have been replenished somewhat as of recent weeks.*

Depleting assets? Why had his father not mentioned this before? Was that the reason for stubbornly withholding his last year's tuition at university? Or was it the burden of Ollie's taking on a bride without financial means that gave rise to such an intense degree of animosity? Why not tell him the truth?

> *Seems an investment here and there has done better than we had anticipated thanks to burgeoning industry. Fortunately, we have not had to release more staff, and Harrington Manor once again appears to be thriving.*

He shook his head in disgust.

> *It is clear our Betsy yearns for you.*

And then he smiled.

> *She never has eaten her oats heartily when you've been away.*

Seems a bit listless. Of course, she is getting on in years. The stable boys have been doting over her. She appears to enjoy that.

And now to my intended reason for this letter.

Ah-ha! He does have an ulterior motive.

I fear I have dreadful news, Son. I prefer sharing it with you in person. Some things are more appropriately communicated that way. But since that is not possible, and a telegram is even less personal, it is with heavy heart that I tell you that we have lost your beloved Emily.

Ollie's heart thumped wildly. He slapped the letter on his knee. You are wrong. You are cruelly wrong. Lost? No, you meant not to say that. She merely left England. I'll find her. She will come back. You'll see. He quickly read on.

Her mother stopped by several days past. Mentioned Emily had been riding in a carriage to the north of the village when in pouring down rain a wheel hit a chuckhole. The carriage over-turned. And if that is not grief enough to share, the child she had been carrying ....

Paralyzed with shock, he stared past the letter, now a blur from trembling hands. He crushed it, flung the wad across the tent, and with a single blow he upended the makeshift end table. It crashed to the ground.

A private barged through the tent flap. "Everything okay, sir?"

"No!" he shouted. "Now leave me alone."

He collapsed on his cot, prostrate with grief, where he stayed until well into the evening. When he finally began to stir, he stared at the mess of broken glass, writing instruments, and strewn papers—a cruel reminder that this was no nightmare. It was real. After collecting his wits about him, he slowly stooped to retrieve the letter, smoothed it again with the flat of his hand, and forced himself to finish reading where he had left off.

> *... was a boy. Your son and our only grandson. It appeared there was more to the story, but Emily's mother erupted into a flurry of tears. I fear she ran off mid-sentence. We are so very sorry and offer you our deepest sympathies.*
>
> *With this most tragic news, we hope while being in exceedingly dangerous territory you shall be especially careful until your heart has had ample opportunity to mend. We so look forward to your safe return.*
>
> *God speed.*
>
> *Your loving father and mother,*
>
> *Lord & Lady Harrington*

CHAPTER FIVE

O llie returned to London. No matter where he searched, peace remained elusive, the pain of losing Emily and his unborn child unbearable. He upended a draught of ale and slammed the mug on the bar. "Barman? Gimme another."

"You've had enough, sir," a deep voice said from behind.

Through swirling smoke and an alcohol induced blur, a white neck-band vaguely worked into focus, the face not as much. "On the contrary," Ollie said. "I've barely begun."

The vicar slid onto a barstool. "Mind if I join you?"

He shrugged. He preferred not to engage in small chatter or meaningful talk. He wished merely to be left alone.

"Still in the military, are you?" the vicar pressed. "Rumors abound that you're back at Harrington Manor, but no word about how long."

"I have nothing better to do," Ollie said.

"What about your studies at university?"

"I'll get to them one day ... perhaps."

"But not before numbing yourself with another visit to a local pub, I presume?"

You presume correctly. "You've been informed of my visits, have you? How about you? Why would a man of the cloth take an earthy stroll through a rundown tavern such as this? No, don't tell me," he said, forcing words through a thick tongue. "You thought no one would see you walking about in the fog, is that correct?"

The barman motioned for confirmation of a drink but the vicar shook his head, neither did he respond to Ollie's slight. "You have me curious, Oliver. Why would a man of the aristocracy take an unabashed roll through the mud? And in a pub so many miles from home?"

"Home?" He chuckled. "Not home. Prison. I wished to find a place where I might enjoy permission to feel. Feelings are disallowed at Harrington Manor, or perhaps that you did not know."

"Things have gotten a bit trying for you, have they?"

He wobbled on the barstool. "How did you find me?"

"Your father presumed you were here."

"Ahh, my father ..." Ollie laughed again. "He ordered me not to marry my Em. Did he reveal that to you as well? And have you any idea what her enormous misdeed was?"

The vicar positioned an elbow lightly on the bar. "Why not tell me about it?"

"She was a commoner. That was her misdeed. Her big, big misdeed. And have you any idea what happened in the end? Her carriage overturned. She lost her life. My son died, too."

The vicar squeezed his eyes closed and then stared off, his countenance empathetic. He appeared to collect his thoughts. "Your loss is far more painful than I even want to imagine," he said. "But you, my good man, are a Harrington. Harringtons are a tenacious lot. They face life, not run from it. Why are you choosing to numb your pain?"

"Not pain," he said.

"Then why the excessive consumption of ale?"

He teetered again. "What better way to numb my anger?"

"But why?" the vicar said.

"Take a look at me." Ollie held out a hand. "These fists. I'm anything but a small man. I'm numbing my anger so I won't hurt anyone."

"Who is it you wish to hurt?"

He choked at the thought. "My father?"

The vicar appeared surprised. "He angers you, does he?"

"Let's state it this way … all my life he found a need to control everything about me but my thoughts, and he would control those as well, were it possible—what to eat, how to dress, who my friends ought to be, where to attend studies, whom I could and could not date, and whom to marry. He even threw a tantrum when I told him I wanted to be a barrister. So you ask if he angers me? How could he not?"

The vicar plucked up a napkin and wiped away water spots from the counter. "From what you've told me, you have every right to feel cross. Unyieldingly so. But with your father's land income, why did you find it necessary to choose a profession?"

Rather than answer, Ollie chugged down a generous swig of ale.

"Given your current disposition," the vicar said, "rest assured I find your anger healthy."

He blinked. "Surely you jest. It makes me feel rather wicked."

The vicar shook his head. "You're grieving, and anger is a natural part of the grieving cycle. Don't scold yourself. It's a clear sign you're getting better. Regarding your father, though, have you thought to dig deeper, to learn why Lord Harrington is as he is? I mean not in a confrontational way, but rather in a loving way, to understand and value him the way you wish him to understand and value you?"

"But I was a boy, vicar."

"And now you are a man," he countered.

Ollie glanced around the smoke-filled room, his thoughts sobering faster than his gray matter. A rational conversation with his demanding father had never before occurred to him. The thought cut loose an anchor, his torment dissipating.

He smiled to himself.

Em would have wanted that.

OLLIE SPENT THE NEXT WEEK WEANING off hard drink while mulling over unfinished business. If he desired to get beyond grief, he must face his past—have that chat with his father, decide how best to navigate his future, and make a visit to the flat of Mrs. de Haven in the heart of the impoverished section of the city. He would begin by visiting her.

He stood outside the tenement house with hand poised to knock, cherished familiarity flooding his heart with renewed pain. When the door opened, Emily's aging mother fell into his waiting arms. After a measured moment, she pushed back and invited him in.

A crib sat in an alcove in the modest living room, stabbing his heart as would a sharp knife. Left by his dear Emily? For their beloved son? For an instant Ollie felt certain he heard the beginning of a baby's whimper, but then silence. How cruel the imaginings of grief.

Mrs. de Haven ushered him to a small table in the sparse kitchen and left him and his tortured memories alone while she disappeared for a moment, then returned to heat a pot of tea.

She handed him a dainty cup on a saucer and said, "What was I thinking? Let me find a larger cup."

"This one's fine," he said, but then he grinned. "I must admit its handle does feel a trifle small, but I rather enjoy the challenge."

Although a commoner, Mrs. de Haven sat primly, folding her hands in the way of a consummate lady. "Tell me," she said, "how did you fare in Sudan?"

"How did I fare in Sudan?" he repeated, his gaze falling to the worn flooring. "It was difficult. Quite an education, actually."

"In what way?"

Hearing Emily in her mother's voice, he considered a world of privilege as it contrasted to a world of want. He raised a brow and lightly placed the cup back on its saucer. "During war, soldiers kill," he said. "That's what we're trained to do. We have no idea which day might be our last. And every now and then there comes along a young officer who flaunts a flagrant attitude of entitlement. Disrespecting the enlisted. Treating them as if they were servants ... or lower than servants."

Like the day Ollie had grabbed a private's wrist to stop a knife the bloke was about to throw. The stunned leftenant for whom it was intended learned respect the hard way. That officer was fortunate he had any life left to learn it at all.

Ollie shook his head. "Suffice it to say, it was an education in a number of ways."

"You're a humble man, Oliver. No wonder my Emily was so devoted to you." Mrs. de Haven's eyes took on a hollow look as she lightly fingered the stem of her cup. "You aren't here to share your experiences in Sudan. You've come to learn about her final hours. We had had a lot of rain that day," she began. "I felt so sorry for Emily. The weather had been dreary for weeks and she felt housebound. Said she needed to get out for a while. No one could blame her." Mrs. de Haven shook her head, and as if spewing memorized lines that had been spoken one too many times, she said, "As Emily rode off in that buggy, I called after her, begged her to be careful. Several hours later I received word. The ruts in the road cut deep. The puddles were too large. What a dreadful time to break a wheel." She looked at Ollie, tears cascading down her gaunt cheeks. "By the time I reached her, she had lost too much blood. The poor dear was white as that porcelain cup you're holding." Mrs. de Haven hesitated before choking out, "The doctor mentioned something about tremendous damage to capillaries. And the baby—"

"My son," Ollie said, a knot forming in his own throat as if an invisible hand twisted it tighter and tighter.

Mrs. de Haven quickly changed the subject, appearing to force a positive tone. "Emily always did want to move to America. We have family in southern Minnesota. A place called Amber Leaf."

"I remember it sounded idyllic. She asked if we might move there one day." He got up and paced about in the cramped room. "When I first received word about the accident, I felt numb, lost my desire to live. I hoped in time it would return, but that hasn't happened."

She took a sip of tea and lowered her cup. Why did she have to look so like Emily? "I've resumed studies at university now," he said. "As soon as I complete them, I'm considering getting on to America to fulfill her dream. I hope to find myself there. If not, I can always return to England." That is, if my father chooses not to shun me again.

The remainder of their chat taking on a strained quality, he said, "I must be on my way. It's impossible for words to express what a delight it has been to visit with you."

On his way to the door, he looked toward the alcove. It sat empty. No crib. Had his imagination been playing tricks on him? He needed to get on with life or he would lose his mind for certain.

In the months that ensued, he did not venture far from studies. He socialized little and stopped drinking completely. Late one evening in front of the fire he had that chat with his father. Much to his dismay, it brought no resolution. In late autumn, after expressing concern about his emotionally impoverished existence, his mother hosted a holiday party. In the room filled with guests, there were but two unattached attendees—Mary Ashbury and Ollie. He minded his manners playing the practiced gentleman while dancing woodenly to chamber music. Gazing at the happy faces about him, emptiness invaded him to the core.

He would never find warmth in this aristocracy. He must get away from this wretched existence lest he shrivel and die.

CHAPTER SIX

Nearing the shores of an unfamiliar land, a throng of enthusiastic passengers strolled about the deck, rested against the rails, or gazed over the side of the ship, mesmerized by hungrily lapping waves. Near the stern stood a young woman who appeared to seek Ollie's attention. She bore a striking resemblance to Mary Ashbury, that fine aristocratic young lady who defined the term pretentious. Whom he did not love. Could never love. To think his father had had the audacity to mention her name in the very letter announcing Emily's passing. He spun on his heel and headed toward the aft port, choosing to leave England and all reminders thereof behind.

"Harrington was the name, was it not?" a voice called out. The affable chap with moustache bopping up and down like a trap door and pipe clamped between his teeth distractedly searched his pockets. "Might you happen to have a light, kind sir?"

Ollie struck a match and held flame to the man's pipe. "Forgive me," he teased, "but I hadn't recognized you. As I recall, the last time we chanced upon one another, you appeared a paler shade of gray than the paint aboard ship. Thought perhaps you might have taken a plunge overboard."

The man laughed. "I did spend the bulk of the journey below deck, lying in close quarters in a prone position, becoming only too familiar with drab walls. My wife and infant son did not fare much better. How about you?"

Wife and infant son? "I was fortunate to gain my sea legs early on," he said after a brief hesitation.

"Most fortunate indeed. What a delightful springboard for your new pilgrimage in America. How long do you wish to stay?"

For the rest of my days. "Time alone will tell, my good man," he said and then smiled at the thought of making his own way. "And what about your plans?"

"We are on extended holiday. I hope to research. Begin writing my next novel. That sort of thing. Thought we should spend several months ferreting about in New England and return to Britain late summer."

Ollie considered the words 'the next several months,' intrigued by what those months promised to hold.

The man perked up. "Ahh, here come my lovely bride and our little fledgling now." He reached for his child. "Come to Papa."

Ollie's heart grew mournful. He bid the man a hasty farewell, returned to his quarters, and peered out the porthole for a long moment. He then picked up his writing instrument, tapped pen against paper, and began to write.

20 June 1901

Dearest Family:

Although the seas remain calm, we are surrounded by fog, and for the four hours past the foghorn has sounded every two minutes to keep the ship from striking other vessels. We are scheduled for arrival in New York Harbor later this evening, bringing an end to a long and arduous journey across high rolling seas. I fear we spent the bulk of our time sailing against the wind, which cost us an extra day. Though there has been much about which to write and many adventures aboard ship to share, I regret to inform you that the majority of travelers spent a great deal of time below deck, unbearably seasick from heaving waters.

Earlier this afternoon an American doctor inspected us again and after breaking through the fog, we spent the rest of our time watching for land. It is finally visible as we near the coast. The beauty before us is beyond expression. Splendid villas. Magnificent forests. A harbor bedecked with hundreds of ships. And as I write, tugboats are towing us toward the docks. It is an exciting time. An adventurous time. A time filled with wonder.

I plan to take in the sights of the great city this evening and tomorrow evening shall board a train for the upper Midwest. Perhaps I shall better manage writing from the rails.

He stilled his pen and leaned away from the desk as the ship listed. The chap journeying with wife and child niggled at him. The man had reached for the little one and referred to himself as papa. Having left England alone and soon to arrive at New York Harbor alone, Ollie couldn't imagine such a thing.

He glanced at the letter, the ink glistening wet. Never in his life had he felt comfortable calling his parents father and mother. Though he wanted to call them warm and tender names like papa and mama, he penned his letter to dearest family, but to his mother and father it was intended. He must find deeper things about which to write than the weather, inanimate ships, and far-off vistas if he ever wished to break that impenetrable invisible barrier holding him at arm's length.

Do know that I appreciate your disappointment with my decisions, which run counter to your desires, and I further respect your desire to again break ties with me. My only wish is that you will one day come to appreciate my grief as well and find it in your heart to respond, even if it is merely a word every now and then indicating that you are well.

Please pass along my greetings to other members of our family, and give an extra carrot to Betsy along with my undying affection.

Now the cordial greetings from your loving son Oliver

Having finished the letter, he stuffed it in an envelope, sealed it as if sealing his fate, and wondered at his future—alone in a foreign land.

CHAPTER SEVEN

"Next stop, Amber Leaf," the porter cried.

A shiver of excitement rippled through Ollie. *This is it ... the unknown about to reveal itself.* He stepped onto the railway platform, and a blast of oppressive humidity doused him. With fedora in one hand, bag in the other, he sighed. This was one day he preferred London fog.

"Harrington?" a scratchy voice cried from behind. "Barrister O.M. Harrington?"

A lanky man, wrinkle lines from what appeared a perpetual grin, gray thinning hair, and bib overalls headed toward Ollie with hand extended. "Arend de Haven," he said with a pleasant chortle. "I'm Emily's uncle. Go by the name of Deacon."

"By all means, feel free to call me Ollie."

Deacon's grin grew wider. "Minnesota is Scandinavian country, my good man. Home of the lumberjacks ... and you look like one. You'd fit in better if you went by a name like Ole. Or by the looks of you, even Big Ole. Seems more fitting."

Ollie felt contented with his name as is. He was British, not Scandinavian. So he merely shook Deacon's moist hand then pulled out a handkerchief and wiped his brow. He yearned for a moment to also wipe away a dreadful attack of emptiness. Though standing face to face with Emily's uncle, realization set in. This man was incapable of assuaging that unremitting hole in his heart.

"Humidity getting to you I see." Deacon slapped the air and gazed up into the glaring sky. "Whatever you do, don't concern yourself. Every now and then we get a hot spell like this. It'll pass. Always does." Glancing at Ollie's suitcase, he said, "Say, you came with not much more than the shirt on your back, I see."

"Harrington?" another voice cried out. "Oliver M. Harrington?" Farther down the line two porters struggled with a steamer trunk.

"Gentlemen? Over here." He waved and murmured, "Perhaps a bit more."

Deacon reached for the trunk handles and grinned. "Should've known better." Though standing eyeball to eyeball with Ollie at six feet and three inches, from east to west the gangly farmer appeared half his size. But as he opened his mouth to say 'I'll get that,' Deacon hoisted the hundred pound trunk, flinging it on the back of the buckboard as if it were no heavier than a briefcase. "I think the wagon and Old Horse can handle the extra weight."

Undoubtedly noticing Ollie's astounded stare, Deacon said, "Been liftin' hay bales. Climb aboard." A tug on the reins and a light "tck, tck, tck … Giddyup, Old Horse," and they set off.

Struck by that name again, he said, "Old Horse?"

"Around our place we call 'em like we see 'em."

"I get the impression I'm going to like your place."

Deacon's smile disappeared. "Say, we sure were sorry to hear about Em. You must have loved her something awful to pursue her dream as your own. She deserved as much," he said. "Wonderful little gal. An amazing beauty outside and in. Are you sure you don't want to stay out at the farm for a few days 'til you get acquainted with the town? We have plenty of room. The kids can double up. They'd get a kick out of it."

"Thank you kindly for the offer," Ollie said, "but I prefer being fresh for that new venture awaiting me first thing in the morning."

The buckboard stopped in front of Hotel Amber and he looked around. "Nice place."

"Best you'll find for miles," Deacon said. "We'll expect you out at the farm for Sunday dinner. I'll swing by with the buckboard at half past noon."

A bellboy helped with the luggage. They climbed the few steps of the hotel's impressive entry. Immediately inside, he stopped to familiarize himself with his new surroundings, the view of the room giving him great pleasure.

You would have loved this place, Em.

Shoes clicking against marble. Grand staircase. Glistening crystal chandelier in the center of the lobby. Elegant dining room and coffee shop. The lingering scent of cigar smoke. Undoubtedly a Mecca for travelers, many of whom were salesmen who stayed or dined at the hotel before heading out for worlds unknown. Not Ollie, though. This he considered his new home.

Compliments of the management, copies of *The Minneapolis Journal* and *The Amber Leaf Tribune* along with a bowl of fresh fruit awaited him in his room. After scanning the papers, taking a long bath, and enjoying a hardy steak in the dining room, he set off on foot to explore downtown. Pleased with his findings, though no one with whom to share a word or two, he returned to his room. Determined not to participate in a continuing one-sided war of no words with his father, he sat down and penned another letter.

1 July 1901

Dearest Family:

May this letter find everyone in good spirits and in good health.

Arrived in Amber Leaf a few minutes past noon today. Emily's uncle met me at the railroad depot. I found Deacon de Haven captivating. He has a quality about him—my dear Emily's warmth, wit, and decent to the core. I presume we shall get along famously.

My first order of business was to take a long bath to get relief from the oppressive heat, but fear I was as wet after toweling off as before climbing into the tub. According to Deacon, it will last for but a short spell. Perhaps it is best not to complain. Better the humidity than the pending tornadoes and subzero temperatures, which promise to darken our future.

I took a casual stroll up Broadway and am pleased to say that Amber Leaf is a pleasant town with canopied windows, clothiers, tobacconists, and restaurants much like one would find in a larger city. And where the north of Broadway ends, a verdant, sloping hill butts against a lake and prodigious residences abound along its shoreline. At the north side there sits a rather small island that appears idyllic for an occasional Sunday afternoon picnic.

As for Hotel Amber, it is as exquisite and charming as I had hoped. The smoke-filled air smells pleasantly of cherry tobacco. The place is most inviting. I would be surprised to ever find the lobby emptied of guests.

As for the courthouse, it stands immediately across the street. As I write, I hear the bell pealing in its tower. If its architecture is any indication, I believe it shall be quite satisfying to engage hearings there. The structure boasts five chimneys, four steeples, and, yes, that bell tower. I took it upon myself to take a quick stroll down its halls before supper, and tomorrow I will explore the law office farther up the street as I begin my first day of employment. I remain enthusiastic at the thought.

You may write to me c/o Hotel Amber, Amber Leaf, Minnesota, USA.

Now cordial greetings from your loving son Oliver.

With folded letter in hand, he reflected on the day one last time before calling it a night. A new country. A new life. A new friend. But a new name? Though Big Ole Harrington suggested confidence and strength, he wasn't ready for it. Overwhelmed by his new surroundings, neither was he certain he was ready for a new life.

CHAPTER EIGHT

ootsteps pounded on hardwood—Ollie's footsteps. He smiled inwardly, deeming it impossible to manage his way undetected up the stairs and down the hallowed halls to Addison & Crowley even if he walked in stocking feet. But that mattered not at all. At the end of the day, how might he look upon his new charge?

A pleasant older woman stood at the door appearing to anticipate his arrival, a pencil behind an ear and hair sticking out terribly. She introduced herself as Hilda, supervisor of the clerical staff. Immediately behind her, wooden desks with teetering stacks of files stood scattered about in the fashion of a patchwork quilt. Paperweights secured reams of loose papers atop wooden file cabinets near open windows raising Ollie's hopes for an occasional light breeze, of which they were in desperate need.

Hilda ushered him from desk to desk introducing the clerical staff, quickly calling off their names. She gestured toward an enclosed office near the entry. "That's where Mr. Addison hides out," she said. "You will do well to give him a wide berth. He's all business and prefers being called Boss."

She guided Ollie on, introducing him first to Nelson Prixton ... Nel's son. Pricks a ton. Nelson Prixton. Then to John Brown ... Yawn. Yellow and black make brown. John Brown. And finally to

Charlie Mendenhall … hair charred and frizzy. Mend a hall. Charlie Mendenhall.

"You appear absorbed in your own world, Mr. Harrington," Hilda said. "Would you like me to repeat any of those names?"

"I believe I can manage them. Nelson Prixton. John Brown. Charlie Mendenhall. Might you care for a recounting of the secretaries' names as well?"

Hilda appeared astonished. "I think that will do."

A thin-lipped man of about forty with a few strands of brownish hair combed severely across his pate approached as if on his way to a wicked fire. "Harrington?" he said with a crushing handshake, "Addison here. Feel free to call me Boss. Welcome aboard." As he hurried on with a half grin, he turned back and, bumping against the side of a desk, he said, "You'll find your first assignment laid out on your desk. Now get busy."

Hilda hurried through the office procedures then said with an amused grin, "I'd better not keep you from your work."

He rifled through desk drawers, plucked out a tablet, inkbottle, and pen. Anxious to take on his first case, he opened a folder, titled Crusty Schmidt, and delved in.

After perusing several papers, it appeared the man with no next of kin was getting on in years. The railroad wanted to seize his land. After a number of failed attempts to reason with him and an occasional wild shot fired, the County's help had been solicited. Several attempts later, the County approached Boss to intercede on its behalf, to which Boss reluctantly agreed.

When Ollie lifted the folder, a pile of hand-written notes spilled out. Leafing through them, it became readily apparent why the County found it necessary to assume guardianship. That would be no easy task judging by the forbidding words on the chits of paper. Complaints. All of them—withdrawn, unruly, cantankerous, cross, uncooperative, snarling dog, sitting on his porch looking mean as a bull during mating season yet still as a possum, clutching his shotgun … again.

He had been sitting at his too small-scale wooden desk for the better part of an hour when a rush of footfalls begged his attention. A frazzled secretary nearly tripped over herself trying to get to her desk. He took a moment to still his excited heart. Next to Emily, she was the loveliest creature on which he had ever laid eyes. Smartly dressed. Chestnut hair bouncing gently at the shoulders. Doe eyes beaming from a gentle face. Sweeping lashes.

As he watched her slip her handbag in a desk drawer, however, an unexpected puff of warm, moist air met his neckline followed by a tempered warning. "Don't even think of it. She's taken."

The unsubtle pull of an eyebrow and the subtle upending of hairs like porcupine quills rising at the nape of his neck, Ollie turned and said, "Excuse me?"

Nelson Prixton, a sepia-haired attorney who appeared uncommonly self-important, sidled back to his desk like a suave fox that had marked its territory.

He sat dumbstruck. How was it that an exceedingly attractive young lady would find that pitiable piece of work worthy of her affection?

Mid afternoon he stood near the files when she happened by. "I haven't had the privilege of meeting you yet," he said. "I'm Oliver Harrington, and you are?"

Her cheeks grew a lovely pale shade of pink and she looked even more attractive, if that were possible. "Gretta Van Dyke. Nice to meet you. Please … call me Gretta."

"Van Dyke. That would be Dutch, would it not? My wife was Dutch."

"You'll have to excuse me," she said. "Mr. Brown is a brilliant attorney and interesting to work for, but when he's on deadline, watch out!" As she hurried away, she glanced back and smiled awkwardly. "Welcome aboard."

He returned to his work and by late afternoon, after pouring through the contents of Crusty Schmidt's file, he had gotten a decent grasp of what was expected of him. He would arrange an excursion out to the man's farm sooner rather than later.

At five o'clock a light tapping noise echoed throughout the room. He looked up.

Nelson was standing at Gretta's desk, hovering over her. "Let's go."

"I can't," she insisted. "Mr. Brown needs this letter first thing. I've got to finish it."

Though Nelson's face was not visible from his vantage point, the edge in his voice bothered Ollie. "You can finish it in the morning," Nelson said.

"But what if he—"

"If there's a problem, I'll take care of it."

As she stood to leave, she glanced back at Ollie, her expression one of utter embarrassment.

Only the first day on the job and already he found two sets of ears that appeared to need bending. Nelson's for being so demanding, and Gretta's for not standing up for herself.

Or did their ears need bending? Emily's words revisited him, words about that poor boy in ragged clothes and the street seller in a fit of temper, 'I answered anger with anger,' she'd said. 'How am I any better than the seller?'

And how might I be any better than them?

CHAPTER NINE

A string of muggy gray days yielded to a clear blue sky, setting the stage for what Gretta hoped might be an ideal Fourth of July, but with Nelson, she never knew what to expect.

She wedged the tip of her parasol against the dock and gave a deliberate push, easing the rowboat out onto placid waters.

"Well done," Nelson said.

The boat swayed gently, rippling the waters along the tranquil northern perimeter of the lake. When they approached the southern shore, Gretta peered from beneath the shade of her parasol. A throng had gathered on a grassy knoll along the south shore. Baby buggies and white straw hats dotted the lawn as if it were a checkerboard. Flags waved. A band struck up John Philip Sousa's *The Stars and Stripes Forever*. Just then a tall man weaving through the crowd stopped and turned as if captivated by the sound. Oliver Harrington? To Gretta's astonishment, her heart fluttered. She gazed briefly at her scuffed shoes, dull dress, and fraying parasol then back at him.

Nelson craned his neck. "What are you looking at so intently?"

A blush warmed her cheeks. "No one."

"I said what, not who." He tented his eyes. "Say, isn't that Harrington?"

"Where?" she said, feigning innocence.

"Over there. You can't miss him." Nelson stopped rowing and took in the sight, his expression curious, then pulled again at the paddles. "I wonder how he's going to fare at the office. Boss gave him a pretty tough first assignment."

Gretta gasped. "Not Crusty?"

He nodded, his unexpected smirk troubling her. He wouldn't have had anything to do with setting up that assignment, would he?

"The County struck out," he said. "No one else will go near the man."

"Sounds like an initiation stunt. That doesn't seem fair."

"Why not? Why coddle him?"

Nelson was right. Why coddle anyone who is paid to do a job? But if the barrister didn't know how to swim, he was in real trouble. His first assignment promised to plunk him in the middle of a severely deep lake.

"Speaking of Mr. Harrington," she said, "why did you insist on whisking me off during his first day at the office? You embarrassed me."

Nelson's brows spiked as he drew harder at the paddles. "I didn't mean to."

"I'm sure you didn't, but I was under pressure and told you so. A meaner man than Mr. Brown never drew breath, and yet you insisted that we leave. I only went because I didn't want to make a fuss in front of everyone."

"In front of everyone," Nelson said, gazing back at the crowd, "or in front of Harrington? You did make your deadline the next morning, didn't you? I have a better question. Why did you blush like a schoolgirl when you were talking to him?"

Her cheeks grew warm again. "I didn't mean to. He caught me by surprise. Looked so sad when I told him my name. Said his wife was Dutch, too."

"So what if she is?"

"He said *was* Dutch. I get the impression she died or something."

"Why not ask?"

"That isn't something you ask a person. I know I'm being silly, but for some strange reason I feel intimidated by that man."

Nelson smirked. "Not because he's a barrister?"

She gazed back at the shoreline, looking for the tall man who was no longer there. "You have to admit his title does sound impressive."

"But it's only British for attorney. He's no different from any of the rest of us."

I wouldn't be so sure of that. "I get a feeling he's going to join ranks with the likes of you and really go places some day."

It wasn't possible for Nelson's grin to grow wider. "Thanks for including me in your summation," he said.

After a relaxing journey around the lake, Gretta hooked the handle of her parasol on a plank and helped ease the boat back to the dock.

"You sure are handy with that thing," Nelson insisted.

He secured the boat and escorted her down a narrow path winding alongside the lakeshore. After picking up a prepared picnic basket from his buggy, they strolled along to a lightly wooded area, and spread a blanket beneath a tall oak. Nelson made pleasant conversation as they ate, but then grew thoughtful. "I've started writing a poem," he said. "It's about you. I'm still working on it, but it goes something like this.

Her footsteps warmed the hallowed halls
She smiled and his world stood still
But when she vanished past a far off wall
The light in his heart grew nil

"It's your footsteps I speak of, Gretta. It's your smile that makes my world stand still. But the days in the office when you aren't around, the life drains out of the place."

Though she questioned whether Nelson would ever make it as a romantic or a poet, she said, "Give me a moment to still my fluttering heart."

"I'm serious," he said. "You've got to believe me. You bring a warmth to my life I've never experienced before … and I like it."

She tingled at his sincerity.

He went on to ask thoughtful questions about her family, her past, and her goals for the future as if finally taking her more seriously.

Could that be because of the new attorney in town?

CHAPTER TEN

At half past ten in the morning, Ollie's rented buggy arrived at Crusty Schmidt's not so rundown farm. An old man with a cheek filled with snuff, undoubtedly Schmidt, sat on the front porch and glowered. A rusty-colored mongrel with teeth bared and a low steady growl flanked him on one side, a shotgun on the other.

"Morning," Ollie said.

The man's menacing gaze pivoted to the gun.

"Morning," he repeated, preferring not to look up the wrong end of the double barrels. He considered his options, which were few. Though his hands leaked sweat and his heart vibrated, he climbed down from the buggy, feigning courage.

Barking angrily, the vicious mutt lunged off the porch and made a mad dash toward him. Meanwhile, the old man stopped chewing, casually took aim at a spittoon, and discharged all the while eyeing Ollie. The man slowly gathered up his shotgun, appearing nonplussed by the dog's attack.

The horse whinnied, and Ollie stood frozen, heart hammering while his eyes riveted on the savage beast lunging at him. He willed himself not to speak. *Call. Your. Dog. Off ... Now!*

In the midst of an airborne leap, the man cried, "Blacky!"

As the dog dropped to its paws, tucked its tail between its legs, and meandered back to the porch, Ollie eased out a guarded breath.

"Good dog," the old man said. He scratched it behind an ear with a free hand while raising the shotgun with the other.

Ollie drew open his coat and took a cautious step forward. "You won't be needing that. I'm not packing a pistol."

"You with the State?" the man said.

"No, sir. Law Office of Addison & Crowley. We're collaborating with the County."

The old man swiveled the shotgun barrel directly at him. "I'm warnin' ya. Don't come any closer. I could shoot a tooth clean off a grizzly given half a chance." He spat again into the spittoon while that low growl continued to rumble in the dog's throat. "I heard you people was gunnin' for me. An' you young whippersnapper ain't takin' me nowhere. This is my place and I aim to stay put."

Ollie eased forward, both hands raised, palms out. "If you please, sir, I've come to solicit your help."

The man's eyes narrowed. "Say, you some kinda foreigner or something? You talk kinda funny."

"British. Arrived recently from England. I shall attempt to ease out of the accent, but everything takes time."

"That a fact?" He spat again. "You said something about wanting my help?"

"I presume you're Crusty Schmidt?"

"You presume right."

"The County has acquired what I believe you would consider a wagonload of complaints about you."

Crusty let out a laugh. "There ain't nothing new about that. I earned those complaints, every last one of 'em. They better get used to it, too, 'cuz they're gonna get a whole lot more before I get done."

As he took another step forward, Crusty lifted his shotgun higher, but this time didn't take aim.

"You stay right there, young fella'."

He eyed the gun and then the dog. *Very well.* "The County is uncertain as to how to attend to you. They feel they might need to impose guardianship. I fear that would cause you much distress. It would also be a rather costly expense for the citizenry. Since they prefer that their hard earned tax dollars be spent with a fair amount of wisdom, contrary to everyone's wishes, I'm attempting to find a way to make that happen … to keep you in your own home. I believe I have a way to manage that. Would you be opposed to my joining you for a minute or two?"

Crusty raised the gun higher, taking aim again, but he stayed put, staring him down.

"You don't scare easy, do ya, boy?"

As easily as anyone with a shotgun aimed directly at his solar plexus. "I prefer to hold my own."

"How can I trust you not to nab me?"

Again he eyed Crusty's shotgun and then the snarling dog. "How can I be certain I can trust you?"

"You can't," Crusty said. He lowered the gun, pulled out a handkerchief, and started to polish it.

After a prolonged moment, Ollie said, "Would it be your intention to have me stand out here all day in this formidable heat?"

"Suit yourself."

The old man was not about to cooperate. Ollie looked off toward the field, and tented his eyes. "Good crops this year, I see."

"Not too bad. Could be better," Crusty said, his tone softening.

He took another step forward. "Might I at least enjoy the shade of your porch? I can help you, of that I am certain. Besides, I fear I may suffer sun stroke dare I stand in the sun much longer."

Crusty surrendered a smile. "Come on in." He wedged the gun beneath his arm and held the squeaky screen door open for Blacky first and then him. Inside, he pulled the drapes back, brightening the dark, though well-kept, living room. "What made you so sure my dog wasn't gonna take a bite outa your hide?"

"You neglected to look concerned."

"I didn't neglect nothing. People who have the presence of mind to think when a vicious dog is running at 'em are few and far between."

Drawn to pictures situated on a table immediately to the right of a potbelly stove, he took a step forward to study them. "May I?"

"If you must."

One photograph in particular fascinated him. "Your wife?"

Crusty nodded. "Wedding picture. Lost her going on five years now. One beside it's my parents."

"Children?"

Crusty shook his head.

He picked up another frame, but this of an object. "What might this be?" Getting no response, he looked at it more closely and balked. "The Congressional Medal of Honor? I found nothing in your file about this. Anyone else know about it?"

The man shrugged.

"We must have a chair," Ollie said. "I think it best if we engage in a rather earnest chat. You are the one wielding the power, my good fellow. A gentleman of your stature certainly doesn't belong in a home. If I am to assist you, I need to know what it is that has tousled your feathers."

Crusty eased onto an armchair well past its prime. "They say they're gonna take my land from me. They can't do that, can they? It's mine. And all my good-for-nothing neighbors are in on it. The more they push, the madder I git. Now they're saying awful stuff. Saying stuff like I'm tetched."

"Does the railroad want to pilfer your land from you, or purchase it?"

"It's all one and the same, ain't it? Talking about building some no account railroad across my property or some fool thing. Imagine that."

Ollie peered out the window. "They wish the land on the north side of your property here?"

"Yup."

"How many acres might you have?"

"Couple hundred."

"Give it some thought, Mr. Schmidt. The sooner a railroad passes through, the easier it will be for you to ship grain."

"Aww, no. You ain't gonna go talking me into that. This is my house and my property."

"That's correct. It is your home—a very nice home at that, with good land. Rich soil. Before you get your rankles up, let's discuss this from a higher plane where we might see things more clearly. Anyone clever and brave enough to receive the Congressional Medal of Honor is also too wise not to sort things through."

Though Crusty scowled, he went on. "No one wants to live next to a railroad, but in your case, it might be beneficial."

"You're talking crazy."

"I noticed when I rode up," he said, "that a fair amount of your acreage is under swampland."

"It's my swamp."

"Indeed, it is, but have you any idea what lies beneath it?"

"You mean that peat soil?" Crusty scoffed.

"Yes, sir. As it stands now, how does that land benefit you?"

"It doesn't, but like I told you, it's mine."

"Eventually they plan to dam it up. Were you made aware of that?"

Crusty sat back and gave his head a subtle shake. "No, I sure wasn't."

"You would still have the same aggregate of acreage, but you and your neighbors would also have more land available to farm, with some of the richest soil in these parts and a nice slice of lakeside property in addition. With more crops that you'd likely be raising, you might speed up shipping if a railroad passes through. You'd win all the way around. You may wish to give this a fair amount of thought."

Crusty scowled. "How do I know what you're saying is true? You can't trust nobody these days."

"Indeed. But it does appear plausible, does it not?"

He scratched his chin. "Well, by gummie, I guess it does at that."

"Take time to think about it. When the County and railroad learn you've earned the Congressional Medal of Honor, they'll leave you alone."

At half past two, he returned to the office with a grinning Crusty Schmidt in tow. With the exception of Nelson Prixton, jaws dropped like a row of dominoes as they passed through and proudly presented themselves at the threshold of Boss's door.

Nelson, however, scowled.

CHAPTER ELEVEN

ager to once again enter Emily's world, that world too quickly
denied, at half past noon, Ollie waited near open windows for
Deacon to pull up with Old Horse. Deacon had been a pleasant
surprise, but what of his family? Ollie wondered whether they might
get on or feel put upon to have a stranger disrupt their comfortable
lives. And what of the farm? He felt apprehensive not knowing what
to expect.

At one o'clock, still no buckboard.

He stepped outside, concern growing that he might have burdened
Deacon, who at present was his only lifeline. He needed to keep on
good terms with the man.

He let out a relieved sigh when Deacon arrived tens of minutes
later wearing that perpetual grin of his. "Would have come sooner," he
said, "but Old Horse threw a shoe. Bridge is out on the main road, so
we'll have to take the long way home."

For the next three quarters of an hour, the horse clomped and the
buckboard squawked over badly rutted country roads. To Ollie's great
pleasure, Deacon's wife awaited them on the porch with hands on pudgy
hips, wiry gray hair drawn into a severe bun, and bright eyes dancing.

A brief wave of longing invaded him as he paused at the entry
of the two-story home and surveyed the scene inside. Five children,

mostly grown—guffawing with one another and arguing fervently about who'd get the biggest slice of cake, while glancing at him as if he were an integral part of the merrymaking. How pleasant to grow up with spirited siblings and free run of the land, he mused. The fun. The camaraderie. With the favorable tone Deacon had set, Ollie felt at one with his family and he had but arrived.

"We'd better eat," Mrs. de Haven said, "before the food gets a chance to burn."

They converged around the table, Deacon at the head, Mrs. de Haven opposite him, and Ollie and the children, stair stepped by age, lined the sides. During the feast of pot roast and its trimmings, the children took turns introducing themselves, each asking Ollie a question. 'What was it like living among aristocrats? ... Why do you have to work? ... Where did you attend school? ... What was it like living in London?' As Ollie answered, he was taken with the orderliness, maturity, and manners exhibited at what his father would deem a commoners' table.

After dinner, Deacon invited him out to the rocking chairs on the front porch. He dug at his teeth with a toothpick while Ollie admired the cornfields from afar and sipped a sarsaparilla.

"Peaceful out, isn't it?" Deacon said, breaking into a long silence. "Sure hope we can hold onto the place."

He was taken aback. "It's been in the family for years, has it not?"

"It has, but a house full of kids can dwindle a man's resources. If times get tough and we need a loan, I don't know that the bank will be there for us. Word's out they've been having some trouble."

"If times get tough?" Ollie said, curious.

"Crops didn't do well last year. They look good now, but you never know when something unforeseen comes up. Last year a bull took sick and some equipment broke down. One of my boys broke an arm. And there's always maintenance. House could use a new coat of paint. Barn and shed, they could use a little work, too. It'll all work out, though. Always does."

"I meant not to pry."

"Consider yourself family," Deacon said. "Families share their business."

Warmed by the thought of a loving family, Ollie listened happily to an occasional horse whinnying, cow mooing, and flies buzzing about. A scattered dry breeze happened every now and then rustling the leaves. As minutes past, his emptied soul seemed to fill. Perhaps with the help of Emily's family, he might one day indeed move on with his life.

"Em would have loved this place," he said.

Deacon absentmindedly stretched and snapped his suspenders. "We sent pictures from time to time. The wife is good at corresponding, so we did well keeping in touch. According to Em's letters, she longed for country life."

"You met her, I presume?"

"Once, when she was about ten or so. The wife and I got an itch to take a trip to the old country. Had a wonderful time with relatives, getting to know them. Saw a lot of Em's family. She sure was a pretty little thing. Loved getting attention, but she sure loved giving it, too."

"I hope I'm not a burden presuming my way into your lives," Ollie said. "When I received word that I lost her and our son …" His words caught. He gathered himself and attempted again. "Coming here, I—"

"Connects a man to life again?" Deacon's smile radiated Emily's same warmth. "I would have done the same thing. And you aren't presuming your way into our world. A man can't have enough family." He nudged Ollie's shoulder. "Sorry to hear about the boy. I know heartache. We lost our firstborn, too."

Deacon didn't share how he achieved it or how long it took, but he appeared at peace. Ollie longed for that peace also—peace about Emily and his son, those losses that never go away.

"Say, I've been wondering," Deacon said, "how was your first week at work?"

He set the chair to rocking and it let out a low moan. "Rather jolly, actually. However, I found a couple of contrary characters with which I fear I must contend."

Deacon looked at him and his easy grin reappeared. "I'm sure you'll get along fine," he said. "When your ways please the Lord, He makes your enemies to be at peace with you."

"God forbid they should become enemies, though they are certain to add a touch of color to my stay. A man by the name of Addison runs the place," he continued as an afterthought. "As you Americans say, he has his nose to the grindstone. Commands respect. Prefers being called Boss."

"I'm sure a man like that has a pretty good clerical staff."

Ollie nodded. "There's one in particular that's arrested my attention."

"Why's that?"

I feel drawn to her as I was to Em and that troubles me. "She's difficult to decipher. Seems bright and articulate, yet lacking confidence. Her supervisor raised his voice at her several times, and she cowered. She also spends time with one of our attorneys. He strikes me as being overbearing. I find it peculiar that with all she has to offer she would allow that sort of treatment."

"Give her time," Deacon said. "Maybe she'll grow a spine."

He looked out across the rolling fields, the corn as high as his shoulders. "You are most fortunate to live in the country where your life is your own."

"Yes, but every job has its challenges. Weather keeps us on our toes. At times we get an animal in distress. The crops don't like hail, wind, too much rain or the lack of it, saying nothing about the blight, but I'll take my problems any day over the quirkiness of others."

He set down his glass. "Do you ever enlist laborers come harvest time?"

"Mostly my boys and I handle it, but I do take on a hired hand every now and then. Don't tell me you want to get your hands grubby?"

"The way you lobbed my trunk on the back of your carriage when you engaged me at the railroad depot inspires me to toss a hay bale or two myself. A man can get soft sitting at a desk day after day."

"Tell you what," Deacon said, "come September you and me, we'll talk."

Ollie smiled to himself. First a barrister, now farming.

CHAPTER TWELVE

O llie's triumph with Crusty Schmidt had released a bursting flare of praise like fireworks, yet dwindled every bit as quickly. Rather than partaking in the victory or desiring to learn from one another, his fellow attorneys appeared to withdraw as if they assumed themselves in competition with him. That ought not to be.

At ten o'clock on the morning of July 30, Boss called a compulsory meeting. "As you all know, we have an important case coming up," he said. "I'll share more details with everyone involved as they unfold. But for now, I need an outstanding, impartial attorney to take it over. Do I have any volunteers?"

With the exception of Ollie, all hands raised. A hush fell on the conference room, eyes and ears riveted on Boss the way children wait in anticipation, listening for the call of their name, hoping to make that special team.

Boss glanced from attorney to attorney then peered down the bridge of his nose. "Harrington, you're the only one who hasn't raised a hand. Why not?"

He wanted a case, but not this soon, and not this one—whatever it might be. Considering the resentful attitudes of his fellow attorneys, he found the price tag much too high. He valued peace over having anything to prove. "I'll be happy to volunteer next time," he said.

Boss tapped a pen against his hand. "That a fact? Gentlemen, because he's only been with us a few short weeks and already had the moxie to take on and diffuse Crusty Schmidt, whom I might add," he scowled, "no one else had the guts to confront, I'll go with Oliver Harrington."

Not only did air siphon from the room, he winced at the mention of his name.

"I expect everyone to pitch in when asked," Boss said. "Questions?"

"Why Oliver Harrington?" a voice with a sharp edge asked from across the table.

"I've already covered that. Any more questions?" Boss waited a moment. "That's it, everyone. Now get back to work."

Hopeful expressions withered as shuffling feet retreated to their desks. Eyes cast downward. A whisper. A frown. An outright glare. Ollie was certain someone had said, "I thought we'd kicked the British out." Surprisingly, Nelson Prixton looked him in the eye. His expression, though sober, hinted of admiration, which surprised Ollie. As for the other lawyers, if fertilized, this may prove the seed that too easily encouraged resentment to grow.

At five o'clock the attorneys left the office together. John Brown looked over his shoulder and said, "Where are we all headed? The beer'd better be mighty cold."

Nelson was last out the door. He waved to Gretta, glanced back at Ollie, his expression nondescript, then walked off, calling to the others to wait up.

Ollie didn't hesitate to charge into Boss's office uninvited. "About this case to which I've been appointed," he said, anchoring his hands on Boss's desk. "Your choice of attorneys appears not to have been well received by my compatriots, and I can't in good conscience blame them."

Boss sobered. "Don't tell me you think you've won a popularity contest?"

"Why choose me over the others, other than I had the courage to confront Crusty Schmidt? True, I may be impartial since my knowledge of the town's history is limited and I know nothing about the case, but I'll have to learn everything everyone else knows before I presume to take on this task."

"If you listen to scuttlebutt," Boss said, loosening his tie, "you'll learn that your fellow attorneys believe this case is already lost. Crazy thing is, no one's bothered with due diligence yet, but you don't strike me as being short sighted."

Boss leaned back. Crossing his feet at the ankles, he propped them on the desktop and folded his hands over his belt as if attempting to set a casual tone for an anything but casual summarization. "It's an embezzlement case. Amber Leaf National Bank. I don't want it to go to trial, but if it does, we need to win."

An embezzlement case? Deacon had commented on problems at the bank. Might that have been Amber Leaf National?

"The owner is a friend of mine," Boss continued. "Fellow by the name of Josh Whiting. His son got caught red handed. Admitted to pilfering funds. Josh and I have been good friends for years. His son had a squeaky clean reputation 'til this happened. It's clear something's going on that no one cares to talk about. The bank's board was quick to press charges. We're representing Whiting. His boy's been suspended, but they let Senior keep his job—until this thing reaches a satisfactory end, that is. If it does go to trial, I want it to be fair, but I also need to honor a friendship. We have to win."

Ollie felt conflicted. First Crusty Schmidt, now this. Boss certainly was anything but shy about appointing him to the challenging cases. "Any waiting time before due diligence?"

"Get on it. Head this off quick as you can."

"One more inquiry," he said. "Whom might we hire for the investigative end?"

Boss impatiently drummed his fingers against the desk. "Hilda has a list of investigators. She'll help with that."

"Are we manacled to that list?"

"Why? Have someone in mind?"

He flashed on Deacon and his hard times. "I believe I do."

CHAPTER THIRTEEN

Gretta peered around the oversized menu. Nelson was looking nervously about the crowded dining room, his demeanor troubling her. "You haven't been yourself all day," she said. "Come to think of it, all of you attorneys acted touchy."

Nelson restrained his voice to a notch above a whisper. "We've got a sensitive case coming up. Boss put Harrington on it."

"Why didn't he give it to you?"

"He approached me a few weeks ago. Wanted me to have first crack, but I said no. Had to."

Nelson's response stopped her. He invented ways to climb the corporate ladder, not dodge them.

A harried waiter appeared. "Are we ready to order?"

Nelson placed their orders then waited until he disappeared. "The boys are pretty worked up."

"Is that why you all walked off together last night?"

He nodded.

Things didn't add up. If Gretta was to build a trusting relationship with Nelson, she needed to understand him. She plucked a biscuit from the breadbasket. "Why did you turn it down? That's not like you."

"Conflict of interest. I know the guy too well."

"Do I know him?"

"Keep this quiet, okay? Does the name Stephen Whiting ring a bell?"

A chunk of biscuit lodged in her throat. She forced it down. "Not *the* Stephen Whiting? From Amber Leaf National?" Stephen Whiting had it all. Cushy job. Gorgeous wife. Well-behaved children. Well dressed. Pillar of the community. "He isn't guilty," she said.

"I beg to differ."

"Why steal from his own father's bank? That doesn't make any sense."

Nelson ignored her question. "Whiting Senior is desperate," he said. "He'll do anything, including bribery, to keep the family name out of the paper."

"Bribery? What's he thinking?"

"Desperate people don't think. I'm sure that's why Boss chose Harrington to handle the case. He doesn't know the background and doesn't strike me as being easily bought off. As for Stephen and me, we've been buddies since grade school."

"I didn't know that. Why didn't you tell me?"

"Never thought to. We boated together. Fished together. Chatted over beers on occasion. Then he went off and got married. Doesn't have time to pal around any more."

"Just because he got married?"

Nelson grinned sheepishly. "Seems I dated his wife."

Gretta felt an unwanted jab of jealousy. Slippery, slippery Nelson. Conflict of interest, indeed. "If he married her, what's the problem?"

He shrugged, then lowered his voice. "He *is* guilty, Gretta."

"If he doesn't have time to pal around, how could you possibly know that?"

Nelson gave another cautious look at neighboring tables and leaned in close, bathing her with his breath. "He admitted as much."

"When? I thought you said you don't see much of him any more."

He sat stone-faced.

Why did she not believe him?

CHAPTER FOURTEEN

Stephen Whiting was not what Ollie had expected. Standing at the perimeter of Central Park shifting his weight from one foot to the other, he looked like an innocent boy in a sophisticated man's body. He had cow eyes, was well dressed, clean-shaven, and appeared inexplicably at peace with the prospect of incarceration.

Anxious to learn more about his new assignment, Ollie extended a hand. "Stephen Whiting? Oliver Harrington. I trust this venue meets with your approval."

"It's fine," Stephen said, his tone indifferent.

He led the way to a weather-beaten bench, taking care to avoid splinters. "You aren't as I had anticipated," he said. "The jury will be quite taken with you. That is, if we're forced to go to jury. I'm confused, however. Why would you freely admit to embezzlement, yet refuse to defend yourself?"

Stephen shrugged.

He drew a tablet and pencil from his briefcase. "How long have you lived in Amber Leaf?"

"All my life. Both Dad and I were born here."

"You're quite fortunate," he said. "It's a splendid town."

Stephen shrugged again. "Not too bad."

"About pleading no contest to the charge … that's a rather solemn admission. Did you, in fact, embezzle money from the bank?"

Stephen didn't flinch. "Yes, sir, I did."

The lead on Ollie's pencil snapped. "Pardon me." Thinking it prudent to find a more effective approach, he took his time searching through his briefcase for another. "Perhaps we would manage best if we began again. Your age?"

"Twenty-five."

"Married?"

"Yes."

He looked up. "Children?"

"Two."

"Ages?"

"One and three."

"You are living beyond your means, I presume?"

"No, sir."

Perplexed, Ollie scrutinized the sincere looking man sitting at his side. "Why the need to embezzle?"

Stephen looked away. Although not appearing outwardly hardened or bitter, what little light was left in his eyes dimmed.

"How is your relationship with your father?" Ollie said.

Stephen rallied. "Good."

"Good," he repeated. "Siblings?"

No response.

Ollie tapped his pencil against the notepad. "If I am to represent you, I'll need assistance. Any siblings?"

Again no response.

"You do know that I am all that's standing between you and prison walls, do you not? You have a wife and two small children to consider. Now, let's try this again. Siblings?"

Stephen shut down, his expression unnervingly blank.

"I fear this is my fault," Ollie confessed. "Perhaps I'm pushing too hard for our first meeting. I'll do more homework. Perhaps we should plan to revisit this again soon."

WHEN HE RETURNED TO THE OFFICE, Ollie greeted John Brown who chose not return the favor. Ollie went on to retrieve a stray letter from the floor and placed it on Charlie's desk. Charlie offered no thank you. Offered no nod. He then progressed to the file drawers where Nelson stood, his expression neutral. He hesitated then turned and walked away.

Mid-afternoon, he backed out of Boss's office and into Gretta. His heart fluttered at her nearness. However, before her blush disappeared, Nelson reappeared. He winked at her, which deepened the pink in her cheeks. He then turned to Ollie, his tone strikingly sincere. "How'd it go with Stephen Whiting this morning?"

Gretta excused herself and headed on toward the wall of files.

"How is it you assume I engaged a meeting with Whiting?"

Nelson raised his chin. "Saw you leave. Noticed you were gone for a while. Just assumed."

"It might have gone better, I suppose."

"He's still not talking, I take it?"

What was it about Nelson? While he exuded sincerity, Ollie hesitated to trust him. "Rather difficult to figure, is it not?"

"If you need any help at all, give me a holler. Stephen and I have been friends since grade school."

Surprised yet pleased with the offer, he said, "Might you happen to know if he has any siblings?"

"He doesn't."

Why *blurt* out his response? "Of that you're certain?"

"That's right. Why?"

"When I questioned him, that appeared to be his freezing point.

Are you certain he doesn't have a brother or sister the family might feel a need to keep private? Parents must be horrified when they produce an imperfect child—hydrocephalic, severe amentia, that sort of complication."

"I doubt it, but I'd be happy to it check out."

Ollie flinched when a gruff, "Van Dyke, where in the world are you?" resounded throughout the office. John was standing at Gretta's desk impatiently tapping a folder.

Her cheeks growing as red as her nail polish, she swiftly returned to her desk.

"Why that—" Nelson hissed.

"About the help," Ollie said. "Thank you."

His footfalls did lighten as he returned to his desk. But what was it about Nelson that befuddled him? Perhaps with him coming to Ollie's aid, the other attorneys' attitudes would thaw as well—John Brown's included.

He then glanced back at Gretta and protective instincts overcame him. Witnessing a secretary being unnecessarily mistreated caused him much concern.

CHAPTER FIFTEEN

Gretta plodded home, fighting dark thoughts with every indignant step. Mr. Brown humiliating her again in front of the entire office still smarted. She needed to make him stop, but he wielded the power.

A voice called out from behind. "Wait up." Nelson was sprinting to catch up with her. She relived his scowl today when Mr. Brown had shouted, and her heart warmed. Rather than being embarrassed for her, Nelson had held her with his eyes, and she'd felt sheer relief.

"It's a mild evening," he said. "Thought it would be fun to walk you home for a change."

"Aren't you afraid of spoiling me?"

He extended an elbow and wrapped a hand around hers, patting it. "You could use a little spoiling. Brown isn't easing up on you any, is he? He seems even more—"

"More what? Demanding? He is getting worse. Do you think he feels threatened?"

"By Harrington?" Nelson nodded. "He certainly shows classic signs of needing to prove himself, but that doesn't justify his behavior. I'd be happy to have a chat with the man on your behalf. I don't appreciate seeing my girl getting talked down to in public."

My girl? How she wanted to believe him.

"There's no excuse for the way he calls you out, Gretta," he continued. "I have to stop myself from boxing his ears every time he opens his mouth."

"I know," she said, "but I've got to be careful. I need my job too bad. My mother isn't getting any better. Her medicine's costing a bundle these days."

"I could be subtle. Let him know he's making himself look bad."

"Let me think about it," she said. "For all his faults, he'd probably respect me more if I handled this myself … if it's possible for him to show anyone respect."

Nelson grasped her hand, swinging it as they walked on. "What are you up to tonight?"

"Supper with my mom. Want to join us?"

"You bet," he said, then started whistling *Ta-Ra-Ra Boom-De-Ay* in perfect pitch. When they reached the foot of Broadway, he pulled her toward him. "You blushed when I found you talking to Harrington."

There was something in Nelson's tone when he said the name Harrington that smacked of unfettered jealousy. "Didn't mean to," she said. "But I did hear you offer to help with the Whitings. That was awfully kind of you."

He shook his head. "The boys have been giving him a pretty rough time. I figured someone needed to take the lead. As for Brown, though, I'm going to give you one week and not one day more to handle him. If I don't see any improvement, he's going to have to answer to …"

His gaze shifted down the sidewalk where a wee child in knee pants and suspenders wandered along listlessly. He looked no more than three or four years old.

"Something isn't right. I wonder what's going on with that little shaver." Nelson picked up their pace. When they reached the boy, he dropped on one knee. "You look like you're lost, little man."

The boy stared at him blankly and didn't answer.

"I don't think he understands," Gretta said. "I wonder if he's deaf or if maybe he's a foreigner or something."

"There's only one way to find out. Sprechen sie Deutch?"

The boy's gaze fixed on Nelson's lips.

"Parlate Italiano? Parlez-vous Français?"

The boy lit up. "Oui!"

"Est-ce que vous êtes détruit?"

"Pas si je peux trouver le Central Park."

Gretta leaned in closer. "What's he saying?"

"I asked him if he's lost." Nelson glanced up at her, his eyes compassion filled. "He said not if he can find Central Park."

"You wouldn't happen to know anyone who might want to escort him back there, would you?"

He got up and tenderly brushed her cheek with the back of his fingers. "See you tomorrow." He turned to the boy and said, "Venez," hoisted him on his shoulders, and carried him off, whistling.

Gretta smiled at the touching scene, but then as darkness deepened, so did her returning thoughts of Mr. Brown.

CHAPTER SIXTEEN

Hilda stood front and center at Ollie's desk, arms folded across her plentiful middle. "Do you have a few minutes? Miss Van Dyke and Mr. Brown are waiting in the conference room."

Ollie glanced at a growing stack of folders on his desk. "What might this be about?"

"Clerical coverage. Boss briefed me on the Whiting case. You're going to need all the help you can get."

A scowl wreathed Mr. Brown's pocked cheeks when Ollie pulled a chair to the table. As for Gretta, she looked down and nervously massaged the edges of her stenography pad. What was the matter with that girl?

Hilda took her position at the head of the table. "As I was saying, Mr. Harrington, you're going to need clerical assistance. Gretta is our newest secretary and far and away our best. Since her workload is the lightest in the clerical pool, she has agreed to assist you as well as Mr. Brown."

Not caring for the mood in the room, he considered Gretta's plight. "Are you comfortable with that, Miss Van Dyke? I can't promise I won't be demanding."

She nodded, confidence finally revealing itself, and it looked good on her. "I'm more than okay with assisting you."

He turned to Mr. Brown. "How about you? Will you be able to share her time without resentment?"

Hilda cleared her throat. "I'm not sure why the question, Mr. Harrington."

Mr. Brown glowered. "And I'm not sure about sharing her services without a fair amount of resentment. Seems Harrington wants to take over the office. First the best cases, now the best clerical help."

Hilda didn't hesitate to lift her nose. "I assure you we're doing the best we can with the resources we have, Mr. Brown," she said, "and as for you, Mr. Harrington, I would jump at the chance."

He picked up a pencil and gently rolled it through thick fingers. "I'm grateful for the opportunity, but I also feel it important to set a positive tone."

Hilda gaped at Mr. Brown. "It's pretty obvious the tone's already been set."

Ollie redirected his attention. "Mr. Brown, do you mind if I call you John?"

He shrugged.

"As I view it, John, we all enjoy the same chances for opportunity in this law firm or any other firm for that matter. It's how we handle these opportunities that separate the professionals from the amateurs, but that goes without saying. From what I've discerned, you are an exceptionally hard worker—" It was as if Ollie saw and also heard a sudden crack in John's hard shell. "… and perseverance in my book equates with success. If we are to partner on the same team, we must be mindful of the weight of Miss Van Dyke's workload. The less pressure we place on her, the better she will perform. The better she performs, the better you look, the better I look, and the fewer the number of mistakes that shall be made. To be painfully blunt, I believe in running a tight ship and giving the utmost respect to everyone regardless of professional standing."

John's gaze anchored for a moment on Nelson and Charlie who

passed by the conference room, and his frown evaporated. "Partnering on the same team?"

For the first time since Ollie had been watching their exchanges, John turned to Gretta and looked at her respectfully. "I think we can handle that, can't we, Miss Van Dyke?"

Relieved, Ollie seized his hand. "I will be at your disposal as well. I plan not to return to England. That is unless …"

"No need to say more," John muttered.

Teetering between laughter and tears, Gretta stared at the towering stack of work. Oliver Harrington did not run a step ahead of everyone, he ran ahead an easy country mile. He had made it unnecessary for her to handle the likes of John Brown and also tempered her working life with a mere handful of circumspect words.

But what was she getting herself into by agreeing to work for the man? Not that she had a choice. My, how she wanted to try to keep up with him.

She glanced at Mr. Brown … John … and smiled. He appeared carefree as he rifled through a ream of papers. How uncharacteristic. Clearly Mr. Harrington's strength was rubbing off on him, and somehow she sensed the hostility had lessened.

As he passed by, Oliver Harrington tapped a finger on the housing of her typewriter one time. She jumped, but then a smile worked up her cheeks. She wondered about his playful side as he headed straight for his desk and dove into his work.

At closing time, she reached into her drawer. As she pulled out her purse, a pair of oxfords loomed into view, and a shadow dimmed her desk. "Hey, good lookin'," Nelson said, appearing frazzled. "All day I've been busier than a wallpaper hanger with two bum arms. Haven't even had a chance to say hello. How about grabbing a quick bite with me?

Could use a little diversion before burning the midnight oil. What do you say?"

A half hour later, Nelson appeared to have difficulty sitting still, and the instant their supper arrived, he hungrily jabbed a fork into a chunk of roast beef. As he ate he told her about the lost little boy, how they'd found his frantic mother roaming the streets and how she'd burst into tears when they met up.

"They're only here on holiday for a couple of weeks," he said. "So how about you? How was your day?"

Gretta grinned. "I think my Mr. Brown problem has been resolved, if that's what you're wondering."

Nelson appeared pleasantly surprised. "How'd you pull that off?"

"I didn't. Mr. Harrington did."

"What?" Nelson said.

Uncomfortable with the irritation penetrating his tone, Gretta's mashed potatoes inched back up her esophagus. She took a hard swallow. "I said Mr. Harrington handled it."

"*Oliver* Harrington?"

Sensing it best not to say more, Gretta ate the rest of her supper in silence.

As did Nelson.

CHAPTER SEVENTEEN

Ollie stepped out into the dog days of summer, humidity wet as ocean spray and no place to escape unless taking a plunge in a lake or frequenting a root cellar.

Several blocks up Broadway, he straightened his tie outside the door of Amber Leaf National and sauntered in. Catching the eye of a teller, he said, "I'd like to have a word with Mr. Whiting, please."

A dozen footsteps later, Ollie looked about the large office with mahogany furnishings and bookcases a librarian would covet. "Mr. Whiting? I'm Oliver Harrington."

Whiting reminded Ollie of a Saint Bernard he once had. Hanging jowls weighting down pale skin. Sad, drooping eyes. Thick shouldered. But unlike an unwavering Saint Bernard, Whiting appeared nervous, edgy. "Believe I've heard the name before. From the law office, right?" He flipped open a box on his desk. "Care for a cigar?"

"No, thank you. I was surprised your teller asked if I wanted to see your son or you. I was under the impression Stephen no longer worked at the bank."

"Doesn't, but he stops by on occasion. Got along well with everyone. So what brings you here?"

"Thought I'd introduce myself," Ollie said, "ask a few questions before we consider scheduling a deposition."

With a quick tug at his tie, Whiting cleared his throat. "I believe I've told Addison everything you need to know."

Another less than cooperative Whiting.

"We have a few loose ends I should like to tie up," Ollie said.

"Such as?"

"How is your relationship with your son?"

Whiting brightened. "We have a great relationship. Always have. He's a good young man. Good husband to his wife, devoted father to my grandkids, good son to his mother and me."

Ollie scratched a note on his tablet and looked up. "Any idea why he would embezzle? Was he having financial problems?"

"None that I'm aware of … and we prefer to call it borrowing, Mr. Harrington. I'm sorry to say that's a word our bank board appears reluctant to acknowledge. My boy borrowed the money, but always paid down fast, and borrowed more as needed."

Whiting Senior seemed overly confident and that concerned Ollie.

"I was under the impression it's uncontested that he borrowed the money under the table with no verbal or written permission," Ollie said, "the amounts were significant, and the balance had been accumulating, not decreasing. In all due respect, Mr. Whiting, how would that not be considered embezzling?"

Whiting offered no answer. He nervously tapped a forefinger on the massive desk, sounding like a woodpecker rapping away at a tree.

"What need had he for the money?" Ollie waited. Getting no answer, he continued. "I had a chat with your son. It took little for him to shutdown. Any idea why he would refuse to cooperate?"

Whiting got up, paced to the window, and looked out as if to find answers somewhere out on the street. "Whatever the reason for his indiscretion, you can rest assured it was important."

"Any idea what that reason might be? Any idea at all?" Ollie asked, pressing. "This information is critical … or do you prefer that your son goes to prison?"

Whiting looked back, his expression unreadable.

Do not press harder. Not yet.

"How many other children do you have?" Ollie listened with a sharp ear. Why the hesitation? It cannot take that long to count your offspring.

"I have one son," Whiting said finally.

"Any daughters?"

With a nervous tick and a scowl, Whiting repeated sharply, "I have one son."

Ollie broke an awkward smile.

"I fail to see the humor," Whiting said.

"I don't wish to be disrespectful." Ollie stood and buckled his briefcase. "I was certain you and your boy were holding something back and am surprised to find that an understatement. Trust takes time. Building a foundation takes time. And I have every intention of building a solid one. For now, though, I find I need to sort things through, but I will return."

Ollie preferred quiet time to collect his thoughts while still fresh, so on his way back to the office, he found a table at a nearby café, ordered a lemonade, and penned pertinent notes from the meeting.

All the while he wondered what sordid secrets lurked in the great unknown.

CHAPTER EIGHTEEN

Gretta wasn't suspicious by nature, but there was something in Nelson's tone when he said, "Harrington?" that didn't sound right.

She glanced back to find him standing far too casually, resting a hip against Mr. Harrington's desk, while adjusting his already adjusted tie. His utterance sounded crisp yet confident. "I did what you asked."

"Which is?" Mr. Harrington said.

"Last night I had a chat with my buddy over supper. I was right. Stephen verified he doesn't have any brothers or sisters—full, half, adopted, or otherwise."

Gretta's stomach knotted. Had her hearing failed her? She ate supper with Nelson last night, not Stephen. They left the office together at five o'clock sharp and he walked her home. She warmed a quick supper of leftovers, which they ate with her mother, and played chess until he left at around ten, leaving no time for him to talk with anyone.

Mr. Harrington scratched his chin. "That's curious."

"Why?" Nelson said.

"I had a notion to the contrary. Thank you for following up on it, though. I'll give it more thought."

"But I just told you," Nelson said, his tone lacking patience.

Gretta couldn't keep from looking back.

"He doesn't have—"

The unconvincing look on Mr. Harrington's face appeared to silence Nelson.

As he headed back toward his desk, Gretta reached for a reference book, which slipped from her hand and smacked on the floor with a thud. Nelson appeared at her side, swept it up, handed it to her, all the while proudly displaying a charming grin and a wink.

Which gave her a chill.

Gretta flinched a few minutes later when Mr. Harrington stopped at her desk. Learning how to get and remain calm in that man's presence proved a job in and of itself.

"When you have a moment," he said, "would you mind typing these notes?"

She reached for the paper, hoping he wouldn't see the tremor in her hand. "Not at all. How many carbon copies?"

"No carbons necessary. These are for my purposes only."

Intent on pleasing her newest boss, she set her other work aside and slipped a sheet of paper in the platen.

But she felt nervous.

And she always made mistakes when she felt nervous.

Several words into the document, however, her fingers flew as she found herself lost in Mr. Harrington's well-formed penmanship and the engaging words he had poured on paper.

NOTES: Meeting with Josh Whiting, Senior

PLACE: Amber Leaf National Bank

DATE: Friday, 2 August 1901

(1) Met, unannounced, with Josh Whiting, also known as

Whiting Senior, in his office at Amber Leaf National to assess him verbally as well as nonverbally. He appeared defensive, indicated that he had already passed vital information on to Mr. Addison, and grew increasingly wary when probed for details about his family.

(2) *An interesting thought to ponder to set up a compelling defense … had I disgraced my family heritage, inadvertently or otherwise, how would my father have reacted? Reluctant? Edgy? Nervous? Or disappointed, concerned, and helpful? Why would Whiting act as if he were hiding something if the very thing he was hiding had the power to send his only son to prison?*

(3) *A second thought to ponder … if my son, had he lived, found himself in a compromising situation, what would be my response? In fear, would I be overly protective? Or would he warrant my undying support while fleshing out the truth?*

(4) *When I asked Whiting about his children, he said, "I have a son." When I asked if he had any daughters, Whiting repeated harshly, "I have a son." The word no appeared glaringly absent from his response. Why?*

(5) *Next step … search further into another sibling possibility and call a joint meeting with Whiting Senior and Junior, taking care to give them short notice.*

As she proofread her typing, Gretta was pleased to notice an absence of mistakes. But as she reread the memorandum, the words, *and if my son, had he lived*, leaped off the page. The poor man had lost a son. She recalled their conversation near the file drawers and a wave of sadness descended on her. 'My wife *was* Dutch, too,' he had said.

Gretta rolled the paper out of the platen and placed it carefully in the center of her desk as if it were an ancient document too delicate to handle.

CHAPTER NINETEEN

O llie climbed the stairs of the hotel one reluctant footfall at a time. Tonight he gaped into the bowels of a long empty weekend and that did not sit well. When he strolled past the registration desk, however, a clerk cried out, "Mr. Harrington, this is for you. Hand-delivered an hour ago."

Curious, Ollie stopped at the base of the staircase, tore open the envelope, and drank in the words inviting him to an official send-off for Deacon's oldest son who planned to begin a new life up in Minneapolis. Ollie smiled at the thought of a Sunday filled with warmth of hearth and home.

Buried in work, time passed swiftly. Two weeks later, he hired a buggy and in the early afternoon hours navigated the heavily rutted country roads from memory. He easily found his way back to the farm where Deacon and Hoyt awaited him.

"This is all your fault," Deacon said with a teasing burst of laughter. "My kids seemed content at home with Ma and Pa. But you show up and they learn there's this big exciting world out there. They get a hankering to cut a slice out of it."

"Pa's right," Hoyt said. "The more I thought about it, the more I wanted what you have. Let me take your horse."

As Hoyt led the roan out to pasture, Deacon slapped Ollie on the back and steered him toward the house. "It's hard to admit, but you've done us a favor. Sometimes home can get a mite too comfortable. It's good for a boy to learn what this old world is all about. He waits too long," Deacon said, sounding pleased with his own humor, "rheumatism will set in for sure."

After a satisfying meal of the best fried chicken Ollie had ever tasted, the half happy, half sullen family gathered around on the front lawn. Deacon held his son gently at the nape of the neck. "I can't let you go, boy … not without giving you a few words to ponder as you journey out on life's road."

As Deacon looked into the anticipating eyes of his wife and children and words freely flowed, Ollie recalled his own voyage to America— no acknowledgment, no send-off, no words of wisdom or pat on the back—and yet he felt surprisingly content. What he had lacked in England, he gained in Amber Leaf. Deacon welcomed him like a son. No need to heed empty rules. No choking restrictions. Merely being himself proved more than adequate.

"The most valuable going away gift I know to give I've already given throughout your growing up years. Do you know what that was, boy?"

Hoyt smiled. He knew.

"That's right," Deacon said. "Knowledge of the scriptures. A favorite passage I treasure and offer as the most appropriate for your new adventure is from Psalm One. 'Blessed is the man who walks not in the counsel of the ungodly, nor stands in the path of sinners, nor sits in the seat of the scornful; but his delight is in the law of the LORD, and in His law he meditates day and night. He shall be like a tree planted by the rivers of water, that brings forth its fruit in its season, whose leaf also shall not wither; and whatever he does shall prosper.' Seek godly counsel, Hoyt. Stay clear of mocking, and above all, delight in God's Word with your whole heart and soul. Make your dad proud. Do well and prosper." Deacon lightly cuffed his shoulder. "Now be off with you."

After the blessing, Hoyt shook hands with Ollie and thanked him again for stopping by. Ollie then retreated to the porch to allow the family a moment of private time. Deacon modeled the ideal father. Respectful. Happy. Generous. Responsible. Hard working. Easy with which to occupy time. As Ollie watched them, hope rose in his heart that he would one day raise a fine family, too, and like Deacon, be a loving father who refused to treat his children as if they were first and foremost a possession—his possession.

Hoyt then mounted the stallion and set out for an unknown world, not looking back, while Deacon returned to the porch. He eased onto a rocking chair. It appeared as though half of him had ridden off with his son.

"He's a good boy," Ollie said. "All of your children have a quality about them. They must make you very proud."

Deacon chuckled self-consciously. "More grateful and fulfilled than proud."

"Last time I was here," Ollie said, "you mentioned problems at the bank. How are you getting on? And what about Hoyt? Any difficulty withdrawing funds for his trip?"

Deacon shook his head. "Not that boy. He doesn't trust the bank. Had a stash of cash rolled up in a Mason jar he kept under his bed. He's going to do fine. As for me and the farm, we're getting along okay. Haven't needed much in the way of supplies. Don't know how it will go when I do, though." Deacon nodded toward the field. "We've got a bumper crop this year. Outside of a bad hailstorm, we'll do fine." He rocked his chair and said, almost as an afterthought, "The banker's son went to school with my boy."

As Hoyt faded into the distance, Ollie said distractedly, "You bank with Amber Leaf National?"

"Yes, sir."

"Hoyt and Stephen Whiting are friends?"

"I didn't say they were friends. They attended school together. There's a big difference. You might say they walked in different social circles."

Ollie grinned. "Whiting didn't measure up, I presume?"

And Deacon laughed.

"I wonder where I got the notion that Whiting Senior had more than one son," Ollie said. "I was told I was wrong."

"But you questioned that?" Deacon stopped rocking. "Good instincts. You may want to revisit it. Just to be sure, I mean," he said too quickly, then smiled. "Sometimes we men get a hunch. I used to do a little private detective work, you know. Developed a feel for things."

"Em had told me about that," Ollie said. "Sounded fascinating."

Deacon gave the back of his neck a quick rub. "I grew up on the farm, but got restless. Wanted a little adventure. So when I was old enough, I joined the police force. Worked my way up the ranks and one day became a detective. Loved the job. Finessing information out of people without them having a clue. Following them without getting caught. Nosing through public records. Figuring out what makes people tick. When my grandpa died, though, someone needed to come back to pick up where he left off and that was the end of that."

"Did you have any dangerous cases?" Ollie said.

"You mean did I ever get shot at? A time or two. Once during a robbery. Another time when I hauled in a drunk who swore he was Wyatt Earp."

"Have you engaged in any detective work since?"

"Nope, but I sure would like to."

An hour after Ollie dropped off his buggy and returned to his room, a sudden summer storm blew in. A ruinous storm with skies dark as soot. The wind howled and rain cascaded in sheets. But then came a thunderous noise that set his nerves on edge. Hailstones the size of marbles battered the building. Fearing the windows might break, Ollie stepped back. After the hail, he gazed out the window again, reflecting on Hoyt, reflecting on Deacon's bumper crops.

The rain subsided, and an eerie quiet set in.

CHAPTER TWENTY

Ollie reached for the light, but not before the steady rat-a-tat-tat of a distant typewriter cried out. He stopped, then smiled. Boss in his office pounding away at the keys? The man needed an inkling that there's life beyond work. Intrigued, Ollie followed the sound.

"Miss Van Dyke?" he said, surprised. "How is it that you're still working at this late hour?"

"I'm finishing a report for Mr. Brown," she said.

"He has managed to request that you stay late, has he?"

She shook her head. "My choice. This is too important not to stay 'til it gets done."

"I was about to turn off the lights," Ollie said. "I'm pleased I had the good sense to look back." He peered around the office. "No Hilda. No Nelson, either. You're alone?"

She nodded. "Hilda got another one of her headaches, and Nelson had some sort of family get-together tonight. I'll be fine."

Ollie headed toward his desk, feeling surprisingly happy to be in the same room with Gretta, sharing her air. What a pleasant way to spend an early evening. "Let me know when you plan to leave."

She called out to him, her voice tentative. "You aren't staying late because of me, are you?"

Absolutely. "I will certainly not leave you here alone."

"I'll hurry … and thanks."

Ollie tugged at his pencil drawer, but it wouldn't budge. He gave it an extra hard pull. The housing broke apart and crashed to the floor, pencils rolling.

"Are you okay?" Gretta cried out. "What happened?"

Ollie plucked them up one by one and surveyed the damage. "Nothing important. Might we have any adhesive or sandpaper about? I fear this drawer suffered a fit of rage."

Gretta appeared a short while later and placed a burning candle on his desk. "You'll be needing this," she said. "The glue and sandpaper are in a toolbox up in the attic."

Air squeezed out of Ollie's lungs in a whoosh. "Attic? Where might that be?"

"Above the storage room. There's a ladder at the end …"

Ollie had peeked into the storage room, but refused to enter it. Long. Narrow. Dim. A ladder at the end. *Breathe deep. Breathe deep. Don't allow her to observe you in distress.*

"Mr. Harrington? Are you alright?"

He broke out of a stupor. "Of course. You mentioned a ladder at the end?"

"That's right. The hatch is light and easy to open. We keep the toolbox right there, but you'll need the candle to see. The attic is black as pitch."

Ollie's heart hammered, every inch of his body leaking moisture. "No windows?"

"No, it's tiny. More of crawl space. Whenever I go up there, I have to stoop over to walk through the place."

Please don't disclose any more. He pressed his hands hard against his thighs. "Thank you, Miss Van Dyke."

Is it necessary for you to hesitate so?

She appeared concerned. "I'd be happy to get it for you."

Ollie's cheeks grew uncomfortably warm. "I'm certain I will have no difficulty finding it," he said, a hint for her to be off. "Thank you again."

She walked away.

And he let out a choking breath.

He willed his fingers to stop trembling. Of all of the times and places to engage a claustrophobic attack, it had to be in the office and in the presence of an unusually lovely young woman. Drat! From where did this senseless fear originate? Surely there must be a way to break free of it. He glanced at the supply closet. A small, dark attic. No windows. He must exercise courage. Move swiftly. Not allow another treacherous moment for thought.

He seized the candle and, making a pretense of courage, traipsed into the supply room, lightly skimming the shelving on the sides of the narrow passageway as he pressed through. Concentrating severely on the task at hand, he slipped the candle on the outer rim of an upper shelf, hoisted the hatch, and peered in. To his bad fortune, some dullard had set the toolbox a far reach inside. Knees turning to rubber and trembling uncontrollably, he held tight to the ladder and took a deep breath. He then braced one hand against the attic's edge while lunging in with the other. He pulled out the retched box and descended the ladder quicker than a fireman down a fire pole.

The instant his shoes hit wood, his breathing relaxed. Task complete.

Half an hour later Gretta appeared at his desk.

"You've finished?" he said.

She glanced at the pencil drawer. "I see you've finished, too."

"That I have. After a small amount of sanding, the drawer opens with ease." He did not admit, however, that he slipped the no-longer-needed toolbox immediately inside the closet door … on the floor … for someone else to return to its proper place.

As his weary feet echoed down the hall, Ollie said, "I trust Mr. Brown has been behaving better as of late?"

"Much better, thank you."

Ollie stopped walking. "I find myself a bit confused. How is it that anyone with your level of competence would tolerate such rudeness?"

She looked straight ahead, her expression troubled. "Some of us don't have much choice, Mr. Harrington."

"You number among them?" he said, surprised.

Gretta hugged her pocketbook beneath her arm and they resumed walking. "I was afraid to say anything. This is the highest paying job I could find and we need the money too badly."

"We?"

"My mother and me. My father died when I was in my early teens." When Ollie looked at her uncertain, she said, "an accident," as if he'd asked for an explanation.

To his surprise, for all of his father's faults, Ollie preferred not imagining how life would have unfolded growing up without him, having a mother who was not well, and that coupled with a lack of financial security. "I regret most deeply hearing that."

She looked up at him. "I never thanked you for speaking up for me."

"You have me at a disadvantage," Ollie said. "When did I speak up for you?"

"I'm sorry ... I was referring to Mr. Brown. The day I was standing by the file drawers and he shouted at me, Nelson got pretty upset. He wanted to confront Mr. Brown himself, but I knew that would backfire. Nelson can get a bit passionate at times. Anyway, I needed to buy time, especially since I'm still on probation. I told him I'd handle it, but had no idea what to do. You made it seem embarrassingly simple."

Ollie broke a reflective smile. "Simple for me because I had nothing to lose and everything to gain. No matter our walk in life, Miss Van Dyke, rest assured all of us have an underbelly we need to protect. That's nothing of which to be ashamed."

"Even *you?*" she said.

If you saw me in the supply closet, you would have no need to ask. "The bigger you are ..."

They continued strolling along. Feeling he better understood Gretta's difficult situation, Ollie felt at one with her and was not ready for the conversation to end. But after exchanging idle chatter for the better part of five minutes, he looked up to find them too soon at his hotel. As they stopped to go their separate ways, Gretta said, "I've been meaning to tell you—"

"Yes?"

"Nothing."

Appearing ill-at-ease, she quickly walked on.

CHAPTER TWENTY-ONE

Gretta dipped the tips of her toes into shivery waters lapping hungrily against the shoreline. Autumn approaching, Catherine Island appeared especially lovely as the sun dipped below the horizon. Soon deciduous trees would shed their leaves and Father Winter would do his magic, casting a chill on the lake the way Nelson had cast a chill on their relationship. All that took was articulating one thoughtless falsehood to Oliver Harrington. No one could stop Father Winter from making the lake freeze over, but she needed to stop Nelson from freezing her heart. "How was supper last night?"

"Great," he said. "We had a huge crowd. Lots of fun. The last person didn't leave 'til midnight. It's a shame you weren't there. You would've had a good time."

Another thoughtless remark. "You didn't invite me."

"I knew you'd feel uncomfortable around a bunch of strangers. If I'd asked you to come, you'd have felt obligated," Nelson said, sounding as if he believed himself.

Gretta anchored her gaze on the rippling flow of water. "Why would I feel uncomfortable?" she said.

He playfully nudged a shoulder against hers. "You know how you are. You blush easier than anyone this side of the Canadian border."

"My blushing doesn't mean I wouldn't enjoy—"

"What about you?" he said. "What did you do last night?"

Why was it that he appeared to have an interest in relationship building only when it benefited him? "Worked late."

"On what?"

"A project for Mr. Brown." She hesitated. Nelson had deliberately changed the subject, taking her for granted. He needed to know there were other men who valued her. To tease him with the knowledge would be wrong, but to warn him, to set him up to succeed wouldn't. "Mr. Harrington stayed late, too," she said. "He didn't like to see me working alone. He's a real gentleman."

Nelson raised a disapproving brow. "He's a little too much for work, don't you think? He's got to be a real bore to spend any time with."

Gretta gazed up into the evening sky where stars popped up, growing increasingly brilliant in the deepening darkness. Why stop now? "On the contrary. I get the feeling he could be very interesting, and speaking of Mr. Harrington, I overheard you telling him you had supper with Stephen Whiting, and you said Stephen told you he didn't have any siblings."

"You heard right."

"Did I?" *No. Please. Tell me I heard wrong.* "You and I had supper together that night, Nelson, not you and Stephen. Besides, I thought he was too busy with family these days to spend time with you."

"So I was off a night or two," Nelson said. "What's the difference?"

The difference was huge. She needed to trust him. Falsehoods kill trust. "Did you really have supper with him? Did he really tell you he didn't have any siblings?"

Nelson frowned. "Why do you want to know?"

"Because I thought I heard a rumor once."

"That's none of Harrington's business."

"Why not?"

"Hey, what is this?" Nelson said with an edge. "Why are you sticking up for him? I thought you were my girl."

"Nelson … does Stephen Whiting have a sister?"

He looked away. "Not that anyone needs to know."

"He does, doesn't he? And she has something to do with his embezzling."

"When did you become a private detective?"

"Nelson, tell me what's going on."

He lifted his nose in the air much in the likeness of a small schoolboy. "I'm not talking."

Disappointed by his response, she continued, "Years ago his dad had a tryst with Maude Millning, didn't he? Maude, the one everyone says is discreetly running a one-woman brothel? She disappeared for a while … long enough to have a baby and came back looking like she'd put on weight."

"Who told you that?" he said.

"My mother. She figured it out."

Nelson's expression grew unreadable.

"It happened when I was little," Gretta said. "My mom never liked the woman. Said she tried to seduce my father once, not long before he died. My father wasn't happy about it. Told Mom everything. She said it was like Maude snapped or something, making moves on all the men. Didn't seem to care if they were married, widowed, divorced, or single. Mom said she saw Stephen's father sneaking into Maude's place one night when she was walking by. The next thing she knew, Maude was nowhere to be seen. That's when she figured out that Maude might have had his baby and given it away. That is what happened, isn't it?"

"That's nobody's business."

"You're wrong," Gretta said. "It's Mr. Harrington's business if it has anything to do with your friend's embezzling. Why isn't Stephen talking? What's he hiding? And what about his father? Why won't he stand up for his son?"

Nelson turned on her, hard. "Leave it alone, Gretta. This is not a road you want to walk down."

"When did you have supper with Stephen?"

"I said leave it alone."

CHAPTER TWENTY-TWO

Ollie stopped by the livery and reserved a horse for tomorrow night's trek to the Whiting estate. Though he dreaded the task before him, if he wished to ferret out the truth, what other choice had he than to skillfully work father against son?

A handful of minutes later, he returned to the hotel. Too early to call it an evening, he set off for the lobby, lit a cigar, and again put pen to paper.

20 August 1901

Dearest Family:

Amber Leaf continues to please me. On sunny weekend days, I enjoy hikes around Fountain Lake with its islands, boating, and fishing as well as exploring the outlying areas, which are heavily wooded and verdant. Countless fields bursting with bountiful harvests also abound.

As for disagreeable weather, a storm blew in on Sunday past, which spewed hailstones as large as marbles. The sky turned black as pitch and the noise was deafening. I scarcely heard myself think. At one point, I feared the window might shatter. Much damage was done to neighboring farms, one of which was

Deacon de Haven's. He stopped by this evening past to share the unfortunate news. His son had left for Minneapolis earlier in the day to search for work. Fortunately the boy had found shelter at a passing farm and then returned home long enough to see about his family. I fear for Deacon, praying for the restoration of his livelihood.

The door opened, feet shuffled, and a match struck. Ollie looked up. A distinguished looking fellow with greased down pate, wire-rimmed spectacles, and dapper attire took a seat on a nearby settee. He glanced around as if anticipating someone's arrival. The man appeared uninterested in conversing, so Ollie returned to pen and paper. Write warm thoughts, he told himself. One day your father will long for your presence.

Deacon is very much like Emily, and his family tremendously decent and kind. Rides to their country home remind me of her. They also bring back fonder memories of the days we spent at our own stable in England, buggy rides with Betsy, and the happiness we enjoyed at family gatherings.

The door flew open again and another gentleman walked in. He bore the eyes of a raven, and hair and beard black as coal lightly stained with strands of gray. "Ahh, Mr. Ainsely," the first gentleman said. "I hope you haven't been waiting long."

Ollie froze like a pointer dog sensing viable prey. Amber Leaf National's attorney was a gentleman by the name of Ainsely. Ollie then purposely returned not only an absent gaze on writing, but also an active ear on their conversation.

"Just arrived," the man continued. "We still have a few minutes. How about if we enjoy a smoke before going to the meeting?"

They went on to share pleasantries, catching up on family news and plans for the holidays that would be upon them in a few short months.

As the gentlemen prattled on, Ollie set his pen aside long enough to ponder the thoughts that disturbed him. This year he would spend the holidays with Deacon and his family, but what of the long weekends surrounding those days? No wife. No children. He had never before spent such occasions in isolation. How would he fare?

Then the man named Ainsely lowered his voice. "Say, I've been meaning to ask, what's Addison thinking? He's making a fool of himself."

Jolted by the question, Ollie stared again at the paper. Morally, he felt a need to leave, to give these men privacy. Intuitively, he felt a need to glean unsolicited, though valuable, information he had difficulty extracting from the Whitings.

His intuition won.

"He'll never win," the other man scoffed. "He only took the case because he and Whiting are friends."

"They won't be for long, not when Addison's firm takes a hit." Mr. Ainsely exhaled a slow stream of smoke. "Who wants to do business with a loser?" he said.

Ollie didn't appreciate Mr. Ainsely's condescending tone.

"I wouldn't, that's for sure," the other man said. "Who are we going to find to replace Whiting? After this mess blows over, we've got to let him go."

"Imagine," Mr. Ainsely muttered, "a bank president with a son in prison."

A stranger appeared in the hallway. "You're here, gentlemen," he said. "The meeting's about to begin."

As the men walked off, Ollie mulled over their careless words, discarding Josh Whiting with no in-depth knowledge of his plight, and shunning Addison in the process. Now more than ever, he determined to win this case.

Picking up his pen, Ollie returned to his writing. He had more to share with his father than weather reports and memories of long ago.

My work also lends much in the way of fascination. I am currently laboring on a case I find most interesting. A young man with a small family and much to live for has courageously and honorably declared guilt over nonviolent, though significant, financial misdeeds. He faces hard time in prison and yet refuses to answer the very questions that might set him free. I fear I have a significant challenge ahead of me. I shall meet with him and his father tomorrow evening next and question them together. The young man appears sincere. I cannot in good conscience allow him to go to prison. Not if I can help it.

I must retire to my room now to indulge an accumulation of reading. Do know that each day when I arrive at my sleeping quarters, I relish the thought of word from England. I so hope to one day hear from you.

Now the cordial greetings from your loving son Oliver.

CHAPTER TWENTY-THREE

At dusk, Ollie rented a horse and followed the road marks to the Whiting estate a mile to the north and west of Fountain Lake. The narrow road threaded through a thickly wooded area with dense brush. A deer bolted across his path, giving his horse pause and Ollie the feeling he wasn't alone. And then another bolted past. In the distance, still others fed on vegetation. Gazing up into the sky absent a radiant moon, Ollie purposed to make this meeting brief. Finding his way back to town in utter darkness would prove difficult.

He reached a fork in the road and tugged on the horse's reins. Had Whiting instructed him to veer to the left or the right?

An unexpected faint clomp of a single horse's hooves echoed in the woods behind him. Ollie glanced back.

The clomping stopped.

Peering deep into the shadows, he saw no one. A neighbor turned off the main road, perhaps?

Whiting had indicated that his house sat a city block to the left or right of the fork. If Ollie made a mistake in directions, what did it matter? He veered to the left. A hundred feet or so up the path he stopped again. Wrong way. Again that faint clomping of hooves. Was he being followed? As he pulled at the reins to backtrack, the sound grew faint, the distant horse riding off in the opposite direction at a full gallop.

Whiting Senior met Ollie at the entrance of the impressive home and escorted him into a study. Stephen, who was sitting comfortably, got up and extended his hand. Whiting Senior assumed his position behind the desk, while Ollie pulled up an armchair. With neither of the men's wives anywhere in sight, it was clear who wanted control of this meeting. Whiting Senior eased back in his chair and studied Ollie for an awkwardly long while. "You strike me, sir," he said, "as someone who fastidiously weeds the grass beneath his feet. While I respect that in a man, Stephen and I have been taking a hard look at our options and have decided what we want."

Ollie smiled at their presumption. "Are you not putting yourself in an inappropriate position of strength, Mr. Whiting?"

"I sense you are a very knowledgeable and cunning young man, Mr. Harrington," he said, totally ignoring Ollie's question. "What we want is for you to cut a deal with our bank's Board. Mrs. Whiting's health is fragile. We want to protect her. I'm afraid we also find ourselves in a most precarious situation. My son has already lost his position with the bank. If I step forward and reveal too much information, my job would also be in jeopardy. In the end, we stand to lose everything. Stephen has chosen to risk a few years in prison to keep us from losing our entire fortunes."

Taken aback at the directness, Ollie sat forward. "Mr. Whiting, certainly you are aware that your job is already in jeopardy. Perhaps if you told me what you are attempting to conceal, I might find a way to use that in your favor rather than against it."

Whiting Senior forcibly shook his head. "No, we can't risk that."

"Do you not understand?" Ollie said. "The very thing you are attempting to maneuver us away from is the very thing that is drawing our attention."

"I understand only too well," Whiting Senior said. "But let me repeat. We can't risk that."

Ollie crossed an ankle over a knee and plucked at his pant cuff.

"Allow me to go back in time. When I asked both of you separately about the possibility of other children in this family, I couldn't get a yes, but neither could I extract an honest no from either of you. Now why might that be?"

Whiting Junior's eyes filled with something indistinguishable, and his jaw visibly tightened. "I want to answer that," he said. "To move past the embezzlement and pry into our personal family business is to violate our boundaries … and in a flagrant way."

"What you're saying makes no sense," Ollie countered. "According to a very good friend of yours, you have no siblings, so why the hesitation?"

"What friend?"

"Nelson Prixton."

"Nel—" Stephen turned to his father as if looking for help.

CHAPTER TWENTY-FOUR

Ollie slid his breakfast plate to the side and sipped a second cup of coffee while penning notes from last night's meeting. The Whitings were being blackmailed, of that he was certain, yet they appeared too honest and conscience-stricken to be involved in anything dubious. Was someone extorting money from them? If so, who and why?

He took one last gulp of the cooling coffee and hurried off to the office where Gretta sat primly at her desk looking lovelier than ever. He glanced at his handwritten notes. "Would you mind typing these? I would prefer that we keep this private."

A short while later Gretta stood at his desk. She appeared reluctant as she handed him one paper while holding the other back. Her midnight blue eyes reminded him of Emily—vulnerable yet courageous. Why did she have to look like that he wondered, as he plucked the first sheet from her hand and offered a kind thank you. But rather than typed, to his surprise, it was hand written. He began reading. *Would you be available to meet with me at your hotel this evening? Seven o'clock in the lobby?* His heart thumped and again he wondered. Why the need for privacy? Why not share her thoughts in the office? He glanced at Nelson who appeared to not be paying attention and gave Gretta a subtle nod.

Her shoulders slackened. She handed him the typed notes. Unfortunately, a delightful hint of cologne lingered in the air as she returned to her desk.

OLLIE FOLDED THE EVENING PAPER AND placed it on an end table. Three minutes before the hour of seven. He wondered about Gretta and her need to see him. After handing him the note, she had remained painfully attentive to her work for the remainder of the day, barely looking up.

The door opened and in she walked, fresh as the breeze behind her. Ollie's heart did that funny little fluttering thing again, the way it had the first day he laid eyes on her. Under softened lights of evening, she looked every bit as lovely as Emily, if not more so, and she possessed that same air of guilelessness.

Gretta hurried toward him, a woman on a mission. "Mr. Harrington, thank you for agreeing to meet with me."

He guided her toward a private seating area.

"I don't want to take much of your time," she said. "It was too risky to say anything at the office. Nelson's playing cards with the boys tonight. He'd be furious if he caught me passing on information. It's about the Whitings," she said. "I'm sorry. Here I go rambling on. Taking over, like some kind of man."

As she swept a lock of hair away from her eye with a dainty hand, Ollie's heart grew warmer, if that was possible. "You're doing fine. You've definitely whetted my curiosity, so continue, please."

"When I typed your notes about the Whitings before and then again this morning, I found myself squirming something awful."

He smiled reassuringly. "Perhaps that was my fault. I may have been too candid."

"No. If anything, your being candid helped. I may have a lead for you. What I'm about to share is unconfirmed. Nothing more than a hunch on my part, okay?"

Ollie sat straighter. "Go on."

"I did some checking," she said, "so this much is confirmed. There was a baby girl born on July first in 1880 to a woman named Maude Millning. Have you ever heard of her?"

Ollie shook his head.

Gretta hesitated. "I feel guilty passing along gossip, but I think you might want to check it out. The father was listed as unknown. And Maude? She's also known as Scarlet Maude. Rumors have been floating around for a long time that she runs a … discreet, though illicit, house of ill repute."

"What might that have to do with the Whitings?" Ollie asked, impatient for her to get to the point.

She smoothed her skirt and looked down. "I've got a strong feeling that Josh Whiting is the father of that baby."

Her words hit hard. This news certainly would explain the man's unwillingness to cooperate. "What makes you so certain?"

"My mother. She told me about it years ago and I never forgot. If I'm right, it's no wonder the Whitings refuse to talk."

Ollie absently shifted his gaze to the chandelier. "It would at that."

"What are you thinking?" Gretta said, and then she gasped. "Please don't tell me you're wondering how to squeeze information out of a prostitute without prostituting yourself?"

He grinned. "That is precisely what I'm wondering."

CHAPTER TWENTY-FIVE

The neighborhood grocery store appeared harmless enough on the main floor of the modest two-story house. Before entering, however, Ollie peered over his shoulder and scanned the windows of neighboring homes. Was anyone watching? Although that was important, he faced a greater concern. How does a man converse with a lady of the night … during light of day? He had never before visited a bordello. From what he had gleaned, Scarlet Maude ran her primary business in a dimly lit back room.

He scanned the neighborhood one more time. Might as well move along. The longer he waited, the greater the chance of being noticed.

A bell jangled above the door. The store smelled of last winter's stale smoke from a potbelly stove and earthy produce fresh from surrounding fields. There was no one around, only the steady tick, tick, tick of a clock. The store was tidy. Every tomato stacked perfectly as if a work of art. Not a speck of flour on the well-scrubbed floor, canned goods stacked smartly about the windows, and not a single item to block the sun's rays pouring in at a slant.

Ollie lifted the lid on a licorice jar when a curtained entry opened and a middle-aged woman stepped in. He studied her for a moment and wondered about her story, her life's choices. Auburn ringlets bounced on well-laced shoulders. Curious gray eyes shone through a flawless complexion. Though appearing well fed and slightly exhausted, she bore a gentleness, a complete lack of hardness. She looked as though she could easily be a happily married woman with grown children and spirited toddlers of their own.

"Maude Millning?" he said.

"I'm Maude."

Ollie gave the small store the once over. This was no place to ask probing questions lest someone else enter. "I haven't come to buy licorice, or anything else for that matter. The name is Harrington," he said, "Oliver Harrington from Addison & Crowley. Might we have a word in private?"

As she led him down a narrow hall, Ollie wavered between nervous and curious. He kept a look out for the famed back room and wondered what kind of man would frequent it. But there was only one door and it opened into a rather pleasant sitting room, which smelled of spice and was adorned with arrangements of colorful summer flowers.

"How may I help you?" she said.

"I fear this is a rather delicate matter."

"Yes?"

"Whiting Senior?"

"Josh?" Warmth, familiarity, and genuineness seemed evident in the revered way she spoke his name. For a moment she squeezed her eyes closed. "What about him?"

"I represent his son. I'm certain you've heard about the trouble?"

She nodded.

"We're working hard to keep this case from going to trial."

"What does that have to do with me?"

If my instincts are correct—everything. "I heard a rumor. I'm trying to clear you."

"Clear *me*?" Her expression pivoted from pleasant to hard. "For heaven's sakes why? What have I done? Did he send you here?"

"No, and that's my dilemma. I've repeatedly asked both he and his son if he has other children, only to repeatedly hit a brick wall. They won't say yes, but I find it curious that neither will they say no."

She glanced at the window, as if searching for a place to flee. "What about this rumor?"

"I understand that back in 1880 you disappeared for a number of months."

Moisture gathered in her eyes. She sat quietly, her pause lingering. "I did."

"Might you wish to tell me about it?"

She fussed with a doily on an end table and said, "No."

"Whiting's child?"

Maintaining her poise, she said, "I think perhaps you'd better leave."

"I think not. Don't you see how this might implicate you? How you could have set him up for blackmail?"

Anger exploded from her no longer gentle eyes, her tone ratcheting. "Blackmail? You couldn't possibly think—?"

"Ma'am, I don't know what to think." Ollie gave his summation another thought. One thing he did know. This woman appeared incapable of blackmail. He felt it in his bones. "Something sinister is being guarded tighter than a corset."

Why did I say that?

"I'm not here to judge," he went on, "but I do intend to unearth a deep secret in an effort to protect you and the Whitings. I find it curious that no one appears to trust anyone."

"Why would we?" she said.

That's precisely what I wish to find out.

CHAPTER TWENTY-SIX

Ollie's Monday morning did not begin well. While crossing Broadway in pouring down rain, an impatient driver chose not to bypass an immense puddle. The wheel of the carriage hit it head on, the spray drenching him. Sopping trousers clinging to his ankles, he returned to the hotel to change them along with socks and shoes, making him last to arrive at the office.

And then things turned bad.

Hilda peered through the door as he walked in.

"Good morning," he said.

She looked at him strangely and lifted her nose. "Is it?"

You managed to get drenched, too, did you?

Not one of the secretaries looked up as he passed by with the exception of Gretta, who smiled awkwardly. His fellow attorneys huddled around Nelson's desk. "Good morning," Ollie said. Something about their dismissive looks, absence of greetings, and taking a step back troubled him. Nelson, though slightly pink in the cheeks, sat expressionless. And then came John Brown. He greeted Ollie with biting words. "Had a little too much weekend, did you?"

"Your purpose for uttering such a remark would be?" Ollie said.

"Playing coy, too, are you?"

For the next several hours, Ollie overheard the word 'prosecution' used repeatedly, but it sounded more like a mispronunciation of the word prostitution. That made no sense. He glanced at the clock. He still had time to finish several letters before the noon hour. He peered into the empty conference room before approaching Gretta. "Might you have time for dictation?"

She nodded. Following him into the room, she started to close the door. "It isn't necessary to—" Ollie said as it clicked shut.

"Oh, but it is." She approached the table looking as if someone had threatened her in a back alley. "Everyone can see us. I need to sit with my back to the window. Please try to look as nonchalant as possible."

Ollie picked up his notes and pretended to read. "Go on."

"Somehow word's gotten around that last Friday you had a tryst with Scarlet Maude."

Ollie restrained a flinch as his breakfast somersaulted. "Start writing," he said. "Pretend you're taking dictation. No wonder all morning long I've been treated less than pleasantly." He purposely looked up, as though pondering what next to say. "Any idea how the rumor started?"

"None." She fixed her eyes on her notes, her lips barely moving. "Nelson thinks it might be coming from Boss."

"That's most interesting. I had hoped we enjoyed being on the same side." Ollie thought for a moment. "That explains something else."

Gretta looked up at him.

"I heard a lone horseman the other evening when I took a ride out to the Whitings'. When I doubled back, the horse took off in a full trot. Never did see who it was. And now this. I thought I was exceedingly careful when I visited Miss Millning. I looked around. Checked every alley, every window. I swear there was no one in sight."

"What are you going to do about it?"

A smile broke loose.

"What could you possibly find that's humorous?" she said. "They're making a laughing stock out of you."

"I'm considering how I might handle this," he said. "I refuse to let myself be easy prey."

"But how? What *can* you do?"

He glanced at his pocket watch as though it were a calendar. "When is our next staff meeting?"

"It's the first working day of every month. Since Monday is Labor Day, the meeting will be a week from tomorrow. Starts at nine in the morning and is over promptly at eleven, regardless of what's on the agenda."

"I wish to pen a note," Ollie said. "Would you be so kind as to fetch an envelope, please?"

"Now?"

"Yes, ma'am."

When Gretta returned, Ollie folded a hand written note, stuffed it in an envelope, sealed it, and penned the name Miss Maude Millning on it. "Would you see that this gets delivered this afternoon, please?"

Gretta's eyes bulged.

"Miss Van Dyke," Ollie said, "respect is not something we deserve. It is something we need to earn ... and I *will* earn it."

"Yes, sir," she said.

"One other thing—"

"Yes?"

Ollie's heart warmed again at the sincerity beaming from her eyes. "Thank you for being straight up with me, for telling me what was happening behind my back. That took courage."

"It was the right thing to do, but it doesn't get you out of a jam."

CHAPTER TWENTY-SEVEN

Nelson reached across the table and seized Gretta's hand. "Anything wrong?"

She studied him, and her thoughts bothered her. "There's plenty wrong," she said. "Why are you attorneys trying to bring Mr. Harrington down?"

Nelson pulled back. "Excuse me? I'd say he's doing a fair enough job of that on his own."

Gretta shook her head. "We all know better than that."

"Do we?"

"Why did you say you thought Boss was the one leaking word about him visiting a brothel? No one knew Mr. Harrington was going to see Maude Millning. Someone had to have found out and told him."

Nelson jiggled a few peas around on his plate with the tongs of his fork. He froze his eyes on them and said in a flat tone, "I don't know if I like you working for a man who keeps company with prostitutes."

"Do you honestly believe he'd be that base?"

Nelson thought for a moment, realization appearing to set in. He shook his head. "No. I don't. What was I thinking? You can tell by looking at him he isn't that kind. Did you have any idea he was going to see Maude?"

Gretta refused to let Nelson know she was the one who tipped off

Mr. Harrington. He'd be furious. She repositioned her napkin, then glanced casually around the café. "Do you have any idea how the rumor started?"

"No, but there is something I need to tell you," Nelson said. "You've got to promise to keep it to yourself, okay?"

She nodded.

"I heard another rumor. Words out Harrington's being followed."

"Who's putting these words out?" she said.

Nelson shrugged. "Did you know anything about that?"

"Of course, I did."

Nelson's brows collided above the bridge of his perfect nose. "How come you didn't tell me?"

"I was afraid to. I didn't think anyone else knew."

"What did Harrington say?"

Gretta's breath grew shallow. "I'm really beginning to feel uncomfortable, Nelson. I work for the guy. I can't tell you about that."

"Don't be silly. I already knew, remember? The first time it happened was last week when he rode out to the Whitings."

Gretta blew out a breath. "You're right. And now there's this rumor about Scarlet Maude. Think about it, Nelson. Mr. Harrington isn't the kind of man who would spread a rumor like that about himself."

"No," Nelson said sounding sympathetic, "he isn't, is he?"

"I get the feeling whoever did this is going to get found out."

Nelson painstakingly wiped moisture from the sides of his water glass, his gaze again frozen into a stare.

"Mr. Harrington is up to something," she continued. "Said as much. Didn't take long for him to figure out how he was going to handle it either."

Furrows cut deep into Nelson's forehead. "What's he going to do?"

"I'm not sure. He found it humorous." She grinned. "Even wrote a note to Miss Millning. Asked me to make sure it got to her."

Nelson's eyebrows drew together again. "What did the note say?"

"I don't know. He sealed the envelope."

"Any idea how soon he's going to handle this?"

"Nope," she said.

"Did he say anything about setting up any meetings or anything?"

"Nelson, you're asking too many questions."

"You baited me." He smiled a mischievous smile. "Got me curious."

Gretta shook her head. "What am I going to do with you? The only thing he asked about was the next staff meeting, when it was, but that was it."

"Do you still have the note?"

She shook her head. "Our errand boy bicycled it to her late this afternoon. Why are you asking? You wouldn't even begin to think about—"

"Of course, not," Nelson said and then he laughed. "But you have to admit, flirting with the idea is kind of fun."

LATER THAT EVENING, GRETTA SAT IN front of the mirror and slowly brushed her hair. As she replayed her conversation with Nelson, she started to squirm. He never did tell her how he'd found out about the rumor, or how the attorneys knew that Mr. Harrington was being followed. But Nelson had accused her of baiting him. She certainly hadn't meant to.

She then recalled the warm look in Mr. Harrington's eyes when he thanked her for playing it straight, and she squirmed harder. She shouldn't have spilled the beans about Mr. Harrington's note to Miss Millning.

But it was Nelson who confided in her first. He had appeared sympathetic toward Mr. Harrington. He was, wasn't he?

Gretta dropped her head in her hands.

What have I done?

CHAPTER TWENTY-EIGHT

Ollie pulled back the reins at the outer edge of Deacon's farm, scanned the fields from one end to the other, and grieved. Hail damage. Irreparable. Though shocks of grain dried on the quarter section, the corn appeared unsalvageable. Livestock grazed lazily where stalks normally reached to the sky, and yet Deacon greeted him with a grin and a solid pat on the back. "Good to see you again, my boy."

Lifting his cap and smoothing back his hair, Ollie looked out across the field. "You were right about the damage. It's devastating. But how about you? How are you getting on?"

"The boys and me," Deacon said, "we held back a couple of bushels of seed. If all goes well, we'll be back on our feet again next year. Been a little damage to the barn, though. We did our best to fix it. The roof still troubles me a trifle, what with the heavy snows coming this winter and all. One of these days we're going to have to build a new barn. If we can get a loan from the bank, we'll be fine."

"By the look of things, you won't be needing me for the harvest."

Deacon grew sad. "We sure looked forward to it, too."

An hour later they gathered at the table where Ollie noticed one less setting. "Heard anything from Hoyt?"

"That boy's going to do just fine," Deacon said. "He already found a place to stay at a boarding house of some kind, and he landed an apprentice job at a publishing company. Said he'd be home for a visit in a few weeks."

After Sunday dinner, Ollie asked if they might take a stroll to the barn to survey the damage. One look at the sagging roof and he questioned the wisdom of entering, fearing it might collapse, but Deacon pressed on. They tromped across squawking boards, Deacon pointing out temporary repairs in every weakened nook and cranny.

The ceiling sagged dangerously above the loft. "It'll take little to reinforce the roof," Ollie said, straining his neck upward. "A half dozen four by fours could provide good support, prop it up surprisingly well. How about doing a grown man with dwindling muscles a favor. Allow me to stop by the next few Saturdays to lend a hand. I'll pick up the wood and be on my way."

Deacon rocked on his heels and stroked his chin. "You really do want to get your hands dirty, don't you? Okay, but I insist on paying for the lumber."

Ollie shook his head. "The cost of wood is what a man like you would call chicken feed and as for me, I feel the need to contribute something for the Sunday dinners your wife's been preparing. Besides, am I not family?"

They walked on, Deacon leading the way out into the fields. He stopped and lifted a barbed wire for them to pass under. "You might want to watch out for—"

"Cow pies?" Ollie lifted a Sunday-go-to-meeting shoe out of a mushy mess, but not without it making a sucking sound that sickened him.

"Why didn't I think to say something sooner?" Deacon squinted. "They're hard to see amidst what's left of the corn. Don't worry. Happens all the time. We'll clean your shoe good as new when we get back to the house."

As they plodded along, Deacon made no mention of what was

destroyed, but rather pointed out in detail what they managed to salvage, and when he reached a grove at the field's edge, he leaned against a tree. "Enough about us," he said. "Last you visited, you wondered if the banker's son had a sibling." Deacon appeared strangely interested. "Were you ever able to find out anything more?"

"I continue to work on it. No one wishes to talk. I've gotten wind of a new angle of which I'm in pursuit, though."

"What angle is that?"

"Would you happen to know anything about a woman they call Scarlet Maude?"

"Sure do. She's my sister."

Ollie's jaw fell open and stayed there.

"Hey, Pa?" one of Deacon's kids cried from the front yard. "Ma needs ya."

"Let's go." Deacon led the way. "We'll talk more later."

Deacon de Haven and Scarlet Maude—brother and sister? Of all of the unlikely siblings, and of all of the inopportune times to get interrupted. While Deacon tended to his wife, Ollie retreated to the mudroom where he raked his shoe against a boot scraper. He headed out to the well with rag in hand, drenched it under a dipper, and buffed off the rest of the muck. Deacon was right. Good as new.

As Ollie slipped the shoe back on, Deacon reappeared holding up two plates and forks. "The wife wanted us to enjoy a nice piece of pie. Let's head out to the porch."

They devoured their pie in silence. Who was the most eager to re-engage in conversation, Ollie could only wonder. Curiosity getting the best of him, he lowered his emptied plate to the floor next to the rocker. "What happened to your sister? I wouldn't have thought of you as having had a questionable upbringing," Ollie said.

Deacon took on the sad look of someone who found himself regurgitating a memory he'd prefer to forget. "We didn't," he said. "At least not 'til after Pa died. Maude was twelve, thirteen maybe, at the time.

Used to be such a carefree and cute little thing. She was younger than me by a couple of years. And Ma, she got lonely. With good men few and far between, she decided to become one of those mail-order brides. After they got married, the man moved in with us. Didn't take her long to realize she'd made a big mistake, but how was she to know?

"I used to lie in bed at night and listen to that donkey yell at her. Come down for breakfast the next morning and he'd be sweet as this here pie. I saw a bruise on my ma from time to time, but it invariably seemed to happen when us kids were away. I'd ask her how she got them and she'd say, 'aw, I was just clumsy.' She always looked embarrassed."

"What about Maude?" Ollie said. "Was he cruel to her, too?"

"Now Maude's a different story. I never saw any bruises, but she changed. Talked when spoken to. That was about it. I thought she was just feeling protective of Ma 'til one day I heard a ruckus out in the barn. Heard her whimpering. I snuck up on 'em ... her and that brute Ma married. Maude's dress was ripped, and she was backing away from him. Her face smeared with dirt and tears. Eyes big as eggs. I can still hear his voice, filled with disgust and loathing. He said, 'You're worthless. You ain't nothin'. You got that girl? No man is ever gonna to want you after I get done with you. You ain't good enough.'"

Ollie choked on those words. "What did you do?"

"After beating him to within an inch of his sorry life," Deacon said, resentment still ripe in his aging eyes, "I grabbed a pitchfork and started prodding. He scampered away on his hands and knees like a scared animal. Made me sick. I yelled after him, 'You get outta here. You ever come back, I'll put this pitchfork to use for sure.' He never did come back. Ma, she died of consumption a year, maybe two, later. Then Maude and I moved to the farm here with our grandpa. As for me, after learning what I was capable of, I got serious about religion. Figured I'd need all the help I could get."

"Have you seen much of Maude since?"

Deacon shook his head. "Na'ah. She won't have anything to do with us. A year, maybe two, after that, she got married to some loser who didn't deserve her. Months later, he ran off with another woman. I heard Maude went through a rough time for a while, taking off after married men as if it was her right. About that time word got around that Josh Whiting's wife was going through a hard time, too. Wouldn't talk to anybody. You know how tongues can wag. Rumors abounded that Josh was spending time with Maude. Then she up and disappeared for a while. Seems it was about a year or so before she came back. People thought she might have gone some place and had his baby, but no one knew for sure.

Deacon jabbed at what little was left of his pie, but didn't cut into it. "We've learned to leave her alone. Come Thanksgiving and Christmas we always have a turkey or ham delivered along with a note telling her how much we love her. She never responds. We keep praying that one day—"

Ollie slowly began rocking.

"Ole?"

The nickname sounded like an endearment. "Yes?"

"You find out anything, you be sure to let me know, won't you?"

"Count on it. I sent her a note. Asked her to stop by the office Tuesday morning. We can only hope she shows up."

CHAPTER TWENTY-NINE

Ollie wondered at the caption in the morning paper. *Speak softly and carry a big stick* Vice President Theodore Roosevelt had advised during yesterday's speech at the Minnesota State Fair. Ollie found the line particularly prophetic since today he planned to do precisely the same thing.

An hour later, he stood at Gretta's desk. "Were you able to reserve the conference room?"

"Eleven o'clock sharp," she said.

"I'll need to know if and when Miss Millning arrives."

Gretta's eyes swelled. "She's coming?"

"If she does, be sure to interrupt the staff meeting … and Gretta? Don't hesitate to use her full name. Follow me?"

Ten minutes before the hour of eleven, the door swung open and Nelson hurried in looking frazzled.

"Where have you been?" Gretta said. "I've been worried sick. The staff meeting will be over in a few minutes."

"I rode down to Mason City yesterday," he said. "Horse threw a shoe. Had to wait for the blacksmith to open his shop this—"

Nelson's head swiveled as the door swung open again. His eyes protruded and his mouth wedged open when in walked Miss Maude Millning, hair coifed in an attractive upsweep. She was donned in a fine robin egg blue frock and smelled like a French perfumery. "My name's Maude Millning," she said. "I'm here to see Mr. Harrington."

Gretta shot up. "I'll let him know."

Her heart picked up its pace. Before opening the door to the conference room, she glanced back at the lovely woman standing at her desk and felt a pang of guilt. How ridiculous to feel jealous of a lady of the streets who was old enough to be Mr. Harrington's mother.

"Mr. Harrington?" As all eyes fastened on Gretta, she couldn't keep from smiling inwardly. "I'm sorry to interrupt, but there's a Maude Millning here to see you. She said she has an appointment."

All around the conference table and in sync, surprised heads jerked toward Mr. Harrington. Even Boss appeared caught off guard. "Scarlet Maude?" he said as he glanced at his timepiece. "Gentlemen? I believe this meeting is adjourned."

OLLIE MET MAUDE AT GRETTA'S DESK and extended an elbow. "This way, please." He escorted her back to the conference room where his fellow attorneys strangely, or not so strangely, continued to huddle. Ollie looked each of them square in the eye, making sure not to display a show of emotion as the men filed out of the room. However, the air did take on the thick quality of maple syrup as it would during a biting day in January.

The instant Ollie closed the door, Maude parked her hands on her hips. "You purposely paraded me through the office," she hissed, "and I don't appreciate it one little bit."

"Please be seated, Miss Millning."

She did not move. "Why did you ask me to meet you *here*? Why not meet at some place, any place, more private? What are your motives? To make a spectacle me? Put me on display? Well you've certainly succeeded."

Ollie nodded. "You're right. I purposely paraded you through the office. I wished not to use or abuse you, but fear I may have done so just the same. One thing is certain. It's not you who is a spectacle or, worse, the subject of a joke, Miss Millning. It's both of us. Seems word has spread like a firestorm that I paid you a visit. There's been a tremendous amount of snickering going on ever since. I thought it best to handle the situation head on."

Maude rested a hand on the crook of her parasol and narrowed her eyes. "Who did you tell?"

"No one."

"You don't think for a minute that I—"

"Not at all."

"Then how—?" she said, her tone aghast.

Ollie peered through the office window where Nelson passed by, taking a not-so-subtle peek in. "I have the distinct feeling that some-one's paying close attention to my every move," Ollie said. "There's nothing I'd enjoy more than to smoke out the culprit."

She took a step forward. "Any idea who?"

He pulled out a chair for her and sat also. "I have not a clue. My only reason for inviting you was to quiet the rumors, or at least steer them in another direction. Whoever is doing this must have an awfully good reason, and I can't help but wonder if it's related to the Whitings. All that confuses me at present is the tight lips about Whiting Senior having another child."

Maude recoiled. "I'm not about to—"

"I have no intention of squeezing more information out of you, Miss Millning. Do you mind if I call you Maude?"

She appeared to have settled down. "I prefer it actually."

"As I was saying, I'm certain you will share that information when you're ready. And speaking of being ready, I thought you'd want to know that your brother is concerned about your welfare."

"My bro—"

"I arrived from England seeking him out. I was married to his niece. Lost her and my son when their carriage overturned. It was Em's—"

"You mean Em's—"

"You knew her?"

"No, but I did know of her. I'm so sorry."

"It was her dream to come to America," Ollie continued, "so I thought I'd come in her stead, see the place, spend a few months to a year in Amber Leaf before deciding what to do with the rest of my life. Returning to England is not necessarily an option.

"And now that I've taken you away from your store for selfish reasons, may I have the honor of treating you to lunch? There's a nice little café close by."

Maude's eyes grew moist. "You and me? You mean you'd … I'd like that."

Ollie grinned mischievously. "The entire time we've been talking, my fellow attorneys have been wearing a trail on the hardwood and not without taking numerous peeks through the glass. How about we give them more about which to gossip?" He escorted her through the office with a tempered gait.

As they passed Gretta's desk, he said, "We'll be on an extended luncheon, Miss Van Dyke," then stopped near the door and plucked his fedora off the coat rack. He resisted turning and tipping his hat toward the hoard of gaping mouths.

But he certainly felt tempted.

CHAPTER THIRTY

The room stilled. Gretta smiled at the complete absence of sound, embarrassed by how much she enjoyed Mr. Harrington's seeming triumph. A roomful of tongue-tied attorneys? This had to be a first.

Boss stepped out of his office and leaned against the doorjamb with a stogie clenched in his teeth. Smoke billowing up his nostrils watered his eyes. He looked the room over, but said nothing. Resting thumbs behind his belt, he muttered something indistinguishable beneath his breath and shuffled back in.

Hilda appeared refreshingly amused. "Did you know about Maude Millning's appointment?" she said.

Gretta smiled her answer then hunkered down, focusing her attention on menacing footsteps and shallow breathing. John Brown was the first to arrive at her desk … and attack. "Did you have any idea that woman was coming?"

Mr. Brown appeared conspicuously taller and patently more intimidating at close range. "Yes, sir, I did."

"Yet you said nothing?" he said.

Why did he have to sound belittling? "I didn't know 'til this morning. Mr. Harrington asked me to get him out of the meeting when she came, and specifically asked me to mention her full name."

More footsteps as Charlie and Nelson crowded around. Nelson did not look happy.

Neither did Charlie. "How dare that man cheapen our office by parading around a prostitute? And to think he did it on purpose."

"He turned the tables on us," Mr. Brown hissed. "Turned *us* into stooges. We can't let him get by with it."

Nelson picked up a paperweight and restlessly rolled it around in his hand, his expression unreadable. He appeared neutral and searching, and also appeared to ignore Gretta. A moment later, he burst into laughter. "That man sure has brass. The more life throws at him, the tougher he gets." Lodging his focus on the paperweight, Nelson volleyed it one last time and caught it. "Gentlemen, do what you want, but I'm not about to take him on."

When the last of the staff headed out to lunch, Nelson appeared at Gretta's desk. Abruptly. Why the quick change in demeanor? His eyes darkened, his words accusing. "Why didn't you bother to tell *me* you reserved the conference room for Harrington?"

Gretta pulled back. "I don't appreciate your tone. You were in Iowa, remember?"

"Do you mean to tell me he really didn't reserve that room until this morning?" Nelson picked up the calendar and leafed through it. "Harrington must have been keeping a close eye on the schedule."

"That's what I was thinking," Gretta said, then added, "I can't figure you out. One minute you defend him and the next minute you attack him."

When Nelson answered, "You're being ridiculous," she recoiled.

"The attorneys in your office," Maude said as she and Ollie strolled up Broadway, "you didn't sneer at them, lift your nose, or overplay your hand. Why not?"

"That I did wish to do, but it would have been less than gentlemanly."

Half a block later, they entered a quaint restaurant and the hostess seated them at a booth.

"Might I have a hair out of place?" Ollie asked as the hostess walked away.

Maude appeared perplexed. "Isn't that something a woman would ask? You of all people are anything but feminine."

He raised a brow and released a playful grin. "Seems I'm attracting an inordinate amount of attention."

And she grinned back. "Why do I feel an integral part of that equation?"

They enjoyed a leisurely lunch with far more to converse about than Ollie had anticipated.

After the waitress replaced their emptied plates with dessert, Maude picked up a fork and dangled it loosely in her hand. "Most people play judge," she said, "ask me why I've chosen the lifestyle I have. But not you. And no man dares spend time with me in public. What makes you different? Aren't you the least bit curious?"

"Perhaps I'm mildly curious, but in the few times we have spoken, it takes little to gain an understanding," Ollie said, careful to keep his tone matter-of-fact.

Maude lightly rested her petite chin on a finger. "Now you have me mildly curious."

Ollie refused to violate Deacon's portrayal of their past. But why not share an accounting he would have as easily thought of on his own? "It's simple, is it not? Even with a few years on you, you're still a strikingly handsome woman," he said. "Unpretentious, too. I admire that quality. It goes without saying that you were also a beautiful young girl at one time, or might it be more accurate to suggest you were a beautiful, innocent, and vulnerable young girl?"

Maude leveled her gaze on him, appearing taken aback.

"There's a tremendous amount of jealousy in this less than ideal world," he continued, "and predators abound. Somewhere along the way I have an unpleasant feeling someone disrespected you with their actions, words, or both, giving you the impression that you lacked in worth … and you believed it."

Maude opened her mouth as if to speak, but words appeared to have gotten lodged deeply inside and did not break loose.

"Forgive my bluntness," Ollie said, "but you have an appealing innocence about you."

"What a kind thing to say."

"Have you ever thought to take it back?"

"What? My innocence?" Maude smoothed a soft ripple in the tablecloth. "I did try church a few times …"

"And?"

Her voice took on an edge. "I know where I'm not wanted."

"I assume you felt rebuffed?"

"That is a more pleasant word than snubbed, isn't it? The goody-goody people there didn't hesitate to show their disapproval." She looked at Ollie, appearing to take umbrage. "What's behind the grin? Aren't you being a bit insensitive?"

"They need you as much as you need them, Maude."

It appeared as if Ollie's words had hit a nerve. "Excuse me?" she said.

"We're all deceived."

"Not those goody-goody church people."

"Them, too. They were only showing their weakness."

She leaned in. "But their weakness—"

"I know, but be kind. Show them your strength. They need to see it. I'd go so far as to say they hunger for it. Remember Mary Magdalene? If she was good enough for Jesus, we all are." Ollie laughed self-consciously. "I can't believe I'm engaging in this conversation over lunch in a crowded restaurant. I hope not to have disrespected your privacy. It's personal and I fear I'm rather out of line."

"I like it," she said. "But about being a Christian? I grew up in Sunday School, and I'm no Mary Magdalene. After taking a wicked fall …" As her voice trailed off, she looked away then said, "Besides, I don't know that I'm strong enough to walk the straight and narrow, not for the duration."

"Have a nasty pile of unpleasant memories, do you?"

She nodded. "Don't know how to get rid of them. My conscience would eat me alive if I attended church all the time."

Ollie reached for her hand, holding it, and her cheeks blossomed a cotton candy pink. "Take courage, Maude. Be an over comer. Forgive the people who've snubbed you. Love them no matter what." Ollie caught himself. "My sincere apologies—"

She raised a brow. "None of us are above a sermon."

And then Ollie knew. "You never did abandon the faith, did you?"

Her smile confirmed it.

Ollie glanced at the thinning restaurant. "Perhaps we'd better head back. I'd like to make a quick stop at another place along the way."

Several doors down from the café, he stopped by a florist's shop. "This way, please," he said, heading straight for the roses. "When we chatted in your sitting room, I noticed you appeared to favor these. Thought you might enjoy refreshing yours."

A short while later, Ollie shook Maude's hand outside the law office. "Thank you so much for coming," he said. "My time with you has been an absolute delight."

As she turned to walk away, he called after her. "I'm hauling wood out to Deacon's early Saturday morning. His barn is in need of repair. I know he'd enjoy seeing you, so do give it some thought. I'll stop by at eight o'clock sharp. If and only if you choose to come along, be waiting on your front porch."

She merely turned away and walked on.

CHAPTER THIRTY-ONE

8 September 1901

Dearest Family:

With thoughts of you often, I hope this letter finds you most happy and well.

On Sunday past, I hired a horse and buggy and rode out to Deacon's farm for yet another visit. Unfortunately, the hailstorm I had mentioned previously had all but destroyed his crops. Wherever we looked, ears of corn were sheered from their stalks. Deacon was left with no choice but to turn the harvest over to his livestock to graze, and yet his greeting was cheerful as ever. While not a man of means, he continues to be a man of amazing character. I rode out again yesterday to help reinforce the roof of his barn. It felt good to once again exercise my biceps.

Monday past was a public holiday in America, which they call Labor Day. The weather having been balmy, I boated by daylight and spent the evening hours reading. I continue to so enjoy this fine land. Autumn will soon be upon us with the leaves of the trees in full color. Pumpkins. Squash. Indian corn. There is much in which to look forward.

That intriguing case I alluded to in my most recent letter is leading me down roads I had not contemplated imaginable. While I fear no physical harm, I find my every move is being watched, and I have no inkling by whom or why. Keeping an eye out for hidden clues makes me feel like Sherlock Holmes. I rather enjoy it. Even more fascinating are the people involved with the case. On Tuesday past I found myself sitting in a café, as a practicing attorney during business hours nonetheless, speaking with an alleged lady of the streets about things we deem holy. Although difficult to believe, I assure you that did happen. What amazed me more was that it felt natural and good. Perhaps I have missed my life's calling. Perhaps I ought to have become a man of the cloth.

On a more tragic note, I am certain you have heard news of President William McKinley and how he suffered a bullet inside the Temple of Music in Buffalo, New York. An anarchist made an attempt on the President's life because of the loss of his job over, of all things, a labor dispute. This leaves me not knowing what I should think. I begin and end my days with prayers for the President's speedy recovery.

Each day I continue to arrive at my sleeping quarters desirous of a letter from England. I hope one day your opinion of your wayward son will soften for I so look forward to hearing from you.

Now the cordial greetings from your loving son Oliver.

Ollie sealed the envelope and set it aside. As he reached for a book, his ears perked up. Rushing footsteps in the hallway. A passing shadow in the gap under the threshold. A white envelope skittering across the floor. The staccato clip of retreating foot drops.

He plucked up the envelope, opened the door, and peered up and down the hallway. It was empty. He returned to his desk and sliced open the envelope. Letters forming single words had been clipped from a newspaper and pasted on a note-sized piece of paper.

Stay away from Maude Millning.

CHAPTER THIRTY-TWO

Boss struck a match. Before lifting the flame to the tip of his cigar, he took a long, curious look at Ollie. The flame died out. He lit another.

"About last week," Boss said, "that guest you paraded through the office." He drew in several repeated puffs, lifted his chin, and choked out a cloud of gray. "I don't care for surprises, but that one was an exception. I've held off asking until now." He grinned mischievously. "Didn't want the explanation to spoil a perfectly good illusion. Now tell me, Harrington. Why in heaven's name did you invite a woman of Maude Millning's reputation to grace our hallowed halls?"

Ollie made the mistake of smiling.

"You find this amusing, do you?" Boss said.

"I believe I find it more awkward than amusing, sir."

"Well?"

"Confidentially, I have reason to believe your friend Whiting Senior and Miss Maude Millning may have produced a child together."

Boss plucked the cigar from his mouth. "Why, that's preposterous."

Ollie allowed him a measured moment to reconsider then said, "Is it?"

"You know," Boss said with a quick scratch of his chin, "you may have something there. Some years back, as I recall, Josh and his wife did go through a rough patch. It was no secret, not to anyone. About that same time, Scarlet Maude was on the prowl. There couldn't have been a woman within a fifty-mile radius of town who didn't feel threatened. They hated her, to put it mildly." He flicked ash into a tray. "But why not talk to Josh about it? Why talk to the Millning woman?"

Ollie studied the man intently. Contrary to what he'd been told, Boss could not have spread the rumor about his visit to Maude's. He couldn't have known, and he's too direct for coyness. But if not Boss, who?

"That's my dilemma," Ollie said. "I did question Whiting Senior and also his son. They refused to cooperate. That's why I went to visit Maude."

"Correction. That's why you asked Miss Millning to come to the office. Why do that? You knew tongues would wag. Why not meet her at her place?"

Ollie shook his head. "I did go there initially. When I found myself snubbed and mocked over the visit, I felt I needed to hush the rumors, so I purposely invited her to the office thinking perhaps—"

"That was a brilliant move, but why not fill me in first?"

Because I wasn't entirely certain where anyone stands, including you. Ollie hesitated then said, "There's more."

Boss held his gaze as Ollie brought up the note he'd found under his door.

"Was it threatening?" Boss said.

"I prefer to call it a suggestion. No one knew I was going there and yet word got around. Miss Millning is not about to kiss and tell. That would ruin her business. That is, if she has a business. The jury's still out on that one."

"Did she admit to having Josh's child?" Boss said.

"No, sir, she did not. The one thing she, Whiting Senior, and Junior have in common is that none of them will admit to a child having been born out of wedlock, neither will they acknowledge that one does not exist."

"Sounds like you're on to something," Boss said. "Keep going. The preliminary hearing is scheduled in November so you still have plenty of time." Boss took another drag on the cigar. "But let's go back to that note under your door. Any idea who's behind it?"

Ollie shook his head. "I'm not certain."

"You gave the impression you didn't feel threatened by it. Why not?"

"Uneasy, perhaps, but not threatened. I get the strange feeling it might have come from one of our attorneys."

Boss scowled. "That's a bit of a reach, isn't it?"

"Not necessarily. They know too much."

SEVERAL HOURS LATER, BOSS SUMMONED OLLIE again.

"I'd like you to drop everything and take a trip over to Aspen first thing in the morning. Hilda and I were scheduled to go, but she hasn't been feeling well lately. Seems to have issues with headaches. And my wife is scheduled for surgery. Nelson has a case at the courthouse. Charlie requested a vacation day. I think he said something about going up to the Twin Cities. And John has problems with his back. A buggy ride would only exacerbate his condition."

"This meeting is for …?" Ollie said.

"I'm trying to woo a man by the name of Petersen. He's in the meat packing business. I've heard rumblings of trouble. I'd like you take over for me."

"But the other attorneys—"

"Still concerned about their opinions, are you? Don't be. Their plates are full. Besides, this could be short lived. Winning a contract with Petersen won't be easy. I'm the pursuer, not him. I'll have a file prepared with all the pertinent information before you leave tonight. By the way, you'll need a stenographer to take detailed notes."

"Why the need for detailed notes?" Ollie said.

"Take Miss Van Dyke. She's competent and professional. According to Hilda, she's the best we've got." Boss leaned in. "You'll need an escort, too. Our driver can fill that roll. I'd also like you to wine and dine Petersen and anyone he chooses to bring along. There's an upscale restaurant near your hotel. Take your time with supper. We could use the added business."

"But about the detailed notes ...."

CHAPTER THIRTY-THREE

B oss had plunked Ollie in the middle of another difficult situation. Though an idyllic morning for a carriage ride, to bring Gretta to Aspen rather than Hilda was comparable to inviting a starving man to a feast and not allowing him to eat. Nelson wasn't beyond jealousy, Ollie wasn't beyond guilt, and Gretta exuded a staggering amount of appeal.

A driver pulled in front of the hotel at half past nine. From there, they stopped by the office where she awaited them with a smile as wide as her baggage. "I'm so excited," she said. "This is my first business trip."

The road running due east to Aspen was narrow with deep ditches on either side and for the most part decidedly straight. After a few pleasantries, Gretta disengaged. Whether absorbed in the beauty of the countryside or she merely fell short of words, what did it matter? Her feminine presence lifted Ollie's spirits, which had been doing nicely from the onset. After a while, though, that same absence of words grew awkward. "I hope Nelson is getting on well at court today," Ollie put forward.

Gretta shook her head. "He may stop in at some point, I suppose, but there was nothing on his schedule."

"But Boss said—"

"John Brown has problems with his back, right? Charlie Mendenhall decided to take a day of vacation, probably to go to the Cities? Hilda's been having a lot of headaches lately? And Boss's wife is in surgery this morning?" She snickered. "Those are standard lines he uses whenever he wants to manipulate someone into doing his bidding. Same scenario every single time. The attorneys laugh about it."

"The chap is box clever, is he not?" Ollie said. "I shall bear that in mind. I fear I misjudged the man thinking him direct and unable to be coy." His grin faded when he noticed a column of dust up the road. "Driver, any notion what that might be? What say you? A horse race or a caravan?"

The driver glanced back. "Definitely a caravan, sir." He maneuvered the horse to the side of the road to allow the cavalcade to pass, but the lead carriage stopped. Its driver looked about appearing worried. "It's going to be tight," he said. "Would you mind nudging a bit to the right, sir? A few inches should do it."

Ollie took note of the cavernous ditch abutting the side of the road. The carriage's wheels balanced mere inches from its edge. "Driver, we have but little choice. Why not give it a go?"

The horse inched forward, the front wheel cutting deep into the ditch. Ollie positioned himself at the ready as the carriage started a slow slide. When it threatened to flip, he bounded out, reached back, and plucked Gretta out of the seat as if she were lighter than air. As the driver grabbed the bridle and steadied the whinnying horse, Ollie uprighted Gretta. Meanwhile, the carriage continued sliding sideways and to an angle until the rear wheel found its resting place at the bottom of the incline.

The driver held the bridle, continuing to steady the excited horse as the column of carriages, gaping driver after gaping driver, maneuvered past. With the final carriage gone, he led the horse forward and eased the carriage from the ditch.

Ollie turned to Gretta. "No casualties," he said.

"No casualties," she repeated. But as she reached for his hand and climbed back in, something happened to Ollie. Something down deep. The warmth and tenderness of her touch made him not want to let go.

IN GRETTA'S NARROW WORLD, SHE HAD never before been on a tour, saying nothing of walking the floors of a meat packing facility. Although well organized and pristine, her nostrils flared at the smell of raw meat, her skin pimpled at the vacillating temperatures, and bouts of moist air suffocated her lungs, making her feel light headed at times and hesitant to enter the next chamber. But walking alongside Mr. Harrington, she wouldn't hesitate to go again.

As Mr. Petersen stopped here and there to share a stray thought or a bit of background, Gretta kept an ear tuned in to high points, scribbling detailed notes as she deemed necessary.

After several hours, Mr. Harrington thanked a smiling Mr. Petersen for the tour of the well-run facility.

The driver already at the hotel, Mr. Harrington and Gretta checked in as well, and at seven o'clock they again met Mr. Petersen, who had insisted on coming without his bride to a quaint restaurant two doors away. Colorful floral arrangements and candles glowing on miniature mirrors served as centerpieces on coral linen. Coral napkins. Fine china. Sterling silver. And a menu with a glaring absence of prices. Gretta felt like a country yokel on display in the elegant décor.

She carefully followed Mr. Harrington's lead. He ordered a glass of merlot. She ordered a glass of merlot. He ordered a t-bone and baked potato. She ordered a t-bone and baked potato. But the breadbasket she passed along, choosing to wait for the second round before plucking out a warm roll.

"You're British," Mr. Petersen said to Mr. Harrington.

Mr. Harrington smiled. "Relatively fresh off the ship."

"What part of England?"

"London."

Mr. Petersen's face brightened. "You wouldn't happen to be related to Lord and Lady Harrington, would you?"

"I certainly am," Mr. Harrington said, appearing surprised. "They are my father and mother."

Gretta's chunk of roll lodged high in her throat. It took several gulps of water to force it down.

"That would make you the barrister," Mr. Petersen said. "What a delight to have the opportunity to get to know you. I met them at The Palace Theatre of Varieties back in '95, I think it was, when the wife and I vacationed there. We met the Addisons for the first time that same evening, and all got along fabulously."

Mr. Harrington looked at Gretta as if to say, 'Boss knew what he was doing, didn't he? He deliberately arranged this meeting.'

Gretta held back an amused smile.

"My father corresponds with Mr. Addison quite frequently," Mr. Harrington said.

"I would assume that's how you secured a job at his firm."

"That's correct."

"I'm surprised a man of nobility would assume a position as attorney."

When Mr. Harrington smiled and said, "Suffice it to say, my father isn't in complete agreement with my chosen occupation," Gretta got the distinct feeling there was much more to that story.

"Are you in the States permanently?"

"I'm not certain." Gretta found it wonderfully odd that Mr. Harrington looked to her and added, "Thought perhaps I'd spend a fair amount of time in Amber Leaf and then get on from there."

"Do give your father my best." Mr. Petersen set his plate to the side. "Now, let's talk business. How would you say your firm compares with others in the area? Why would we want to sign up with you?"

Gretta pulled out her steno pad and again took notes. Mr.

Harrington told him the firm was financially competitive, the attorneys hardworking and conservative, avoiding lawsuits if at all possible. "If it's your preference to walk down that road," he said, "I assure you we aren't the firm for you. If, however, we determine the opposing party is unreasonable and we are strongly in the right, we would have no choice but to engage a suit and would promise to scale mountains to win. We stake our reputation on winning. We lose that, we lose clientele."

Gretta took note of Mr. Harrington's confidence and candor and for a moment she felt as if she'd taken on his strength.

Mr. Petersen absently wiped breadcrumbs to the side of his place setting. "But you don't appear interested in knowing our track record or what we have coming down the pike."

"I assure you, we've done our probing," Mr. Harrington said. "No stones unturned as you Americans say."

The businessman cracked a grin. "What's our next step? Do we draw up a contract?"

Mr. Harrington took on a brief far-off look. Sensing something was amiss, Gretta waited for a nod then handed Mr. Petersen a folder containing a standard agreement.

"We took the liberty of preparing this document," Mr. Harrington said. "You are welcome to carry it along with you, and do take your time reading it. If you decide to sign on, feel free to return it at your convenience. If not, nothing more needs to be said or done."

Discerning that the men needed private time to chat further over a nightcap, Gretta graciously excused herself.

"Could you manage to get a message to our driver?" Mr. Harrington said, as she was about to walk on. "After you and I meet for breakfast at first light, tell him we'll be ready to head back to Amber Leaf." Mr. Harrington smiled warmly. "Rest well."

Gretta didn't walk to her room, she floated. This had been far and away the most wonderful day of her life. Closing the door to her room behind her, she leaned against it and inhaled a beautiful hurt. She relived

Mr. Harrington's amazing strength when he effortlessly plucked her out of the carriage, how secure she'd felt at his heavenly touch, and the grace with which he had accepted being manipulated by Boss not once, but twice. And when he admitted that his parents were Lord and Lady Harrington, she thought about how accepting and respectful he had been of her from the very day they met and her heart melted. But that changed nothing. Oliver Harrington was even further beyond reach than she had imagined and already anticipated the day he would move away. She then would be left either trying to mold Nelson Prixton into another Oliver Harrington, or sifting through commoners looking for another prince, not that she deserved one.

She crawled into bed, her unworthy heart stubbornly crying out for Oliver Harrington's heart.

How she yearned for, yet dreaded, first light. This was a business trip she did not want to end.

CHAPTER THIRTY-FOUR

At twenty-five past seven, Ollie took another sip of coffee. Gretta had proved refreshing company. She possessed an instinct for business and an uncanny ability to separate the important from the unimportant. At every high point during the tour, without fail, he found her busily attending to note taking.

"Good morning," she said, gliding toward the table with the grace of a swan.

At the mere sight of her, Ollie's heart did that crazy little thing again. He got up and pulled out a chair.

After placing breakfast orders, Gretta said, "how did it go last night?"

"Do you mean, did we procure this?" He held up the signed contract.

"Noooh!" she said. "He signed it so soon?"

"Your note taking was of great assistance. Our new friend Petersen made mention of it and expressed his appreciation for our attending to the task assigned us in such an earnest manner."

Gretta winced at her first sip of coffee.

"Too strong?"

"Wonderfully rich beans," she said then placed the cup on the saucer and moved it curiously far from her plate. "Do you have any idea why Boss wanted me to take notes on a walking tour? I've taken minutes at meetings, and dictation, but I've never even heard of anyone taking notes at anything so informal."

Mr. Harrington turned thoughtful. "I've wondered about that as well. As for Petersen, he did appear overly anxious to sign the contract. That concerns me," Mr. Harrington said. "Did you notice how many times he pulled us aside and shared vignettes about potential labor difficulties?"

"I did."

"As I've been sitting here, I've given this a fair amount of thought," Ollie said. "Czolgosz lost his job during an economic panic. Eventually he turned to anarchism and went on to shoot President McKinley who is, fortunately, recovering. People tend to personalize their livelihoods. That's why proprie … employers like Mr. Petersen heed close attention. Labor disputes are nothing to trivialize."

After a leisurely breakfast, Ollie retrieved Gretta's bag and they met up with the driver. At half past eight they headed east with the sun at their backs and a long stretch of road before them.

For the longest while, Gretta stared off as if her heart were far away.

"Might I ask what it is that has so entirely captured your attention?" Ollie said.

She smiled. "I was looking at that grove of pines up ahead. Autumn and winter are my favorite times of the year. I love the dry air. The sun takes on a warm golden hew. Baskets of pinecones sitting near the fire on a long winter's night. I hope one day to have a modest home with lots of land and my own little groves of trees. An apple orchard and a miniature pine forest."

Ollie sensed there was more going on in that lovely little head of hers, but what? "I understand the need for an orchard," he said, "but what about the forest?"

"I love the scent of pine … Mr. Harrington?" she said. "When Mr. Petersen expressed confusion about a man of nobility assuming a position as an attorney, you—"

"Avoided responding?" He nodded. "One Sunday afternoon when I was in my mid teens, my carriage broke down. A young blacksmith happened by. As he labored, we talked. Not only did I find him unusually hard working, I was amazed at his brilliance. I lived in a world of plenty while he lived in a world of want, yet his passion for life left me wanting." Ollie looked at Gretta and smiled. "That's when I learned one of life's biggest secrets. Fulfillment is found not in accumulating things, but rather in earning them. I always had an interest in the legal field and am anxious to see how far it can take me. Thus far I've found that the journey is worth everything."

An occasional snort of the horse, the squeak of the carriage, and the constant crunching of wheels on gravel accompanied a quiet replete with warmth for the next number of miles. Then like the blue aftermath of Christmas when packages have been opened and guests have long past returned to their homes, that same quiet grew empty as the horse's hooves met with the graveled roads of Amber Leaf.

"I'll type my notes first thing," Gretta said as the carriage neared Broadway.

But the driver drove on.

She nudged to the edge of the seat. "Where are we going?"

"I thought it best to drop off your bag before we return the carriage to the livery," Mr. Harrington said.

Her heart picked up its pace. "That's not necessary. I can carry it home tonight."

Mr. Harrington grinned. "I fear the horse has a mind of its own. It doesn't appear to want to stop."

Gretta steadied her breathing. She recalled the words *Lord and Lady Harrington* and imagined the environment most familiar to him—servants, a magnificent home. She then considered the rundown bungalow she and her mother called home and felt as if she were straddling life's lowest rung. She had never gone to a restaurant before dating Nelson. Last night's hotel stay in Aspen was her first. Had she not borrowed a bag from her neighbor, she would have had to tote her clothing in a gunnysack. But what could she do? If Mr. Harrington had the courage to face the Crusty Schmidts of this world, the grace to befriend the Maude Millnings, and the wherewithal to hold a blacksmith in the highest regard, Gretta chose to accept her plight as well.

"Our horse lacks a keen sense of direction," Mr. Harrington said. "I believe our driver could use some assistance."

She smiled. "Our home is at the bottom of the hill and to the right."

"Thank you. For a moment there I feared you were choosing to be rather hard on me."

She hurt at the thought.

"Had we not gone now," he said with a grin, "I would have been in for a long walk this evening, and I'm not in the tiptop shape I enjoyed during my youth."

As they turned down Gretta's street, she felt like Cinderella at half past midnight. Her mother was sitting on the front porch still in a nightshirt sipping on a mug of coffee, hair disheveled, and undoubtedly with bare feet.

While the driver retrieved Gretta's bag from the rear of the carriage and slipped it inside their front door, Mr. Harrington escorted her to the porch. She stood speechless as he turned to her mother with hand graciously extended. "Mrs. Van Dyke? I'm Oliver Harrington. I can't begin to tell you what a privilege it is to meet you."

Her mother slowly stood, her eyes swelling with wonder. She hadn't lit up like that in years. It was as if she were meeting royalty. In a way, she was.

"It's a pleasure to meet you as well, sir," her mother said. "Gretta has said some very flattering things about you."

Mr. Harrington looked at Gretta. If she hadn't known better, she would have sworn his heart was in his eyes. "You must be very proud of her. She's extremely professional and an outstanding stenographer."

Soon after, the carriage stopped in front of the law office and Mr. Harrington helped Gretta down, his expression growing somber. "Well, this is it." After what appeared a thoughtful pause, he said, "Your Nelson Prixton is one very fortunate young man."

CHAPTER THIRTY-FIVE

id-morning on Saturday, Ollie backhanded a fistful of perspiration. No matter how much sweat and toil, he seemed powerless to break free from persistent thoughts of Gretta.

"Work too much for you?" Deacon asked. "You've barely said a word since you got here. We can quit any time."

Ollie stopped sawing and gaped at Deacon. "Is that what you think?" He shook his head. "Please take no offense. Hard labor seems the best medicine at the moment."

"Life at the office getting to you, my boy?"

"I confess the week did prove most interesting," he said. "I wish to sort through a few things."

"Anything you care to talk about?"

Yes. Gretta Van Dyke. I'm falling in love with another commoner, only this time she's in love with someone else, and I want not to help myself. "No."

"You never did tell me if Maude showed up at your office."

After a solid pull on the saw blade, Ollie stopped again.

"What is it?" Deacon said. "Spit it out, my boy."

"She did, and it went as well as could be expected. Then last Saturday I stopped by her home to see if she was amenable to riding out with me. I was certain that would be agreeable to you. Asked her to wait on her front porch, but she chose not to. I would have said something before, but—"

Deacon turned sad. "We would have welcomed her with opened arms."

"There's more." Ollie stopped long enough to guzzle a large swig of lemonade. "It's been suggested that I stay away from her.'"

"By who?"

"I have no idea. Some coward slipped a note under my door."

Deacon lowered onto a hay bale and mopped away the sweat beading on his forehead. "You were threatened?"

"I prefer to believe I was advised."

"But who would do such a thing or why?" Deacon said, alarm mingled in his tone.

"I don't know, but rest assured I intend to find out."

"Have you noticed anything amiss?"

Ollie shook his head. "I've been keeping an eye out. Things are too quiet. There must be a way to snare the chap."

"I want in on it," he said. "You're talking to the detective, remember? We've got to watch out for Maude. Besides, I haven't had a good scare in a long while. Might be kind of fun for a change."

"You want in? I have a thought." Ollie glanced out at the ruined field. "And it pays."

CHAPTER THIRTY-SIX

What happened to Mr. Harrington? Why the change? Gretta fidgeted relentlessly. She slipped a marker back in her book, set it on the sofa beside her, and adjusted her shawl one more time.

On Wednesday, Thursday, and all day Friday he had pulled back somehow, appearing withdrawn. She felt awkward in his presence. It was as if they hadn't gone to Aspen, as if the trip had been nothing more than a pipe dream. He barely spoke to her, and when he did, he uttered no more than a simple word or two. No good morning. No have a nice evening. No dictation. No requests for folders. She scoured her thoughts. Had seeing her home cast her in a dimmer light? Although he was a gentleman, gentlemen are people, too. They have second thoughts. But why the need for blatant rejection?

For all of his faults, Nelson had never done that. He worked with her, too, yet he'd been to her home and kept coming back.

She picked up the book again, slipped a finger into the marker page, but didn't open it. During the thrill of the Aspen trip, something about the thought of tonight's date with Nelson had left her feeling numb, and she'd felt guilty about it. But now as the hours ticked past, she looked forward to their time together. She needed to figure out a way to salvage their waning relationship before losing it completely.

Nelson arrived at seven o'clock straight up with a dozen red roses. This was the second time he had surprised her with a gorgeous bouquet. Maybe it wouldn't be as difficult to get back on track as she'd thought.

"Did you hear the awful news?" he said.

Gretta sniffed the flowers and thanked him, then set the bouquet on the table. "What awful news?"

"President McKinley … he died."

Gretta pricked her forefinger on a thorn and drew back. "That can't be."

"They say he was doing okay 'til gangrene set in."

She mulled over the word. "The President of the United States died … because one man lost his job?" She massaged her tender finger, soothing it, and remembered Mr. Harrington's explanation about the dangers of labor disputes. No wonder Boss had wanted her to take notes. Had Mr. Harrington withdrawn because he sensed imminent danger and was planning his strategy?

For supper, Nelson escorted her to Hotel Amber's main dining room. She looked around awkwardly finding herself wondering if … hoping … she might see Mr. Harrington, but he was nowhere in sight.

After supper they strolled up Broadway toward the lake and around to their favorite part of the shoreline. Nelson grew uncharacteristically quiet. "Am I losing you?" he said unexpectedly, the ache in his voice clear-cut.

It's worse than that. I'm losing me. "What are you talking about?" Gretta said.

He stared into the lapping water. "I missed you something awful when you were gone on your trip. I don't like it when you aren't around. And I hate to admit it, but I found myself feeling jealous of Harrington."

More emotional tearing. Nelson's candidness warmed her heart. Why couldn't she just jump in with both feet and get it over with. "You don't need to waste your jealousy on him," she said. "He's not interested in me. He's an aristocrat, remember? And I'm just a commoner."

"I know that. He'd never have you."

Nelson's unthinking words cut to her core, yet that changed nothing. He was right. She didn't belong in Mr. Harrington's world. Not now. Not ever.

"But he's a man," Nelson continued, "and you're easy on a man's eyes."

"Nelson, please," Gretta said. "To him Amber Leaf is nothing more than a stepping stone."

Nelson's tone grew bitter. "A lot can happen between now and the time he steps on another stone."

"It could happen soon," she said, feeling put upon. "He said as much to Mr. Petersen at the packing plant."

Nelson wouldn't let it go. "I don't want you going on any more trips with him."

She looked at him pleadingly. "Please don't do that."

"I said no more trips."

Gretta's mouth fell agape as she grappled with Nelson's blatant childishness. She picked up a pebble and hurled it into the water. The contrast between him and Mr. Harrington continued to widen like the ripples glimmering in the moonlight.

The aftermath of her trip with Mr. Harrington aside, she felt valued and deserving of respect when in his presence. It was as if she drew from his strength. Not so with Nelson. She couldn't trust his motivations, and his behavior proved inconsistent. He often vacillated from good to bad and back again. At times he made her feel treasured. At times he made her feel as though she didn't measure up. With the mood he was in, she needed to tread lightly, but she did need to tread.

She touched his coat sleeve. "Something isn't right between us," she said softly. "Hasn't been from the beginning, and I want it to change."

"Ho-oh. Here it comes."

"No, don't do that. Let this be a good thing." She drew her legs up and swaddling them, she rested her chin on her knees, her words thoughtful and slowly spoken. "I do want everything to be well with us, but it isn't yet. Maybe it's nothing more than we're moving too fast. Let's slow things down for a while. Give our relationship a chance to grow healthier."

"How can it grow anything if we're not together?" he spat.

Gretta winced at the words shooting out too strong and fast, the intensity and swiftness of his anger. She found herself losing patience with the reckless intimidation. "That's just it. We're together all the time. We'll still be dating and seeing each other at the office every day."

He plucked up a handful of dried grass by the roots and flung them back to the ground. "You know what they say about giving an inch. How do I know you won't start dating other guys?"

Why did he have to overreact? Why insist on completely ruining things? "Look Nelson, I adore you, but I'm not sure I can trust you yet, and believe me, I want to with all my heart. That's going to take time."

Or would it? She trusted Mr. Harrington with her life yet she barely knew the man.

"You're not sure you *trust* me?" Nelson slipped further into a rage. "You don't want us to slow things down," he spat.

She recoiled, her heart quickening.

"You want to call it quits," he said. "Well, I'm not going to let you. You break off with me, you'll be sorry."

She hopped up. "Are you threatening me?"

"Call it what you want, but no girl breaks up with Nelson Prixton." So *this* is who you really are! "I just did."

"Sit down."

"No," she said and stomped off.

"You walk away from me," Nelson cried out, "you can kiss your job good-bye."

She stopped short. "What?"

He got up and slowly inched toward her, his scowl menacing. "You heard me. You're still on probation, remember?"

"What are you getting at?"

"All I have to do is have a little chat with Boss."

"What about?"

"You. Why you lost your last job. How you don't deserve this one. You didn't pass your typing test," he said with a sneer. "Did you know that? I'll make sure he finds out how you disintegrate under pressure, too."

Be calm. Stay strong. Make sense. "About my last job," she said with a distinct absence of emotion, "I didn't lose it. I quit."

"Not before shoving your boss against a wall, you didn't."

"You've got to be kidding me," she hissed ... so much for staying strong. "It was a company Christmas party. He drank too much. Made an inappropriate advance."

"You could've called for help. You didn't need to slam—"

"I didn't. He was too drunk to stand and fell back against the wall. I was trying to get away from him. I. Did. Not. Push. Him."

Nelson lifted his chin. "You can bet he sees that one through different eyes."

"And as for the typing test, what are you talking about?"

"I had a chat with Hilda," he said. "You had the speed all right, but when you get nervous, you make mistakes. Lots of mistakes." He sneered again. "When we got done subtracting them from the total, you didn't pass. I talked her into hiring you anyway."

Gretta labored for breath. "You what?"

"You heard me. I'm sure Boss wouldn't appreciate hearing you got hired under false pretenses."

She couldn't let him get the best of her. "What about you and Hilda? You'd have to explain why you hired me anyway."

"No, we won't. Hilda can say whatever she wants, but I'll just play dumb."

Gretta stepped up nose-to-nose and toe-to-toe with Nelson. "You may have won this battle for now," she said, "but you might want to rethink your strategy. Threats don't buy love ... they destroy it."

CHAPTER THIRTY-SEVEN

The note instructing Ollie to stay away from Maude continued to niggle at him. He'd kept a sharp eye out all week long, but nothing appeared amiss. Perhaps it was time to take action, to make something happen.

When he rode out to Deacon's farm and asked how soon he wanted to start on their detective scheme, Deacon yanked on the straps of his bib overalls and grinned. "Day before yesterday."

At noon the next day, Ollie stopped by the City Livery Stable and rented a horse and buggy. Heading down Broadway, he casually passed Deacon at the side of the road who, without looking up, mounted Old Horse.

Minutes later, Ollie entered Maude's store. She stood at the counter filling a candy jar. "Mr. Harrington," she said. "What brings you in? I thought you worked for a living."

"Are we alone?"

"As far as I know." She shoved the jar aside and looked up expectantly. "You're here on business?"

"Of sorts," he said as he handed her the cryptic note. "I thought you might appreciate seeing this."

Maude read it, frowned, and shoved it back at him. "What's that all about?"

"I was hoping you might have an idea."

"I'll take that as an insult."

Ollie smiled. "Don't. A week ago Saturday morning when I was on my way out to Deacon's, I waited out front for a few minutes," he said, "hoping you'd take up my invitation and decide to come along. On Sunday this note appeared under my door."

Deep lines of concern penetrated Maude's features. "Why did you wait a week to tell me?"

"I didn't hurry because you aren't at risk. I'm the one being challenged."

"Did you involve the police?"

He shook his head. "Deacon followed me, stayed a block or two behind. We're hoping to flush out anyone who might be following. We're meeting up later at the hotel. I'll be certain to advise you if and when I learn anything. I'd appreciate your returning the favor. And as long as I'm here, might I purchase a box of cherry tobacco?"

After he returned the horse and buggy to the livery, Ollie met Deacon in his room.

"I stayed a good distance behind," Deacon said. "Didn't see a thing. Rode my horse around the block a few times, too. Nothing other than an old woman knitting on her front porch swing."

Ollie massaged the back of his neck. "I know I should feel grateful, but I'm not. I'm disappointed. We'll need to remain patient. See if anything else happens."

"I'm spending the afternoon at the hospital doing visitation," Deacon said. "I'll stop by on my way home. Make sure everything's alright."

Ollie returned to the office where all seemed in order. That evening, however, another newspaper cutout note awaited him beneath his door, this one more ominous. *Another visit to Maude Millning's ... she gets hurt.*

He flopped on the bed. A moment later he jumped at a light knock.

"Anything new?" Deacon said.

Ollie held up the note.

Deacon's eyes filled with trepidation. "Someone's threatening Maude?"

"Appears that's the case, does it not?"

"You will to go to the police, won't you? This is nothing to play with."

"Let's think this through first," Ollie said. "If you saw no one following me, there must be a snitch in the neighborhood. Think back. Are you certain you didn't see a curtain move or someone peering out a window?"

Deacon shook his head. "No … not unless you think old Granny Prixton's part of the underground."

Ollie's heart danced. "Granny *Prixton?*"

"Yes, sir. She's that old woman who was out on her front porch doing needlework. I waved to her, but she barely looked up. Never was much on the friendly side."

"Perhaps that explains everything."

"How's that?"

"If she's a Prixton," Ollie said, "I would presume she's Nelson Prixton's grandmother."

Deacon shrugged. "Not too many Prixtons around town. You can bet they're all related."

Ollie couldn't keep from pacing. "Nelson's an attorney in our law firm. If she's his grandmother, she would have easily seen me each time I've stopped by to visit Maude. On second thought …" Ollie hesitated. "The day Maude stopped by the office to meet me, Nelson was the only attorney who was absent from the meeting. He showed up after it was over."

Deacon wedged a thumb behind his belt. "But that doesn't make sense, does it? How would he know you set him up?"

Ollie's heart sank. "He's dating Miss Van Dyke. Perhaps she's unintentionally passing along clues. Deacon, you've been an amazing help."

"What are you going to do now?"

Ollie glanced at the note again and slapped it on his hand. "Learn what I can about Nelson and confront him."

"But what about Maude? He threatened her."

"I'm sure she'll be fine. If he is the culprit, you can bet he's … what do you American's call this? All hat and no cattle?"

"What if he isn't?" Deacon said. "What if someone's working with him?"

Ollie hadn't considered that. "Let me think on this overnight. If little push comes to big shove, we might want to encourage Maude to stay out at your place for a while. Could you manage that?"

Deacon's eyes glistened. "I'd welcome it."

Ollie plucked a silver dollar from a pants pocket. "How about asking one of your boys to stop by her place? Pick up a few supplies? I doubt that would raise Granny's suspicions. Have your son give Maude an update. Offer to keep someone there until this blows over."

"I'll send Harley first thing," Deacon said. "Have him drop a note by the hotel, too, so you'll know how it went."

Ollie thought for a moment. "One more thing. Boss heard rumblings about trouble brewing at the meat packing plant over in Aspen. We just signed on with them. Are you interested in taking on a part-time job? See what you can find out? How dangerous the situation's getting?"

Deacon beamed Cheshire-cat-happy. "How soon can I go?"

CHAPTER THIRTY-EIGHT

Ollie awakened in the wee hours and studied slow shadows crawling across the ceiling. While the moon drifted lazily across the late night sky, his thoughts did anything but.

He worried about Maude. Was she safe alone in that two-story home? She needed protection. If anything happened, Ollie would be at fault. Whatever path he chose, he needed to choose it swiftly and exercise tremendous wisdom.

OLLIE ROLLED OUT OF BED BEFORE the alarm went off and, knowing Boss arrived at the office first, he showed up early. He stopped by Nelson's desk, slipped the first cryptic note he'd received in his pencil drawer, and knocked on Boss's door.

Boss, who appeared not to have had his first cup of coffee yet, looked up. "Someone didn't get much sleep last night either, I see. Something on your mind?"

Ollie pulled up a chair. "Allow me to ask a few questions. I'd like to keep this purely objective."

"Shoot."

"If you received an anonymous note telling you what to do, how would you choose to handle it?"

"Does this have anything to do with the one telling you to stay away from Maude?"

"That aside, I need you to answer the question, please."

Boss shrugged. "Depends on what it would be about, I suppose. I'd probably be amused and fling it in the trash."

"What if the note was threatening? And what if you couldn't rid yourself of the nasty notion that it came from one of the men who worked with you?"

"That doesn't take much thought, does it?" Boss said. "I'd wave it in the air for all the world to see and ask what dirt bag wrote it."

"That's as I thought. Seems that anonymous suggestion that I stay away from Maude has turned into a threat."

"You mean—"

"I mean I got another one."

With hiked brows grazing his hairline, Boss no longer appeared to have need for coffee. "And?"

"To date, I've received two notes. On both, the letters were cut and pasted from a newspaper." Ollie handed a note to Boss. "And this is the second one."

Boss quickly scanned it and tapped his pointing finger on it. "This isn't good. Do you still have the first one?"

"I'm getting to that."

"Any idea who might be doing this?"

Ollie nodded. "Nelson."

Boss balked. "Not Prixton?"

After Ollie filled him in on the details, Boss said, "What do you plan to do? I'm itching to turn this over to the police."

"We can if we have to, but I think it best to wait it out. If this is linked to Whiting, we might want to keep it quiet until we know for certain then use it to our advantage."

"But how can we prove it?" Boss scratched his chin. "You know, I did give Nelson first crack at the case. He backed off. Said he had a conflict of interest. Something about being too good a friend of Whiting Junior. My gut tells me that isn't, shall we say, accurate. But how do we pry the truth out of him?"

Ollie planted his hands on the arms of the chair. "You asked about the first note. I slipped it in his pencil drawer on my way in. If he's guilty, he's going to run straight to me."

Boss appeared dubious. "How do you figure that?"

"He'll be the only one who knows the source of the note. If he's innocent, he'll undoubtedly pull a Boss and wave the paper in the air. If he doesn't, we may have no choice but to involve the police."

"I'll keep an ear out for him this morning," Boss said. "If I sense your hunch is even remotely correct, I'll call you both in for a powwow and we'll hash it out." Boss shook his head. "What's the man thinking? Why would he threaten Scarlet Maude?"

OLLIE STARED AT A JOURNAL, THE words appearing no deeper than black on white. Listening intently for footsteps, every few minutes he glanced toward the door loathing how slowly the time was crawling.

Ahh, footsteps … Mendenhall. *Drat.*

The next shuffling of feet? Brown.

At five before nine, more footsteps. Taking care not to look up, Ollie sensed Nelson's presence.

Like clockwork, Boss emerged from his office and sauntered toward the back of the room.

A chair rolled back. A desk drawer opened. Ollie felt a hard turn and a red-faced glare, although he didn't see it.

CHAPTER THIRTY-NINE

Gretta stood on the sidewalk hugging her handbag, then turned and glanced up the road toward the druggist. Her mother had taken a turn for the worse this morning and needed medicine. Rent was due. She gaped down at her fraying blouse and skirt. Definitely needed better clothes.

She then looked up toward the office and dread descended.

Nelson.

The weasel.

After learning who he really was, she'd laid awake half the night thinking about him. One more torturous week and no more dating game. One more torturous week and no more probation. Then she'd come clean with Hilda and her problems would be handled. But the thought of laying eyes on him in a few short minutes gave her another unwanted taste of breakfast.

"Good morning," a voice muttered from behind.

Gretta jumped at the greeting.

"What's the matter, child?" Hilda said. "You look as if you've contracted a bad case of the blues."

"I'm fine." At least that's what everyone says when they merely want to be polite.

A smirk formed on Hilda's rotund face. "Are you planning to spend the day working out on the sidewalk or are you coming in?"

As Hilda grabbed the railing and huffed up the stairs, one slow step at a time, Gretta stopped at the halfway point. "Hilda," she said, "is it true that I didn't pass my typing test?"

Hilda straightened. "Why wherever did you hear that?"

"Is it true?"

"You did have better rhythm and speed than anyone who's ever taken the test," Hilda said, "but you also did have a few too many typos. After thinking it through, we decided to waive the rules and use the better part of discretion."

"What about my references? They all came in okay, right?"

Hilda took on a look of concern. "Why are you asking"?

"I'm still on probation and wouldn't want anything to mess it up. I need this job too badly."

Hilda slipped a hand on Gretta's forearm as if needing support and climbed another step. "So that's it. Well, rest your weary mind. I was in a hurry to get someone on the payroll, and in all my years of hiring, I have yet to get a negative report, so I waived that, too. Everything *is* okay with your past, isn't it?"

"Absolutely." From Gretta's end, that was the truth. When they reached the tops of the staircase, she said, "Boss knows about the typing test?"

"I don't bother him with the nitty-gritty. He's got enough to worry about. Besides, last week when he asked who was the best in the secretarial pool to accompany Mr. Harrington to Aspen, I told him you. You did have a good trip, didn't—"

Gretta's stomach constricted as Nelson emerged from the opposite end of the hall.

"Why the strange look, dear?" Hilda said. "I hope everything's okay between you and Nelson."

She shrugged then forced a tentative wave as he slipped into the office. She then took the last of her steps down that long, long hall-way, following close behind Hilda. They no sooner stepped inside when Boss bellowed from the back of the room. "Prixton? Harrington? To my office. Now."

"What in the …" Hilda sounded as stunned as Gretta felt.

The men paraded toward Boss's office looking straight ahead and appearing grim.

CHAPTER FORTY

Ollie waited respectfully, wanting to push past torture. Meanwhile, Boss sat still as a cat ready to pounce on tantalizing prey. And Nelson? He flicked make-believe flecks of lint from his trousers as if he had all the time in the world and no accounting for it.

"Well?" Boss said.

Nelson's career weighed heavily in the balance. He was young and had taken but a few steps down its long and braided path. Now he sat tense, beads of sweat beginning to glisten on his guilt-ridden brow. He easily manipulated his fellow attorneys, or so he must have thought, but not Boss who wielded the power to wreak havoc on his professional future, or lack thereof. Nelson's words would need precise measure for each one counted.

He shifted in his chair. Then, as if having accepted fate, his tension faded. "Just tell the truth?" His forehead twitched and his eyes grew sad. "Your hunch was right, Harrington," he said. "I was the one who slipped the warnings under your door." He gave his head one hard shake. "I wouldn't have done anything to Miss Millning. I was trying to get you off the scent. When you're scared, you don't think straight. You do stupid stuff."

He got up, strolled to the wall, and stood with his back to it, the way one would stand in a line up. He stuffed hands in his pockets like a conscience-stricken schoolboy. Boss watched and waited, as did Ollie.

"When I was about eight or nine years old—"

"No background," Boss said. "No excuses."

Nelson's features hardened. "When I was about eight or nine," he repeated, "my father developed a habit of disappearing. I heard my mother crying in her bedroom all the time. So one night I decided to follow him. All the way to Maude Millning's place."

Ollie cringed.

"Some months later when I was emptying the trash, a rumpled letter that my father didn't have the conscience to hide … yeah, that's my father I'm disrespecting. He was that arrogant. Anyway, it fell out on the floor and rolled. So I read it. Stephen Whiting and I were friends when we were kids. One night soon after, he confided in me. He found a letter his father had gotten, too. Same one … seems Maude didn't know who the father was."

Ollie saddened at the overwhelming pain of ill-fated lives. With Maude, it had all begun so innocently. Her father died. Her mother remarried. And Maude got abused. Undoubtedly numb from caring, she passed on the abuse, abuse that grew roots that twisted and anchored in the hearts and minds of others.

"I was surprised when I saw the letters weren't threatening or demanding," Nelson continued. "She had distant relatives. They couldn't have kids. They wanted to take the baby in, but were dirt poor. She said she'd send money regularly, but would appreciate getting a little help. According to Stephen, Josh Whiting felt obligated. But my father? I'm sure he couldn't have cared less. And it seemed Maude wasn't the kind to beg.

Boss, appearing taken aback and troubled, glanced at Ollie then returned his attention to Nelson.

"I never told Stephen about my father or his letter," Nelson said. "I was too embarrassed. Besides, it didn't matter anyway. My father rarely took responsibility for his actions. He laughed them off. But I couldn't dismiss it. I was haunted. I had to find out if it was me or Stephen who had a brother or sister out there. Here all the while, Stephen's father was sending money to what he believed was his own little girl."

Ollie squeezed his eyes closed, bracing for more of Nelson's hard truth.

"Every now and then I asked Stephen indirect questions to wheedle out information," Nelson went on. "I doubt he ever gave a thought to what I was getting at. He told me he had a sister and told me where she lived. So I saved up and caught a ride to Kansas. One look and I knew."

"It's not necessary to say any more," Boss said, sounding uncharacteristically uncomfortable.

"No. If you want to win this case, I think you need to hear it all," Nelson said, then continued on. "She wasn't his sister. She was mine. We could have been twins. She cried when I introduced myself. But she was sick. Really sick. She has consumption and desperately needed money for medical bills."

Nelson looked like a bullwhipped puppy. "I know what I did was downright awful, but I didn't know what else to do. Didn't have any money at the time."

"This happened before you started working at the firm?" Ollie said.

Nelson nodded. "I told my father about my sister and how sick she was, but he yelled at me. Said I was crazy. Said I should keep my nose out of his business. I didn't have anywhere to turn."

"So you turned to Josh Whiting?"

"That's right. Since he had money and already invested a small fortune in her life, I decided to set Stephen up to get his father to help out. Told him I'd been down to Kansas. Looked her up since I was there anyway. He was thrilled until I delivered the news that she was sick and might die. That devastated him.

"What I didn't know was that Stephen never told his father about it."

"So he was the one who turned compassionate?" Boss said.

"Yes, sir. He started sending money under the table. Knew it would be stupid to apply for a loan to pay for the medical expenses for an illegitimate kid. Besides, that would expose his father. Long story short, gentlemen, that's the reason no one's talking."

Boss glanced at Ollie, his expression forlorn.

"May I?" Ollie said.

"By all means."

"Nelson, it appears as if this entire problem rests at the feet of your father."

"Like I've told you, he doesn't give a rip."

"Do you mind if I have a word with him?" Ollie turned again to Boss. "That is, if I'm not overstepping Boss's boundaries."

Boss shook his head. "Have at it."

Nelson gripped the chair arms. He appeared emotionally drained. "Am I ... fired?"

"To be honest," Boss said, "I don't know what to make of this. For now, though, I want to see how this whole mess shakes out before I make a decision."

"Thank you, sir. One other thing. I know I don't have the right to ask and feel free to shoot me down, but I'm wondering if we can keep this quiet for a while."

Boss glanced at Ollie then answered Nelson with a less than pleasant look.

CHAPTER FORTY-ONE

Gretta slowly rolled a sheet of paper into the platen and looked up, as did everyone else. Nelson and Mr. Harrington were filing out of Boss's office the way children slither out of a woodshed, minus the tears.

What happened in there?

Why did Mr. Harrington look so concerned?

Why did Nelson have to look so vulnerable? Why did he ignore her on the way back to his desk? Half good, half bad Nelson. When he wanted her, she wasn't sure she wanted him. When he pulled away, she feared the loss. What was the matter with her? And after his miserable tantrum, what was it about him that he could still tug at her heartstrings?

With words of explanation unspoken and no one about to ask questions, an air of gloom swept over the office. Slow minutes ticked into slow moving hours, as if a pendulum had taken on added weight. The tat-a-tat-tat of typewriter keys pulsed from apprehensive fingers. Talk reduced to circumspect whispers. Who would dare break the quiet? When, and how?

A sudden flutter, a breeze, and Gretta jumped as a sparrow zoomed in through an open window and swooped low overhead. It picked up speed. Its wings fluttered, clipping several windowpanes. While heads bobbed and arms flailed to protect vital papers, Gretta hurried to another window and threw it open. Footsteps pounded as one by one windows popped open all around the room. The bird found a perch on a casing, its head bobbing about. She waved a hand in invitation. "Here, little guy."

The little feathered friend did not move.

"What do you say, everyone?" she said. "How about if we all go over to the far wall? Maybe the bird won't feel threatened and will find its way out."

Feet shuffled. Eyes riveted on a tiny creature holding the entire office spellbound. Sandwiched between Nelson and Mr. Harrington, Gretta felt conflicted. With his well-tailored coat, vest, and shining shoes, for all of his faults Nelson did possess presence. Though he claimed he wanted her, he reminded her of that sparrow wanting in and out at the same time, and she'd had enough. Mr. Harrington on the other hand was not available, yet his powerful presence filled a room whether he spoke with her or not.

The bird cocked its head and flew off again, sweeping several times across the office before finding its escape into the great outdoors.

Mr. Harrington touched her elbow and her heart fluttered. "Good work, Miss Van Dyke."

She smiled. He talked to her.

Nelson appeared indifferent and walked away. Why?

In the early afternoon Mr. Harrington stopped by her desk. "I'm behind on dictation," he said. "If the conference room is available, would you have a few hours to spare?"

Gretta had taken dictation many times. It often proved arduous. Hours of sitting. Waiting. Words spurting out in clusters—words like 'scratch that.' A finger would tap her steno pad as a voice over her shoulder asked 'what did I say here?' Not so with Mr. Harrington. He dictated from handwritten notes. Fluently. Never a request for a reread. His corrections to typed copy were discreet. If he found a mistake, he minimized it or claimed it as his own. The rich tenor of his voice. His confidence and clarity of thought. As she gathered her writing instruments, she wondered if it would be wise to look for an opportunity to break the barrier that had popped up between them. With a man of his stature, that would prove unnerving yet it was crucial if she wanted peace in the workplace.

After an hour or so of solid dictation, not only had Mr. Harrington told her that that would be all, he also told her to take her time, that he wasn't in a hurry. There had been no reference whatsoever to the meeting he'd had with Boss and Nelson.

Gretta play-acted courage. "Mr. Harrington?"

He appeared troubled, which tugged at her heart … much like Nelson. "Yes?"

She gathered her steno pad and pencil and forced confidence. "You haven't said much since our trip. I want to make sure I haven't done anything inappropriate."

He appeared taken off guard, yet sincere. "Please accept my apologies. I have been preoccupied of late. I assure you, Miss Van Dyke, you have done nothing wrong … of that you are incapable."

LATER THAT EVENING, OLLIE STOPPED BY the front desk. "Anything for me?"

"No, sir. But there is a young man over yonder who's been waiting for you."

Harley, who was sitting in the lobby engrossed in a newspaper, hopped up. "I've got something for you," he said. "It's in the wagon. Meet you up at your room."

He arrived at the door soon after and hauled in an overstuffed crate of fresh peaches. Ollie eyed them curiously. "What are those—"

"I didn't know what to buy with the money you gave Pop. Hope these are okay."

Ollie held back a grin.

An entire crate?

For one person?

"That money was for you," he said. "Please, take them home to your mother. Tell her I'll stop by Sunday afternoon and will be looking forward to fresh peach pie. By the way, how'd it go with Miss Millning?"

"You mean Aunt Maude? ... I've only seen her from a distance. Heard a lot about her, though." Harley grinned and his eyes glistened. "She sure is a beauty, isn't she? She got all choked up when I told her who I was. Said she didn't think my dad would want us kids to have anything to do with her. Even said she'd love to come out to the farm some time to meet all of us."

"Did she say anything about the threat?"

He nodded. "She doesn't want us to worry. Said she can take care of herself. She thought you'd want to know that old Granny Prixton's been spending a lot of time out on her front porch, more than usual, keeping an eye on everyone who passes by."

Ollie clapped Harley on the back. "You've done well. Tell Deacon she isn't in any danger. We're getting to the bottom of this whole mess now. I'll stop by in a few minutes and have a chat with her and then fill him in on the details on Sunday."

Harley stopped at the door. "Would you mind seeing if Aunt Maude—"

Ollie grinned. "Wants to come along?"

CHAPTER FORTY-TWO

O llie paused halfway up Maude's steps and glanced across the road. No Granny Prixton sitting on her front porch.

"She doesn't do needlework in the early evening hours," Maude said through the screen door from behind. "Not enough light."

Ollie turned. "Well, hello. I didn't realize you were standing there."

Maude snickered pleasantly, then stepped outside and joined him.

"I presume there's something you find rather humorous?" He looked down at his shirt, pants, and shoes. "When I got a gander at myself in the mirror, I thought I looked rather handsome."

"Have you eaten all of your peaches yet?"

Ollie removed his cap and laughed. "What was Harley thinking?"

"I don't think he much cared," Maude said. "He had far more important things on his mind. And Mr. Harrington?"

"Yes?"

"Thank you … I was shocked when he introduced himself. He's such a good boy. He seemed thrilled to meet me." She looked at Ollie in wonder. "Imagine that. Even called me Aunt Maude."

"Why would he not be thrilled?"

"You're talking to Maude Millning, remember?"

"I know." Ollie smiled. "Maude Millning, whose brother and family clearly see her as a sister and aunt whom they love and need." He sighed then changed the subject. "I stopped by to tell you that Nelson Prixton warbled like an African finch."

Maude appeared stunned.

"He revealed all we needed to know," Ollie said. "No more threats. You're safe. I do plan to handle this with his father one day next week … under the table."

"Nelson's father? Is there anything you'd care to tell me?"

About knowing the truth? Ollie couldn't in good conscience do that to her. "Let's just say that Prixton Senior has some fence mending to do."

"How do you plan to pull that off?" She quirked a brow. "He only cares about himself."

"I must find a way to use that against him, mustn't I? On a more pleasant note," Ollie said, "Harley asked that I deliver you out to the farm on Sunday. I'll stop by at half past noon."

Maude reached for the doorknob. "I can't do that. They need an aunt they can respect."

"I beg to differ. They need an aunt they can love. See you then."

As he turned and walked away, Ollie resisted a smile.

She did not say no.

CHAPTER FORTY-THREE

y Friday, Gretta was whooped. She and Nelson had spoken little to one another the entire week. She dreaded their standing
Saturday night date, looking forward to it the way one looked
forward to going to the dentist. She held her breath. If he stayed at
arm's length, she was off the hook.

Unfortunately, he stopped by her desk on his way out. "See you
tomorrow night at the usual time," he said.

Though no longer on shaky ground with her job, she shrugged.
Why take chances?

To her chagrin, he arrived five minutes early—warm-eyed, carrying
a dozen red roses for her, this time an additional dozen for her uncharacteristically overly appreciative mother, and had a buggy waiting that
made Cinderella's coach look chintzy.

As Nelson drove up the road to buy Gretta a supper she didn't want,
she hugged the far side of the seat. "Why are you doing this?"

Again the warm-eyed look. "I'm ashamed to admit it, but I've
behaved miserably. I want to make it up to you."

She folded her arms over her handbag. "Life is hard. Why make
it harder? I need a relationship that's easy. Flowers won't work. Fancy
buggies won't work. Expensive meals won't work. Nelson Prixton, if you
want any kind of relationship with me at all—" *What am I doing talking*

like this? "You're going to have to show consistent respectful character. Nothing shy of that will work."

"I will. I want you to marry me. I want you to be my wife, bear my children."

What about your whipping boy? That's part of the deal, too, isn't it? "If and when I do get married," she said, "it will be to a man who values me, not someone who jerks me around and makes me question my own worth."

He reached for her hand. "I'll change. I promise."

Why did the warmth of his hand have to feel pleasurable?

After engaging a cook's tour around Spring Lake, Fountain Lake, and the shores of Lake Amber Leaf, they enjoyed a candlelight dinner at a fine restaurant on Broadway, while soft chamber music played in the background. However, a man's conversation at a table immediately to their right grew increasingly loud as the evening progressed. To hear Nelson talk became a task of its own.

"Waiter," the man cried.

Gretta nudged closer to the table to allow a swift-moving server easier access.

"Gimme another drink," the man insisted.

"Sir, I'm very sorry, but our restaurant's policy—"

The man slammed a fist on the table, and Gretta jumped. The silverware clinked and the tableware clattered. "I don't care what your restaurant's policy is. I told you to bring me another drink."

"Yes, sir. Right away, sir."

The waiter glided off red faced while the man grumbled louder with each passing second. The woman with him appeared too frightened to speak.

Gretta leaned closer to Nelson and lowered her voice. "Any idea what's got him so cranked up?"

"I'm not sure." Nelson reached for her hand as if to comfort her. "People like him look for things to get mad about."

The waiter returned, appearing to brace himself for what was to come. "I'm very sorry, but we're not allowed—"

The man jumped up, their noses within an inch of one another.

Gretta's heart pounded. They hovered feel-your-breath close. The waiter's eagle eyes bulged, and he gasped. "Please ..."

The instant the inebriated man raised an angry fist, Nelson leaped up and grabbed his arm. A chair flew over, the woman screamed, and several glasses crashed to the floor. The man twirled and took an empty swing at Nelson who ducked with exemplary timing. Nelson took the next swing, a spot-on hit on the man's middle. The wretch gasped and fell back into the hands of two expectant waiters who dragged him out onto the street for the police to deal with.

As the busboys scurried to clean up the mess, the owner apologized to the dinner guests. When he said, "I hope everyone enjoyed the spontaneous entertainment," the tension dissipated.

The owner immediately appeared at Nelson's side. "Are you okay, sir? Do you need medical attention?"

Nelson shook his head. "That was too much fun."

The owner showed every sign of out-and-out relief. A grin. A weighty sigh. Slackened shoulders. He mopped his forehead with a handkerchief. "Rest assured this evening's dinner is on the house. Please come back any time. We promise to offer you our finest tables and the best of service."

When they stepped outside, Gretta said, "How'd it feel playing hero? Weren't you scared?"

"Na'ah. The guy was too drunk to stand. My punch barely touched him and you saw what happened. He folded like a napkin. What do you say? Want to cap off the evening by building a bonfire down by the lake?"

A hero, and a modest one at that. "It is chilly," she said. "Sitting by a warm fire sounds good."

When they arrived at the lakeshore, Nelson seized her hand and guided her to a preset site. She gaped at it in disbelief. "You came earlier and set up the logs, didn't you?"

"You mean the world to me, Gretta, why wouldn't I? You're worth it."

Please be telling the truth.

Parched logs burst into flame, sparks spattering and spiraling. Millions of stars. Crescent moon cutting sharp into an early autumn sky. They sat close on a log, hands reaching out, warmed by the fire.

After a long moment, Nelson sandwiched her hand in his. "There's something I've been meaning to tell you." In the flicker of firelight, he gave her that warm-eyed look again, that pleading, vulnerable look that she found irresistible. "I got called into Boss's office the other day." He shook his head and looked down, his tone filled with remorse. "No, that's not exactly true. It was worse than that. I got called on the carpet."

Gretta felt a need to withdraw her hand, but not now, not when Nelson had the courage to bare his soul. Besides, she'd been dying to know what happened. "Why?"

"This is private, okay? Josh and Stephen Whiting were set up."

"Do you mean Stephen didn't embezzle?"

"He did," Nelson said. "He was covering for his father."

Gretta gasped. "You mean Josh Whiting—?"

Nelson nodded, then explained the entire mess. That Maude Millning had, in fact, had a child out of wedlock. That she didn't know who the real father was. That Josh Whiting had been supporting a girl who in the end wasn't his daughter, and that Stephen took compassion on an alleged half sister he'd never met and risked his career to help save her life. Nelson didn't divulge how Stephen found out about the girl or who the real father was, only that he was some ne'er-do-well.

"Why did *you* get called on the carpet?" Gretta said, then braced herself for an answer she feared she didn't want to hear.

"I did something, shall we say, inappropriate?"

"How inappropriate?"

"Very. I wanted to protect Stephen."

Those words sounded off key.

"I'm ashamed to admit this," he said, "but I followed Harrington. Slipped a couple of anonymous notes under his door to keep him from getting too close to the truth."

Gretta's forehead pulled tight. "Why would you do a crazy thing like that? We're all on the same side."

"I already told you why," he said. "The way I had it figured, to delve into the Whitings' lives was one thing, but it was getting too deep. It needed to stop somewhere. Unfortunately, it didn't take Harrington long to figure out who was behind the notes."

A light breeze blew a cloud of smoke toward them. Gretta choked on it the way she choked on Nelson's words. "Why not? Dare I ask?"

"I'm already in too deep, Gretta. I'd rather not say any more."

After Nelson walked her to the door at midnight, she stopped by the table, plucked a drooping petal off a rose, crushed it in her hand, and set off to call it a night. But by two in the morning, she needed to rearrange her bedding. Tossing and turning had it all but lying on the floor. Lying still for the longest while, staring at the ceiling, she asked herself hard questions. That's when she understood why Nelson was so deeply involved in the Stephen Whiting embezzlement when they were no longer the best of friends, and why Nelson wouldn't say who the real father was.

Maude Millning was the mother of *Nelson's* half sister, not Stephen's.

Gretta's weary breath squeezed out in a rush.

What kind of man was Nelson that he'd let Stephen go to prison to protect his own family's reputation?

CHAPTER FORTY-FOUR

Ollie hopped out of the buggy and scurried up the sidewalk with a spring in his step. Maude *was* waiting … swinging gently on her front porch, appearing lost between the pages of a novel. She plucked up her handbag and parasol.

Offering an arm, he glanced discreetly across the road where a withered old woman sat on her front porch. He helped Maude into the buggy then murmured, "Be right back."

"Where are you going?" she called after him, but he kept moving.

The old woman peered over spectacles as he ambled up the walk. "Good afternoon," Ollie said. "I've seen you here before and thought I'd introduce myself. I'm Oliver Harrington and you are?"

The woman looked surprised. "Granny Prixton."

"Granny Prixton," he repeated. "I see you're knitting. I'm curious. Might I see your work?"

"Why certainly." She offered a pleasant grin as she sprawled the project across her lap. "It's a neck scarf for my favorite grandson. You may have heard of him. Name's Nelson Prixton. He's a successful young attorney. Works uptown at Addison & Crowley." She hesitated then said, "You wouldn't happen to work alongside him, would you?"

"That's a most professional job," Ollie said, keeping his eyes on the woman's painstaking work. "I only hope he appreciates your efforts."

"He will. He's a good boy."

"Is he now?" Ollie said more as a statement.

The woman appeared to ignore the leading question. "And where might your parents be?"

"England."

"You certainly are a long way from home, sonny."

Oddly, I've never felt closer to home, Ollie mused. "Nice meeting you, Mrs. Prixton. I'll be certain to inform Nelson I've had the privilege of making your acquaintance."

A block up the road, Maude looked back. "What was that all about?"

"Paying my respects. Sometimes it's good for folks to find out who the enemy isn't."

"You certainly aren't afraid to face life head on, are you?"

He smiled. "So, then, are you nervous?"

"No ... yes ... very."

"You look lovely."

She eyed her flowing skirt, vest, blouse, shoes and handbag. "Don't feel lovely. Talk to me, Ollie. I find I'm calmer when I don't have time to think. What if Deacon doesn't want to see me? What if our visit doesn't go well?"

"He does, and it will." The horse trotted up the hill on Broadway, through the uptown area, then turned down a country road that rib-boned through golden fields toward the east.

"Keep talking," she said. "I need to hear your voice."

"What would you like to talk about?"

"I don't know."

She wasn't making this easy. "Yesterday morning, I took a walk down Newton," he said. "Want to talk about that? Found a nice little trail that cuts into the hillside overlooking Lake Amber Leaf."

"I've walked it a number of times," she said. "It's one of the most beautiful places in the world this time of year. Bright sun. Dry breeze. Brilliant autumn colors. It's heaven."

"That it is," Ollie said. "I didn't want the trail to end. At a lower point, I hiked down to the shoreline, skipped a few flat stones across the water, took a little time to think."

Maude dipped her parasol into the light breeze.

"Would you prefer that I raise the top?" Ollie said.

She shook her head. "I spend far too much time indoors. The sun feels good."

"I noticed you were reading when I drove up."

"I love to read," Maude said. "Always thought it would be fun to join a literary society one day."

"What sorts of books do you prefer?"

"The classics. Non-fiction. Magazines. The paper. Pretty much anything in print. Does that surprise you?"

"Not at all. I'm quite the reader myself." Ollie looked up the road ahead and pointed at a deer in the clearing. "They certainly are engaging creatures, are they not? There's a young lady in our office that reminds me of a deer. She's also captivating … graceful … innocent."

Maude raised a brow, her tone teasing. "Would that be the same young lady who fetched you the day I stopped by?"

"That it would."

"She is unusually attractive. Are you in love with her?"

Ollie choked. "She's dating Nelson Prixton."

Maude's eyes filled with alarm. "That's not what I asked," she said.

"I gave you my answer."

Maude sighed. "Tell me more."

Ollie felt shy, as if he had waded too deep into a lake and needed to swim or turn back. At the moment, swimming seemed more productive. "I don't understand why she's wasting her time on him."

Maude dipped her parasol to the side as if to hide her face. "If he's anything like his father," she said in a concern-filled voice, "I'm sorry to say I understand only too well … I've got a question. You are and always will be a society man. How is it that you married Emily?"

"I was in love with her."

"That's not what I was asking. From my reading, I get the impression that in England aristocrats don't give commoners a second look. Is that true?"

Ollie shrugged.

"What made you different?"

Feeling the bump and sway of the buggy and watching the swish of the horse's tail, Ollie measured his thoughts. "My father. The more he devalued commoners with no more than a word or a look, the more I saw their value. It happened slowly, naturally. In time I learned to envy them and their freedom. The kids got to get muddied, express their feelings, laugh without reserve, and even cry if they so chose. Over time I found myself drawn their world. Life seemed warmer there, far less stilted. Then one day I met Em. It was love at first sight. So I married her ... against my father's wishes. In the end, my parents distanced themselves. Then I lost Em and my infant son. One might say that I lost it all. Now I'm attempting to discern where that leaves me, where I go from here. Does that make sense?"

"We all have crosses to bear, don't we? Now, back to your friend," Maude said, that look of alarm revisiting her. "You would do well to warn her away from Nelson."

"I'm not in a position to do that," Ollie said. "My motives would be in question. But why would you state it so strongly?"

"It sounds as if your friend is butting up against a miserable case of 'like father like son.'" For an instant she turned toward Ollie, but only for an instant. "If he's a louse, too, he won't hesitate to prey on her emotions. That's what Nelson's father did to me.

"Elias and I dated back when we were in school. At times I swore I was losing my mind. We'd get together and he'd be loving and tender. Made me feel as if I were the most valued creature on earth. The next time I saw him, he'd be cruel. Embarrass me in front of our friends. He knew what he was doing. Afterward, he'd apologize in private. Shed a tear or two. Treat me great again until the next time he got into one of his moods. Back and forth, back and forth. I knew he was no good for me. Always making me want to prove myself, prove that I was worthy of his affection."

The more Maude talked, the more Ollie wanted to handle Elias and Nelson with his fists. "But you're a strong woman," Ollie said. "I don't follow."

"That's because you've never walked in my shoes. You see, Elias came from a respectable family, and I was hungry for that. After my father died unexpectedly, we lost everything. What I'm saying is that we didn't do well. Mom tried. Oh, how she tried. Unfortunately, she made a few unwise decisions. Dreadful might be a better word. Wasn't her fault, but Deacon and I suffered the repercussions. So when Elias started paying attention to me, I thought I'd gotten an opportunity to crawl out of an ugly pit … until one day I got tossed aside for the lady who eventually became Nelson's mother. She didn't get much of a prize, did she?"

Those words were underplayed. "Why didn't you surround yourself with people who made you feel good about yourself?"

"For the most part, Elias did. We were so young at the time, and I didn't know any better. In the end, what I saw as strength was really weakness and immaturity. Blatant at that. But tell that to a kid. I don't think the man ever grew up. Unfortunately, I had a hard time of it myself."

"Have you seen your daughter?"

Maude stiffened. "You found out about her, did you?" She squeezed her eyes closed and shook her head. "I only saw her once … when she was born."

Maude sat motionlessly as the buggy traveled on, the furrows in her forehead deepening as memories appeared to draw her in. "I've never stopped thinking about her, wondering how she's doing. I've gotten pictures over the years, but shoved them in a trunk. Never could bring myself to look at them. I sure created a mess."

"Did you?" Ollie said.

"What do you mean?"

"They say water seeks its own level. From what you've inferred, someone dipped too freely into your well and drained it dry. No one can begrudge you that. Unfortunately, it can take a long time for a well to fill again."

She nodded her agreement. "Will you be able to get Josh out of this mess without doing any more damage to his family's reputation?"

"I don't know, but I'll certainly make every attempt."

"About your friend?"

"She isn't my friend." Ollie felt a self-conscious grin form.

"If you're as smitten as you appear, why not fight for her?"

Ollie balked. *Smitten?* "A heart should be given, and freely, not taken. I fear many have paid a handsome price over a lifetime for taking that which did not belong to them. When I do marry again, it will be out of desire on both sides, not one. As for Gretta, she isn't available."

"But—"

"It's no good," Ollie said. "A man can get himself into a heap of trouble merely walking past another man's stable. She needs to figure Nelson out on her own. Besides, I don't plan to stay in Amber Leaf long. I'm quite happy here, but it's far too difficult in a smaller town such as this to find someone appropriate and tender who reaches deep inside your heart."

"And Miss Van Dyke does that for you?"

Ollie looked up the road. "Say. Look who's there. Do you recognize that fellow?"

Deacon, in a full run, tore out to meet them, beaming and waving his cap without restraint.

And Maude wept.

CHAPTER FORTY-FIVE

O llie watched in wonder. A well-written novel could not do justice to Maude's reacquainting with family. Warm happy faces. Laughter vibrating the walls. Catching up on riveting tales about the good times and the not so good. But after eating a feast, a spread fit for a queen, Deacon invited Ollie to join he and Maude on a tour of the farm.

Maude managed to slip out ahead as they approached the garden and the fields, oohing and aahing over God's amazing creation. But as they approached the outbuildings, she managed to stay a step behind. Ollie would take a step back to join her and they would move forward until she slipped behind again.

When they reached the barn, Deacon took a grinning lead. "You've got to see the fine work Ole has done in the barn," he boasted.

Maude stopped without warning as tears welled in her eyes and a hand slipped over her mouth.

THE BUGGY MEANDERED ONTO THE COUNTRY road, its back against deepening shadows of evening. Ollie still had much to do—stop by the livery, get on with reading, and prepare for the coming week, but all of that paled to reveling in the remainder of their visit, with the exception of the incident outside the barn, that is. Why hadn't Deacon and he thought to steer clear of that dreadful reminder of Maude's ugly past? He turned to her. "You had a good time, I trust?"

"The best," she said. "The children? They're nearly all grown, and they seemed to like me."

"That surprises you?"

She nodded. "I've missed out on a lot, haven't I? It's my fault. So many years of self-loathing. So many wasted years."

Ollie found her words grievous. "Aren't you being a trifle hard on yourself?"

"Can't help it. At least I couldn't help it in the past." Maude took on a look of utter shame. "About what happened at the barn—"

Ollie gave a purposeful laugh. "I'm pleased you mentioned that. You spared me a significant amount of embarrassment," he said. "I fear my ability to saw is in need of refining. I would be hard-pressed to prove the joints fit together soundly given the fact that light shines through more gaps than the spice cake we ate had raisins. Deacon used up all of his screws and braces, and still he brags on me."

Appearing relieved by Ollie's response, Maude dropped the subject and brightened. "Deacon gave me a standing invitation for Sunday dinner. With the exception of bad weather, I plan to be there … Ollie? When are you planning to talk to Elias?"

"First thing in the morning."

"Then there's something you might want to know." She hesitated, her chuckle awkward.

"It's not necessary for you—"

"I didn't know who the father of my child was. You're probably wondering what kind of woman stoops that low, right?"

Ollie looked off into a forested area, longing to be there. Perhaps some things were better left private.

"You've probably heard of my nickname," she continued. "Scarlet Maude?"

He kept his gaze fixed on the road.

"It's alright to talk about it," she insisted. "Remember what you said to me that day in the restaurant? You said somewhere along the way someone told me I wasn't worth a lot, and I believed it. Well, the thing is, I wasn't only told that, my stepfather took it upon himself to prove it. Then after my husband ran off with another woman, I felt more worthless than dirt. About the same time, Josh Whiting's marriage had hit a low point and one of our mutual friends threw a shivaree. I went by myself and so did Josh. We both felt miserable. One thing led to another. Word got around.

"And then there was Elias. There's more about him that I didn't tell you. You don't want to get on the wrong side of that man. After he heard about Josh and me, he showed up on my back doorstep one night in the wee hours teetering drunk. When I refused to let him in, he refused to accept no. Immediately after that less than pleasant episode, the word scarlet became coupled with Maude. People backed away from me on the streets. You should have seen them. And you wouldn't have believed the parade of men that started knocking on my back door and the fire in their eyes when I told them to get lost. I saw the hate in women's eyes, too, and it angered me. If they trusted their husbands, they wouldn't have needed to fear me. I got a glimpse into a lot of marriages. Learned what I wasn't missing."

After hearing her recounting of a sad reality, Ollie sat quietly, thinking. The carriage reached the edge of town at nightfall, lights flickered in passing windows, and the breeze stilled. "There is something I find difficult to comprehend," he said. "You strike me as being a principled woman. After all you've been through, why did you choose to—"

"Roll over and play dead? What was I supposed to do?" Maude said. "In case you hadn't noticed, it's a man's world. Josh and Elias went on with their lives, but I didn't stand a prayer."

Her words reeked of an excuse. "Why not?"

Maude gasped. "Didn't you hear what I just said?"

"You said Josh and Elias raised their chins. Why would you choose not to raise yours as well?"

"You don't mean to tell me—"

Ollie looked straight ahead, giving her time to think, then said, "This may sound harsh, but as I see it, you've been acting no differently than all of those wives whose husbands knocked on your door. They assumed the role of victim, but so did you. It's not too late to lift your own chin."

Maude giggled as if entertained by the thought. "But where would I begin? What would I do? I'm too well rooted to leave town and start over again. Even if I did, my past would always be there to haunt me."

"Only if you let it." He thought for a moment. "Tell me more about your reading."

As hope appeared to overtake hopelessness, Maude's features softened. "I have a small library in my back room. I don't know that I would ever qualify as a librarian ... my books are arranged by color and size, but I've always wanted to join a book club."

"Have you ever considered starting one?"

Maude's jaw dropped.

"You could call it *The Amber Leaf Literary Society*. You could read books. Host benefits to make sure the poor are well taken care of. Visit the elderly. Deliver toys to needy children at Christmastime. Help teach the illiterate to read and write."

"But what if no one wanted to join? I'd be back to feeling like the dung of the earth."

"What do farmers do with dung?" Ollie said.

Maude appeared to mull the question over for a moment. "Use it for fertilizer?"

"That's right. And what do you think God does with the dung in our lives?"

"Uses it for fertilizer, too?" She grinned. "The last shall be first? Maybe you are right. Maybe it's my turn to step to the front of the line."

Ollie smiled at that. "If you do," he warned, "you won't gain traction unless you come with a pure heart."

Maude balked. "How do I go about doing that?"

"Think about it. Each spring Deacon plants seeds. They go into the ground and rot. Virtually they die and come back to life. If your garden is to grow, perhaps you need to first plant the seeds of forgiveness. Let those who have hurt you off the hook. And there's more." Ollie paused. "Where did your problem begin? I'm referring to Amber Leaf."

She raised a brow. "With Elias?"

He nodded. "That's correct. We often find solutions to our problems inside the problems themselves. If you do wish to begin a literary society, you will need support. That said, who do you feel owes you the most?"

"Not Elias?" she blurted.

"He took your reputation. Who better than he to give it back?"

Maude giggled lightheartedly. "But what about the rumors? All the men sneaking to my back door? Elias is slick. But conning any of them into coming forward and supporting me? That would implicate them."

"Use that to your advantage," Ollie said without hesitation. "They will not come forward to support you, but neither will they come forward to castigate you. If you do decide you'd like to have a chat with Elias, I'd be honored to listen in. By the time the two of us get done with him, somehow I have the feeling he may well become your most enthusiastic supporter."

She looked away. "And if he doesn't?"

CHAPTER FORTY-SIX

A white picket fence surrounded the spacious Romanesque home on the north side of town. Certain he had the right place, Ollie eased the buggy through a stunning entry and along a narrow gravel road threading through a grove of oak, elm, and maples. If only the conversation he was about to engage could prove as pleasant.

Elias Prixton met him at the door. Sepia hair with an absence of gray and alert eyes, he stood a strikingly older image of his son. He appeared well dressed in a smoking jacket, the evidence of age having eluded him, and exhibited even more charm than his son, if that was possible. No wonder Maude had been both drawn to and repelled by the man.

"Would you care for coffee?" Elias said. "Tea?"

"That won't be necessary, thank you."

Elias led Ollie through the living area and into an open elegant library with rolling ladders affixed to the shelving on two walls of nicely arranged floor-to-ceiling books. And spacious French windows folded out onto a well-maintained garden. Elias invited Ollie to join him on two plush chairs facing out, a superb place to read and relax. What a dream to have a home like this. One day, Ollie mused.

"My son said to expect you this morning," Elias said.

"Did he give any indication as to why?"

"Nothing other than it had to do with the Whiting case. Why would you feel this involves me, Mr. Harrington? Whiting and I know each other, but it goes no farther than that. I rarely speak to the man."

Ollie had met Elias no more than a few short minutes ago and already sensed the need to carefully choose his words. Though he found it difficult to ascertain why, Ollie perceived Elias as accomplished at deceit and a challenge even for him. Though Ollie could hold his own, it would be easy to fall prey to his calculated devices.

"I'm certain you know Miss Maude Millning," Ollie said.

"Maude Millning?" The newly formed furrows in Elias's forehead appeared professionally placed. "Name sounds familiar. I believe I may have gone to school with a Maude Millning."

"I believe you would have gone to school with a Maude de Haven," Ollie said. "Millning was her married name."

Why say that? Never put a man on the defensive when in need of information.

Elias struck a match, holding flame to his pipe, and drew in a few short puffs. "Ahh, yes. What was I thinking?" He gazed out toward the garden and left Ollie carrying on a one-sided conversation.

"I have reason to believe Miss Millning may have had a child out of wedlock," Ollie said. "Would you happen to have knowledge of that?"

Elias ran a thumb across his fingertips and absently studied his nails. "I don't believe I do."

The man would not become involved.

"Have you any idea why Stephen Whiting might embezzle money from his father's bank when he doesn't live above his means and could easily have requested a loan?"

"No, I don't," Elias said, his tone impervious. "Besides, that doesn't concern me."

"That's where we differ."

Ollie stopped talking. Elias needed to squirm, not that he had it in him.

Rather than endure the man's passive behavior, Ollie strolled to the window where he stepped directly into Elias's field of vision. Though it didn't interest him, he took a closer look at a grove of trees flanking the garden and rocked on his heels. "On second thought, perhaps I would like that cup of coffee if the offer still stands."

Not appearing particularly happy, Elias excused himself. He returned with a coffee tray in hand and an edge to his voice, but Ollie was not about to shrink from his duties.

Elias managed to sit immobile as an opossum as Ollie opened his briefcase.

"I have a letter," Ollie said with a baiting tone, "that you might wish to read. I believe you received it some years back. I rewrote it in my own hand from an original, which we have in safe keeping at the office."

Elias gave it an indifferent glance, but a word or two appeared to capture his attention and his shell cracked. "Where'd you get this?" he said.

"You've seen it before?"

"I asked where you got it."

Ollie allowed few men an upper hand. Elias was not about to number among them. "And I asked if you've seen it before."

"If I said yes?"

"I'd say you have some explaining to do."

Elias folded the letter and stuffed it in a pocket. "Who else knows about this?"

"Mr. Prixton, I'm the one asking questions."

"We'll see about that."

"Very well." Ollie snapped his briefcase closed and stood. "When you're ready to talk, we will resume this little chat. No need to see me out."

As Ollie neared the door, Elias called out. "Okay, I'll talk."

Ollie returned to the chair being careful not to expose his sense of relief. "Please, start at the beginning."

Elias took a slow drag on his pipe as if weighing the cost of each word he was about to utter. "Everyone knew what kind of woman Maude was."

"Correction," Ollie said. "Everyone heard about who Maude allegedly was *after* you began to spread rumors. Scarlet Maude ... isn't that what you called her? But she was not the deep scarlet you painted her, was she? Now let's hear the correct version of your story."

Elias's face reddened, his eyes firing icicles. "Under the circumstances, any man would have done what I did. You want to know about Josh Whiting? He got what he deserved. Ever since I can remember, he competed with me in everything we did. Always had to win. Stole my girl from me. Married her and then had the audacity to look down his nose whenever he saw me. He dated Maude, too, back when we were in school. After he changed her out for someone he thought was better suited, Maude and I picked up where Josh and she left off. One thing led to another until I met the missus. I'll admit, I didn't do right by Maude either. But I was a youngster. Not that many years later word got around that Josh was having problems with his marriage. His wife went into some sort of depression, I think they call it. And poor Maude. Her husband had left her high and dry. Next thing I knew, she and Whiting were in thick. Things weren't all that great under my roof either at the time. I remember one night I had a little too much to drink ... okay ... a lot too much. I paid a visit over at Maude's. But for her to claim that baby was mine when she was in thick with Josh, I just couldn't buy it."

"Have you seen your daughter?"

Elias's eyeballs bulged. "My what?"

"Your daughter?"

"You mean Josh Whiting's daughter."

"No," Ollie said, "I mean yours. She's the spitting image of you, as is your son Nelson."

Elias's Adam's apple took a dip and shot back up. "You mean to tell me—?"

"Josh Whiting has been supporting your daughter from infancy to age sixteen. The past few years she's taken sick with consumption. She has a pile of doctor bills, and the high cost of medicine above that. Stephen Whiting heard about it. Since he and his father had never shared words about an illegitimate child, Stephen wasn't about to let on that he knew. Feeling sorry for the girl, he chose to embezzle. Now he's facing prison for something you started."

Elias turned white, then ran a nervous hand through his hair, down his cheeks, and chin.

"We're working around the clock to keep Whiting from going to trial," Ollie said. "You know as well as me that his name will be plastered across the headlines of *The Amber Leaf Tribune*. And since you're an integral part of the puzzle, rest assured your name will make headlines, too. Seems you've tripped and fallen on your own slippery surface."

"But what can I do to stop it?" Elias said.

"There's only one thing you can do, but it will cost you."

"Which is?"

"Open your wallet and be generous."

Elias hopped up. "Wait a minute, Harrington."

"Here's what I propose." Ollie stood and peered down at the man. "I'll call a meeting with the bank's board. Ask for a reprieve. You pay the embezzlement in full with a kicker to the bank, and do it anonymously. I'll request the receipt be made out to me and add your name for your records as soon as the bank receives the money. You also have substantial payback to Mr. Whiting. I can't promise that he or the board will buy it, but I know he wants to keep a low profile. The case goes away, and you all live happily ever after."

"What's in it for me?"

… Said the selfish child. "Certainly keeping your name out of this

mess and taking responsibility for the welfare of an unusually lovely daughter must be worth something."

Elias relaxed, but only slightly. "Give me time to think about it. This is a lot to swallow."

"You have until a week from today. Oh, and there's one other thing. Maude Millning's launching a literary society. She needs good press, and you are in her debt. I've encouraged her to have a word with you. You might want to give that serious thought as well."

CHAPTER FORTY-SEVEN

Immediately after the meeting with Elias, Ollie peered into Boss's empty office. Where was the man when he needed him?

As he turned to walk on, Nelson sidled up to him and muttered, "How'd it go?"

Ollie spoke in a whisper. "Your father's thinking things through, but I believe he'll do what's right."

Creases cut deep into Nelson's smooth forehead. "Does he know about me?"

"I was discreet," Ollie said with a slight shake of his head. "That was the professional thing to do, was it not?"

Nelson's shoulders appeared to relax more than they should.

Ollie then strolled past Gretta's desk. Though she was off somewhere, a wave of guilt rippled through him. Unable to pursue her since she was already spoken for, he had withdrawn for all of the right reasons, but that appeared to trouble her. This was a fight he couldn't win. For the next long while his longing eyes drifted toward her empty chair until her feathery footsteps finally clipped past him. She murmured a soft "good morning."

Everyone accounted for.

A too-long-moment later, Boss arrived and waved Ollie into his office. "How'd it go?" he said.

Ollie smiled. "It was a bit tense at first, but by the time I chose to leave, it seemed as if Elias finally saw the world through grownup eyes. I allowed him a week to think things over. He agreed to get back to me."

"Good work. What do you propose to do beyond that?"

Hold my breath.

"If the man remains steady," Ollie said, "we'll have the clout to bargain. We'll need to call a quick meeting with the bank's board and their attorney. Hopefully they'll see things our way and we can bring this to a satisfying end."

GRETTA GLANCED BACK. MR. HARRINGTON LOOKED utterly professional poring over the papers on his desk. She'd give the world for their interactions to remain as warm as they had been during that glorious trip to Aspen. Although she had broached the subject and he warmed for a moment, nothing changed. He still saved up his work, doled it out sparingly, spoke to her rarely, and even those words remained few. Didn't tell her where he was going or when. That smarted.

She then gazed at Nelson who'd been setting Stephen Whiting up for an extended stay in prison. Gretta understood how low a traitor was capable of feeling. She was still dating Nelson, that less than exemplary attorney. Her trusting him was about as likely as Mr. Harrington feeling he could trust her.

If only he knew her heart.

Nelson must have sensed her attention. He got up and hovered at her desk. Why did he have to make a spectacle?

"May I have the privilege of walking you home again after work tonight?" he said. "It's important."

Important to him. Though Gretta ached to say no, she didn't want to make a scene, so she nodded.

When the clock struck five, Nelson held the door.

Drawing a cape over her shoulders, Gretta took the lead. The instant they reached the sidewalk, she turned on him. "Before you say a word, my three-month probationary period is over tomorrow. I've already talked to Hilda about that typing test. As soon as I get a chance, I'm telling her all about that Christmas party, too. I refuse to let you hold it over me ever again."

"You're right, Gretta." Nelson's eyes began to water, taking her aback.

But this time she would hold strong. She'd been giving their relationship a tremendous amount of thought. It was far too volatile and needed to end. No turning back.

"Protect yourself," he said. "I knew I was being a jerk when I threatened you."

You *knew* it? "Then why'd you do it?"

"I was terrified of losing you. Tried grabbing on anyway I could. But it wasn't right, and I couldn't be more sorry. I only succeeded in pushing you farther away."

"That's the problem," Gretta said. "When it comes to me, you never think 'til after you mess up."

He kicked a small stone off the sidewalk as though taking a kick at himself. "It won't happen again."

Another day, another promise. "Why was it so important for you to walk me home?"

"Thought you'd want to know Harrington paid a visit out at my parents' house this morning."

"And?"

"I couldn't tell you before," he said, his tone oozing remorse. "I was too ashamed. It was my father who spawned Maude Millning's little girl, not Josh Whiting."

Nelson was pulling a number on her again. Why did he have to be so disarmingly honest? "I know."

He blanched. "How?"

"I figured whatever or whoever you were protecting had to be close to home or you wouldn't stick your neck out."

Nelson stopped in the middle of the sidewalk and his brows inched up. "Why didn't you say anything?"

"What happened?"

He shrugged. "Harrington used his powers of persuasion. He's doing everything he can to make this mess go away without drawing attention. So far it's working."

"How can he do that?" Gretta said. "It's too big."

"Not for him. I've got to hand it to the man. He's shrewd."

No average joe for Mr. Harrington. He had to play a starring role again. Gretta raised her chin. "There's one thing I haven't been able to get past, Nelson Prixton. You were going to let Stephen go to prison. And all these years, you sat back and let his father pay for someone else's kid. How could you do that and live with yourself?"

"Oh, Gretta," Nelson moaned. "How could you think so little of me?"

That shouldn't be too hard to figure out.

"I didn't know I had a kid sister 'til I went to Wichita."

"Why'd you go there?"

"Had a suspicion."

"Why?"

"I know my father," he said, "and just couldn't let go of it. Figured Josh must have seen her or he wouldn't be shelling out his hard earned cash. I had to be careful, though. If my father knew I'd interfered, he'd cut me out of his will for sure."

"Aren't you being overly dramatic?"

"No," Nelson said soberly. "He did that to my brother. As for Stephen, I can see where you'd be appalled. Thing is, I did it on purpose. Planned to pay him back after I started making money."

Gretta gulped. "Then why haven't you?"

"I'm still saving up. Have been since my first day at the firm. And about Stephen … he isn't exactly a saint either. A part of me was paying him back for stealing my girl."

Another *my girl*. How many have there been?

"He married her and flaunted her whenever I was around," Nelson said. "I didn't feel good about getting even, but I did feel good about helping out my sister. She's beautiful and warm and kind outside and in," he said then softened his voice, "just like you."

Why did he have to say that? "But what about Stephen's going to prison? You deliberately blocked Mr. Harrington from exonerating him. That was despicable."

"That's not true," Nelson said.

"What?" she spat. "Isn't it a bit naïve to expect this to go away on its own?"

Nelson went on to explain how he'd planned to send full payment to the bank's board along with a note declaring Stephen's innocence, telling enough to prove it, but not enough for anyone to know what happened or why. He planned to tell about the love child, but not who she was. That he'd learned the amount of the payments from her. Said they would believe him. After all the truth couldn't have been stranger. "You have to believe me, Gretta," he said. "I need you to."

She looked deep into those imploring eyes. She did believe him. Every exasperating, sincere word.

Later that evening she snuggled under the covers. In some sick way, with everything finally making sense, she questioned herself. Would she be wrong if she opened her heart again and gave Nelson another chance?

Would she be more wrong if she didn't?

CHAPTER FORTY-EIGHT

After supper, a ruckus drew Ollie to the window. A rider on the street below was busily stroking his spooked horse. Ollie must have Elias too heavily on his mind. The man even looked like him.

A short while later, a sudden sharp knock sounded, and Ollie jumped. Who would stop by at five past eight on a Monday evening? Unexpected visitors were rare.

To his astonishment, Elias stood in the hallway, bone-chilling eyes peering over spectacles, and said, "Have a minute?" He slapped a glove against a hand, strutted in, and paced nervously. "I've been doing some thinking since your unwelcome visit. Made my decision."

That was far too fast and judging by the look on Elias's face, Ollie sensed the decision would be less than satisfactory. "But we only spoke this morning. You have another week."

"I don't need more time," Elias said, his gaze biting. "What I need is for you to keep your nose out of my affairs. You barge into my world making fool accusations and have the gall to tell me what to do and when to do it. It's common knowledge that Josh and Maude found refuge in one another's company some years back. He is the father of that illegitimate child, not me. You caught me off guard once, but I won't tolerate it again. I'm a good friend of the chief of police. The next time you step foot on my property, you will deal with him directly. Do I make myself clear?"

"You make yourself crystal clear," Ollie said, "but there's something of which *you* do not possess knowledge."

Ollie casually approached the water pitcher and poured a slow glass. Raising it, he said confidently, "I can produce proof."

Elias chuckled wickedly. "What … that letter? What does that prove? If I assume it's a fraud, that Maude wrote it to deliberately implicate me, so will the judge. Good luck getting it to hold up in a court of law."

Ollie poured another glass. "Perhaps you're right, but we do have something the judge will believe."

"We?"

"Stop by tomorrow evening at the same time, and I'll present irrefutable proof."

After Elias wriggled away with a not-so-confident glance back, Ollie's lungs collapsed. He had exercised a power play out of hearsay and pride. What if he couldn't manage to produce proof? What if Maude hadn't kept the pictures? She did say she'd put them in a trunk and admitted to never looking at them, hadn't she? But what if they were unrecognizable?

And what if she refused to share them?

CHAPTER FORTY-NINE

On Tuesday evening as the minute hand rapidly ticked to the hour of eight, Ollie worked himself into a state—wondering where Maude was, chastising himself for sending a note rather than speaking with her directly. Had she not gotten his message? If Elias stopped by with her not present, then what?

By five to eight, the suspense grew unbearable. He wedged a note between the stile and doorjamb, just in case, and hurried down to the lobby.

Maude spun around, appearing relieved at the sight of him, but not as relieved as Ollie.

"Where have you been?" she said.

"Waiting for you in my room."

"The note said to meet you at the hotel." She looked like she wanted to pick up something and swat him, which at the moment he felt he deserved. "I had no way of knowing if Elias was with you," she said. "Didn't want to intrude."

"This way." Ollie guided her up to his room. "Elias turned the tables on me. In a moment of weakness, I made the mistake of becoming prideful. Backed him against a wall. In the process, I pinned myself in a corner as well. Please tell me your daughter's pictures are in good order."

The instant Maude smiled, Ollie calmed.

She rifled through her handbag, drew out a thick envelope, and headed across the room. Splaying photographs across the desktop, she turned to him, and a grin blossomed. "Today was the first time I had the courage to look at them. Isn't she beautiful, Ollie? Isn't my little girl absolutely stunning?"

He studied the dozen or so pictures, each one strongly resembling not only Maude, but also Elias and Nelson. "She is beautiful. This is indeed proof of who the real father is."

"I'm so nervous," she said, wringing her hands. "When will Elias be here?"

"Any minute now. Don't concern yourself. You'll be fine."

"In all these years, I've only seen him from a distance," she said, "and even then we sneered at each other. There's a part of me that hates the man and another part of him that still cuts to my heart, especially when I think of our little girl."

Ollie didn't hesitate to place the most telling picture on top. "If he does come, it isn't necessary for you to say anything. We can only hope he does the gentlemanly thing."

"And if he doesn't?"

"We'll see him in court. Will you be able to manage that?"

She nodded. "I'm tired of hiding from the truth ... I brought something else for you to see," she said as she retrieved a flyer from her purse and held it up. "What do you think?"

Ollie's eyes swelled. "It's marvelous. *Inaugural Meeting, The Amber Leaf Literary Society,*" he read aloud. "This poster looks professional. You've done a masterful job," he said and meant it, then touched her shoulder. "I'm proud of you. Taking this project on is very courageous on your part."

"More determined than courageous," she said. "I hesitated at first."

Ollie smiled. "Afraid no one would bother to come?"

She nodded.

"They'll come, especially if your meetings are held here at the hotel. Have you had any difficulty reserving a room?"

"I got lucky. The manager must not know about my reputation. Said it would be good for business. Once the brochure is out, it wouldn't be good for the hotel to deny access."

Ollie glanced nervously at the clock. Ten past eight and still no Elias.

Maude laughed. "Aren't we a pair? You're worried Elias won't come, and I'm worried he will."

Ollie held up a forefinger and listened intently to rushing footsteps and a sharp rap on the door. His heart quickened as he opened it.

Elias looked as if he were about to pass out when he saw Maude. "Why didn't you tell me she'd be here?" he said.

"You didn't ask, and I didn't know. Perhaps you'd consider being a gentleman and shake the lady's hand."

Ollie pulled several chairs up to the desk. "Please," he said before joining them. "I told you we had proof, Mr. Prixton."

"What proof do you have? Her li—" Elias glanced at the desktop. His eyes widened and his words appeared to have gotten caught as he dropped onto the chair.

"There's an old cliché," Ollie said as he scooped up the photos and handed the stack to the man, "about pictures and the untold words they paint. I believe these speak for themselves."

Elias looked curiously at the first photograph. Pulling it close, he squeezed his eyes closed. He waited a moment before slowly peeling through the rest of them, his breathing labored. Realization must have broken his resolve. "She's beautiful." He gazed at Maude, moisture gathering in his eyes, his voice tight with emotion. "Our little girl … my only little girl … is beautiful. Why didn't you tell me, Maude? Why after all these years—"

"I did. Remember?"

He leaned back and nodded. "I do. I want to see her."

"What about your wife? Your son?"

Elias shook his head. "I don't know. This is all too new yet."

Ollie looked from Maude to Elias. As if no time had passed, they appeared to meld together as one.

"I haven't met her either," Maude said.

Elias appeared stunned.

"I finally mustered the courage to look at her pictures for the first time today," she said. "It was hard enough knowing what I was missing without torturing myself further. I couldn't bring myself to correspond with her either. It didn't seem right to let Carole know who her real mother was."

"Carole?"

Maude nodded. "As for her father, if she would have asked … until I finally looked at the pictures … I could explain Josh, but how could I ever explain you?"

"I was such a fool back then," Elias said with a grievous shake of his head. "I did love you, really I did. But when I knew I could have you, I didn't want you. Then I lost you to Josh, and I went nuts. Can you ever forgive me, Maude? Can you ever forgive me?" he repeated.

"I hate to break up this heartfelt moment," Ollie said, "but where does that leave us now?"

Elias looked at him and a grin formed. "I've ached to have a little girl since before the day I first got married," he said. "And now I have one." Glancing at Maude, he corrected himself. "And now we have one. Where are we, you ask? You never did tell me, Maude. Can we arrange a meeting?"

"Absolutely. I want to see our little girl, too."

CHAPTER FIFTY

Gretta retired to her room where she resumed reading George Gissing's *The Paying Guest*. The story set near London drew her deep into Mr. Harrington's magical milieu, drawing imaginary images of his past. She couldn't stop admiring him, his breadth, strength of character, and exemplary upbringing. What must it be like to be Barrister Oliver Harrington?

Several pages into a chapter, she jumped when something struck the window, as if the sharp end of a branch smacked it. She looked up. No wind. No nearby trees. Another clean pop. And then another. She turned off the light. Peering into the darkness, she threw open the window. "What are you doing down there? You're going to break the glass."

"Pebbles are too small for that," Nelson said. "Come down to the porch."

"But it's—"

"Still plenty early."

She sighed. Fortunately she hadn't changed into her nightgown yet. Grabbing a shawl, she tossed it loosely about her shoulders.

Nelson waited on the porch swing. When she approached, he nudged to the side.

"What are you doing here so late on a Sunday evening … and unannounced?" she said.

"You don't seem happy to see me."

"You're impossible."

With a wide grin, his white teeth glistened off the light pouring through the window. "I'm charming, and I have something to tell you."

"Couldn't it wait 'til tomorrow?"

"My father took a trip to Kansas and back."

Gretta gulped. "Kansas?"

"Yup. Wichita." Nelson hopped up. "Gotta go."

"Nelson Prixton, you sit back down. What do you mean he took a trip to Kansas and back? … Nelson?"

"Are you going to be nice?"

"Yes."

"Are you going to make me feel welcome?"

She grinned and nodded.

"Okay. See that you do." He stood with his back to the railing and leaned against a post. The night was still, and away from the light of the windows, black as coal, and the air comfortably cool—the perfect backdrop for another interesting story.

"He didn't say much at dinner," Nelson began. "Wasn't himself. Moving his food around. Barely eating a thing. And yet there was a joy about him. When Mother asked him about it, he dropped his fork. It hit the table, hard. Then he told us there was something we had a right to know. Mother looked at me. I looked at her. She didn't know what was coming, but I had a pretty good idea. 'I have a daughter,' he said. But there was something about the way he said it. Almost prideful. Mother gulped and got all teary eyed. Asked him how he could do such a thing."

"What did he say?"

"What can anyone say to something like that? Told her it was all her fault. If she'd been a better wife, it wouldn't have happened."

Gretta cringed. "Didn't your mother stand up for herself?"

"How could she? It was the truth."

"Nelson?" Gretta blurted in disbelief. "Do you hear what you're saying?"

He appeared unsure. "But it was the truth, wasn't it, Gretta?"

"Even if it were, that wouldn't justify infidelity, would it?"

When Nelson shook his head doggedly indicating that he understood, Gretta sighed. "Did he say anything about your sister?"

"He's thrilled. Said he always wanted a little girl and now he has one. Said she's beautiful, and when they got off the train, she broke into tears."

"They?"

"Maude and my father."

"Maude? … Millning?" Gretta's mouth fell open. "She went with him?"

"Yup," Nelson said. "They took an early morning train. Arrived in Wichita late Thursday night. My sister and her adopted parents met them. Father stayed at a nearby hotel and Maude stayed at their house. He said they spent all day Friday getting to know her, seeing where she went to school, the town, her church, that sort of thing, and they rode the train back early Saturday morning. Everything on the up and up."

"Does your father have any idea you've already been down to see her?"

Nelson pulled back and lightly pressed the post with a palm of his hand as if trying to press his secret in and make it stick. "I don't think so, but even if he did, I doubt he cared. He's way too happy about finally having a girl."

"What's going to happen with Stephen now?"

"I don't know," Nelson said. "We didn't talk about that. But I'm sure Father will be happy to pay up. The whole time he was carrying on about my half sister, he couldn't stop grinning.

"Oh, and there's something else. He said Maude's going to start a reading club in town. After besmirching her reputation all those years ago, she told him he needed to put out the good word for her or else. I think fathering his child must have done something for him. He actually agreed."

Gretta was stunned. "Maude Millning is starting a literary society? In Amber Leaf?"

"Why not?"

"What about your mother? Did your father say anything about it to her?"

"She was sitting right there and ignored it."

Gretta knew only too well how demeaned women feel. "She wasn't ignoring it. And you can bet the gossips are going to go to town on that one. Your father needs to protect your mother."

"He doesn't give a hoot," Nelson said. "He'll tune out her pleas and charm everyone else. You can bet the town is going to hear all about his beautiful little girl, too."

"How can he do that to your family?"

"He doesn't care. At this point, I'm not sure I do either. As for my mother, I'm sure she'll crawl into a hole and hide the way she always does."

"Sounds like your parents have a miserable relationship. Whose fault is that? Your mother's or your father's?"

He looked at Gretta with hopeless eyes. "Probably both. She cares too much. He doesn't care enough."

After Nelson left, Gretta stopped by her mother's room. "Thought I'd have a cup of hot chocolate. Want some?" She pulled a quart of milk out of the icebox and a pan from the cupboard while thoughts of Mrs. Prixton burned at her like harsh stomach acid.

Her mother stepped up from behind. "You're mumbling to yourself, dear," she said then pulled out a chair near the table. "Did Nelson say something that distressed you?"

"Nelson always says things that distress me. I was thinking about his mother, how I get the feeling she's no match for her husband."

"No one is a match for Elias Prixton. Bright, articulate, charming … slippery, cunning, selfish."

Those words hit home. "Why would she marry a man like that?" Gretta asked.

"She was probably too in love to see the truth. Either that or she didn't want to. Who's to say? It's always easier to siphon strength from someone else than to build your own, but it takes a while for young people to learn that. If that was her motive, the poor woman has forever paid the price for her weakness, hasn't she?"

Gretta slowly stirred the heating milk. "What scares me is that I identify with her," she said. "I'm no match for Nelson either. I'd give anything if he could be like Mr. Harrington. That day in Aspen was so idyllic, I didn't want to leave."

Then she remembered how she had felt when he stopped by and saw firsthand their humble house—her embarrassment. She glanced back at her dear mother, embarrassed by her embarrassment. It was as if she were sipping from a well of unworthiness, and she wasn't even in a relationship with the man. "But I don't belong in Mr. Harrington's world."

"Mrs. Prixton is different, though," Gretta said. "She won her man years ago. Why doesn't she stand up for herself? Why wiggle into a hole that makes her feel even weaker?"

Her mother's eyes and her voice emitted compassion. "Are you afraid of turning into a younger version of her if you marry Nelson? The signs of what life with him would be like are already there, aren't they? Have been all along."

Gretta nodded as she painstakingly stirred cocoa and sugar into the scalding milk, the cocoa growing lighter, the milk growing darker, mixing together until neither were recognizable, much the same as her conflicting thoughts. She poured it into mugs and carried it to the table. "He's told me enough times he wants to marry me, that's for sure. If I did, I don't know if I could make it over the long haul. Would I weaken while he gets stronger or would I cave in and be miserable, too, just like his mother?"

Gretta's mother blew over the steaming cocoa then said, "Sometimes people change, sometimes they don't."

She felt a need to cry. "What if he doesn't change, Mom?"

"That's what concerns me. The Elias Prixtons of this world wield the power and care the least leaving those about them gnashing their teeth. And then you have the Oliver Harringtons. They care the most, don't they? And leave those around them at peace, free to grumble, free to praise."

Her mother took a sip of the chocolate then continued. "What a shame Mrs. Prixton's in such a mess. Looks like she's dug herself in deep."

"What can anyone do about it?" Gretta said.

"I don't know. It would take an enormous will to climb out of something like that, wouldn't it? But I don't think I'd worry about her. If man is made in God's image, all of mankind has the capacity for a strong will."

"Mrs. Prixton included?"

"No," Gretta's mother smiled. "… Gretta included."

Gretta considered Maude Millning, another beaten down woman. After all those years, she'd gained the courage and strength to start a literary society, and if that wasn't enough, she demanded Elias Prixton's support.

And he said yes.

With the possibility of two dream men in her life during the peek of eligibility for marriage—Mr. Harrington not an option, Nelson Prixton a dangerous amount of work—Gretta needed to continue on, one step at a time, until her path became clear.

But would it?

CHAPTER FIFTY-ONE

arly morning fog eased into light drizzle spattering against the windowpanes, the steady patter of rain lasting the greater part of the day. In dreary light, Ollie reviewed the notes for tonight's formidable meeting before running his proposal past Boss.

"You're walking a tightrope," Boss cautioned. "Too much to hide, too little to share, and only one opportunity for success if we want to bypass that hearing."

Ollie lifted his chin. "Perhaps the weather will wear down the board's resolve."

"We can only hope," Boss said. "Does Whiting know the kid isn't his?"

"I doubt it. I'm certain Elias will wait and approach him after he pays off the bank. That conversation I don't envy."

"You're going to have to do some fancy dancing, too, Harrington," Boss said. "You pull this off … we'll talk more about your career. That is, if you don't have a confounded notion of going back to London."

Ollie smiled his answer.

Stepping out into the office area, he stole a moment and recalled his arrival, that day he first stepped off the train. After the emptiness had subsided, Amber Leaf felt right, like hearth and home. As did Gretta. Across the room she leafed through folders at a filing cabinet, a high collared blouse cinched snugly at her thin waist. The hem of her skirt lightly dusted the hardwood with each graceful movement. And her warm midnight eyes were deeply engaged in work. Ideally he wanted to remain in Amber Leaf for a long, long while, be successful, marry, and build a home with someone lovely, someone with poise, warmth, and tenderness of heart—someone like her.

By evening, puddles checkered the roads and a light fog fell again, swirling about lampposts. A pensive Josh Whiting greeted him at the bank. Ollie took note of the dripping umbrellas and galoshes lining its entry. "How's the mood so far?" he said.

"No hostile looks, if that's what you mean."

Ollie chose not to air what was he was thinking—that there was no need for hostile looks. The board had already made its decision.

"Are you sure we aren't making a mistake by not having my son join us?" Josh said.

The slightest inkling that Stephen had sacrificed his career under false pretenses for someone who wasn't related to him would be explosive. It required tactful handling. "I'm certain."

Much like the outside fog, pipe and cigar smoke billowed about the chandelier in the half filled conference room. Ollie and Josh took their positions at the far ends of the long cherry wood table for a subconscious edge. The bank board's attorney, Mr. Ainsely, the distinguished looking fellow Ollie had seen at the hotel, sat in the center on the left side, and the board's chairman, Mr. Johnson, the other gentleman who had met Mr. Ainsely there, sat in the center on the right. Ollie doubted the men recognized him or realized he had been privy to their conversation.

After the chairs filled, Mr. Johnson called the meeting to order. The board members' striking confidence as they went around the table introducing themselves concerned Ollie, their compassion for Stephen appearing wanting. But that's what happens when minds are made up. The chairman then turned the meeting over to Ollie.

"We all ... believe ... we know why we're here," he said. "Money has, in fact, been embezzled from Amber Leaf National Bank by Stephen Whiting and by his own admission. To that we plead no contest." Ollie paused purposely before proceeding. Exhibit confidence, he instructed himself. Compel them to question themselves. "However, I think it important to set the stage by offering a plea bargain, followed with background and offer our argument as to why we believe our offer is best not only for Stephen, but for all concerned."

Ollie paused again. "Our bargain? By ten o'clock tomorrow morning, the bank will be recompensed in full with a generous ten percent interest, the payer remaining anonymous, and charges against Stephen Whiting will be promptly dropped."

Josh drew up. "What's this about an anonymous—"

"That's outrageous." Mr. Ainsely's scowl shot daggers. "Whiting needs to spend time behind bars where he belongs. The good citizens of Amber Leaf deserve as much."

Josh frowned at Mr. Ainsely, then quickly shifted his attention to Ollie. "But what's this about an anonymous payer?"

"We'll discuss that later, Mr. Whiting," Ollie said, hoping Josh wouldn't push harder. Meanwhile, he needed to break Mr. Ainsely's rigid stance. "And as for you, Mr. Ainsely, your point is well taken. Under different circumstances, I could not agree with you more."

Needing a more sympathetic audience, Ollie then turned to Mr. Johnson and waited out his lead. To his relief, the man folded his hands and leaned forward. "Mr. Ainsely, why don't we refrain from passing judgment until we hear the man out? Go ahead, Mr. Harrington."

"Before I proceed," Ollie said, "I have a request. I do find it necessary to remain mildly candid, since reputations are involved, reputations I feel a strong need to protect. The information I am about to disclose is to remain confidential." He cast his gaze from board member to board member. "I trust we're all amenable to that?"

"Why don't we take a step outside?" Mr. Ainsely could not have been more brusque. "You give me a quick briefing," he said, "and we'll make our decision from there."

Josh pushed up, holding onto the table as if for support. "That won't be necessary."

Ollie fought to regain his footing, but before he could, all eyes and ears pivoted toward the man, to the grief in his eyes, and the broken-ness in his voice. "Gentlemen," Josh said, "in all due respect, I can no longer sit back and allow my son to take the heat for something I'm responsible for."

"Mr. Whiting, please," Ollie insisted.

Josh shook his head. "No, let me talk." He looked about the room. "Mr. Harrington is only trying to protect my reputation. To the degree possible, I hope the board will respect our privacy, not for me, but for my family."

Mr. Ainsely gaped at him. "Surely you don't expect us to—"

"I'm not expecting anything," Josh said, "but I am requesting it. This entire predicament rests on my shoulders. If you're wondering why I would allow my boy to take the blame for something I started, that was his request. He feared I'd lose my position at the bank, too, and that our family's assets would get totally wiped out."

Mr. Ainsely appeared taken aback, his gaze drifting to Mr. Johnson's subtle nod of sympathy. Mr. Ainsely then said in a tone exuding bewil-derment, "I move we respect Mr. Whiting's privacy. Is everyone in agreement?"

To Ollie's relief, a chorus of curious "agreed" filled the room.

Josh began his story. "Years ago, my son stumbled upon a letter he had no right to read, a letter that, if true, would damage our family's reputation. Out of fear and respect, he kept it to himself."

Mr. Ainsely peered over his spectacles. "And what was the content of that letter, if I might ask?"

"You don't need to answer that, Mr. Whiting," Ollie quipped.

"I fathered a child," Josh said, "outside the bounds of holy matrimony … my holy matrimony."

"Objection," Ollie said. "Mr. Whiting, have you ever seen this child?"

He appeared confused. "No, sir, I haven't."

"Then how do you know the child is yours?"

Josh's cheeks turned a warm shade of pink. "Because I had a relationship with her mother."

"And who was the mother?" Mr. Ainsely asked, as if believing it was his right to know.

Ollie flexed a hand that was seizing on him. "That information is not at issue, neither is it pertinent."

"Without my knowledge," Josh continued, "several years ago Stephen got word that a close relative whom he had never met had taken critically ill with consumption."

Again Mr. Ainsely spoke up. "From whom did he get word?"

Though Ollie preferred to raise a fist, he raised a forefinger. "Again, that is not pertinent."

"The relative for all intents and purposes," Josh said, "was purported to be Stephen's half sister. He somehow found out that I'd been supporting her since she was an infant. Although he hasn't told me, I assume he figured that out by looking over the bank's books. In his position, it doesn't take much to find a standing bank draft. Knowing I no longer support her, when he found out about her condition, Stephen felt a responsibility to help. He didn't feel he could approach me and admit to—I found out recently—having read my personal mail, and since it would be highly inappropriate to request a loan for medical expenses for an unknown sibling, out of family love and moral decency, my boy put his career at risk to save her life."

The room grew uncomfortably quiet, every man looking down as if looking into the bowels of his own shame.

"Surely you must have known about your daughter's illness," Mr. Ainsely said. "Why wouldn't you pay her medical expenses yourself?"

Ollie lifted his chin. "Correction. Alleged daughter's expenses."

Mr. Ainsely glowered. "Alleged," he said.

Josh exuded the innocence of a small boy and the honesty of a broken man. "As I said, all of my payments over the years were made by automatic bank draft to an account in Wichita until the age of sixteen at which time the payments stopped. I never corresponded with my child and only found out that she was a girl after charges were made against my son. Other than seeing her occasionally from afar, I have had no contact with her mother since before our child was born."

"Correction," Ollie said. "Alleged mother. And there but for the grace of God go the rest of us, do we not?"

Again eyes cast downward.

"At the heart of the problem," Ollie said, "we have a desperate young man borrowing funds from a bank and paying them back as promptly as possible in an effort to save the life of his half sister."

"Correction," Mr. Ainsely rebutted. "Not borrowing. Embezzling."

Ollie ignored the correction. "The problem reaches no deeper than that. Stephen Whiting's need for money was not borne out of greed as one might have imagined, but rather out of necessity and as a result of love—the purest form of love, a blind love for someone he had never before seen. That being said, I hereby request that the board take this into account and show leniency."

Mr. Ainsely laughed awkwardly. "We can't let the boy off the hook. He blatantly violated the bank and broke the law. The good people of Amber Leaf need to know the bank is watching out for their financial interests."

"In all due respect," Ollie said, "how would you have handled yourself under similar circumstances, Mr. Ainsely?" He then shifted his attention individually to members of the board who appeared more sympathetic. "How would any one of you have handled yourself if you were caught in this spider's web? No one can dispute Stephen Whiting's motives. Can any man here bring himself to believe that he had no intention of paying down the debt? A young man who would sacrifice the livelihood of his family to save a poor girl's life? Please take your time to think on it."

Mr. Johnson spoke up a bit too quickly. "We won't be needing any more time, Mr. Harrington. We have your answer. First and foremost it is our charge to represent the bank."

For a passing moment Ollie had thought his powers of persuasion prevailed, but then his breath grew shallow as realization set in. "I would implore you not to speak too quickly," he said. "If your bank is wise, as I believe it to be, it will reconsider the far-reaching consequences of a premature decision. There is more at stake than readily meets the eye. Amber Leaf National is in competition with other banks that would love nothing more than to gain your business. What about maintaining a positive image within the community? Being seen as possessing generosity of spirit? Or having the reputation of being financially wise for accepting full reimbursement along with ten percent interest? It would be foolish to sacrifice that for a petty sense of revenge."

As the room grew still, Josh leaned forward and said, "Mr. Harrington, you still haven't told me. What's this about an anonymous payer?"

CHAPTER FIFTY-TWO

Gretta pierced a fork into a chunk of carrot, but rather than chew it, her thoughts chewed on Mr. Harrington's phenomenal ability to exercise wisdom. "How's the pot roast, Mother?" she said.

"It's wonderful. You're an excellent cook. I hope the young man who finally wins your heart values your worth."

"You mean Nelson?"

"No," her mother said with a smirk, "I mean the one who wins your heart."

Gretta laughed. "I'll be sure to keep reminding him … and thanks for putting the roast in the oven."

"You did all the work. All I did was replenish the wood." Her mother stopped eating mid bite. "You're in an unusually good mood this evening."

Gretta wanted to shout from the highest hill. "Mr. Harrington got all of the charges dropped against Stephen Whiting."

Her mother gaped at her. "All of them?"

"And the bank board gave Stephen his old job back. Mr. Harrington acted like it was nothing more than another day at the office."

"Pass the salt, please."

"Pepper, too?"

"No, just the salt. Thank you." She wielded the shaker as if trying to loosen the last granule, then said casually, "You can't help being sweet on the man, can you, dear? I have the distinct feeling your Mr. Harrington is sweet on you, too."

Why was her mother doing this? "He's not my Mr. Harrington."

"I noticed it the day he drove up and escorted you to our porch," she said, appearing indifferent to Gretta's protest, while still having a heyday with the saltshaker. "He couldn't take his eyes off of you. What a gallant young man."

"I thought I salted the roast well."

"You did, but potatoes can always use a little more."

"About Mr. Harrington being sweet on me, that's not possible." Gretta mindlessly stabbed a hunk of roast and placed it on her plate. "Remember, Cinderella is a fable. Men like him need someone with social standing."

Her mother finally set the saltshaker down. "I'm telling you, girl, that man is smitten with you."

Why be so insistent? Gretta was not getting any younger and had no desire to build mansions in the air. "You mean smitten by my ability to take dictation. You've only seen him once. You don't see him every day at the office. I feel like I'm invisible."

"How do you know what's going on inside that man's head?" her mother said, sounding unconvinced, but then she raised a brow. "Or is it more appropriate to say heart?"

Please don't raise my hopes about the hopeless. "Even if you are right, what would it matter? It isn't likely he'd marry a commoner. And what about Nelson? I forgot to tell you. He's invited me to meet his parents this weekend."

Her mother shook her head, worry lines etching creases along the sides of her eyes. "I adore Nelson. He's charming, and he's been awfully good to me, but I don't trust that young man. Never have. Can't you see he's precisely like his father? He doesn't know what he wants. You need someone stable, someone who won't break your heart."

"You make it sound so easy." Gretta paused for a moment, wondering. "Mom, did you mean to say Nelson's like his father? Or did you mean to say he's like my father?"

Gretta's mother set her fork on the table and played with it. "Both, I guess."

"Why did you ever marry Dad in the first place? I don't remember him ever being kind to you."

"He was at first. Besides, I thought I was in love, and I understood his world," she said. "My father was mean to my mother, too."

Tears glistened in her mother's caring eyes. She reached across the table and patted Gretta's hand. "About Mr. Harrington, there's something I've kept from you all these years, but I think you need to know about it now. I'll be right back."

Poor and in failing health, her mother returned to the table several minutes later, walking slowly, and held out an age-old photograph of a handsome young man. "His name was Abe Manning," she said, the regret in her voice unmistakable.

Gretta studied the picture. "Was?"

Her mother nodded, then sat down and folded her hands on her lap. "I didn't think I was good enough for him, either. His father was a well-to-do doctor up in Minneapolis. My parents? You knew them. They didn't have any money. And my dad always embarrassed me. Couldn't hold down a job and was drunk more than he was sober. Told me all the time that I was good for nothing.

"But Abe was different. He treated me with respect. To be honest, I didn't know how to act around him. When he went off to medical school, he sent letters all the time asking me to come see him. I never took them seriously. Besides, I couldn't afford the train fare and wasn't about to ask for it. Then one day I met your dad and that was that.

"And this is where you and Mr. Harrington come in. A few years back, I found out that Abe had taken his own life. I was devastated."

Gretta's lungs solidified. "What happened?"

"What happened?" her mother repeated, ache returning to her voice. "The very thing that made him successful appears to have been the very thing that did him in … I heard he'd been working far too many long hours. Hadn't gotten enough sleep. Got called in for an emergency surgery because he was the best of the best. The patient was a five-year-old girl. He made a mistake of some kind. I never did find out what it was. But the little girl? She died. And Abe couldn't live with himself … so he ended it.

"I felt so awful, I cried. I knew about his wife. She was hard nosed. I kept thinking that maybe if I would have married him, I might have helped him through his grief. I never could part with his letters. Kept them in a trunk up in the attic. When I heard about the awful thing that happened to him, I went back and reread them. That's when I realized how much he cared. It doesn't get any plainer than 'I care for you deeply.' I just couldn't see it at the time." She looked hard into Gretta's eyes. "We're all just people, dear. We're all equal in the eyes of our Lord, you and your Mr. Harrington included. Don't you ever forget it."

OLLIE SLUMPED ON A CHAIR AND stared into the darkness beyond his window. What was the matter with him? He couldn't find happiness if it landed in his lap.

The bank's board had willingly accepted his terms of confidentiality and reinstated Stephen. Then there was Elias. He didn't hesitate to spend a small fortune paying off the bank and reimbursing Josh for those many years of child support. And Josh, from what Ollie had heard, was in the end devastated to learn the love child wasn't his. Ollie shook his head in wonder about this phenomenon called love. But then he thought about his own father, and sadness crushed his heart. What he wouldn't give to have a loving relationship with him. Ollie eyed his pad and pen.

2 October 1901

Dearest Family:

I continue to have thoughts of you often and again hope this letter finds you happy and well.

Here in Amber Leaf we are now descending deeper into autumn. On Tuesday past, a steady rain thinned the leaves of the trees somewhat. Soon the branches will be barren and snow will come. There is already a nip in the air.

I'm smiling awkwardly as I write. Although I find it mildly interesting, it really is not my wish to write about the weather, but rather to address not having received word from England. You certainly have earned the right to distance yourselves from me, but something has happened that I find greatly troubling. I hope you will indulge me my thoughts.

In an earlier letter, I spoke of an intriguing legal dispute. In the end, I learned that a fellow attorney was trying to divert my attention and ease me off the case. To make brief a long tale, he was protecting his father's reputation as well as his own. His father, a wealthy man but with what appears to be wanting moral standing, fathered a child outside of his marriage bed and for years denied culpability. And yet, some twenty years hence, that same man after seeing photographic evidence of his fatherhood, so valued his child that he paid a fortune in arrears.

Seeing the light in that man's eyes when he spoke of his little girl and the price he was willing to pay for something as intangible as love touched me as few things have. And while I feel deep joy for the man, my own heart grieves. What I would have given for you to value my Emily over her social standing and me over the choices I've made, but I fear that was not to be.

Each day I continue to arrive at my sleeping quarters with hope of receiving a letter. While I have no inkling how well I will fare over the longer term in these United States, as time progresses and thought of receiving word from London continues to wane, I grow increasingly less certain that I shall ever return to my homeland. I hope one day your heart toward your wayward son will soften. Perhaps my feelings would be different then, for I so look forward to hearing from you.

Now the cordial greetings from your loving son Oliver.

CHAPTER FIFTY-THREE

Gretta draped the buggy blanket over her knees. "I'm nervous, Nelson. What if your parents don't like me?"

He patted her hand and smiled. "My parents will love you. My father's so smitten with my sister these days, it's not possible for him to not like anyone. I swear for the first time in his life, he even likes Josh Whiting."

"Nelson?"

"Hmm?"

"Have you had a chance to talk with Stephen yet?"

He nodded. "Day before yesterday."

"How did it go? Was he upset with you?"

"Did you feel that? It's starting to rain." Pulling back the reins, Nelson said, "I need to raise the top or we're going to get soaked."

They were close enough to Nelson's home that she let the subject pass until later.

Her eyes swelled and her breath caught as the buggy pulled up in front of Elias Prixton's remarkable estate. She'd felt intimidated around Mr. Harrington, but his world was an illusion. This was reality.

The Prixtons met them at the door. Mrs. Prixton, in particular, appeared warm, kind and accepting, as if Gretta were their equal.

Gretta looked again at Elias and wondered how much of that acceptance found its origins in Mrs. Prixton's own need for respect.

A grand piano sat proudly near the windows of the spacious living room and a fire roared in the fireplace. Gretta gazed in wonder then inhaled an enticing hint of what promised to be a wonderful dinner with some sort of beef, which wafted from the kitchen. She smiled broadly. The thought of living in such an elegant setting surpassed her wildest imaginings.

"Come," Mrs. Prixton said, guiding her by the elbow. "I'll take you on a cook's tour while the men retire to the library. Seems they have some business to discuss."

As they ascended a wide open-railed staircase that emptied into an antechamber on the second floor, Gretta resisted the pull of being drawn deeper into Nelson's tempting world. The room lightly furnished with wingback chairs sandwiched a coffee table adorned with a large autumn bouquet. She sniffed the flowers, twirled around, and gazed at a stunning oil painting of Mr. and Mrs. Prixton that had to have measured no less than four feet tall by three feet wide. "What a handsome painting," she said. "Your home and everything in it is absolutely beautiful."

Gretta found it disheartening that Nelson's mother merely smiled.

Double doors to the right opened into a master bedroom suite with a walkout balcony while double doors to the left opened into a long hallway with a sewing room, sitting room, and several spare bedrooms. The size of this expanse alone was far larger than the entirety of the square little box Gretta called home. She pinched her eyes closed and sighed. If she married Nelson, would they one day have a home like this? She caught herself. The lure of a beautiful home was definitely the wrong motivation for marriage.

The door to Nelson's bedroom opened at the end of the hallway. Gretta looked around wide-eyed. "How brilliant to mount his skis and tennis racket on the wall," she said. "And his dresser—?" She started counting. "There must be thirty trophies here if there's one."

She withheld a grin as the words ostentatious and embarrassing popped into her mind. What would it be like to live in a world of plenty? Nelson's questionable character aside, how fun it would be to try.

As they strolled along, Gretta was also taken with the explicit care given to every detail of the immaculately kept rooms. "I'm in awe," she said.

Soon after, they stopped by the library. Mrs. Prixton called the men for supper. The dining room, though long and narrow with floor to ceiling French windows, looked out onto a meadow, which had a calming effect, even with pouring down rain.

Later, after a wonderful evening of exquisite food, interesting chatter, and parlor games, sadness overtook Gretta as Nelson called for the buggy, and they were off.

"I had no idea I'd enjoy your parents so much. And your home? Please tell me this night is real, that it isn't a dream."

Nelson pulled her close. "I assure you it's anything but."

As they rode along through the fairytale night, he shared the earlier discussion he'd had with his father in the library.

"You mean he wants your sister to live with you for the winter?" Gretta said.

"He and Maude made the offer and she seems interested."

"You're happy about it?"

"I am."

"That's going to be awfully hard for your mother, isn't it? … I'm sorry," she said. "It was rude of me to ask that. You never did tell me about your talk with Stephen. What happened? Is everything going to be okay?"

Nelson shrugged. "Probably as okay as it can be under the

circumstances. He isn't all that happy with me. Can't say that I blame him. But he hasn't exactly had exemplary character either."

"Two wrongs don't make a right," Gretta said.

He let loose a grin. "You have to admit they do balance each other. I rode out to his place the other night. Found him wandering around in the stable. When he saw me, he took a swing, but I blocked it. No matter what I said, it didn't seem to sit right. So I went back in time, reminded him of a few things I'm sure he'd rather forget. He had to admit neither of us can claim innocence. I get the feeling there'll always be bad blood between us."

The buggy pulled up to Gretta's house. "What about your father and Josh Whiting?" she said. "I thought that went okay."

"It did. Josh is doing okay for now, but I'm sure after he thinks about things for a while, it'll probably back up on him."

"Then what?"

Nelson shook his head. "I don't even want to know."

CHAPTER FIFTY-FOUR

Ollie could only hope Maude's impressive posters would draw a reasonable crowd to the first meeting of her literary society. Men and women were invited. No children under age sixteen. He held his breath and walked on.

Though a distant crowd rumbled, he approached the room Maude had reserved. All appeared stone quiet. He hesitated. The poor woman would need encouragement, but what words might he offer? He stepped inside. No one there. No Maude. No flyers, books. No anything. Had management reneged?

He hurried to the front desk to inquire, slowing his pace as an animated assembly unfolded into view.

"Ollie? Mr. Harrington?" Maude weaved through the horde and reached for his hands.

"What is this?" he said. "What happened with the room?"

She let out a delightful giggle. "So many people kept coming, we had to meet in the lobby to hold them all. You'd better grab a chair. There aren't many left."

Ollie grinned at the spectacle. In the center of the hubbub, the mayor chomped a cigar. Elias Prixton entertained a small crowd merrymaking near the entry. A parson. A blacksmith. Merchants. Boss. Hilda. Seamstresses. Secretaries. Housewives. And in the center, Deacon pointed a forefinger at an empty folding chair and mouthed the words, "We've saved you a seat."

"I'm reeling." Ollie looked about. "Where did everyone come from?"

"Whole town must be hungry for something new," Deacon said, but then he immediately turned troubled. "Say Ole, I got on at that plant over in Aspen. Been asking a few questions, snooping around. A word of advice?"

With Deacon's ominous tone, Ollie hesitated. "Yes, sir?"

"Stay as far away from that place as you can."

"Surely it can't be that—"

Deacon was adamant. "It's a powder keg ready to blow. Those boys are hot and from what I've picked up, they have a right. Management isn't paying attention. Dangerous working conditions." The door punched open and Deacon looked up. "Say, that wouldn't be—"

Ollie's heart sank. "Nelson … and Gretta." Like a sudden slap, though sitting next to Deacon, he felt strangely alone.

"May I have your attention, please?" Maude dropped a gavel and waited for the room to settle down.

Deacon drew close. "Tell you more later."

Behind Ollie, feminine tittering. Beside him, upturned noses. Leering men with raised brows huddling in the back. Derisive thoughts radiating through contemptuous eyes. Ollie plucked at his shoelace. First, problems at Aspen. Now this. The crowd wasn't here to learn. They weren't here to participate. They were here to watch the hard fall of Maude Millning.

"Thank you all for coming," she said, her tone unaffected, her gaze steady, her demeanor commanding.

A well-dressed, older woman in the front row raised a hand.

"Yes?" Maude said.

"What credentials do you feel you have to lead a literary society?"

Ollie took exception to the woman's condescending tone.

"We'll have time for questions and answers immediately following the meeting," Maude said graciously.

Several more hands shot up.

"I'll be more than happy to answer your questions after the fact," she repeated, "but for now we must get the meeting underway."

Deacon bumped Ollie's elbow and whispered with pride. "Isn't Maude something?"

And that she was.

She held the audience captive as she shared with unparalleled eloquence the need for, proposed structure of, and her vision for a local literary society. Anyone wishing to join needed to remain active, miss no more than three meetings during a one-year period, and make a positive contribution, or they would be asked to forfeit membership. When she mentioned that the society's meetings would begin with a quick recap of current news, someone interrupted from the back. "What kind of news?"

"Snippets of interest," Maude said. "For instance, how many of you knew that just the other day our President changed the name of the Executive Mansion to The White House?"

"Teddy Roosevelt did that?" someone said.

"Yes, he did. Anything that sparks our interest will keep our meetings and community vibrant. As for our book selections, I thought it a good idea to begin with the classics," Maude went on, "endeavor to have readings by authors, and also expand into philanthropic projects for our community."

Ollie kept a pulse on the crowd, faces changing slowly from mocked indifference to hungry desire. But about halfway into her talk, an inebriated man staggered in, and Ollie grew wary. Well-dressed, although fedora askew. Middle-aged. Thin around the middle. The man pulled a pint from a coat pocket and upended it, backhanding his mouth as he made a spectacle of screwing the cap back on while teetering back and forth on shiny shoes.

Gretta, who was sitting closest to the man, recoiled. Although he didn't want to, Ollie forced himself to stay seated. To his chagrin, protecting her was Nelson's responsibility.

For the first time during the evening, Maude's train of thought lost fluency. She stopped. "Excuse me, sir, but this is a private meeting. No drinking allowed."

All heads turned to the colorful man. From the smug look on his face, Ollie sensed his instincts had been right. The man came with a distinct desire to shame Maude.

"You mean to tell me a woman the likes a' you can be in a place like this, but a gentleman like me can't? When did you get so high and mighty?"

As if preplanned, Deacon and Harley understatedly got up and positioned themselves near the door while Maude stepped up from behind the lectern.

"In all due respect," she said, "I'm afraid I'm going to have to ask you to leave."

"I ain't goin' nowhere," he said with a churlish grin. "It's you who ain't fit to be here."

The proper ladies appeared shocked, the proper gentlemen entertained. As for Ollie, he kept his focus on Maude, waiting for a signal to intervene.

"Please," she said. "We don't want to—"

Her eyes widened as Elias Prixton got up and drew his shoulders back. "It's okay, Miss Millning," he said smoothly then slathered on a charming grin. "I'll handle this."

Ollie looked from Elias to the drunk. Under normal circumstances, he would prepare himself for a good fight, but Elias appeared comfortably in control. All eyes were on the two.

"What's the matter, Reuben?" Elias said. "Don't tell me you've tried Miss Milning's back door like a slithering snake and found you weren't welcome."

The drunk took a fist to his chest and belched. "Ain't that a little like a kettle callin' a pot black, Misss-ter Prixton?"

Elias nodded, his confident grin widening. "That's precisely what it's like," he said. "Some twenty odd years ago she slammed the door on me, *too*."

Ollie's mouth dropped open, but not before a shocked, self-conscious snickering filled the room.

"Maude Millning is every bit the *lady*," Elias said. "Always has been. Always will be. And don't you forget it. Now I think you might want to listen to her and consider coming back another time."

Deacon and Harley seized the drunk by the elbows and escorted him out the door, the man's feet airborne and flailing.

Relief accompanied Maude's smile. "Thank you, Mr. Prixton."

After her talk, she opened the floor for volunteers. Officer positions needed to be filled beginning with the president.

Ollie glanced around at the audience then got up. "I wish to nominate Maude Millning for president."

She struck the gavel against a chorus of cheers. "No, no, no. The literary society is for the folks of Amber Leaf, not for me."

"Miss Millning," Ollie said, "I can confidently state that no one is better qualified to be the first president of *The Amber Leaf Literary Society* than you."

As he looked back to the crowd for support, Gretta stood out like a beacon, as if the light in her eyes shone only for him … and the feeling of being alone vanished.

Maude backed down to boisterous applause. Elias Prixton was nominated vice president, a nurse from the hospital as secretary, and Deacon as treasurer. Maude then opened the floor for questions. There were none, so she adjourned the meeting.

Elias tapped Ollie's shoulder. "Amazing meeting, wasn't it?"

Ollie nodded. This wasn't a meeting—it was a lesson on life. "If

Maude has the will to crawl out of a deep hole with amazing success, why not the rest of us?"

"Why not, indeed." Elias slipped a hand in a pocket. "I've been meaning to ask you. Every year on Thanksgiving weekend, I host a party at my home. Why don't you plan to join us? And feel free to bring a guest if you'd like. I'll make sure you receive a formal invitation."

After the crowd thinned, Ollie hugged Maude. "Congratulations. This was far and away one of the better meetings I've seen conducted."

"Thanks," she said, "but I'm not blind. We both know why they came. How many of these fine people do you think will bother to come back?"

CHAPTER FIFTY-FIVE

Immediately following Maude's meeting, Gretta gripped the buggy seat with both hands. "Aren't we going a little fast? You have the horse in a full trot."

"What's the matter?" Nelson scoffed "Don't you trust me?"

No.

Gretta didn't like the way she felt—confused, pent-up, frightened. "The fog's so thick you can't see a thing. What if someone crosses the road and can't get out of the way fast enough?"

"You worry too much."

"Someone has to."

"Look," he said, "if anyone's out there, they can hear a horse and buggy coming." As if thinking better of his position, he quickly calmed down. "I'm sorry, Gretta. I'm just anxious to get home. Got a big meeting early in the morning I'm not ready for. I can't get on the bad side of Boss. I'm already walking a tightrope."

What would marriage to Nelson be like, she wondered. Always on edge and never at peace? She called herself into question. Was he the problem or was she? Was she unreasonable or possibly too demanding?

To Nelson's credit, the horse eased into a steady gait. "Did you enjoy the meeting?" he said, his tone gentler. "Think you'll be going back?"

She nodded. "How about you?"

"Might." After an awkward moment, he nodded. "Gretta? Is anything going on between you and Harrington?"

Her breath caught. "What?"

"I said—"

"I heard what you said. No. Absolutely not. Where did that question come from?"

"I saw the way he looked at you when that drunk leaned in too close. Thought he was going to fly across the room and belt the guy."

Gretta laughed. So that was why Nelson drove so fast. "Nelson Prixton, you're jealous."

He nodded in the buggy's lamplight. "I'll own that ... again."

"Don't be. Mr. Harrington can't help being protective. He would have even leaped across the room to protect you."

"Now that's a stretch."

"Not necessarily. And about the drunk who gave Maude a hard time ... the way your father handled him ... he was amazing."

When they reached the foot of Broadway, the fog lifted. Gretta's emotional weight lifted as well, but questions still carped at her. "I noticed your mother wasn't there," she said.

"She and my father go their separate ways." Nelson thoughtfully adjusted the reins. "Have for years."

Gretta saddened at the thought. "I can't imagine what their marriage must be like, how lonely it must feel. That's kind of a shame, isn't it?"

"They seem okay with it."

"How has your mother been doing since she learned you have a sister?"

"Doesn't say a lot." He looked straight ahead. "I don't think she much cares."

Gretta gazed into the dark for a long moment then turned to him. "Doesn't that bother you?"

"The truth?" His eyes grew sad. "It depresses me. I wish she was capable of feeling something."

GRETTA'S MOTHER SAT ON THE SOFA, a magazine held high to a lamp, stifling a cough. Her bronchitis was getting worse again.

"Home so soon, dear? How was your meeting?"

"Amazing. When the weather warms up, why don't you think about coming, too? You might enjoy it."

Her mother folded the magazine and set it on the coffee table, fussing with it until it aligned with several other journals, and then she sat back. "Maude Millning handled herself okay?"

As Gretta hung her wrap, she smiled at her mother's accusing tone. "She was wonderful."

Her mother appeared surprised. "There weren't any problems, were there? I mean with Miss Millning's questionable reputation and all."

"Only one," Gretta said, baiting. "Other than that it went well."

"Well for heaven's sakes, don't keep me in suspense. What happened?"

Gretta happily shared the tale about the drunk, and Elias Prixton's response. "I get the feeling the gossip about Miss Millning has been shamefully overplayed."

"That Elias," her mother said. "So tell me, was it scary when things got out of hand?"

"No. There were too many people—"

"Gretta, why are you blushing?"

Confusion consumed her. "I feel guilty."

"Whatever for?"

She lowered onto the arm of the sofa. "Remember telling me how you thought Mr. Harrington couldn't take his eyes off of me? Well, tonight when things got tense, he looked at me like he wanted to protect me … like he was holding me with his eyes. Nelson saw it, too. It was embarrassing."

Her mother smiled. "Maybe that was good for Nelson to see. Have you thought about that?"

"But it didn't feel right, Mom. I was with Nelson, not Mr. Harrington. I know you don't trust Nelson. I don't either. Not yet, anyway. But one thing's for sure. He is trying. Awfully hard. And when it comes right down to it, can he trust me? I haven't jumped in with both feet yet, and that obviously hurts him. What was he supposed to think?"

Her mother appeared indifferent. "Things like that go right over a man's head."

"Not his. He asked me about it, remember?" Too restless to sit, Gretta got up. "When Mr. Harrington looks at me sometimes, I get all mushy inside. I love the way he makes me feel."

"I thought you said he ignores you at the office."

"Except for that," Gretta said, feeling embarrassed. "But I did hear what you told me. Haven't been able to get it out of my mind. There's nothing I'd like better than to believe he has eyes for me, but for all I know, he looks at every woman like that, Maude Millning included. And for as much as I'd like to be, I'm not in his league. I never will be. Besides, like I said before, he's doesn't plan to stay in Amber Leaf permanently."

"Gretta?" Unusual understanding revealed itself in her mother's warm voice. "Letting go of Nelson is rather like letting go of your father, isn't it? It hurts too much."

Her mother's words sliced deep. She nodded. "Warts and all, he was my dad. But there's more. Oliver Harrington aside, there's so much about Nelson's world I really do love, and at least he's available to me. Supper at his parents' home was amazing. They live in a fantasy world, have more than we could ever hope to have. You've got to see their place, Mom. I'd love to cuddle up with a book and stay there forever. They have a cook and a gardener. They host great parties. They go on exotic trips together. They have it all. Gorgeous home outside and in. Enough money to do whatever they please. Social standing. Good health. Is it so wrong to want that?"

"No. But they don't have trust, do they? You need to be careful, dear. Guard your heart with Nelson. I don't want you getting hurt."

"Mother, I also need to guard my heart with Mr. Harrington. I wish ..."

Gretta remembered how Nelson had responded to his mother's lack of response and her heart warmed. He said he wished she felt something.

For a moment Gretta felt at one with him for she wished she felt something, too—trust, peace, and no more confusion.

CHAPTER FIFTY-SIX

O ctober passed, as did November, and December drew near. On Thursday, Ollie enjoyed his first Thanksgiving at Deacon's home. He stopped by for Maude along the way. Ice popped on frozen mud puddles as they buggied past fields modestly powdered with snow. As for Maude, with the second meeting of the literary society surprisingly more successful than the first, she enjoyed an exceptional mood. But that was Thanksgiving Day. With the office closed on Friday, too few guests around, a near-empty dining room, and too much alone time, Ollie paced the halls.

Then came Saturday.

He loaded a shaving brush with soap and lathered his face. You will take pleasure in Elias's party tonight, he swore to himself. But showing up without a date felt much the same as showing up with shoes and no socks. He peered into the mirror and made a first pass with the razor. With no credible excuse not to go, and a golden opportunity to enjoy time with others, he would do well to make the best of it.

But Gretta would be there … with Nelson.

When he arrived at Prixton's at half past seven, carriages lined the road like boxcars at a railroad crossing. Elias met him at the door with a vigorous handshake and graciously led the way toward a fair young woman who, with ebony hair drawn up loosely and striking eyes the color of sky, resembled Snow White. "Mr. Harrington," Elias said, "I would like you to meet my daughter, Carole."

Ollie found it difficult not to stare. She was more beautiful than her picture if that was possible. "You have no idea what a pleasure it is to meet you," he said.

As they clasped hands, Nelson stepped up with Gretta at his side. "Nice you could make it, Harrington."

Ollie's heart fluttered as Gretta shied away. Somehow it didn't feel right … her with Nelson. She was far and away the loveliest in the room, even lovelier than Carole, and appeared displaced at the man's side.

But then neither did jealousy feel right, carrying with it an unpleasant resentment that Ollie felt a need to suppress.

"Son," Elias said, his tone carrying a condescending edge, "Mr. Harrington would like to get to know your baby sister."

Red poked up from beneath Nelson's collar and pushed up into his cheeks. "Guess we'll talk later."

An apologetic quality accompanied Carole's grin. "Would you mind if we talked later, too, Mr. Harrington? I don't mean to be impolite, but a new friend has been waiting for me in the library for close to an hour now."

Elias's admiring smile followed her as she walked away. "She sure knows how to capture everyone's attention, doesn't she?" he said.

Ollie gazed about, warmed by the enthusiastic chatter. "And you know how to throw a party. Let me guess. Fireplaces ablaze in every room?"

"And parlor games in the library if you find yourself getting bored." Elias rotated toward the door and took a step back. "If you'll excuse me, I see more guests have arrived."

"How'd you get an invitation?"

Ollie smiled at that surly voice from behind—Boss idly resting his back against the grand piano.

"Elias get the mistaken notion you were a prominent member of society or something?"

"Appears the man's not too bright," Ollie said. "Where's the missus?"

"She's not what you'd call sociable." Boss blew out a puff of smoke and tapped his cigar against an ashtray, barely a smidge of residue falling in. "But neither am I, so we get along fine. You meet Carole yet?"

"I did enjoy the pleasure."

"No wonder Elias was so willing to own his past." Boss glanced past Ollie. "Nelson looks like he feels replaced. The boy could easily be right."

A cellist, violinist, and harpist played soft chamber music in the background. "Nice sound," Ollie said.

Boss rolled his eyes. "And to think I was about to start snoring."

The men listened as the ensemble finished their piece. When they laid aside their instruments, with Gretta nowhere in sight, Nelson pulled a bench up to the piano. He gave Boss and Ollie a subtle nod then played softly, as if he were alone in the room. At the end of his first piece, Elias appeared from seemingly out of nowhere and said in a not-too-soft voice, "I hired *real* professionals to entertain for the evening, Son. Our guests would be better served if you got out there and mingled."

"Be happy to," Nelson said, pink rising from under his collar a second time.

Boss gave Ollie an are-you-thinking-what-I'm-thinking look. "If I didn't know any better," he said, "I'd say Nelson was playing pretty well, but then I don't have an ear for music. How about let's hunt down something to eat?"

Tables lining the walls of the dining room overflowed with festive food. "Glad the wife ain't here." Boss flaunted a telling grin. "She'd slap my fingers if she saw my plate." He stabbed a large hunk of beef, heaped it on, then looked up. "Say, about that game of chess, you up for a little friendly competition? Or are you a scaredy-cat, afraid of getting whipped?"

Ollie snickered. "I'll take that as projection."

Soon after they arrived at the game table. Boss said, "Bearing in mind I'm the one who signs your paychecks—"

"Bearing in mind, I'm the one keeping the money rolling in …" Ollie went on to win the first game by a sizable margin.

Well into the second, Elias happened by. "How's it going, gentlemen? Having a good time?"

Boss eyed the absence of chess pieces on his side of the board. "All depends on where you happen to be sitting. I smell a little cheating going on."

Elias laughed.

Again Nelson approached. "Father, do you have a moment?"

"In a minute, Son." Not only did Elias not look back, he sounded impatient. "Gentlemen, enjoy your game." He turned and walked off, Nelson finally getting his ear.

Ollie picked up his queen and slid it across the board. "Check."

"Now how do you expect a man to crawl out of a hole like that?" Boss plucked up his pieces. "I get another chance. This time, I'm winning."

"Okay, but no whining if you lose."

"Hey … who's Boss?"

After another three successive wins, Ollie stood. "Time for dessert."

He picked up a large piece of pie and headed off with saucer and fork. "I want to own a home like some day. Think I'll do a little exploring. Want to tag along?"

Boss thought for less than a second. "You're on your own."

A long and narrow pantry with slender windows and a washbasin abutted the kitchen. Freshly potted herbs sat along its windowsills. Fresh baked cakes, pies, and cookies lined long counters. At the other end of the narrow expanse, a connecting door led into what? A mudroom?

After exploring the north side of the mansion, Ollie retraced his steps past the living room, library, parlor, and down a long, wide hallway. Hearing a whimper, he peered through the sliver of an opening at the furthest room. Recognizing a fragment of burgundy velvet, he recalled Gretta's gown and eased open the door. "Gretta?"

She gasped then took a self-conscious step back.

"Nelson?" he said.

She nodded.

"May I come in?" Ollie didn't wait for an answer. "Haven't seen much of you this evening."

Gretta fidgeted with her handkerchief, words apparently escaping her.

"He does appear to be having an unusually difficult time tonight," Ollie said.

"I know." She continued stroking the edges of her handkerchief with trembling fingers. "One minute he's wonderful, and the next he can be so cruel."

"Do you think it might have anything to do with his sister?"

"Definitely. I know he loves her," Gretta said, "but he can't handle sharing the attention and he's taking it out on me."

"I've noticed that Elias is being pretty tough on him, but it doesn't seem right that Nelson's passing that on to you."

Tears welled in her eyes. "First, I'm humiliated in front of you at the office. Now here."

"You mean with John Brown?"

She nodded again.

What was it about Gretta that made Ollie want to open up? He didn't want to help himself. "I can't help wondering why you put up with it, what's holding you back."

She laughed lightly. "I don't know."

"What was your father like?"

"You would have been impressed with him. Everyone was. He was multi-lingual, well educated, worldly, a compulsive poet cloaked in a winning personality, and he had an extremely high IQ. But he was also a narcissistic alcoholic. Couldn't hold down a job. Ran through all his money leaving my mom with nothing. When he wanted to, he could be demanding and cruel and not give it another thought."

"No wonder you're having a hard time," Ollie said. "How could any child stand up to that?"

"How about you? What's your father like?"

"In some ways he's much like yours. Rules with an iron fist." Ollie stared at the oval carpet. "My wife was a commoner. He ostracized me when we got married … I lost her in a carriage accident some time back. Things went okay for a while, but when I decided to come to America, he shut me out again. He has yet to respond to any of my correspondence."

Gretta's gaze grew warm and sympathetic. "Do you feel like you need to win his approval, too?"

Ollie smiled. "Only at every turn. But you, Gretta, of all people, have the world at your feet. I know it's none of my concern, yet … on the one hand I can see why you want to stay with Nelson, but on the other?"

She laughed self-consciously. "I know. He keeps snookering me back in, and I keep taking the bait. He gets nasty again, and I'm back to this awful need to prove myself, like I need to get him to believe in me."

Ollie leaned his back against the dresser and folded his arms. "You don't need Nelson to believe in you. *You need you* to believe in you."

She let out a slight gasp, appearing surprised, and then she cut loose a coy grin. "When it comes to your father, how are you any different?"

Ollie winced. "Looks like we both pack a heavy wallop." And then he smiled. "May I offer you a ride home?"

"I'd like that, but thanks anyway. I'll be fine. And Mr. Harrington?"

"Yes?"

"Thank you for being such a gentleman. I wish with all my heart Nelson could be just like you."

Ollie didn't know what to say to that. Feeling awkward, he turned and walked away.

Carole stood at the entry of the library. "Mr. Harrington, I've been looking for you. We never did get a chance to talk. How can I ever thank you for giving my mother and father back to me?"

He smiled warmly. "I merely picked up the pieces. It's your brother who did the heavy lifting."

"Speaking of brother, I haven't seen him in a while. Any idea where he could be?" Carole turned and searched the room. When she meshed eyes with him, he hurried to join them as if on cue.

"Are you having a good time, sis?"

"The best of my life."

"Good." Nelson looked around distractedly. "Say, have either of you seen Gretta?"

"I believe you'll find her in the back room." Guiding him by the elbow, Ollie walked part way down the hall then stopped. "Nelson?"

"Yes?"

"Gretta is a delicate flower," he said. "Treat her tenderly ... always."

After Nelson walked off, Ollie kicked himself. What a foolish thing to say.

At half past eleven, Ollie took the long buggy ride back to the hotel, thoughts of Gretta lingering. He had talked to her about meaningful things. She didn't shrink from feeling. She appeared honest, straightforward, and unspoiled. They both had fathers who had been a challenge to please. But Nelson aside, he clung to the memory of how she made him feel—admired and appreciated. No party in the world had the power to make him feel better than that.

You NEED YOU TO BELIEVE IN you.

Mr. Harrington had meant well, but what good did it do to believe in herself when Gretta lacked the resources to back her needs? She ran her fingers through the folds of her dated gown and tormented herself with the memory of Nelson lighting up when the mayor's daughter had arrived. He wouldn't stop complimenting her beautiful gown. He was right about one thing. When it came to dressing, Gretta couldn't compete. But why criticize her in front of the girl?

The door pushed open. "I've—"

Gretta jumped.

"Why are you hiding in here?" Nelson said. "I've been looking for you."

She moved closer to the mirror and feigned fixing her make up. "I'll be right out."

Nelson searched her reflection from behind. "Hey … you've been crying."

Gretta wriggled away. "I'm okay."

"No, you aren't, and it's all my fault. I'm not at my best tonight. It was wrong for me to pass my hurt on to you, putting you down. I hope you'll forgive me."

Mr. Harrington's words rushed back. '*You need you* to believe in you.' He was right. She lifted her chin. "Nelson, if you ever put me down again in public or otherwise, I promise you, I'll return the favor. I regret that, but I don't know how else to stop you. If you had any idea how little money I have and how hard I'm trying—"

He reached out and gently touched her cheek with the back of his fingers. "I know. You are my delicate flower, Gretta. I need always to treat you tenderly."

She looked up at him, amazed that he could be that insincere and still keep a straight face.

Then she remembered her chat with Mr. Harrington and more of his words flooded back giving her another burst of hope.

Oliver Harrington had married himself a commoner.

CHAPTER FIFTY-SEVEN

1 December 1901

Dearest Family:

I continue to have thoughts of you often and again hope this let-ter finds you happy and well.

Today is Sunday and a heavy snow is falling. The town has all but shut down. Earlier this morning frigid wind poured through the sides of the windowpanes sending a chill to my bones. I've stuffed handkerchiefs, towels, and washcloths along the offending areas. Although the draft has subsided, I fear the windows appear rather unsightly.

We've been most busy at the office. How swiftly the weekdays tick past. On Sundays I attend services at a house of worship several blocks to the north and west of the hotel and am quite content there. In my spare time, I attend suppers, benefits, sport-ing activities and such.

As I write, I realize that more than five months have passed since I have resided in Amber Leaf, and I have yet to hear from you. At first I was concerned you did not possess my proper address, but then remembered that I included a return address on each of my posts. If you will allow me, I wish to write more about my decision to come to America. Perhaps I hadn't stated it properly. As a grown man, a widower no less, it would have been childish to ask your permission. Do know that my decision to leave had nothing to do with you, but everything to do with Emily. Memories in England were far too plentiful. The son I never knew distresses me to this day. I needed time.

On a more personal level, I recall speaking in a previous letter about a gentleman who had bouts of inappropriate behavior. I wish to revisit that as well to share a greater understanding. I fear I may have misjudged the man. I must remind myself to stay mindful of contempt, which can be equally inappropriate for Saturday evening last, I attended a festive gathering at his family home. From all outward appearances, the young man's father either knew not how or cared not enough to show proper attention or respect. The tragic young man appeared to fight for it in subtle ways throughout the entirety of the evening, but his father looked past him, seeming incapable of meeting his needs. Perhaps this is one of those sins that are passed down from generation to generation.

While unfitting to expect perfection from an imperfect world, I do know that watching that father and son interact brought warmth to my cheeks as I found myself realizing that I, myself, had been negligent in not learning to appreciate the gift of your stern hand. And now all of these years later when I witness firsthand the ill effects of neglect, I wish to thank you with a full heart for caring enough to correct me.

Now the cordial greetings from your loving son Oliver.

Ollie set the heartfelt letter aside, amazed at how easy it was to misjudge. No wonder Gretta had been tolerating Nelson's bad behavior, Nelson a victim of his father's cruel whims. Nonetheless she deserved better.

He got up and peered out into a sea of pure white. On Thanksgiving Day, Deacon had mentioned that when next it snowed, Ollie should consider joining the de Havens on a tobogganing adventure. Today would have been ideal. Ollie was tempted to go alone, but thought better of it. Better to wait on Deacon and his family. With every new adventure they shared, they were building wonderful memories. Sharing in the family's laughter, their pain, breaking bread with them, helping work the farm, spending Sundays and holidays together, building a warm and trusting relationship … was it possible for life to get any better than this?

A stray dog sniffed around on the sidewalk below. Ollie stood entertained for the longest while, wondering about its nose, how cold it must be, and what scent, if any, it could smell through a thick covering of snow.

As he pondered the simple thought, a horse and wagon swung around the corner. A grinning man on the buckboard looked up and waved. Deacon?

Ollie tore the cloths out of the crevices and threw open the window. "Good afternoon," he shouted. "What brings you out and about?"

Deacon pointed a thumb to the back of the wagon. "Wind's died down and there's some nice powder. The kids and me, we thought we'd try tobogganing. Come on out and have some fun."

Minutes later Deacon and his kids burst into laughter as he climbed onto the wagon.

"What is it you find so humorous?" He grinned. "Don't tell me you disapprove of my swaddling clothes."

"I don't know how to tell you this," Deacon said, still in the throes of laughter, "but it can't be any colder than twenty-five degrees out, and that's *not* below zero. With all that garb, you're going to get heatstroke."

Ollie laughed. "Aaah. Your blood has had opportunity to thicken being outdoors on the farm. Give me a chance, kind sir. I'll show you of what I'm made."

"You'll get your chance soon enough." Deacon glanced at the back of the wagon. "We brought a toboggan for you. Harley's been busy waxing them down. Haven't you, Son? Done a mighty good job, too."

Deacon flicked the reins and Old Horse broke into a trot. "There's a nice little hill overlooking Lake Amber Leaf I thought we'd give a try," he said, "but you gotta watch out for trees."

They had the pure white hill to themselves. Deacon insisted that Ollie begin on a far slope with fewer trees and a milder decline until he got the hang of it.

Ollie hadn't had so much fun in years—the wind in his face, the thrill of speed, navigating past trees, flying airborne over bumps. To his surprise, the trek back up the hill proved unusually strenuous, but he appreciated the opportunity to build strength.

After a half dozen runs, he felt more than ready. Advancing to the highest side of the hill nearest the lake, he positioned his toboggan, and shoved off. Acutely aware of trees whizzing past, he redirected his gaze to the hill below and a huge, unforgiving tree trunk looming immediately ahead. He and the toboggan split paths, Ollie rolling off into a snowdrift far softer than a feather bed and the runaway toboggan bouncing off the trunk of that tree at the base of the hill. Ollie doubled over with laughter. No damage to the sled, but the trek back up would be unnecessarily arduous. He pulled the toboggan up the long way, much easier to plod up the road rather than fight through drifts.

As he trudged along, however, a horse and buggy pulled up in front of a Tudor home overlooking the park. When the driver got out and escorted his lady friend in a cuddle all the way to the door, Ollie winced. For a moment, the man looked too much like Nelson.

But that was not possible.

The couple disappeared inside, and Ollie headed back up the hill.

They tobogganed for the better part of two hours, Ollie and Deacon racing like a couple of kids. Finally admitting exhaustion, they called it a day.

They loaded up the buckboard. "You are all welcome to—"

"What's the matter, Ole?" Deacon asked.

"That man over there … coming out of that house."

Deacon nodded. "What about him?"

"That's Nelson Prixton."

"And?"

Ollie felt as if someone had knocked the wind out of him. "He's two timing his girlfriend."

AFTER A HOT SUPPER AT THE hotel, Deacon instructed the kids to return to the wagon and pulled Ollie to the side. "Things are getting a lot worse at the plant over in Aspen. Looks like they're about to start a riot … Ole?"

"Yes?" Ollie said, taken aback by Deacon's forceful tone.

"I'll say it again. Stay away from there."

Ollie returned to his room. Stay away from the meat packing plant? How does one do that? How was it possible to diffuse a riot if no one intervened? And if Ollie chose not to go, who would? There was nothing he would like better at the moment than to knock a few heads together.

Later that night before retiring, he reread the letter he had written to his father. The part about staying mindful of contempt revisited him, along with the taste of tonight's supper. As if the problems at the plant weren't enough, having seen Nelson and his other lady friend left him numb. Misjudging him—again? Ollie felt the need to break his own rules about staying away from other men's stables. Gretta would be in for a lifetime of heartbreak if she refused to see the swine for what he really was.

CHAPTER FIFTY-EIGHT

Ollie tapped on the doorjamb and entered the office uninvited. "We've got a problem, sir. It's about Aspen."

Boss looked up, appearing irritated. "Don't tell me all is not well."

"Deacon stopped by yesterday." Ollie pulled up a chair. "He's concerned. I get the impression our initial tour of the facility was well staged and the problems dramatically understated. No wonder your friend Petersen was so amenable to drawing up a contract."

Color receded from Boss's cheeks. "How understated?"

"A couple of grumblers are busy setting fires. Things were already percolating when Deacon signed on. He's been doing his best to douse the flames, but fears things are out of control."

"Just how good is this Deacon?" Boss asked.

"Used to be a police officer if that's your concern. He's astute, and a great fence mender if ever there was one."

Boss kicked back in his chair. "Any hunch what's behind it?"

"Yes, sir," Ollie said. "Real life. The men have too much time to think. And talk. You can't blame them, really. The work is tedious, ugly at times, and repetitive, saying nothing about dangerous. They need something to do to stomach the monotony. Sounds as if their problems also need to be taken more seriously."

"What do you propose to do?" Boss said, his expression painfully sober.

"Thought I'd compare notes with Petersen. Take a ride over to the plant first thing in the morning. Have a chat with the leader of the pack. See what we can do to make their conditions tolerable."

He raised a brow. "Any idea when you'll be back?"

"Late afternoon, perhaps. I don't care to stay any longer than is necessary. Why send the message this situation is a hazard in the making?"

Ollie turned to leave.

"Harrington?"

"Yes, sir?"

"You sure you're up for this? With McKinley getting shot just because a man lost his job, the timing reeks. You never know if a copycat is lurking out there. You're walking into a powder keg."

"Don't worry. Bargaining is my specialty."

I hope.

"Watch your back," Boss warned. "Getting an angry mob to listen during heat of battle is akin to shouting into a tornado. You can only hope they read lips."

AT HALF PAST TEN GASPS FLOWED across the office like a tidal wave. Ollie looked up. A delivery boy positioned roses on Gretta's desk, by far the largest bouquet he'd ever laid eyes on. She sliced open an envelope. After plucking out and reading a card, she clutched the endearment to her heart, and turning to Nelson with a wall-to-wall grin, she mouthed a warm thank you.

And bile rose in Ollie's throat.

In the early afternoon, he called on her for dictation. "I have a few things I need to get done," he said. "Let's begin with a couple of notes. I'll need them for tomorrow's meeting."

"Tomorrow's meeting?" she said.

"I'm going to Aspen."

Taking on a look of trepidation, Gretta scribbled a doodle on her stenographer's notebook. "Why so soon?" she said beneath her breath.

So soon, or not soon enough, Ollie wondered. "Appears we got hoodwinked when we went on tour. There was a storm brewing behind the scenes."

"How'd you find that out?"

"Deacon de Haven. I needed a mole, someone objective to find out what's going on. He was the right fit for the job. Thought we'd try to do a little damage control."

Gretta's face bore the lines of concern Ollie felt. "What can you do?" she said.

"Calm down the key players?"

"How are you going to do that?"

Ollie shrugged. "Listen to their grievances?"

He felt her concern continue to grow.

"*Please* be careful," she said. "These things can really get out of hand."

Although Ollie did not want to broach the subject, he didn't particularly care for the subject they were on, so he said, "I noticed you received flowers."

She nodded. "From Nelson. They're breathtaking, aren't they?"

More guilt relieving than anything, but not that you'd care to know. "I take it things went well after I left on Saturday evening?"

"He knew he was in the wrong. Apologized profusely." She blushed. "He told me I was his delicate flower and he wanted to treat me tenderly."

Ollie's fist tightened and his stomach coiled into a knot. "He certainly is romantic, isn't he ... but can you trust him?"

CHAPTER FIFTY-NINE

The sun in his face and wind at his back, a horse and buggy, and virtually no distractions, Ollie turned over in his mind the serious complaints Deacon had revealed. He mulled over what it must be like to walk in the shoes of the rebelling men. Don't pick sides, he told himself. Listen to them. Offer concrete solutions. By the time he reached the plant, Ollie felt confident he could calm the players. But then he walked into Petersen's office.

"We have a problem, Mr. Harrington." Petersen's face scored with worry lines. "Red took it upon himself to play hooky."

"He's the leader, I presume?" Ollie said.

"The leader is a guy goes by the name of Bulldog. He's burly with a scratchy voice." Petersen shook his head. "You don't want to mess with him. Red's the most approachable of the group."

Ollie didn't particularly care for this great news. "How did he get word I was coming? Or did the man?"

Petersen blanched. "I'm to blame," he said.

Clearly the man had two left feet when it came to diplomacy. "You?"

"Yes, sir. I asked my secretary to set up our meeting in advance. Thought that might make things easier for you. He must have compared notes with the others and they decided not to play our game."

"If that's the case, this is far worse than I'd imagined." Ollie eased onto a chair. "Looks as if we'll need added protection. Have you called the sheriff?"

Petersen took on the look and smell of fear. "Do you really think that's necessary?"

"How many leaders are there?" Ollie said. "Three, right?"

"Try five."

"Five?" Ollie tugged at his collar and adjusted his tie. "Very well then. Let's invite the rest of them in. We'll query them one at a time."

Petersen sent his secretary into the plant to round up the insufferable character nicknamed Bulldog. She returned twenty minutes later with resignation emitting from her eyes.

"Where's Bulldog?" Petersen said.

"He didn't show up for work today either."

"Okay, let's try Big John."

She shook her head.

Petersen gulped. "You mean to tell me he's not here either?"

"I took a walk past all of their posts. None of them are here." The tiny wisp of a woman nervously wrung her hands. "And it gets worse … I got malicious stares every place I went."

Ollie thanked her for help. As soon as she left, he said to Petersen, "You have five men absent from work without permission? And a plant filled with hostile workers? At this juncture, perhaps it would be the greater part of wisdom to call in the sheriff."

Within the hour, the sheriff, who went by the name of Shorty although he stood shoulder to shoulder with Ollie, strolled in. "Gentlemen, I hear we have a situation brewing."

After Petersen laid out the problem, the sheriff said, "All is quiet now?"

"Appears to be," Petersen said, his tone unconvincing.

"Without a problem or hint of threats other than hateful stares and absentee workers, I'd say we don't have much to work with. As far as your absentees are concerned, I would defer to company policy. If I were you, though, I wouldn't pay them a dime for unauthorized time off. As to whether or not you want to reinstate them, that's up to you. And as for the other workers, if and when things turn violent, we'll be at your door. Until then, I advise you to lay low for a few days. Give it the weekend. See if they organize, make a play. Anything breaks loose …"

Ollie and Petersen ate an early lunch at a nearby café. They worked through logical strategies, discussing in detail every possible scenario. At half past one, Petersen said, "Be sure to watch yourself on the way back. Let me know the minute you get to Amber Leaf."

Bothered that problems had been allowed to swell this far out of hand, Ollie shook his head. "I can handle myself." He then hopped in the buggy and headed due west. The early morning sun beaten back by a dreary gray sky further dampened his mood while the horse's breath, visible as it lumbered along, exacerbated the sensation.

The unrest at the plant had been in the offing for quite some time. Petersen had sensed something wasn't right, but said no one had bothered to step forward. When he asked a subtle question every now and then, no one responded. How could anyone reason with men who refused to talk? Were they afraid? If so, of what? If Petersen had a fault, it was being too lenient. He was not the sort of chap who invoked fear.

Several miles west of town, Ollie tensed at a distinct rush of horses' hooves resounding in the far distance behind. Boss's words backed up on him. 'You're walking into a powder keg.' As did Petersen's advice. 'Be sure to watch yourself on the way back.' And then there was Deacon's warning. 'Stay away from there.'

The rumbling intensified.

Ollie's skin prickled and his breathing became labored.

Whoever was approaching did so in a wicked hurry and with more than a horse or two in the herd. He maintained a steady gait, easing the buggy closer to the side of the road. Stay calm, he told himself. Restless riders need clear passage.

In a rush, a gang of bandana-covered faces rounded his buggy and overtook him. His horse reared. Before Ollie could make a move, a rider swiftly lunged in and snatched its bridle.

Stay calm and in control, he chided himself. "Gentlemen?" He glared at the opposition, not caring for the odds. "How might I help you?"

A giant of a man with blazing eyes and deep gravelly voice said, "We ask the questions, not you."

Bulldog. Burly with a scratchy voice. *Don't mess with him.*

The man pointed to another rider. "You there. Grab a rope. Hop on board. The rest of you lend a hand. Gag Harrington. Tie him up. And while you're at it, blindfold him, too. Let's grab the reins and get outta here."

They know my name?

After hurriedly maneuvering the buggy around, they headed off for worlds unknown. Wherever his abductors were taking him, it could not be far. They would not want to risk meeting anyone along an open stretch of road hauling a blindfolded man. They might get recognized. As they traveled on, Ollie listened for distinct sounds and slipped names, and attempted to judge distances, counting the number of left and right turns and their sequence as he mentally mapped what he was unable to see.

Not more than five minutes later, they pulled off a main road, took a few hairpin turns down several other lesser roads, then journeyed across what must have been a field. The buggy swayed and squealed angrily over rock-hard clumps of earth before coming to an abrupt halt. From the distinct lack of sound, they were out in a no man's land.

Someone clutched Ollie's elbow and pulled him out of the buggy with a forceful yank. He staggered, attempting to right himself. A shove forward and he was pushed into a hollow-sounding building, his feet sinking into something crunchy. A tug, and his blindfold fell off.

He glanced around nervously, and his eyes bulged. They were in a silo. Claustrophobia blew in like a cyclone. He had to do something to get out of here lest he go mad. He moaned through the gag, but his abductors ignored him. Terrified of getting locked in this dungeon for any length of time, he held his breath, hoping his face would grow red, hoping more that he would pass out. His heart raced. Opening his eyes saucer large, he bawled through the cloth again. Finally, someone said, "Hey, this guy's in a panic."

Desperately keeping his wits about him, Ollie made a quick study of his captors while he still had a chance.

"What's he trying to say?" Bulldog said.

Concentrate on *them*, concentrate on *them*, Ollie chided himself.

"I don't know," a big man minus a finger said. Soft spoken for his size, he must be Big John.

"Can't breathe?" Bulldog stood nose to nose with Ollie. "Is that what's bothering you big fella? Don't tell me you got the asthma? Can't handle being in a silo, can ya?"

Ollie shook his head vehemently. He could never admit he was terrified of confined spaces. These men would torture him for sure.

"Well, we can't let him *die*." Bulldog scowled. "Yet." He turned to his cohorts. "Rip that gag off him. Give him some air. Let's get him outside. Of all the fancy men in the world," he said with a disgusted shove, "we would have to end up with a hoity-toity who needs to be slapped around with frilly gloves."

Ollie bolted outside and with hands still tied behind him, he continued putting on what he hoped was a convincing show of wheezing and gasping for air, which under the circumstances he found easy to do.

"What're we gonna do with him now?" a man with a deep voice and swollen knuckles asked. According to Deacon, he would be Bubba, the arthritic.

Bulldog looked around. "Well, the silo's out. Granary, too. I think we're gonna have to stuff him in the shed."

"But there isn't any heat in there."

Ollie glanced back at the silo and shuddered. He welcomed the absence of heat to getting stuffed into that thing any day of the week.

"He's gonna have to be okay," Bulldog said. "We'll toss in a sleeping bag and light a lantern. Now that he's returned to the world of the living, gag him again. Tie his hands. He tries to make a break for it, we tie his feet, too. We can't chance him getting away."

CHAPTER SIXTY

Nostrils flaring at the assault of mold, dirt, and axle grease, Ollie peered into the rundown shack, but his feet refused to move. *Yea, though I walk through the valley of the shadow ...*

"One of the boys'll be right back," a husky voice barked after a rough push through the grating door.

He must be the one they call Animal.

"And don't you go trying nothing funny."

Bound and gagged?

Dull daylight seeped through filthy cracked and broken windows cut into three sides of the weather beaten shed. A grimy workbench ran the full length of one wall. Empty shelves. Naked hooks. An upended crate box. Roughhewn wooden floors that creaked. Biting winter air seeping through slits in wallboards. Things could be worse, like being holed up in that wretched silo. He still shivered at the visual.

Roughly an hour later, heavy footsteps crackled on hard snow, the door grated open, and a bundle hit the floor with a thud. A man, less a bandana, backed into Ollie's temporary living quarters. His hair the color of rust, face blotched with freckles, and graying beard chuck-full of cowlicks, he carried a lantern and folding chair in one hand, and a steamy bowl of beef stew in the other.

"Here's some grub." The man plopped the bowl on the workbench.

This had to be Red, the most reasonable of the lot. He nodded at the bundle. "That's your bed. If we can't find comfort at the plant, you ain't gonna find it here. I'm gonna untie you and pull your gag off, but be forewarned. We got rules. You don't speak unless spoken to. You do, you get gagged again. Try an escape, you'll have Hades to pay. Do I make myself clear?"

Ollie nodded, giving a second thought to the word reasonable.

Red stepped behind him. Ollie's head jerked back and the gag popped loose. Another pop, and his hands broke free.

Seconds later, Red stopped at the door. "It'll be dark soon. I'll be back at first light. Sleep well, Harrington … and keep an eye out for rats." He laughed wickedly. "They grow huge around these parts."

Ollie did not flinch. "Thanks, Red."

But Red did. "Say, who told you my name?"

"Easy guess."

The door closed harder than Ollie would have liked, as did the falling latch.

He had no idea how hungry he was until he dug into the stew. Good stuff, especially for prisoner food. After eating his fill, he placed the empty bowl near the door, pulled out his handkerchief and wiped down the windows. Twilight reflected off a white blanket of snow. Nothing but barren fields and clumps of trees poking up here and there as far as the eye could see. He shook his head. How was it possible to plan an escape through Siberian terrain without leaving a Hansel and Gretel trail?

With no books to read and nothing to do but think, he gathered splinters from the workbench and plugged the gaps in the wall boards as best he could then wiped down the workbench and looked over the floor. Where are the brooms when you need them? He cleared a wide swath of floorboard and managed a dozen pushups, each one an effort. An office job was clearly making him soft.

He drifted from grimy window to grimy window and studied the layout of the buildings. Granary. Wretched silo. Stable. Barn. As fate would have it, a farmhouse appeared to stand behind the one wall that had no windows. No way to see how large it was, how far away, or the comings and goings of his captors.

Ollie pulled up the folding chair and planted it next to a window, pondered the narrow drive leading toward a country road, and evaluated his options. First and foremost, he needed to figure out a way to get his hands on a horse in the middle of the night when everyone was sleeping. Move quiet, fast, and ride bareback. But that was unlikely to happen. He could never fit through a window and unless the door was left unlatched, it would be impossible to break out of the shed. He would do well to differentiate and memorize the sounds and direction of voices, footfalls, and stomping of horses' hooves, though. He knew he had five abductors, but were there any lurking around that he hadn't yet seen? He needed to work out their game plan, find out what they were after, and influence their thinking. But that required patience ... and time he was not certain he had.

How long before anyone would know he was gone? And what good would it do when they finally found out? How could anyone find him shivering in a shed out in the middle of nowhere? Besides, he was new to the area. Who would even care? But then he remembered Deacon and regretted questioning. And Gretta, dear, dear Gretta. She had to care, too. He felt it in his heart. Fortunately, she knew about Deacon, as did Petersen. Deacon was Ollie's only hope, but did he know about a hiding place? What would it matter? It would be impossible to venture out even if he did. There was no way to escape down that long narrow driveway without being seen, much less heard. These men were incensed. Ollie had spent enough time in the military to know that those justifiably angered react impulsively and loathe anything smacking of resistance.

Well into the night, he wearied of concentrating on his environment and decided to turn in. He folded out the sleeping bag, slipped out of his woolen coat and laid it across the length of the bag for added warmth, slipped out of his boots, and crawled in. The floor felt concrete hard and every bit as biting. It would take a few long minutes to warm himself. He rolled up his neck scarf, using it as a makeshift pillow, and angled his fedora against his forehead to salvage body temperature. He desperately needed help. Before closing his eyes, though, he looked around one more time. There wouldn't be any rats in here, would there?

Well into his sleep, he awoke with a start. Calculated footsteps easing along hardened snow. Ollie's heart picked up its pace. He thought he heard breathing. Must have been his own. A rifle fired, exploding the dark, and he jumped. And then a shout. "You got him."

More boots, running boots, and another shout. "Clean through the heart."

Ollie hunkered down. Keep out of sight, keep out of sight, he repeated to himself.

"That's what he gets for coming so close to the house."

That was Bulldog's voice.

"Help me get him outta here, boys."

"He's a big one."

Big John?

"Heavy, too," Bulldog said. "Let's drag him to the barn."

Ollie fought for breath. Yea, though I walk through the valley of the shadow … He lay still for hours staring at the ceiling, sickened by the callous responses to the halfhearted taking of a life.

What were these men—no, these animals—capable of?

CHAPTER SIXTY-ONE

At first light, the door groaned open. After last night's rifle blast, what now? Would Ollie spend the day doing hard labor digging a stranger's grave into frozen earth? Would he face a rambunctious firing squad? All he had to protect himself was his wits. His size would stand against any man, but against a weapon?

Red backed in, dropped off a pot of steaming coffee, plate of scrambled eggs, side of bacon—amazing food for a captive—then picked up the empty plate from the night before.

Though he left without uttering a word, through narrowed eyes, his loathing spewed.

Boss stopped at Gretta's desk and tapped a thoughtful finger. "See anything of Harrington yet?"

"This morning? No sir. Why?"

"Said he'd be back late yesterday," Boss looked around nervously, "but I haven't seen hide nor hair of him. Give Petersen a call, will you? Ask him what gives."

A sense of foreboding swept on Gretta like an osprey on its prey. *Please be at the plant.*

A brief telephone call later, she delivered the unsettling news. Boss stood behind his desk and looked at her resignedly. He already knew.

"He left yesterday afternoon at half past one," she said. "Mr. Petersen asked him to call when he got back to Amber Leaf, but evidently Mr. Harrington looked irritated by the request."

Boss pulled out his chair and sat down hard. "Petersen didn't bother to follow up?"

"No, sir. Said he didn't feel comfortable. And one other thing ... I heard fear in his voice."

I hear fear in my own voice, feel it in my heart.

"Run over to the hotel," Boss said. "Tell them to check Harrington's room. Go with them. Don't be afraid to look over their shoulder. See if anything appears out of the ordinary."

He lifted his chin and bawled through the open door, "Hilda?"

"Yes, sir?"

"Check the livery stable. See if they've seen or heard anything from Harrington."

Fearing what awaited her, fearing more what didn't, Gretta's boots barely touched the sidewalk as she half walked, half skipped to the hotel. She hurried into the lobby. No one at the registration desk. After anxiously looking about, she ascended the spiral staircase taking the steps two at a time. On the second floor landing, a maid carrying a heaping basket of soiled linen eyed Gretta curiously.

"Please," Gretta said. "I need to get into Mr. Harrington's room right away."

The maid took a step back. "Oh, no, ma'am. I could never do that."

As if she knew where she was going, Gretta took the lead. "Please. Knock on his door. If no one answers, peek in. That's all I ask."

"I need permission from the office to—"

Gretta wanted to grab the woman's keys and run. "I stopped by on my way in. No one's there ... I work with Mr. Harrington. He didn't show up at the office this morning. We're worried sick about him. I'll be happy to stay out in the hallway and wait, but please, please do something. We desperately need your help."

The maid, appearing to sense Gretta's sincerity, nodded. "Come with me."

The maid headed down the hallway with a sense of urgency then lightly knuckled the door. "Mr. Harrington?" She knocked again. "Mr. Harrington, are you in there? Someone's here to see you. Someone from your office."

No response.

The maid slipped a skeleton key in the keyhole and nudged the door open. Peering through a crack, she said, "Looks like no one's here."

Gretta slipped from behind and pushed into the room.

"Please, ma'am," the maid protested.

Gretta's fear escalated, fear as uncontrollable as a rabid animal's. "I'm sorry, but I have to check his sheets. If he slept in his bed last night, they might still be warm."

She slipped a hand under the covers. "No," she said through a break in her voice and quickly eyed the room. All in immaculate order. Few women were this tidy.

"Don't worry," she said to the troubled maid. "You did the right thing."

Not more than five minutes later Boss stood waiting for her, his expression grim. "Well?"

"Mr. Harrington never made it home last night," she said.

"Did you see anything out of order?"

"Not a thing. I even checked his bed. The sheets were ice cold. Any word from the livery stable?"

"Yes, ma'am. They needed the buggy today. Harrington said he'd have it back last night no later than six. Promised even. But he never showed. I called Petersen. You were right. Man's a mess. I'm sure the sheriff is at the plant by now."

Gretta drew her arms around her waist, holding herself. "Did Mr. Petersen say anything about Deacon? If anyone knows anything, it would be him."

Boss nodded. "Deacon's a part-timer out at the plant. Of all the rotten times to not be on the job, it had to be today. I'm sure they plan to grill him first thing in the morning."

THE SUN WARMED THE SHED, BUT not by much.

Ollie spent the morning memorizing the men's voices. Bulldog wielded complete control. Must have done something to gain the men's respect. Not a word about last night's kill. But the men did appear restless, wandering out into the cold every few minutes. A name leaked here, a strategy there.

The noon hour passed with no lunch. By mid afternoon, Ollie's stomach set to growling. The last thing he wanted to face was a mandatory fast.

By mid afternoon, it became apparent his abductors were purposely taking their time to make their next move. They wanted to show strength, how determined they were about their fight, and they wanted to make Petersen sweat.

A steady stomp of boots plodded from the farmhouse. Ollie pulled out his pocket watch. Half past four. Food at last? The door flew open, and in marched Red. "Venison," he said as he plopped another steaming plate on the workbench. He picked up Ollie's empty breakfast plate and slowly backed out, the latch falling hard.

Venison? Ollie gaped at the plate.

Last night's rifle shot?

Nothing more than a man dropping a deer?

GRETTA STARED AT THE DOCUMENT. IT wouldn't type itself, but she couldn't get going. It was as though the office was in mourning. The clocked ticked on and still no word from or about Mr. Harrington. Typewriters stilled. Everyone spoke in whispers, as if to honor the dead. But he wasn't dead. Not Mr. Harrington. As for Boss, he followed up with the plant every hour on the hour. No reports of an accident. No requests for a ransom. No word about anything.

At a quarter to five, Gretta hopped up, packed her things, and requested to leave a few minutes early.

"Why?" Hilda asked.

"There's something I've got to do."

CHAPTER SIXTY-TWO

Gretta dashed off to the livery. "Any idea how I can find my way out to Deacon de Haven's farm?"

She scribbled down directions and made a quick stop home, told her mother not wait up for her. Within tens of minutes, she tore down country roads at a full trot, the buggy airborne, more often than not lurching over treacherous ruts.

Deacon must have heard the clatter of determined buggy wheels. To her utter relief, he and one of his sons ran out to meet her.

"I'm Gretta Van Dyke. I work with Mr. Har—"

"We know who—"

"Mr. Harrington. He's missing."

"Missing?" Deacon's voice filled with alarm. "How long?"

"Since yesterday afternoon."

Deacon grew pale. "Say, he didn't go to Aspen, did he?"

She nodded. "I'm afraid so."

He swatted his cap against a pant leg. "Drat! I warned him. Told him not go."

Deacon had warned him? What was Mr. Harrington thinking? "They say he started back at half past one, but never made it home."

"Why does that not surprise me?" Deacon scoffed. "He walked right into a trap. Of all the days to not be at the plant."

Gretta squirmed on the buggy seat. "We've *got* to find him."

"What are we gonna do, Pa?"

"This here's my boy Harley," Deacon said. "Let's think this through for a minute. I've got an idea where he might be. Problem is, I've never been to the place, so we've got our work cut out for us."

"What kind of place is it?" Gretta said, her first inkling of hope blossoming.

"Deserted farm. One of the boys at the plant spilled the beans a week, maybe two weeks ago when he was digging through his lunch bucket. Said they call it their hiding place. It's where they hold secret meetings."

Deacon looked up into the wintry night sky. "There's nothing like a bright moon and snow to light up the road on a dark winter's night," he said. "That'll sure help with finding the place, but it'll also be our undoing once we get there. We need to plan this right. It's dangerous enough as it is."

"Shouldn't we notify the sheriff?" Gretta said.

"We could, but that introduces a whole new ballgame that could get rough real quick, especially with the mood those boys are in. I'm thinking it might be safer for all concerned if we handled this ourselves."

Her heart leaped. "I get to help."

Harley shook his head. "Sorry, miss, but this is man stuff. It's not safe for a girl to tag along."

"Wait, son." Deacon kicked at the ground. "The boys, they know me, but they don't know you. You might pose a threat."

"But I wanna go, Pa."

"I'm sure you do. But we've got to play this smart. The way I've got it figured, we sneak up on 'em, they're gonna smell a skunk for sure. We need to catch 'em off guard, remove any threat, be in control, and stay in control. And that's not going to be an easy task." He turned to Gretta. "As for you, I could use your help. I handled this kind of situation before when I was on the police force. Got an idea I can't carry out on my own. I know those boys. They won't hurt a woman. They're all married folk themselves and they've got kids. Son, I'm thinking it might be best if you rode into Aspen and teamed up with the sheriff. You willing to do that?"

"Sure am."

"Let 'em know where we are and what we're up to. Give us a couple of hours. Be at the ready out by the main road. You hear anything threatening, come running."

"I'll bring—"

"No. Don't bring your brothers. They're too young and this is too dangerous, you hear?"

"Yes, sir. But where is this place?"

"I've got a sketchy idea. The man said something about a red bandana on a fencepost by the turnoff out on the main road. That'll be easy enough to spot. From there, we head due south and east. If my memory serves me right, he said there's a rusty wheelbarrow in the ditch. That's where we turn off to the farm … God be with you, boy."

Deacon turned to Gretta. "I'll be right back."

Please, please hurry.

He disappeared into the house and a short while later rushed out fully dressed in winter garb, carrying an extra lantern, a shotgun, a Bowie knife, and packing a holster. He climbed into the buggy and they tore off.

"We can't do this just the two of us," he said as they pulled out onto the road. "We'd do well to stop back in town first and pick up Maude."

"Millning? Whatever for?" Gretta said.

"Those men aren't going to feel threatened if they see an older woman at my side. And Maude? She's fearless. Knows how to talk better than any man I know. You've seen her in action. If anyone can calm down an angry crowd, it's going to be her."

That's what I thought about Mr. Harrington, too, but look how wrong I was. "What about me?" Gretta said. "What do you want me to do?"

"Why don't we keep you in hiding under a blanket at the foot of the buggy? While Maude and I distract and defuse the boys, you sneak around and try to find Ole."

"Ole?"

Deacon nodded. "Oliver. Do you think you have the courage to do that?"

Gretta's heart hammered, perspiration pouring out of her palms. "Of course, I do," she said through a cracked voice. "But how will I know how to find him?"

Deacon looked out and about. "There's a light enough dusting of snow tonight to make tracks. Follow the freshest ones. Check the basement windows first. Unless he's tied up in the house someplace, they're going to have to go out and attend to him, bringing him food and such. If you don't find him, get back in the buggy and hunker down under the blanket again until we come out."

But what if you don't come out?

What if he isn't there?

CHAPTER SIXTY-THREE

Wheels grating on gravel, Gretta looked out across passing fields, anxiously anticipating the task before them. What they would find. What she feared they wouldn't find. The dangers that lurked about. She glanced at Deacon and Maude. They were lost in their own worlds of thought as well.

Far too soon the farm loomed into view.

"Let's pull over and assess this situation for a minute," Deacon said.

Gretta white-knuckled the buggy seat. "Aren't you scared?"

Deacon laughed. "Sure, I am. That's what makes this so much fun."

"But what if something goes wrong?"

Maude seized Gretta's arm, her voice steady. "Let not your heart be troubled, neither let it be afraid."

Deacon's head snapped in her direction. "Maude Millning—"

She smiled into the dark. "I may have left the church, but I never did leave God."

He peered around her. "Are you afraid, little lady?"

"Wish I could say excited, but yeah, scared to death."

"Don't be. God already knows how this is going to end, and from the powerful knowing He's given me, we're going to be just fine. Now get down on the floorboard, pull that blanket over you, and hang on.

"Heee-ya!" he cried and the buggy took off with a start.

"Hello, the house … hello, the house!" a call cried out loud enough to wake the dead.

Ollie shot up and pressed his nose to the window. A horse and buggy bolting up the narrow drive at a full gallop? "What in the …" Some halfwit waving a lantern as if deranged?

He pulled back for a second. That voice. It had a familiar ring. He pressed his nose to the window again and squinted. Deacon?

No!

To make matters worse, a woman sat at his side. Through the light of the lantern, she looked too much like Maude. What was the man thinking?

From behind the shed emerged a rushing rumble of boot drops and a chorus of shouts. The gang of angry men descended on the buggy, blocking it from view. Ollie suppressed a shout. That would only serve to further endanger Deacon and Maude.

"Hey, what're you doin'?" Bulldog said with an unmistakable sneer in his tone. "How'd you find this place?"

"Put those rifles down, boys," Deacon said, his voice solid, confident. "You won't be needing them. We're here to help. You're in a heap of trouble. If we figured out Oliver Harrington's been kidnapped and we found you, so will the authorities."

"What makes you so all fired up sure he's here?" Bulldog challenged.

"Don't play coy. That's beneath a man like you. Now how about if we all go inside and have a nice little chat?"

Ollie scowled. Why the house? He'll lose his ringside seat.

"I'll stay out here, Bulldog," one of the men said.

"No," Deacon insisted. "We need to make sure we're all reading from the same book, same page. Can't afford to make a mistake."

Bulldog's voice took an unpleasant edge. "We don't want your help."

From what Ollie could see, Deacon appeared unruffled. He slipped a hand around Maude's back and nudged her on. "I don't care what you want. You're going to need it. We'll discuss it further once we get in the house."

Red stepped forward, blocking Ollie's view. "Wait a minute. Why the woman?"

"We'll talk about that, too."

"Have it your way," Bulldog said, "but you won't be needing that shotgun."

"And you won't be needing your rifles," Deacon shot back, "but you're carrying 'em anyway. We'd better get going. Don't have much time."

A door slammed shut and the only sound Ollie could hear was his own breathing. He peered out the window again, longing for the sound of life, when in the distance something moved. Something black. He squinted. The figure slithering across the yard like a viper appeared fixated on the ground then disappeared behind the shed. He watched. Waited it out. A forever moment later, it appeared again. A man? Sneaking around under cover of a blanket? That made no sense. Had he seen light from the lantern? Ollie snuffed it out. Whoever he was, he was inching toward the shed. Ollie stretched to get a better look. What if this was a trick? What if one of the men held back to apprehend him, relocate him, or worse? … Not the silo!

Ollie slid behind the door, back flat against the wall. The catlike creature glided past a side window and out onto the main yard. Holding the wrap above his head, the creature appeared to continue his search of the ground. Whatever for? The man turned and made a beeline for the shed. Swift, stealthy footsteps grew closer. Footsteps light as an Indian scout. The latch eased open, as did the door. Ollie leaped forward and grabbed his abductor from behind, reaching to cover his mouth when a strange scent of something sweet assaulted his senses. What was that he smelled? Not cologne? He let go his grip.

And she turned on him. "Mr. Harrington, what are you doing?"

"Gretta?" he said, stunned.

"Of course, it's me."

"What are *you* doing here?" Ollie snapped. He wanted to shake her. "Do you have any idea how dangerous this place is? I'm supposed to be the knight in shining armor. The one who rescues damsels in distress. Not the other way around."

"You sure are ungrateful," she snapped back.

"What's Deacon thinking bringing a couple of women out here?" Ollie was beside himself. "We aren't dealing with the likes of Billy, Mickey, Joshua, or Stephen, for crying out loud. These men are no-nonsense players. Tough as loggers—Bulldog, Big John, Bubba, Animal, and the lightweight of the group is another one not too many would want to wrestle with. Man by the name of Red."

Thin moonlight bathed Gretta's beguiling smile. "Deacon knows what he's doing," she said. "Maude's in there with him. He thought she'd be good at calming down a crowd of out-of-control men."

"But he doesn't have any backup," Ollie spat.

"Does, too. A militia's out on the main road. Harley rode ahead to get them. They're going to give us a couple of hours to get the job done and then they'll come running."

Ollie's eyebrows drew together involuntarily. "Is that a fact?" he said. "And what's Deacon planning to do for protection?"

"He's got a shotgun."

"A *shotgun?*"

"And a gun in his holster."

Ollie could not believe his ears. "Against all those rifles?"

"A Bowie knife in his boot."

He shook his head. "A Bowie knife," he repeated.

"Yup. And a derringer in his other boot. He walks kind of funny."

Under more favorable circumstances, Ollie would have chuckled. "One man and two women?"

Gretta peered out the window. "We can't see the house from here. We've got to get outside."

Ollie reached for her coat sleeve. "Why?"

"Soon as Deacon and Maude get control of the crowd, she'll give us a signal and we need to rush in."

"Us? No, ma'am. You aren't going anywhere. Get back in that buggy where you belong and be sure to cover yourself up."

"Can't," Gretta said. "Someone might be lurking around out there. I'll be a lot safer with you. Besides, it's too spooky outside alone."

Enjoying her spunk, Ollie sighed. "What am I going to do with you?"

"Forget about me. You'd better get your act together … You're going to have to perform."

"Me? Perform?"

"Yup. I hope you're good at impromptu speeches. Deacon assured us that if anyone knew how to make everyone live happily ever after, it would be you. We'd better get outside."

What a night! "What kind of signal is Maude planning to give us?"

"You'll see."

They crouched behind a towering pine where Ollie got his first good look at the house. Typical white two-story farmhouse with a small front porch. Untypical circumstances. Lights on. Too quiet. And a room bursting with snarky faces.

CHAPTER SIXTY-FOUR

Maude stumbled out onto the porch doubled over with a coughing jag.

"That's the signal," Gretta whispered. "Let's go."

"Why not tell us to come in?" Ollie muttered beneath his breath.

Gretta shot him a look. "Deacon didn't want to give the men time to get riled."

"A little late for that, isn't it?"

The instant Maude, Ollie, and Gretta slipped through the door, the men eyed one another and scrambled for their rifles.

Deacon sprung into position, aiming his shotgun directly at Bulldog. "Wouldn't do that if I were you."

"What's going on here? And who's she?"

"This young lady found him, and he's here to try to talk some sense into your heads."

Bulldog snickered. "Ollie Harrington? You expect us to listen to some lightweight who goes by the name of Ollie?"

"Name's Ole," Deacon said, "but to you it's *Big* Ole. Get my drift?"

Ole smiled. He understood. *You win, Deacon. Big Ole Harrington, it is.*

"You boys play nice," Deacon said. "I have a few words to say before I turn the floor over to him ... and you *will* listen."

Bulldog frowned. "Make it quick."

Deacon cradled the gun. "There's a militia waiting out by the main road about now, so like I said, we don't have much time."

"Why you double-crossing—"

"Let's cut the baloney. You men are too smart not to expect that, so let's get on with it. As for Big Ole, he knows what's been going on. I've been briefing him."

The men grumbled among themselves, but Bulldog quieted them. "Let's hear what the man has to say. Maybe he'll *astonish* us," he scoffed.

"Let's keep this friendly, boys." Deacon turned to Ole. "I know these men. Spent time with them. Met their wives, every bit as lovely and feminine as Maude and Miss Van Dyke here. Met their kids, too. Cute little rascals. These men aren't predators. They're men who care. Care about their profession. Care about their livelihood. Care about feeding their families. But their jobs are tough and there's no excuse for making them tougher. They need to be heard is all. That said, have at it."

All five men crossed arms across barrel chests, chins held high, eyes spewing daggers. Friendly audience if Ole had ever experienced one.

"I had a T-bone supper the other night," he began. "Venison tonight. Amazing cuts of meat carved by artists."

A couple of the men chuckled and Bulldog rolled his eyes. "You ain't talking to a bunch of flunkies. Save the flattery for someone who can stomach it."

"You think I'm not sincere?" Ole said. "I've heard about you men, the trials you've been enduring."

"Oh, yeah? Where were you then?"

"He was doing his job," Deacon said. "Now let the man talk."

Ole nodded. "At my request, Deacon agreed to work for me, to be an infiltrator."

Bulldog pushed to his feet, eyes blazing. "Why you dirty —"

Deacon leveled his shotgun again. "Simmer down. You'll get your chance to talk later … go ahead, Ole."

"We got wind trouble was building at the plant before we signed up with Petersen. Thought it wouldn't hurt to check it out. I know Deacon. Trust him with my life. There was nothing in it for him, yet he agreed to help. Whether you choose to believe it or not, he is your friend, and he's done an amazing job of presenting your side."

Red opened his mouth as if to speak, but quickly closed it again the instant Deacon redirected his aim.

Ole turned first to Bulldog and looked him square in the eye. "After ten years at the plant, your new boss relocated you to the kill line. Why? Simply because he decided he didn't like you. To make matters worse, he replaced you with an upstart. That would get my hackles up, too. And you, Big John, lost a finger because you were exhausted from working too many hours and lost your ability to concentrate. Animal, you're weary of being the one man who has to round up stray cattle that don't make a quick kill. They come charging into your work area as if it were a bullfight and you the matador. Can't think of anything more dangerous. Who could blame you for resenting that constant threat?"

As Ole called the men's names and articulated their complaints, one by one their gazes dropped to the floor.

"Bubba, your arthritis hurts you something awful, and yet they make you work in cold, wet rooms. And Red? One of your buddies lost half a hand to a meat cleaver. Why? He worked in too tight quarters, and the line was moving too fast. You're afraid you might be next.

"Your complaints are justified. Every last one of them. I'd be riled, too, if I were in your boots. And speaking of walking in your boots, you thought I was insincere earlier with my compliments, but I wasn't. You've got the moxie to do the dirty work few others have the gumption to do. Thing is, what would we do without you men? Sitting behind a desk every day, I feel like a … what was that word you used, Bulldog? Lightweight? Perhaps you're right. But before we go tearing down the management, I have a question. Have any of you bothered to let them know where the real problems are?"

"We all did."

"Yeah, we all did."

"We tell 'em all the time."

"Do you?" Ole said. "When's the last time you reported a problem, Bulldog? … Bubba? … Animal? … Big John? … Red?"

The men looked at each other with blank stares.

"That's what I thought. You make assumptions. That's natural. We all do. We assume people see what we see, hear what we hear, express what we ourselves have not expressed. Big John, do you remember how you filled out that report when you lost your finger?"

Big John appeared agitated.

"I read it," Ole said. "You didn't mention a word about the long hours you'd been working and how worn out you were. All you said was that you'd gotten clumsy. Remember that?"

Big John looked away.

"Petersen has a job on his hands," Ole continued. "He's a good man. Doesn't have time to read minds. We aren't a bunch of shy little school-girls. We're men. We see a problem, we deal with it.

"As for Petersen, you get hurt, he has to pay your hospital bills and find someone to take your place when you're off line. Either that, or the rest of you pick up the slack. No matter how you cut it, management needs you to get the job done, and you need management for a paycheck. The company doesn't owe you a job, but it does owe you sharp tools and good working conditions to get it done right.

"Now what I propose is that the five of you work with us to get this mess cleaned up. No supervisor has the right to abuse his workers. Supervisors are employees, too. They need their due respect, but don't hesitate to report them if they get out of line. As for you, you have the right to work in a safe environment that affords enough space and time to do the best job possible. Petersen has agreed to post a suggestion box at the entrance of the facility. You see a problem, write it down. It's not necessary to sign your name. This is about handling problems, not snitching on fellow workers or punishing them." Ole looked from face to face. "We all agreed?"

Bulldog raised his chin. "And if things don't change?"

"They have to. I can't say it enough. Management needs you."

Animal raised a hand and waved it like a school kid.

"Yes, sir?" Ole said.

"Are they gonna take us back? We did walk off the job."

"They don't, I'll pull our contract and give you my word I'll do all I can to help. Enough said."

Something crashed outside, sounding as if an empty milk bucket tipped over and went rolling.

"What's that?" Bulldog shouted.

The men bolted for their rifles and hit the floor.

CHAPTER SIXTY-FIVE

"Come out with your hands up."

"Hey, what is this?" Bulldog snapped. "You double-crossed us."

The men scrambled, backs to the wall, sneaking peeks through windows.

"It's the militia," Deacon said. "I told you we didn't have much time."

Ole motioned to Gretta and Maude, indicating they should crouch down on the floor. "Don't shoot, men," he warned. "I'll handle this."

"You think we're gonna trust you now?" Bulldog jammed the butt of his rifle through a window. Loud crash. Shattering glass. Shards spattering. "You're in with 'em."

"I said *don't shoot*." Ole flew to the door and shouted, "I'm coming out." One swift kick and it flew open. He trudged out onto the porch, hands lifted high. "We have women in here. Do. Not. Shoot."

The sheriff, who had been crouching behind an artesian well, slowly stood and lowered his gun.

"We're okay." Ole looked around and called out, "Sheriff, why don't you step inside with me. The rest of you men, consider yourselves dismissed."

"Hey," the sheriff protested. "This is my operation."

"You stand corrected. It's mine. Come along."

They entered the kitchen, Ole taking the lead. "What in the ..."

Red, Animal, and Big John restrained Deacon, Maude, and Gretta, hands behind their backs, while Bulldog leveled a rifle on them.

"For crying out loud, what are you doing *now?*" Ole said with a purposeful whine. "You're going to undo everything we just fixed. What's the matter with you men? Let the women go. Deacon, too. And Bulldog? You put down that rifle. Now."

The men looked at each other with question-filled eyes then reluctantly did as told. Meanwhile, Ole's knees buckled, not that he would let anyone see. And color returned to Deacon, Gretta, and Maude's cheeks.

The sheriff looked at Ole warily. "We do have a charge of kidnapping here."

"Is that a fact?" Ole said. "Who was kidnapped?"

"You mean to tell me—"

"These boys have been doing hard time at the plant. They have legitimate grievances. We've been negotiating. We get things straightened out and you come along rifle toting. The boys and I are meeting up with Petersen first thing in the morning to hammer this all out. You've come in vain."

The sheriff looked individually from man to man and back at Ole. "You're giving it to me straight?"

"I'm giving it to you the way it should have been from day one."

The sheriff shook his head. "Guess it's time to go home then. Gentlemen," he said. He tipped his cap, walked out, and cried, "Boys, time to head out."

Ole mumbled to Bulldog in passing, "I think you'd better see to getting that window fixed.

"Ladies? Deacon? Our carriages await."

"Wait, Mr. Harrington," Red called out from behind. The man was in a full run. "I'll fetch your horse and buggy."

Ole said his thanks and turned to Gretta. Her warm eyes glistened in the soft moonlight. There was nothing he would love better than to ride back to Amber Leaf, just the two of them together, but that would be foolhardy. Nelson still held her heart.

"Gretta, would you mind giving Deacon a ride in your buggy?" he said. "Maude and I will follow. We'll meet up at Deacon's place. From there, maybe Maude can ride with you to her place. After we turn in your buggy, I'll give you a ride home. It's going to be a long night."

A short distance down the road, Ole glanced at Maude who sat listless. "Tired?" he said.

She nodded and smiled. "What an adventure, though. I had the time of my life."

"You love a challenge, do you not?" Ole said. "Deacon must have been mad to haul you and Gretta into the thick of things."

"Don't be fooled," Maude said. "My brother is as shrewd as you. He knew precisely what he was doing."

"In the end, I believe he did," Ole conceded. "I find it curious, though. Gretta said Deacon asked you to calm the men down. How did you manage that? They were heated."

Maude plucked up the buggy blanket and snuggled it close to her chin. "You need any of this?"

He shook his head. "My heart's been pumping too fast. I'm nearly overheated. So back to my question. How did you calm the boys down?"

"Do you believe in God, Ole?"

"Ole?" He smiled at that. "I'd better get used to my new nickname. And in answer to your question, yes, deeply. He's the needle pointing North on my life's compass. Why do you ask?"

"Because we leaned on Him pretty hard." Maude rearranged herself on the seat. "I think the men sensed they had a friend in Deacon and in me. But they needed help getting past their anger, so I quoted a little scripture."

Scripture? "They didn't protest?"

"Sure they did. They were boiling mad and wanted to be, so I asked them if they were afraid. You know how you men are. Don't like admitting to fear … especially powerful men."

"I'll own that. What scripture did you recite?"

"The love chapter," she said.

Ole started to chuckle, but then thought better of his response.

"'Though I speak with the tongues of men and of angels, and have not love,'" she said, reciting the words as if they were coming from somewhere deep in her heart, words that she believed and lived, but then she stopped.

"Go on," Ole said. "We have time. Recite the entire chapter." As she recited the words explaining what love is and what it isn't, he grew acutely aware of how they could cut deep and challenge wounded hearts.

"But the mood in the room didn't change," she said, "until I reached the verse that said, 'When I was a child, I spoke as a child, I understood as a child, I thought as a child. But when I became a man … I put away childish things.'"

Maude nailed it. Though the men were anything but childish, she wisely drew their thirst by salting their oats.

Ole tugged gently at the reins, allowing Gretta's buggy a more generous lead, more distance from his longing heart. When they rounded the drive at Deacon's farm, Harley rushed out to meet them. "Tell me, Mr. Harrington," he said, "I thought you'd been kidnapped. Wasn't that true?"

Ole gazed into the eyes of his rescue crew. "Let's just say things would've unfolded much differently and not necessarily for the good had your father, your aunt, and Miss Van Dyke not come to my aid."

MAUDE SAFELY AT HOME AND GRETTA's buggy returned to the livery, Ole drove Gretta home once again. How he dreaded saying goodnight.

Another one of the most meaningful experiences of his life was already taking its toll, further strengthening an already deep bond. They rode silently down the darkened streets of Amber Leaf keeping their thoughts to themselves.

"It's hard to drive through your neighborhood at this late hour without making a clatter," Ole said, forcing conversation. "I hope we don't awaken your neighbors."

Gretta didn't respond.

"Are you upset with me?" he said.

She shook her head then looked away too quickly, which further concerned him.

He drew up in front of her home. "May I have the privilege of walking you to your door?"

"No," she said. "That's not necessary."

"I'll wait then. Make certain you get inside okay."

She nodded.

Ole hopped out of the buggy and helped her down. "Gretta?"

"Hmm?" she said, appearing to avoid his gaze.

"Thank you … for everything."

She seized his hand lightly. A moment later, she disappeared into her home, and Ole felt as if he was watching his world slip away.

GRETTA PEERED THROUGH THE WINDOW UNTIL Mr. Harrington rode out of sight. With a piercing ache in her throat, she yanked off her coat and boots, dashed up to her bedroom, and fell facedown on the bed, tears gushing as if from a spigot.

CHAPTER SIXTY-SIX

"Your early morning coffee, sir," a voice called through the door.

Ole groaned. He didn't want to get out of bed. Not in this freezing cold. He slipped bare feet into icy slippers … "brrrr" … and punched arms into a heavy bathrobe. At least the piping hot coffee kept his teeth from chattering.

After breakfast, he swathed a woolen scarf around his neck and over his chin, and inhaled deeply before heading out into the forbidding arctic air. What little breath he was able to take stung his windpipe like sharp cuts of a razor. The third long day of a cold snap, temperatures plummeted to well below zero and stayed there. Dangerously bitter winds. And this was to last several more days?

But in contrast, the town appeared transformed into a winter wonderland. Sun glistened off ice crystals, which frosted the lanterns and streets and barren trees. Footsteps, stomping horses hooves, and rolling wheels of carriages sounded muted as if transported through an enchanted tunnel.

Less than a block up Broadway, a carriage journeyed past. Nelson was driving, the mayor's attractive daughter beaming at his side. He glanced nonchalantly at Ole and waved. A block farther up Broadway, he stopped the carriage and helped the young lady down.

OLE LINGERED AT THE COAT RACK and looked back at Gretta's empty desk. The little wisp of a thing endured a good mile to get to the office and did so day after day without complaint. The thought alone of the days that had come and gone since the kidnapping with no more than words of business spoken between them chilled him like the numbing cold, yet it was only right to distance himself. Meanwhile, Nelson buzzed around her like a fly over a picnic basket. Though she appeared strangely indifferent to his attention, Ole read nothing deep into her lack of response. Why torture himself?

But what about this morning?

"Hello there," Nelson said, jolting him back to the present. "Is it my imagination, or were you waiting for me?"

"I know it's none of my concern," Ole said, "but about your passenger ..."

"You're right. It's none of your concern." Nelson ripped off his neck scarf and coat and flung them on the rack. "Shame on you. I saw her walking from the livery stable. She was shivering, so I gave her a lift."

Ole wanted to grab Nelson and give him a lift, but restrained himself.

"You would have done the same thing," Nelson insisted, "and you know it."

Ole looked again at Gretta's empty desk. "I notice your lady friend isn't here yet."

"Your point?"

Surely you need not ask. "If I were you, I would have driven to her home and given *her* a ride."

Nelson sneered. "I'm sure *you* would have, but you aren't me, are you? And it's tearing you apart."

CHAPTER SIXTY-SEVEN

The evening's meeting about to begin, Gretta kept a nervous eye on the entry. Nelson had explicitly asked her to save him a seat. 'I might be a few minutes late,' he said, 'but no more than that.' Where was he?

"Sure glad that cold snap is over," a man behind her said.

"Me, too," someone else said. "I wasn't going to come unless it let up."

For no good reason, she scanned the room. To her delight, Maude's literary society continued a hit, expanding each meeting by a handful more of participants. Tonight a few empty chairs remained. Three to be exact.

Her cheeks flushed when she briefly interlocked gazes with Mr. Harrington who sat across the room, alone. Who looked away first anyway? Her? Or him? She recalled their conversation in passing yesterday morning. He had glanced at Nelson and started to say something, but must have thought better of it. He stopped mid-sentence then walked off.

When Maude called the meeting to order, still no Nelson and the minutes ticked on. Gretta's concern mounting, about a half hour or so later, she discretely got up and slipped out into the balmy winter's eve. Soft laughter bubbled from somewhere nearby. She peered around a corner. A young couple in love. Lost in one another's worlds. Unaware of her presence, they continued to whisper and giggle.

Gretta squinted. Nelson? First an initial shock, then a sudden wave of relief. How right her suspicions. The scoundrel was cheating on her.

She was finally free.

As she took a step back, he looked up, discarded the young love interest like a worthless piece of trash, and bolted toward Gretta. "What are doing sneaking up on me?"

She suppressed a smirk. "What am *I* doing? You can't be—"

He scowled. "This is all your fault, you know."

Though she heard a loud clatter in the distance, Gretta was too absorbed with Nelson's shenanigans to look. She took another step back. "My fault?"

"I'm the one who wants to get married," he insisted, taking willfully slow steps toward her. "You're the one who keeps dragging your feet."

He reached for her arm.

She pivoted hard, wrestled out of his grip, and continued backing away, one slow step at a time and yet he kept coming. Her boot twisted. She lost balance. Stumbled.

A hard-charging buckboard careened onto her path.

The horse reared.

A bloodcurdling scream wailed into the night.

And Nelson bellowed her name.

"SOMEONE'S BEEN HIT," A MAN NEAR the door shouted.

Ole scanned the room and his heart pounded. He had watched Gretta slip out only a minute ago. *Please, God, no. Don't let it be her.* If he followed the crowd, he'd barrel over them, so he bolted out a side door. A man with purpose, he pressed hard through gathering bystanders, willfully, roughly shoving them to the side.

And there she lay. Covered in dirt and grime. Clothes torn. Cheek smudged. Unconscious. Beautiful, gentle Gretta.

Nelson hovered over her, nervously combing his hands through his hair. "It wasn't my fault. It wasn't my fault," he repeated as if in a daze.

Ole barked orders. "Get me a blanket." One flew at him from the buckboard. "I need a couple of you men to pull this tight for a make-shift stretcher. We must move her with extreme care. You and you, grab the ends. Deacon, help me roll her onto it. We must keep her stable."

They gently rolled her onto the blanket and hoisted her onto the back of the buckboard. Ole turned to the driver. "Let's get her to the hospital. Take it slow and easy until we get moving. We don't want to jolt her anymore than we need to."

As they headed up Broadway, he looked at the gaping crowd staring back at him with Nelson standing there slack jawed, helpless, white, and stunned.

Hours later the doctor, who looked as if he'd been up the past forty-eight straight, eased onto a chair next to Ole. "You family?"

"No. I expect her mother any time now. How is she, Doctor?"

He shook his head. "Doesn't look good. We'll have to wait it out. See how she does … if she'll even make it."

Ole's heart moaned.

"Internal damage. Broken bones. I'd advise you to ask family and friends to spend a fair amount of time on their knees. That little lady is going to need all the help she can get."

"May I see her?"

The doctor nodded and walked away, looking as if he were Atlas propping up the weight of the world.

Asleep in the pristine hospital room, Gretta appeared angelic, fragile, her chestnut hair splayed delicately across the white pillowcase. He pulled up a chair and placed a gentle hand on hers then swallowed hard against a painful lump chugging up his throat. "Gretta," he whispered. "Gretta, can you hear me?" He glanced at the clock. Half past midnight.

He could not leave her alone. No sign of her mother yet, and no sign of Nelson. What was that man thinking?

"Nelson isn't good enough for you," Ole said softly, the ache in his heart growing more painful by the second. "He needs to wake up. I would give the world to have your heart."

Her eyes broke open, warm eyes that appeared filled with love. Her lips moved, but no words would come. She fell into another deep sleep.

"My little girl," Mrs. Van Dyke cried as she rushed into the room.

Ole got up and swept the broken woman to Gretta's side.

"What happened to my little girl?" She choked through a sob. "Is she going to be okay? Has she awakened yet? Said anything?"

"No, but she opened her eyes briefly," he said, then shared the doctor's assessment.

"Who did this to her?" she said, taking on a bitter tone.

He had been wondering the same thing. Why Nelson's unlikely response? "I didn't hear what happened, but I'm certain it was an accident."

"Where did it happen, do you know?"

"In front of the hotel."

Mrs. Van Dyke's head spun toward the door. "Where's Nelson?"

Ole shook his head. "I have no idea."

"He's no good for her, Mr. Harrington. I've told my Gretta that."

A loud commotion sounded from out in the hallway. Reeking of cigar smoke and hard liquor, Nelson stumbled in. "Gretta," he said, tears dripping down his cheeks. "My dear, darling Gretta."

"What happened?" Ole asked. "You were there. What happened?"

Nelson hiccupped and flopped in a chair. "It was an accident. We were standing around talking and she got distracted. She turned and the next thing I knew, she fell right into the path of that oncoming buckboard. It all happened so fast. The horse reared. I think she got clipped by a wheel. It was an accident, I tell ya. A horrible stinking accident."

CHAPTER SIXTY-EIGHT

Gretta struggled to open her eyes, yet she didn't want to. Her brain throbbed. Felt like a giant cotton ball wadded tight inside her skull. It hurt to move—anything. Her arm. Her leg. They felt like hundred pound sacks of potatoes, too heavy to lift. Packaged tight. Tied down. She slowly forced her eyelids open and heard a gasp.

"Gretta? Sweetheart?" The familiar voice sounded as if it were in a wind tunnel.

The room spun. Everything appeared fuzzy. Then someone came into view, peering over her, and then another. "Mom? Mister ..." She focused harder. "Nelson." The word came out flat.

Her mother collapsed at her side and burst into tears while Nelson merely said, "Gretta," a pitiful crack breaking his voice.

"Don't cry, Mom. Please don't cry."

Her mother pulled herself up and wiped her eyes. "I'm sorry, sweetie. We've been worried sick."

Gretta looked about the unfamiliar room. "Where am I?"

"In the hospital."

"Hospital? What day is it? How long have I been here?"

"It's Monday morning," her mother said. "You've been here since last Wednesday night."

"Last Wednesday," Gretta repeated. She looked up at Nelson standing at the side of the bed. "You look like you haven't had any sleep in days."

"Can't say as I have," he said. "Not since the accident."

The accident. Gretta fought her thoughts. Searching. Trying desperately to remember. She did remember something, but what? A scream? A shout maybe? "What time is it?"

"About half past eight."

"In the morning?" Gretta questioned. "I've got to get to work. So do you."

Nelson snickered, his relief more than evident. "You aren't going anywhere. But now that I know you're back among the living, I'd better get cleaned up and make an appearance." He kissed her lightly on the forehead. "I love you, Gretta Van Dyke, with all my heart. I'll be back tonight."

As he disappeared from sight, a peculiar, sick feeling pestered her. Something wasn't right.

"You have no idea how frightened you had us," her mother said. "The doctor wasn't sure you'd make it, but it looks like you're going to be fine. It's going to take a while, though. Say, what happened with Nelson? He's been acting strange."

"I'm not sure," Gretta said. "Why? What happened? What kind of accident did I have?"

"He said you stepped into the path of a fast-moving buckboard."

"I wh—?" A bu—"

"That's right. Do you remember anything about it? Anything at all?"

"A little, maybe." Trying to remember brought her to the brink of exhaustion. "I'm awfully tired."

As the day progressed, Gretta slipped in and out of sleep, waking to an occasional thermometer poking into her mouth, a nurse taking her pulse, forcing down a spoonful of broth or sip of water.

By mid-afternoon, sun streamed through the windows as if stubbornly forcing her to become more alert. But she fought it. For with alertness came a muddied yet growing remembrance of what she preferred to forget. Nelson. The giggling. The cheating. Blaming her. If he hadn't had a wandering eye, she wouldn't have gone outside, wouldn't have backed into an oncoming buckboard, wouldn't be in the hospital. She would be at the office where she wanted to be. Where Mr. Harrington was. No pain. No bad memories. No needless wasting away of precious life.

Her mother sat lost in a book, slowly turning its pages. Gretta could never tell her about Nelson. About his indiscretion. Not under those unnecessary circumstances. Her mother would never forgive him. Why had Gretta ever given that scoundrel the time of day?

A cart rolled in carrying three vases of flowers. Next to them was a miniature pine tree jutting out of a basket of pinecones wrapped with red ribbon and a gorgeous bow. Gretta's heart leaped at the sight. She steadied it. Mr. Harrington knew of her desire for a miniature pine forest, but so did Nelson.

"Oh my, aren't they beautiful?" Mrs. Van Dyke helped arrange them on a table at the foot of the bed.

Lifting her head for a better look, Gretta flinched at a stabbing pain. "Who are the flowers from?"

"We're about to find out," her mother said. "Why don't we start with the smallest and work our way up to the large winter bouquet? Let's see." She plucked open the first card. "Get well soon." She glanced back at Gretta. "These are from your friend, Sarah." She opened the next card. "And this one offers best wishes for a speedy recovery and it's signed Opal and James."

"We sure have wonderful neighbors, don't we?" Gretta said.

"We sure do. And this large one wishes you a speedy recovery from all of your friends at Addison & Crowley."

No flowers from Nelson. Dirty. Rotten. Cheat. Nelson. Please, miniature tree … don't be from him.

Her mother opened the card dangling from the tree. "And this one says—"

Fearing her hopes had spiked too high, Gretta looked away, again flinching from another shooting pain. "No, Mom. Don't bother to read it. I know they're from Nelson."

"Oh, but you're wrong."

"I am?" Her heart fluttered. That's not possible. But please, please let it be. She held her breath. "Who sent them?"

"It says, 'A new tree for a renewed life for the loveliest patient ever. Oliver. M. Harrington.'"

"No! Mom. Please don't tease me. They aren't really from him, are they? Did he really say that?"

"See for yourself." Her mother handed her the card.

Gretta stared at it, recognizing that exquisite penmanship, reading the words over and over again trying to make them sink in. "I had a dream," she said, remembering back. "It felt real. So very, very real. I dreamed Mr. Harrington came into my room. He was sitting next to my bed, lightly touching my hand. And in my dream he said that Nelson wasn't good enough for me and that he would give the world to have my heart. I wish I didn't care so much. Before too long he'll be leaving Amber Leaf … read to me, will you? I need to get my mind on something else."

Her mother returned to her book. Although she read aloud, Gretta's thoughts drifted back to her Mr. Harrington dream and she slipped into a restful sleep. The next time she awakened, it was to a night sky, a dimly lit room, and another bowl of steamy broth.

Nelson arrived at seven o'clock straight up. Though clean-shaven and smelling as handsome as he looked, Gretta's first inclination was to ask him to leave. At the moment, he did not make her world a happier place.

He plucked a bouquet of roses from behind him. "For the lovely damsel in the hospital bed," he said. Then he looked at the other flowers and the miniature pine tree and did a double take. "Who'd you get *that* from?"

"Mr. Harrington," Gretta's mother answered for Gretta, and beamed. "Mr. Oliver ... M ... Harrington."

Nelson looked as if he wanted to throw something. Gretta wondered which that might be—his flowers, or Mr. Harrington's tree.

"How are you feeling?" he said through tightened jaw. "Better?"

"I guess. How was work?"

"More of the same."

How quickly Gretta ran out of words. It appeared as though Nelson did as well. Within tens of minutes, Boss stopped by for a brief visit as did Hilda, merely to say a warm hello. As they headed for the door, Mr. Harrington stepped in, his presence noticeably sucking the air out of the room.

Gretta's heart soared. "Thank you for the pine tree," she said. "You remembered."

Rather than respond, he nodded an acknowledgment, looked to Nelson who sat sour faced, and then shook hands with Gretta's mother. "Good to see you again, Mrs. Van Dyke. Too bad it isn't under more pleasant circumstances." He turned to Gretta. "How are you feeling? To say you had us worried is an understatement."

"She's really coming around," Nelson answered for her.

"Yes, I'm—"

"The doctor assures us she's going to be fine," Nelson interrupted.

Though Mr. Harrington gave Nelson a strange look, he did smile warmly at Gretta. "I can't tell you how pleased I am to hear that ... you need your rest, so I won't stay. I merely wanted to say hello, see how you're doing. You look much better than you did Wednesday night, that's for certain."

"I ... I what? You mean you saw me after the accident?"

Mr. Harrington nodded. "You might say that. Deacon and I brought you to the hospital."

Her gaze found its way to Nelson. "But I thought—"

Mr. Harrington lightly touched her hand, precisely the same touch she'd felt in that very real dream she'd had. "He came later." A warm sadness permeated his kind eyes. "You'd better get some rest."

CHAPTER SIXTY-NINE

For the next number of days, Gretta convalesced in the hospital, her chances for full recovery improving with each passing day and her opportunities to reflect inexhaustible. Nelson often appeared at her side during the noon hour, in the evenings following grueling days at the office, and on occasion during the entirety of visiting hours on a Saturday or a Sunday.

Despite her insistence that he was under no obligation to come, he continued to wander in. During each stay, he picked up a book or pad and pencil and said little, Gretta holding a book as well. The two of them would begin where they left off, merely sharing time breathing in the sterile hospital air, his guilt painfully evident in his countenance, and in what he chose to and not to say.

Although his remorse appeared heartfelt, after days of this, Gretta regarded his presence a millstone.

"Nelson," she said one late January evening, "you're bearing a load that isn't yours to carry. You aren't responsible for my accident."

He set his book aside, his face drawn with sadness.

"I wasn't paying attention," she said. "I'm the one who stumbled in front of that buckboard. You didn't push me."

"What's the difference? You went outside looking for me to make sure I was okay. If I hadn't cheated on you—"

"It was an accident," she said forcefully. "I'm letting you off the hook."

He shook his head. "It's no use, Gretta."

She needed to get through to him, but found his resistance wearing. "It was obvious you had affection for whoever it was I found you draped over. You have my blessings. To be honest, you've done me a favor."

He looked as if he was about to cry. "You can't be serious?"

Gretta no longer cared. "Oh, but I am. You've shown me who you really are. The thing is, I need someone I can trust. Now, please … you're free to go. I'll see you at the office as soon as I can climb the stairs again."

He looked at her blankly as if she had spoken not a word. He eased onto the edge of her bed, and seized her hand. "What I did was despicable," he said, his tone humble and contrite. "That girl meant nothing to me. I guess I have more of my father in me than I want to admit." He stared off. "… using women as play things. That's horribly wrong. I know that now, but …" His voice fractured. "… but it was you who paid the price. I don't know how I can ever make that up to you, but I want to with all my heart. I don't deserve you. But if you wouldn't mind, spending time with you means the world—"

Mr. Harrington walked in at a swift clip, froze in his steps, and took a step back. "I've come at a bad—"

Of all of the inopportune times for him to walk in, why now? Gretta jerked her hand away from Nelson's, her heart ripping. "No, please," she said, "you aren't interrupting anything. Please, come in."

Mr. Harrington shook his head. "No, really, that's quite all right. I prefer coming another time."

As he turned to leave, Nelson got up, kissed her lightly on the forehead against her wishes, said a quick and loving good night, then trailed Mr. Harrington down the hallway.

"HARRINGTON," A VOICE CALLED OUT. "WAIT up."

The fine hairs on the nape of Ole's neck stood on end. He sensed this was a conversation he preferred not to have.

"How about a coffee somewhere?" Nelson said.

"That won't be necessary," he quipped.

"Oh, but it is."

"Very well, then. Perhaps we might meet at my hotel?"

"Sounds good. Want a lift?"

"I prefer walking. See you in the coffee shop."

He buttoned his coat and raised the collar. Stuffing hands in pockets, he trudged on. What was the matter with Gretta? She let Nelson sit on the side of her bed and hold her hand. Nelson was an unscrupulous cheat. Why did she not choose to see it? Ole must have misjudged her character.

A short while later he sat at a table across from Nelson and choked down a cup of coffee he didn't want.

"You've been seeing a lot of Gretta?" Nelson said.

"Not a lot. I stop by on occasion, but she's often sleeping, so I don't stay. Why do you ask?"

"Because she's my woman. I'm going to marry her, and I don't appreciate anyone cutting into my territory."

Nelson defined the term rat. "By anyone I assume you're meaning me?" Ole said. "That's what this chat is about? Me cutting into your territory? From what I observed in the hospital room, you have no worries. Your little soirée with Gretta appeared rather intimate."

He grinned that coy grin of his, the one that made Ole want to slam him up against a wall. "Like I said, she's going to be my wife."

Ole lifted his cup, cradling it with both hands, his gaze fixed on it. "Does Gretta know about your little trysts?"

"What's that supposed to mean?" Nelson said, his tone innocent.

"It means I've seen you."

He continued to play dumb. "If you're talking about giving the mayor's daughter a ride on a freezing morning, aren't you out of line?"

How dare the man? "I'm talking about an afternoon after a heavy snow. A young lady living in a house near the lake … across from that hill where everyone goes sledding?"

Nelson smiled an empty smile. "That didn't mean anything. You know how we men are. Things get serious, we get scared. Need to make sure we're doing the right thing."

"Correction," Ole said. "Not men who know what they want."

Loathing spewed from Nelson's eyes. "You see yourself as superior, do you?"

"On the contrary. I see myself as solid."

"If you're so solid, what are you doing sniffing around another man's property?"

"Man, you say?" Ole got up and tossed a couple of coins on the table. "I hope some day soon that property of yours wakes up. She deserves better."

CHAPTER SEVENTY

O le ascended the staircase one miserable step at a time, fighting the disillusionment roiling in his belly. He must have misread Gretta's heart. Her intimate holding of hands with Nelson revealed more than he cared to know. He didn't want to see her again. He couldn't see her again. Not ever.

One evening soon after, he returned from the office dog-tired. As he passed by the registration desk, the attendant called out, "We have a letter for you, Mr. Harrington. It arrived earlier today."

He glanced at the familiar penmanship and his heart leaped. Too excited to stop for supper, he hurried to his room, and tore the letter open. It read …

1 January 1902

Our dearest Son:

Time slips past so quickly. It is hard to comprehend that we have already cut into the year 1902. Your mother and I hope this letter finds you hail, hardy, and well.

At Harrington Manor, the holidays were kind to us this year. We had the privilege of attending a number of festive gatherings, and I am pleased to say that we continue in good health.

We received with gladness your latest letter indicating that you have finally learned to appreciate my stern hand. Perhaps I was wrong. Perhaps your travel to the United States was of great benefit. You seem to have grown in wisdom, of which you never were in want. We are proud of you, Son.

I write bearing splendid news. I am most pleased to tell you that Meacham has formally submitted his resignation, and a position is now open at his firm, which you have the ability to fill with an impressive degree of competence. I have purchased one-way passage for you on a ship bound for England on 15 April. Your ticket shall arrive soon.

We so look forward to seeing you once again.

Now cordial greetings from your loving father and mother,

Lord & Lady Harrington

Ole carefully folded the letter. Fifteen April. Before Nelson's chat, he would not have considered passage back to England, but now he wondered. He had enjoyed success professionally and treasured his time with Deacon and family, but romantic love was not to be. He glanced at the calendar. Several months to enjoy the de Havens. Several months to wrap up his assignments at Addison & Crowley. Several months to live in the land of Gretta.

Several months of not seeing her.

Several months.

He tapped the letter on his palm and glanced at the door. Time for supper. But he found himself not particularly given to appetite. Not tonight.

CHAPTER SEVENTY-ONE

O n a balmy day in early February, Gretta was wheeled to a waiting carriage, her mother walking alongside. "Now it'll be you taking care of me," she said, concerned.

Her mother smiled. "Somehow I seem to have gained the strength you've lost. Haven't felt this good in years."

They arrived home to a path of planks leading to the back door. Her mother disappeared briefly and returned wheeling out a spindle chair with rollers attached to the bottom of each of its four legs. "Nelson's been busy working on this during his days off. This is precisely what the doctor would have ordered."

"Nelson did that for me?"

Her mother nodded. "It's a shame that rascal has to have a good side, too."

Early the next morning she started her new routine, each day performing strenuous, painful rehabilitation exercises. To her amazement, her strength grew rapidly. When not pushing herself physically, she wiled away the hours with a wicker basket at her side and busied herself with darning, knitting, and crocheting. She read books and magazines, but for the most part, she drew endless sketches of that beautiful miniature pine tree.

And all the while she listened for that special knock. One day soon

Mr. Harrington would stop by again, wouldn't he? A wave of remorse rippled through her, for since the night he caught her inadvertently hand holding, only Nelson had bothered to stop by.

A full week of days later, Gretta rolled her chair to the table where during daylight hours she helped her mother cook and bake, things easily done while sitting stationary. This time she came to frost a cake.

"Gretta, dear, is the pain worse again?"

"Hmm?"

"The pain? You've been working that same small area of icing for the better part of five minutes now. The cake is going to dry out before you get it covered."

She gazed at the calendar on the kitchen wall, her focus on the month of February, the day with the number fourteen etched on it. The thought of sharing Valentine's Day as an invalid in the company of Nelson Prixton seemed utterly unbearable. It was as if her heart had withered and died.

Later that evening he arrived uninvited. After her mother excused herself, retreating to an upstairs bedroom, she once again shared her misgivings.

A pathetic look washed over his face. "I've tried," he said, "but it's useless. I can't live without you."

She sighed. "Your words don't work for me, Nelson. Never have. I have no desire to punish you, and I'm not meaning to be unkind. But I keep telling you that I appreciate your efforts and all of the kind things you've done for me, but it isn't necessary for you to come see me. Yet you insist on it."

His lips quivered and tears formed in his eyes.

She lifted her chin. "Nelson, we're done. Now, please …"

"I don't mean to be a pest," he said, "but I will earn your trust again."

"Then please … start seeing others. I will only trust you when I know you are no longer a part of my life, when I know you can't hurt me any more."

He shot up. "Your decision wouldn't have anything to do with *Lord* Harrington, would it?"

"*Lord* Harrington? I'd give my eyeteeth if you could be even remotely the quality of man he is. If you were, I would give you my whole heart and soul. But you aren't, and therein lies the problem."

"Not for long," Nelson said.

Her heart thumped at the ominous forewarning. "What's that supposed to mean?"

"He's leaving for England the fifteenth of April."

She tensed. Please don't cry now, she castigated herself. You'll have plenty of time for that after Nelson leaves.

"His father already booked passage for your knight in shining armor to leave this fair land. Harrington said he's taking a train bound for New York a week before that. His last day at Addison & Crowley is Tuesday, April eighth. Hilda already booked train passage for him on the ninth."

Gretta shook her head, clutching desperately onto hope. "I don't believe you," she said.

"Why not?"

"Because you've lied before. You tell untruths whenever it's convenient. You tell untruths to protect yourself. You even tell untruths to purposely hurt others."

She caught herself. What was she doing taking her hurt out on Nelson? What if this time he was telling the truth?

"I'm sorry," she said with an adamant shake of her head. "I'm so very, very sorry. I have no right to talk to you like that."

She stared after a retreating Nelson and pinched her eyes closed.

She would get better. She had to. She would be back in the office by April eighth if it was the last thing she ever did.

CHAPTER SEVENTY-TWO

Hilda slipped her hands through the arms of her woolen coat, her ripened features difficult to read. "Any special plans for the weekend, Mr. Harrington?" Her tone sounded uncharacteristically baiting.

"Nothing other than the usual."

"My husband and I are planning a quiet one," she said as if that might be of interest to him, which it wasn't. "Our big day is Monday. We always go out for supper to celebrate Valentine's Day."

Ole didn't care to hear about that either.

"When I was younger, I always looked forward to that day."

Nor that.

She hesitated. "I've been meaning to ask you ..."

Here it comes.

"Have you seen anything of Miss Van Dyke? Heard how she's doing?"

Ole shook his head. Why was Hilda doing this? "Not since she was in the hospital."

"Does she have any idea you'll be leaving for England soon?"

Perhaps. Perhaps not. Gretta was beautiful, single, *and taken*. Nelson had made sure he knew that. As for Ole, he was a widower, and indeed leaving for England. Why Hilda's concern? "I have no idea."

"I'm stopping by on my way home," she said. "I want to see how the dear girl is holding up. Show her we still care."

"Please pass on my good wishes," he said.

She donned her gloves, fastidiously pressing them tighter, finger by finger. "Mr. Harrington, don't you think you should be the one to deliver your news to her?"

Ole managed a sober face, but it wasn't easy. "I fear my boundaries feel a trifle overstepped."

Hilda's nose inched higher, her tone assertive. "So be it. I make no apologies. For the short time you've been in Amber Leaf, you and that young lady have shared more meaningful events than most of us experience in a lifetime. She rescued you from an angry mob, remember? And you helped save her life with your quick thinking the night of that dreadful accident. From what I've heard, she would have died from internal bleeding if it wasn't for your quick action. No, sir, most of us never get an opportunity to bond like that, and not for lack of wanting."

GRETTA JUMPED AT A LIGHT KNOCK. The instant she opened the door, Hilda descended on her. "Gretta. Dear, dear Gretta. You're looking wonderful, but how are you feeling?" She sniffed at the air. "Smells *divine* in here."

Gretta laughed. "I'm feeling much better, thank you, and we'd love to have you join us for supper."

"I'd love to, but I can only stay a minute. My husband cooks. Knowing him, supper's already on the table."

After a few minutes of pleasant chitchat, Gretta said, "How are things at the office?"

"Other than the hole you left behind, everyone's doing fine."

Before giving herself a chance to feel, she forced out the words,

"How's Mr. Harrington? I heard a rumor he's going back to England soon."

Hilda fumbled with her gloves. "It's more than a rumor. He's returning in April. I told him I was stopping by. He asked me to pass on his good wishes … Gretta?"

She hurt too much to talk.

"You aren't okay. That's what I thought," Hilda said. "You have a soft spot in your heart for him, don't you?"

Gretta gulped. This conversation with her immediate boss was off limits.

However, Hilda did go on to say, "He hasn't seemed himself these past weeks. I'm not sure what's going on with him, but it's clear something's up."

CHAPTER SEVENTY-THREE

All weekend long Hilda's chastising words stuck like flypaper. Ole and Gretta had indeed forged a deep bond. A true gentleman wouldn't sail the high seas without a fond farewell. He jabbed an arm through the sleeve of his coat. Why give it further thought? Just do it. He would go, not as a suitor, but in his professional capacity as one of her supervisors. Surely Nelson could not object to that.

But it was Sunday. No florist would be open on a Sunday. What to bring? On second thought, perhaps it would be best to go empty handed. Awkward, but best. No pretense.

When he arrived at her home at half past two with an extra flutter in his big, strong heart, he cursed his hand trembling in anticipation as he lightly rapped on her door. Gretta didn't seem to do much better. She appeared flustered, quickly tucking away loose strands of hair.

"I didn't think I'd … I didn't think you'd … please, have a seat," she said. "Hilda stopped by on Friday night, and now you. Mother, would you please take Mr. Harrington's coat and hat? I'll be right back."

She quickly wheeled on a makeshift chair to a back room only to return with well-coifed hair.

"I'll be brief," Ole said. "I wanted to see how you're doing. It appears you're getting on well."

Her eyes radiated. "I'm growing stronger with every passing day." After an awkward pause, she said, "The miniature pine you gave me when I was in the hospital? That's the most priceless gift I've ever gotten."

"I can attest to that," Mrs. Van Dyke said. "My daughter loves drawing sketches of it from every angle imaginable. Now if the two of you will excuse me."

Ole tensed. Mrs. Van Dyke's presence muted the acuteness of his feelings. "That's not nec—" he said as she disappeared from sight. As for Gretta, her features appeared to sadden at his protest, which confused him.

"I wanted to tell you personally that I'll be returning to England in several months," he said. "My passage has already been booked." He looked about the room. "There are memories and sights in Amber Leaf that can't be duplicated in England. I wish I could bring photographs of them with me, but there is not a camera that could do justice to the images. Deacon's farm." He smiled self-consciously. "That farm near Aspen where you rescued me ... I purpose never to tell my father about that one. There's Fountain Lake. Spring Lake. Lake Amber Leaf. Addison & Crowley. But none of these are to be bested by the wonderful people I feel so rich to have met. You included. If I don't see you again before I leave ..." His throat cinched on him. Why did it have to do that? "I want to thank you more than words can convey for everything—your loyalty, dedication, and admirably hard work."

Were those tears welling in Gretta's eyes?

He stood. "I'd best be leaving. You, uh, get on well. And do give my best to your mother."

His exit was more abrupt than Ole had intended. That strange lump still strangled his throat, drawing pain. But it was over. He had done the gentlemanly thing. Maybe now he could get on with life, redirect his attention to a future in England, and not hold on to a past that offered nothing beyond disappointment and pain.

alentine's Day. A long and lonely day at that. Ole departed from the office on Hilda's heels. After ordering room service, he fluffed his pillows and readied himself for a long lonely night of reading. Correction. A long lonely Valentine's night of reading. He wasn't about to eat supper surrounded by candlelit tables occupied by cooing lovebirds. Nor did he care to listen to a stringed ensemble performing sugary music or warm himself by the fire. Any fire.

If he could not be with Gretta, he did not care to be with anyone.

GRETTA NEEDED THIS DAY TO END.

At half past seven, the door inched open and a hat flew in. A hand poked in. It waved. A shiny black overshoe appeared. And then a head, a grinning winking head.

"Nelson Prixton, what are you doing here?" she said.

"It's Valentine's Day, and I needed to see my girl. Since my hat didn't fly back at me, I'm wondering if it might be okay for me to come in."

She shook her head. "I'm not your girl."

"These are for you," he said, presenting a dozen red roses and a box of chocolates.

"Nelson, I can't accept these. I've told you as much."

"Okay, then they're not for you. They're for your mother. You can't deny her a treat. That would be despicable."

She backed down, but it gave her no pleasure. They played parlor games with her mother and drank hot chocolate until half past nine.

After Nelson's winning several games in a row, Gretta said, "How are things at the office?"

"At the office ... or with Mr. Harrington?"

Her mother appeared to bite her lip, appearing to hold back a grin.

"I know how things are with Mr. Harrington," Gretta said.

Nelson raised his chin. "What's that supposed to mean?"

"It means he stopped by this weekend. So did Hilda. It was wonderful seeing both of them."

"If that's the case," he said, sounding irritated, "why'd you bother to ask?"

"Nelson, you're being inappropriate. I asked how things were at the office ... from your perspective."

"Did Lord Harrington confirm he's leaving?"

"Stop calling him that. And yes, he did say he's going back to England in April. We knew his stay was temporary."

Nelson turned to Gretta's mother. "Did you know your daughter is sweet on him?"

She turned a teasing smile on Gretta. "You didn't need to tell me that, Nelson. I've known it all along. I get the unmistakable feeling Mr. Harrington is sweet on her, too."

Nelson frowned, and with the tension in the room growing, he went on to aggressively win the rest of the games they played. When he finally left with a promise to return, a hollow feeling overtook Gretta. Nelson's presence completely sucked the life out of her, leaving her emotionally depleted.

"It probably wasn't right to say what I did about you and Mr.

Harrington being sweet on each other in front of Nelson," her mother said. "That was unkind. We both know how deeply he cares for you."

Gretta shook her head. "I'm glad you did. He treats me like a possession and refuses to let go. As for me, it's getting late. I'm tired and I'm ready for bed. Goodnight, Mother."

She wheeled to her bedroom, turned on the light, and rolled to the table by the window ... the table where Mr. Harrington's pine tree sat. She lightly ran her fingers along the tips of its deep green needles. Picking up a pinecone, she sniffed it. Warmth filled the emptiness, but every bit as quickly it turned to sadness. She peered out the window and into the darkness. How was Mr. Harrington spending the night? Was it even possible for him to feel as empty as she did?

CHAPTER SEVENTY-FIVE

First thing on Monday morning Hilda stopped by Ole's desk. "I passed your message on to Gretta."

"I know."

Her smile widened. "You stopped by after all?"

"I thought about what you said." He sighed. "Telling her about my leaving was the decent thing to do."

"She looks good, doesn't she?"

"Very." *But she's seeing Nelson, so why torture myself with the thought?*

"Nelson's no good for her," Hilda said.

Ole winced. "What?"

"He's no good for her. What's more, he isn't worthy of any of the young ladies in Amber Leaf. I'm sure he's fun to be around, but I fear that apple hasn't fallen far enough from the tree."

"You wouldn't be suggesting that I see her again?"

Hilda's smile grew into a smirk.

"But Hilda, let me remind you that I'm leaving for England in two short months."

"Do you really want to leave, Mr. Harrington?"

He stood poker faced.

"That's what I thought," she said.

Nelson waltzed into the office an hour later with a grin that cut from ear to happy ear and bolted toward Ole's desk.

"You seem unusually chipper for a Tuesday morning," Ole said.

"I am. I'm getting married."

Ole flopped back in his chair. "You're getting mar—"

"That's right. Thought we'd have a big June wedding."

Ole's brows puckered. "You and who else?"

"Why, Miss Gretta Van Dyke, as if you didn't know," he said, appearing overtly pleased with himself.

"I didn't. I paid a visit on Sunday. She mentioned nothing about being engaged."

"We weren't engaged on Sunday." Nelson tugged on his suspenders and smugly lifted his chin. "I didn't pop the question 'til last night. Want to be the first to congratulate me?"

Bile crawled up Ole's throat.

Nelson pulled open a coat pocket and drew out a small box. "I stopped by the jeweler's this morning to pick this up. That's why I'm late. Wanna see it?"

"Not particularly."

He popped open the box and flaunted it. Inside sat a large, solitaire diamond. Gretta's engagement ring.

Ole gazed at it with reluctant eyes. "Did she say yes?"

Nelson let out a pitiful sigh. "Did she say yes?" he mocked and walked away.

CHAPTER SEVENTY-SIX

For the next number of days, Gretta kept anticipating another visit from Mr. Harrington. She felt it deep inside.

But she was wrong. Instead, Nelson returned. Frequently. One night after one of Gretta's repeated rebuffs, he plucked a box from an inside coat pocket. "This is for you," he said. "One day soon your Mr. Harrington will be gone, and you'll need someone. I hope with all my heart you'll choose me. Set this box aside. Look at it whenever you like. Take your time deciding. I will wait … I will wait and wait and wait."

Weeks had passed and, to her disappointment, Mr. Harrington never did bother to return. Thinking better of it, why would he? He was returning to England. Leaving Amber Leaf for good. He and Gretta had never courted. She merely carried on a one-sided infatuation, an infatuation she had helplessly sensed was shared.

In time, the calendar became her best friend. She drew a circle around the number eight on the month of April. That was the day she would return to Addison & Crowley. She had to be strong enough by then if she ever hoped to see Mr. Harrington again.

Every day she forced herself to ascend and descend the stairs, taking an extra step at each attempt until she made it comfortably from the bottom to the top and back down again.

In her spare time, of which she had plenty, she worked painstakingly on a going-away gift she would present to him on that ill-fated day. She sketched and re-sketched from memory his hotel, Deacon's farm, that deserted farm near Aspen, Fountain Lake, Spring Lake, Lake Amber Leaf, and the law office. Mr. Harrington said no camera could do justice to those images he carried in his heart. They were places. But she could do justice with her sketching, giving prominence to the most meaningful parts of each scene—his desk in the office of Addison & Crowley, the window of his room at Hotel Amber, the shed at the farm in Aspen. She smiled at that one. But how she wished she could capture the images of those Mr. Harrington held most dear. Deacon. Maude. Hilda. Boss. That was not to be. She didn't draw faces well and refused to embarrass herself.

From time to time she opened Nelson's box and gazed at the ring. Nelson's diamond ring. Rather than drawing her to him as he had hoped, it strengthened her desire for Mr. Harrington. So she stopped tormenting herself and set the box on a high shelf in the kitchen cupboard, hiding it from view.

Valuable time slipping much too swiftly away.

CHAPTER SEVENTY-SEVEN

"Do you really need to leave a day early?" Hilda asked.

Ole continued cleaning his desk as if that could wash away all of his heartfelt memories. With the exception of Emily, his time in Amber Leaf had been the warmest, most meaningful time of his life.

"Perhaps it's best if I take another day in New York," he said. "It's always good to give oneself a bit more time when traveling ... I heard a late spring storm might be heading this way. It might be wise to outrun it."

"But we've planned a farewell party ... a supper tomorrow evening," Hilda said. "It was supposed to be a surprise. Gretta will be back in the morning. She'll be heartbroken if you aren't here."

Ole glanced at Nelson and his stomach knotted. "That's highly unlikely."

"But we all wanted to see you off properly," Hilda said.

He snapped closed the clasp on his briefcase. "Bidding farewell is not one of my stronger suits. I had a difficult enough time of it yesterday with Deacon and his family. I do appreciate the sentiment, but perhaps it's best if I slip away without much adieu. I'm certain you understand." He thought for a moment. "Hilda?"

"Yes?"

He handed her an envelope. "Would you see that Miss Van Dyke gets this? I prefer not to leave it on her desk."

Hilda glanced at the hand-penned name on it, her nod tentative, sad.

After a brief hug, he made his rounds.

"Charlie?" he said, stopping by the man's desk. "It's been an honor and a privilege to work with you these past months."

Charlie stood and with one hand shaking Ole's, the other clasping his shoulder, he said, "You've shown us what a real attorney looks like, Harrington, and for that, my good man, we will always be grateful and never forget. My very best to you."

Ole walked on. "John, Miss Van Dyke is all yours now. I can't thank you enough for sharing her."

John chuckled. "And to think I was getting used to it."

Ole smiled at that. "You have the makings of an outstanding legal counsel. I sincerely wish you well."

"Thank you, sir. That's very kind of you." He paused. "Safe travels."

Nelson sat waiting as Ole approached. "Mr. Prixton? You take care of that lovely fiancée of yours. My best to you and your new missus for a long and happy marriage."

Nelson hopped to his feet. "Too bad you can't be here in June to attend the ceremony."

Why did the words *you scoundrel* come to mind?

"Have a safe journey," Nelson said with a brief handshake.

Ole offered a group farewell to the ladies in the stenography pool then dropped in to see Boss who stood and said, "Sure we can't talk you into staying another day?"

"Of that I'm certain."

Boss tucked in his shirt and reached for his coat. "Well, you're not getting away without a nice supper on the house."

"But—"

Boss raised a crooked brow. "I overheard you talking to Hilda. Don't worry. This will be a quiet supper, just you and me. If your father got wind I'd let you go without some sort of send off, minuscule though it might be, I'd never hear from him again." Reaching for the door, he said, "I've been craving a juicy steak since the day before yesterday. Let's get out of here."

Ole stopped at the coatrack and looked back. It was as if his life had ended. All that he had come to love was in Amber Leaf.

"Cheers," he whispered beneath his breath and walked on.

CHAPTER SEVENTY-EIGHT

With her nose to the window, Gretta's mother appeared enthralled. "It must've snowed all night long. There's got to be a good six inches out there, and here I thought we'd seen the last of the white stuff."

"They wouldn't close the office, would they?" Gretta said.

"I doubt it. Are you sure you're ready for this, dear?"

Gretta felt like a teenager anticipating her first date. "Positive. Can't wait to get there. I sure hope bringing my sketches isn't too presumptuous. Mr. Harrington might not have enough room for them in his luggage."

Her mother gave Gretta a half hug. "He'll make room. Your drawings are magnificent."

At a quarter to the hour, she stepped onto the porch and waited. A grin broke and her heart leaped when a carriage pulled up.

With a light breeze brushing her cheeks and the subtle whirl of carriage wheels muted by soft powder, she gazed into the winterish wonderland, the glorious scenery complementing her spirits.

Minutes later, she stood at the base of the staircase and looked up. It loomed far more forbidding than the staircase at home, but she didn't care. With one hand on the railing, the other clutching her handbag, and her sketches rolled and bound, she slowly climbed the stairs, stopping every few steps to wait for a shooting pain to subside.

When she reached the top, Hilda appeared with arms outstretched, but her smile bore an inexplicable droop. She plucked Gretta's things from her hands and helped her with her coat.

"Is Mr. Harrington in yet?" Gretta said, having eyes for no one other than him.

Hilda shook her head.

"I'm sure he'll be here soon," she said with all of the confidence in the world. "Let me show you the sketches I drew for him. Would you mind?"

As she tugged at the ribbon, Hilda touched her hand, stopping her. "That won't be necessary. He left a day early."

The air whooshed out of her lungs. All of these days waiting, and he wasn't here? *You're wrong. He has to be coming.* "But—"

"He asked me to give you this."

As Gretta seized the envelope and plodded to her desk, Nelson leaped up. She shook her head at him. Although he appeared reluctant, he retreated.

She opened a bottom drawer and slipped in her purse, rested the sketches alongside her desk, and slipped a forefinger through a gap in the lightly sealed envelope, loosening it. Her breathing grew shallow as she nudged out the letter and smoothed it open. The note read …

My dear Miss Van Dyke—

At this moment, I visualize you sitting at your desk looking lovelier than ever as you read my fond words of farewell. Do know that you have made my stay in Amber Leaf pleasurable beyond measure. But all good things must come to an end, mustn't they?

I never did congratulate you on your engagement to Nelson, which is not becoming of a gentleman. May your life together bring you unimaginable joy and happiness in the years up-coming. You deserve as much.

Now with cordial wishes,

Oliver M. Harrington

I never did congratulate you on your engagement to Nelson? Gretta grew light-headed. Swiveling around, her gaze swept the room, zeroing in on Nelson who innocently leafed through pages in a manila folder.

She returned to the letter and reread it. Her body rose as if it had a mind of its own, her feet swiftly whisking her to his side. "What's this about our engagement?"

Nelson looked up, appearing indifferent. "I asked you to marry me, remember?"

"And I didn't say yes … remember? It takes a yes on both sides for a person to be engaged."

He returned his attention to the contents of the folder and leafed through it. "You didn't say yes … yet."

She planted both hands on his desk and moved in close enough to get a strong whiff of coffee breath. "When did you tell Mr. Harrington we were getting married? … Nelson? Do you hear what I'm asking? When did you tell him?"

He set the folder aside, his eyes narrowing, a wily grin forming on his lips. "I told him several times, actually."

"Several times," she repeated. "Did you tell him that night you followed him out of my hospital room?"

He nodded. "That was the first time."

"And the second?"

Nelson looked away.

"Nelson? I'm asking you … when was the second time?"

He turned back. "The day after Valentine's Day, so that would be February Fifteenth, wouldn't it?"

"Miss Van Dyke?" Hilda called out. "May I have a word with you, please? It's important."

Gretta glared at Nelson. "How could you?"

She turned clumsily and crossed the room.

"I've called for a carriage." Hilda glanced at the clock, her eyes alarm filled. "Get your purse and sketches. I'll get your coat. You don't have much time. Mr. Harrington will be boarding the train any minute now."

Gretta's heart thumped.

"Hurry now," Hilda said.

CHAPTER SEVENTY-NINE

G retta wrung her hands all of the way to the railroad station. She had to get there on time. Hurry driver ... please, please hurry.

The instant they arrived, too excited to think, she hopped out of the carriage. A horrific pain shot down her leg. Breaking a fall, she limped forward into an alarmingly empty depot.

She rushed outside. An iron horse hissed on the tracks, clouds of steam billowing into the April air. A warning whistle blew.

With hands clasped behind him, a porter near the caboose impatiently raised and lowered on the heels of his shoes.

"Please, sir," she said, moving as fast as her injured leg allowed. "I'm trying to find someone."

"Sorry, ma'am, but—"

She forced another painful step forward. "Please," she insisted. "His name is Mr. Oliver M. Harrington. He's a big, big man, well over six feet. Has a British accent. I'm sure he's on the train."

The porter lifted a forefinger. "A man fitting that description is in the second car. Follow me." When they reached the Pullman, he turned to her. "Wait here."

OLE PEERED OUT THE WINDOW AS if it was possible to memorize the view. In minutes his days in Amber Leaf, the excitement, and new-found friendships, would be reduced to a memory. A wave of melancholy descended on him the way last night's snow had blanketed the countryside.

"Harrington?" The husky voice filled the Pullman. "Mr. Oliver M. Harrington?"

Ole recoiled at the mention of his name. Were his papers not in order? He pivoted toward the back of the car. "Harrington here."

"You have a visitor, sir, but you'd better hurry. You don't have much time."

A visitor? Don't tell me Boss has a last minute note for my father.

Ole stepped onto the platform and his breath caught. "Gretta? What are you doing here?"

"I wanted you to have these," she said holding up a scroll of papers. "I remembered what you said about pictures not doing justice to meaningful places. I had a lot of time on my hands, so I tried to capture them with my pencil." Appearing excessively nervous, she glanced at the rising steam billowing on the tracks behind her and spurted on. "I hope I'm not being too presumptuous, but drawing is my hobby."

Confused, his eyebrows pinched together. Thinking of the future without her—looking at etchings from another love denied him—he forced himself to say, "I can't thank you enough."

The whistle blew a second time and Gretta jumped. "Th-there's something else," she said.

Is that not enough? "Yes?"

"Nelson."

Ole tensed at the mention of that repulsive name.

She lightly touched a hand to Ole's forearm. "He lied. He and I are *not* engaged. Have *never* been engaged. Will *never* be engaged. I needed to set the record straight."

"Do you mean to tell me—"

"I couldn't let you go off thinking I'd spend the rest of my life with someone like him. Is-is that why you didn't come to see me? Because you thought we were getting married?"

Ole looked off. "When you were in the hospital, I walked in on you when you were intimately holding hands, remember?"

"You're wrong." Gretta adamantly shook her head. "I was *intimately* telling him it was over. If you will recall, I withdrew my hand from his grip the minute you stepped in the door."

The whistle blew again and she shouted above it. "The night I fell into the path of that oncoming buckboard, I caught Nelson in the arms of someone else. I could never marry someone I couldn't trust." Her eyes, filled with affection, welled with tears. "Not after meeting some-one like you."

Not after ... "Do you mean to tell me that all this time ..."

She looked as if her heart was pleading for him to believe her and nodded.

Relief revealed itself in a sudden burst of laughter. Ole swept Gretta up and swung her around, her arms latching onto his neck, her tears trickling down his ear.

When he slowed and gazed into her eyes, she said, "I wish with all my heart you didn't have to leave." An ache seemed to pierce through her tone.

"I don't."

She pulled back, eyes wide. "You don't?"

Ole up-righted her. "I don't," he repeated then turned and cried, "Porter? Please retrieve my trunk."

This time Gretta burst into laughter. "Mr. Harrington!"

He grinned. "I think it more appropriate for you to call me Ole."

"I like that. May I offer you a carriage ride home ... Ole?"

He frowned. "I fear you've positioned the cart before the oxen again, my dear. I'm the one who is supposed to offer *you* a carriage ride home."

"But it's my carriage," she insisted.

"You're wrong. It's our carriage. How will we ever get on if you insist upon wearing the knickers?"

She laughed again as if to say, 'But they're such little knickers.'

ACKNOWLEDGEMENTS

A Carriage Ride Home is the first book of *The Chronicles of Amber Leaf*. Research for this new series has been fascinating and greatly increased my understanding of the history of World War I.

My heartfelt thanks to Brett Burner, Publisher at Lamp Post, as well as my editor, Melissa Williams Netherton, for seeing potential in this work and guiding me through the publishing process.

Thanks to my writers critique group (Martha Gorris, Sally John, Ann Larson, Jean Mader, Mary Kay Moody, and Diana Wallis Taylor) for their selfless ideas and editorial assistance.

To Bonnie Aase-Roach, Cindy Belshan, Marilyn Damien, Jean Holien, Lorraine Hooks, Lori Lobnitz, Sybil Obendrauf, Avery Okland, Reese Okland, Sheila Okland, Sonny Okland, Darlene Riopel, Mary Feeler Rogers, Betty Shafer, Ellen Sheldon, Patti Tzannos, and Nadine Washburn, among others, thank you for your inspiration, input, and encouragement.

Special thanks to Dale Busch and Anne Fletcher for their generous input and guidance with the legal aspects of the story line.

Last but definitely not least, my profound thanks to my husband Fred for your amazing input and support. I could not be more blessed.

DISCUSSION QUESTIONS

1. Who was your favorite character and why?

2. Did you find yourself transported back in time as you read A Carriage Ride Home and at the same time see how the problems they faced back then could seem even more serious than the problems we face today?

3. Could you identify with any of the challenges Big Ole faced? If so, which did you find the most compelling?

4. What do you consider Big Ole's greatest weakness and his greatest strength?

5. Can you identify with Big Ole's resolve to forge his own life outside of the aristocracy? Did you find it believable?

6. How did you feel about Big Ole's relationship with Gretta? Were you pulling for him or were you hoping he would continue to walk away?

7. How did you feel about Gretta's relationship with Nelson? Were you pulling for her to live happily ever after with him or with Big Ole?

8. Did you find Big Ole's struggle with claustrophobia believable?

9. How did you feel about Maude and her past? Did you find her transformation believable?

10. What did you feel were the book's greatest weaknesses and strengths?

www.ingramcontent.com/pod-product-compliance
Lightning Source LLC
Chambersburg PA
CBHW020227180626
46810CB00006B/2068